ON THE PLAINS
OF KERRERI

BROCK WALKER

Archway Publishing books may be ordered through booksellers or by contacting:

Archway Publishing
1663 Liberty Drive
Bloomington, IN 47403
www.archwaypublishing.com
1 (888) 242-5904

ISBN: 978-1-4808-5921-0 (sc)
ISBN: 978-1-4808-5922-7 (hc)
ISBN: 978-1-4808-5923-4 (e)

Library of Congress Control Number: 2018901892

Print information available on the last page.

Archway Publishing rev. date: 11/20/2018

FOR MY MOTHER AND MY FATHER, WHO GAVE ME
THE LOVE AND INSPIRATION TO
LIVE MY DREAMS

PROLOGUE

BAHR EL GHAZAL, 1859

There were no laws. There was no order. The only law was tribal law, and each tribe made its own rules. Each tribe had its leader. Each tribe had its value system and beliefs. Each tribe fought the other for survival, and the winner took all, including woman and children. It was the nature of the beast, and it is the nature of man.

There were many eyes on Africa. The vast continent held an endless supply of untapped resources. Rumors of diamonds, silver, copper, and gold circulated in the finest financial institutions in Europe. The nations of the growing industrial world elbowed each other as they greedily fought to lay claim to the lands of the Dark Continent.

But not the Sudan.

The Sudan was no place for a white man. It was a vast, barren wasteland of desert, swamp, and dense mountainous jungles. The only habitable area of the entire northern half of the territory lay in a slender strip along the banks of the Nile. It was a good place for a trading post, but not for a colony. No civilized white nation viewed the Sudan as an opportunity.

But the white man did not see everything. There was another tribe that saw the Sudan as a land of vast opportunity. They were the tribes of Islam.

They did not seek diamonds, silver, copper or gold. The natural resource they craved was human flesh, and the harvest was abundant. The black slaves from Africa brought a pretty penny in the marketplace. The Arabs came not to colonize, but rather to conquer.

Zuetar Rahamna was an Arab slave trader. He was pleased that the

Egyptians and the Europeans had abandoned the Sudan. His rule was absolute. The only enemy he faced was rival slave traders.

Zuetar sat on a wooden stool watching the afternoon sun begin to dip towards the horizon. He brushed a fly away from his face and drank deeply from a clay mug. Beer was his favorite beverage. He fermented it himself from barley grown on his land. He felt his stomach growl. He was becoming hungry. He knew his servants would be preparing his evening meal of goat and "ful," broad beans cooked in oil. He could smell the sweet, pungent smoke from cooking fires that hung over his village. Cooking fires fueled by dried dung from the livestock.

Zuetar owned the village and everyone in it. The only laws were the ones he made. He changed them occasionally, as needed, to ensure he kept power. He held on to his power as all men do, as if it were his very soul. And in many ways, it was.

Zuetar's tribe, the Jaalin, were descendants of the Muslim Fur who inhabited Darfur. They were a proud people who traced their tribal rights to "the prophet" Muhammad himself. They were proud and they were devout. They were Sunni.

And, like all tribes, they needed room to grow. "Bilad al-Sudan," the "land of the black people," was the perfect place. They swept down from Darfur, across the ironstone plateaus and into the swampland fed by the river Bahr el Ghazal, conquering and enslaving all in their path.

The black tribes, the Dinka, the Luwo and the Fartit all fell prey. It was a trade that flourished under the desert sun, as did the Arab slave traders who made it their way of life.

To maintain his aura of power, Zuetar's zeriba was strategically positioned on one side of the village. Clay buildings made of mud and straw dotted the landscape. His clay home had open windows with metal bars to allow the heat to escape. There was a thatched corral to provide shelter for his cattle, and a small clay building with several rooms to give shelter for his slaves.

Zuetar rarely set foot in his home. That was where he kept his wives and children. The only time he went inside his home was to impregnate his wives.

Instead, a large canvas tent was his castle. It stood imposingly inside the compound. It was bigger than his house and the slave quarters combined. It was bleached white from the sun, with multicolored flags and cloth banners hanging from wooden pegs. It was full of furs and tapestries, copper and brass, riches he had plundered from the native tribes.

In addition to his beer, Zuetar loved tobacco. He stood up and walked to the front of his tent. There was a small wooden table with a brass tray on top. He lifted the long-stemmed pipe that he had purchased at the open air-markets in Khartoum and filled the bowl with tobacco from a leather pouch. The souks were full of delightful items brought from around the world. Zuetar had been told that it was a habit of the British to smoke tobacco in the evening. Zuetar wanted very much to be like an English gentleman, although he had never seen one.

He was also told that English gentlemen liked to amuse themselves with their subjects, and this was something else they shared in common. Zuetar had begun to notice that the daughter of his slave Nindomua was becoming a woman.

Feeling somewhat dizzy from the beer and tobacco, he looked up at the darkening sky overhead and felt a stirring in his loins. He turned to Kefala, his right-hand man, part butler, part foreman, and very much in charge of Zuetar's farm. Kefala was Dinka.

"I have noticed that Nindomua's daughter is coming of age, and ready to bear fruit. She has unique qualities that should not go to waste. Send her to me. I want to speak with her," he ordered.

Kefala, an older man, but loyal to Zuetar, understood the tone of his master's voice. He clucked his tongue and pulled nervously at the cloth robe draped around his shoulders.

"Master, she is only recently bleeding," he stated honestly.

"Ah, she is ready for children," Zuetar acknowledged. He inhaled deeply on his pipe and blew out a smoke ring that hung silently in the air. "She will bear strong children, and they will better serve my needs. Bring her to me, and we shall see how recently she has blooded."

"Yes, master," Kefala acknowledged. And though his face bore no emotion, his heart broke. Mindau was his daughter. He walked towards the small servant's quarters, confused by the issue that confronted him.

To have his daughter, a slave, mate with a wealthy Arab out of wedlock, would deprive him of a dowry. But if she bore him a son, of whom Zuetar was proud, she would be guaranteed a decent life, free from the abject poverty which overwhelmed most of the Sudan. There were few suitors for the daughter of a slave in Bahr el Ghazal. She was at best guaranteed a life of poverty, rape, and eventually disease. To carry the child of such an important man as Zuetar Rahamna would give her a better life. What more could a father ask?

"Nindomua," he said softly as he entered the mud-walled quarters. "Where is Mindau?"

"Asleep, of course, you fool," she replied.

"Wake her," he said. "Master wants to speak with her."

Nindomua let out a sigh. A woman's place in the Sudan was somewhere between a cow and a hen. Both had value; both had a taste and texture that men craved. And both were ultimately devoured by those that craved them. Better to be bred than to serve as the main course on a vicious palette.

"Mindau," she called out. "Get up, you foolish girl."

Mindau rose quickly from her bed of straw in the corner of their hut. There was still a slight glow from the cooking fire illuminating the room. Her eyes were wide, her lips slightly parted in fear.

"What, mother, what?" she whispered.

"Go with your father, now. The master wishes to speak with you," her mother ordered.

Mindau felt paralyzed with fear. She had seen the way that Zuetar had watched her while she did her chores in his house. Like a young gazelle, she knew the gaze of the lion, and she felt the same paralyzing fear. She pulled her chadur around her shoulders, lowered her head, and followed her father's footsteps that led toward the master's tent.

As she crossed the ground to Zuetar's tent, she was hopeful she would not see Zuetar's son, Zubehr Rahamna. She wasn't sure whom she feared more.

Zubehr, like his father, also appreciated the importance of the slave trade. When he was twelve, his father gave him a female slave, and Zubehr quickly learned that women were nothing more than vessels for his pleasure. His father had many slaves, including the eleven-year-old Mindau, whose skin was truly as dark as ebony.

Zubehr Rahamna was fourteen, but already had the body of a man. Like his father, he too found himself enthralled every time he was near Mindau. She smelled of warm oil and musk, and her budding breast protruded proudly against the wrap of her chadur, a colorful sheet of cloth that the woman of the Dinka tribe draped around their bodies.

Her large, deer-shaped eyes were as brown as mahogany, and her lips were full and ripe. She was shy and frightened. She knew her place; she was a slave. Mindau was no fool. She knew that Zubehr was the son of the man who owned both her body and the body of her mother. She could feel his blood run hot every time he saw her walking in the compound. His gaze was the same as his father. And so was his intent. She feared both father and son.

Zuetar met her as they approached his tent, and he motioned Kefala away with the back of his hand. The hand then went around Mindau's shoulder, and he led her silently into his tent.

His bed was several layers of goat and sheep skins spread across a mattress stuffed with lamb's wool. He gently guided Mindau towards the bed, and with one hand slid her chadur down from around her shoulders. He turned her to face him, and his dark eyes locked with hers. They were wide, fearful, and her lips were quivering.

He untied the knot by her shoulder and her cloth chadur fell away. Her dark ebony skin was smooth and burnished ebony. His eyes traveled down from her shoulders to her budding breast, heaving with her fear. Her nipples were taut with anticipation. He slid one hand down her shoulder, caressing her arm as it traveled down her skin.

His eyes continued down her narrowing stomach, towards her curving hips, and her womanhood. As he admired her budding flower, he heard the sound of metal on leather, a very soft swish, and then a whistling sound. Something was moving very fast through the air.

He saw a different fear in Mindau's eyes, a look of terror, and he tried to react. His mind told him to fling up his arm, and turn. But his body never had time to comply. The curved, single edge blade of the scimitar caught him on the upper left side of his neck, and like a scythe through a thick stock of corn, sliced clean through, severing his head from his neck in one fell swoop.

Zuetar's head toppled sideways and bounced off the dirt floor of his tent. His body remained standing for a moment, headless. The muscles of his neck twitched as if they were seeking to grasp back that which had just been taken away. A jet of dark crimson blood shot up into the air, splashing into Mindau's horrified face and onto the floor of the tent. Zuetar's now headless and lifeless body dropped hard, landing in a heap at her feet.

All she could do was gasp and stare at his body. She did not dare bring up her eyes. But as she labored to breathe, her eyes rose slowly. Very slowly. They came up from the body at her feet and met the gaze of Zubehr Rahamna, who stood over his father's still bleeding corpse. His right hand, still clenching the scimitar, was at his side. His chest heaved with the bloodlust that coursed through his veins.

The only sounds that had broken the still quiet in the tent had been the scratch of metal drawn on leather, the whistling disturbance of the air, the sound of the blade striking flesh, and the dull thuds of first the head, and then the body hitting the floor.

Zubehr Rahamna felt the fire in his mind spread uncontrolled to his loins, fueled by the naked, dark skinned girl standing before him. He held the knife up to her throat and with his other hand pulled her close to his body. He felt her breast pressing against his chest. Her heart was pounding. Using his free hand, he dropped his pants, pushed her down on the bed, spread her legs, and entered her body with pounding thrusts that were met by the wild bucking of her hips, lost in a wild, primitive, uncontrolled spasm.

Zubehr Rahamna had killed his first man and raped his first woman at the age of fourteen. And no one, not a soul, dared to challenge him the next day when he exited his father's tent and declared himself master of his father's domain. His mother wore the dark black robe of a widow, banished to the slave quarters. Mindau moved into the main house, the first of many wives in his harem.

Zubehr himself moved into his father's tent. It was where he slept, where he took his meals, where he met his clients, and where he enjoyed the pleasures of the flesh, like his father before him.

Ruthless, cunning, fearless and unscrupulous, he plotted the conquest of the surrounding slave traders and tribes. He left thousands of dead bodies behind rotting in the hot desert sun. He was feared and he was legend.

In the Sudan, the veneer of civilization was very thin.

CHAPTER ONE

MONTEREY, 1874

Dirk McDuran walked down the long wooden pier, pulling his collar tight to shield his neck from the rain that blew in from the sea. He clutched the yellow canvas sea bag hanging over his shoulder with one hand. His thick, yellow rubber slicker blocked most of the wind as his boots clumped along the loose boards of the pier. The ocean beat against the wooden planks and pillars. Sea spray shot up through the gaps in the boards as he hurried towards shore. His small cabin was on a hill at the edge of the town.

He walked the two miles quickly. He had been at sea on a whaling ship for six months. His wife, Mary, was due to give birth any day. A sturdy Scotsman, Dirk was one of many who had immigrated to America during the Industrial Revolution of the great nation that he proudly called home. Dirk had come with his parents, and they lived the simple but strenuous life of a fisherman on the coast of California. Dirk was like his father, born to the sea, and he hoped to have a son to carry on the family tradition.

He opened the door of his small wooden cabin and was immediately surrounded by the warm and familiar aroma of lamb stew bubbling in a large iron cauldron hanging over the fire. He strode across the planked floor to the bedroom. As he stepped into the room, his eyes immediately focused on his wife Mary's gleaming face and the child she was nursing in her arms.

"Dirk," she said proudly, "meet your son, Kip James McDuran."

"Oh, Mary," he whispered. He came to her side and felt an overwhelming sense of love for his wife and their child, who eagerly sucked her large milky breast. Dirk admired the shock of black hair that crowned the infant's head. The infant's strong little hands firmly gripped his mother's breast.

"He's beautiful," Dirk said.

"No, Dirk," she corrected. "He's a handsome young Scotsman, like his father."

"Ach, that he is," he agreed. He gently caressed her hair. Mary had the most beautiful head of hair he had ever seen on a woman. Long strawberry blonde tresses framed her large green eyes. He felt himself becoming aroused. It had been a long six months.

"He's got your looks," he told her as he kissed her warmly on the lips.

"And your strength," she added.

"You weren't alone, I hope?"

"No, my sister was here, along with Mrs. Patterson. We did fine without you," Mary teased. She ruefully examined the little mouth that still worked her breast. "And he's just been eating ever since he was born. I might be running dry."

Dirk eyed her large, milk laden breast, and felt a strong urge swell up in his loins. "I doubt that's possible, Mary," he said with conviction. He caressed her cheek. "Even before you were pregnant you were bountiful."

She laughed happily. "I'll never forget the look on your face when you first saw them," she said. Her green eyes were playful. They reminded him of the sea.

"Neither will I," he laughed.

"Oh Dirk, I'm so happy you're home."

"Aye, I missed you badly," he whispered, holding mother and child tightly in his strong arms.

Kip McDuran was oblivious to the happy reunion of his parents, but he felt the warmth of their love and the depth of their passion. His little hands kneaded the flesh as he drank happily. Even though he was a new born, Mary could feel the strength in his tiny hands. Like his father.

Mary looked at her husband's dark, wet, curly jet-black hair slicked back carelessly with one hand, and the turquoise eyes that were latched proudly upon his son, and felt the deepest love she had ever known for a man in her life. She knew that their home was poor, as was their future. But she did not ask for more than she had.

"Dirk," she said. "I am the luckiest woman in the world."

When Dirk smiled, dimples formed at the edges of his mouth.

"No lassie, I'm the lucky one." With one hand he reached out and gently stroked the head of his newborn son. "I have the family I always wanted, and we shall always have each other," he promised.

A worried look crossed his eyes. Mary could see it.

"Dirk, is something wrong?"

He ran his hand through his hair. "Christ, I need a bath," he said.

"That's what's wrong?" she pressed. "I know you better than that."

Dirk let out a sigh. "I'm not sure where to begin." He stood up and went over to the fire, holding out his hands to warm them.

"There was a problem on the ship. The ship's captain, Rodriguez. That Portuguese bastard is out of his mind. He is mistreating the Chinese coolies on the boat. He's trying to make them whalers. They have no experience, and it infuriates him. He puts them into harm's way for stupid, senseless reasons. I think he enjoys it. Several have died because of it."

"It's not your fight, Dirk," Mary pleaded.

"It's wrong. They are people, emigrants just like us, trying to make a better life."

"What have you done?" Mary asked. He could hear the concern in her voice.

"A man came through before I shipped out on my last voyage. He was from Washington. He works for Senator McDonald. He was here asking questions. He wanted to know if the Chinese were physically mistreated. I spoke with him, and told him what I had witnessed on the ship in previous voyages."

"Dirk, the people who own the whaling business won't allow anyone to get in their way. You are putting yourself in danger," she said.

"I have a friend, Chow Lin. He is an amazing man, so intelligent, so hardworking. Two of his men were sent out on a whaling boat to hook some lines that had broken from the harpoon. They were crushed between the ship and the whale. They never had a chance."

"You will not have a chance. Rodriguez will kill you to protect his ship and his owners," she warned. He could hear the desperation in her voice.

"Aye, if he catches wind of it," Dirk agreed. He walked briskly over to his wife and held her in his arms, smiling down into her eyes.

"Don't worry lassie; I can take care of Rodriguez. But you're right. Larkin, aye, he's a dangerous bastard. If he finds out, we will have to be very careful."

"Dirk, we have a son now. I don't want him in danger."

Dirk exhaled. He felt the stress. "I know. We'll be watchful." He wanted to change the subject.

"What's for dinner?" he asked innocently.

"Dirk McDuran, you know full well what's for dinner. Your favorite meal."

"Aye, lassie. It is," he smiled. "And it smells delicious."

He wrapped his arms around her and kissed her lips.

"Long time at sea, sailor?" she said playfully.

"Oh yeh," he said. "Let's put the little Kipper in his cradle for a while," he suggested.

Mary held out her hand. "Not until you've had a bath, mister."

Dirk sat down at the pine dinner table. He built it himself.

"Alright. After dinner. I'm starving."

Mary brought him a hot cup of coffee.

"I missed this," he said.

"I missed you," she answered. Her face darkened. "When do you go back to sea?"

"I'm not sure. It depends on whether Chow Lin allows his men to go back to work. There is talk they may strike. All the white sailors are still chasing gold in the north. They're short-handed without the Chinese."

"I've heard talk," Mary said. "David Jacks is planning to build a railroad between Salinas and Monterey. It would turn the town into a major shipping point for produce to San Francisco. There would be more work than just whaling."

"Jacks. That scoundrel. He'll have to get in bed with Charles Crocker to make that happen," Dirk replied.

"Who is Crocker?" Mary asked.

"A railroad tycoon. He owns the Central and Southern Pacific Railroads. He wants to build a hotel here and turn Monterey into a tourist resort for the rich people in San Francisco. He also wants to get rid of the Chinese."

"I thought the Chinese were the biggest help in building those railroads," Mary said.

"Aye, they were," Dirk agreed. "But Crocker doesn't need them anymore and he wants Chinatown gone."

"Why?"

"He thinks they are blight. A plague. He thinks their village smells bad. It would keep the rich folk away from Monterey."

"Their village doesn't smell any worse than the stench from the whaling station," Mary said. She was right. When the whaling ships came to port with their kill, the humpbacks and gray whales were carved up on the dock and laid out upon huge decks of planking. Then the blubber was boiled in giant clay cauldrons. You could see the thick black clouds for miles, and you could smell the stench too.

"That's not fair," she added.

"Life is always cruel and seldom fair," Dirk said honestly.

Chapter Two

BLENHEIM PALACE, 1874

The palace loomed out of the darkness, draped in fog as the carriage passed swiftly under the stone archway and into a huge courtyard. The driver cracked the whip behind the ears of the horses, and the clatter of their hooves echoed off the stone walls of the imposing castle.

Dr. Fredric Taylor nervously adjusted his brown leather bag which he clutched to his chest as they passed a carpet of carefully trimmed grass and tulips that lined the cobblestone road leading up to the entrance of Blenheim, the ancestral manor of the Duke of Marlborough, home to the Churchill clan. It was enormous, with fifty-foot stone pillars that loomed over the entrance.

Dr. Taylor was not accustomed to paying house calls to such wealthy clientele. He was a country doctor, a physician from the nearby hamlet of Woodstock, who tended to the middle class and poor. He ran his hand nervously over the few remaining hairs on his head, and sighed out loud as he stepped down from the carriage and into the stern gaze of John Winston Spencer Churchill, the 7th Duke of Marlborough.

"Come this way," the duke ordered. He turned and strode up the stairs into the palace. He was followed by an entourage of immaculately dressed maids and hand servants, one who was wringing her hands, sobbing.

"It's awful, absolutely awful," she cried. She took one look at the country doctor's disheveled top coat, his nervous countenance, and ran off down an immense hallway lined with marble statues and gold-gilded trim.

Dr. Taylor ran after the duke, fearing a terrible injury or illness which he must no doubt soon encounter. He felt dizzy as they passed through the cavernous hallways. The thought of becoming lost amidst the 320 various rooms of the mansion filled him with terror. They passed the huge library filled with volumes of carefully bound books and sitting tables, and he gasped at the sheer opulence of the surroundings with which he found himself. Huge, ornate tapestries hung on every wall in every room. Down the hall they raced, past the staircase, and to a "small" bedroom on the bottom floor of the palace. He heard a woman screaming in pain.

"Oh God," muttered the duke, as he threw open the doors of the largest bedroom Dr. Taylor had ever seen in his life. "Please do something!"

"You fucking bastard," shrieked the enraged woman, as she writhed on top of the bed, her hands clenching the sweat covered sheets. "This is your entire fault!"

The small but rather dapper looking man sitting beside her bed immediately leaped to his feet. His hair was dark, and so were his eyes. He wore a thick, handlebar mustache, and had an air of danger to him, despite being rather diminutive. Randolph Churchill had been beside himself with anxiety after the telegram from London had arrived, informing him that the renowned Dr. Febles would not be able to get a train to Blenheim at that hour.

"Thank god you're here, man." Randolph bounded across the room and clutched the doctor's hand. "She went into labor hours ago." He felt a flood of relief now that the physician had arrived, and decided to try to lighten the mood which had been somewhat shaky before the good doctor's arrival.

Randolph tried to humor his wife. "I say, my dear, must you have broken your water on the dance floor?"

Jennie Churchill giggled briefly and then twisted in pain. Her smoldering brown eyes danced with the flames of labor and the expectancy of motherhood. "Randy," she gasped, "I think the baby's coming out!" Her body heaved with a giant convulsion.

"Water and towels," barked out Dr. Taylor. Dukes be damned. There was a child to be born, and Dr. Taylor knew how to bring children into the world.

"You," he said, pointing to the duke and his son, Randolph.

"Out! The both of you."

"But," they protested in unison.

"Out!" roared the doctor, and they obeyed, slinking down the hallway like scolded school children.

"Ooh," gasped Jennie. "Ooh, I..., ooh."

"Spread your legs, my dear, take a deep breath, *and push*," Dr. Taylor instructed. "Push!"

Jennie panted and then felt her stomach muscles tighten. The contraction wracked her, but she focused on his voice. She was dimly aware of the servants bringing in fresh towels and hot water. Someone wiped her brow with a cold cloth. It was the most beautiful feeling in the world. For one second. Then another contraction was upon her.

"Oh God," she sighed. "Let it be a boy."

"Push!"

"Let him be... ooh."

"Push!"

"Brilliant," she gasped.

And with one mighty heave, a small glistening head pushed into the light, bald, with a ponderous forehead, a wrinkled brow, and chubby cheeks. Jenny began to cry. The doctor handed the infant to the nurse maid, and she instantly swaddled him in a warm wet towel.

"What is it?" Jenny asked, exhausted.

"A boy," the doctor said.

"Ah, a boy," Jenny smiled. The future prime minister of England, she thought to herself proudly.

Chapter Three

THE SUDAN, 1874

The banks of the Nile were quiet in the still of the early morning. The creatures of the night were finding sanctuary from the blistering sun that would soon rise above them. Some dug into the muddy river banks. Others nestled in amongst the thick reeds that lined the river. All were looking for sanctuary from the heat, save one.

The Nile crocodiles, acutely aware that many animals would be coming to drink from the river at dawn, lay silent in the river, just under the surface. Their nostrils protruded just above the water, searching the air for the hint of prey.

A bull male, over fifteen feet in length, gently broke the surface of the river with his snout. His eyes emerged, followed by his broad, armored head. He saw his quarry, a three-year old impala. She gingerly picked her way toward the river to drink. Her alert brown eyes nervously darted about, searching for danger.

The enormous reptile waited patiently, four feet from the river's edge, motionless, his eyes never blinking, never wavering from his meal. The endless cycle of violence, the never-ending quest for survival which had played upon the banks of the Nile for thousands of years, was ready to repeat itself again that morning. The laws of nature are both relentless and monotonous.

In a moment, the crocodile would seize the impala in its massive jaws, its teeth tearing first through flesh, and then, with crushing force, sinking deep through muscle and into the bone. Its massive tail would begin to thrash, and the force would spin the thousand-pound creature as though it were a whirling dervish, tearing the impala in half, spilling its blood and entrails into the river, whipped into frothy red foam. Merciful shock would paralyze the impala's nervous system. But her eyes would register the world spinning around her, and she would feel the crushing weight of the jaws upon her.

Gordon smiled, his cheekbone lifting slightly off the right side of his face. His piercing sapphire blue eyes watched as the spectacle was about to unfold. The laws of nature were about to be interrupted by the power of man.

He bent his head down and put his eye behind the length of the 680mm black steel barrel of his William Evans Farquharson rifle, his right index finger gently resting on the trigger. The circle of life had a new player that morning, and he felt a rush of adrenaline knowing that he had the power not only to intrude upon the laws of nature but to rewrite them with his own hand.

He adjusted the back sight of his rifle, raising the metal sight bar to 182 meters, and sighted in just behind the right eye of the crocodile. The weapon he held in his hands had been designed expressly for killing the big game of Africa, just as nature had designed the Nile crocodile to feed upon the impala.

In Gordon's mind, God had designed man to impose his will upon nature so that man too could survive, and, more important to Gordon, carry out God's work. Dominion over nature was a necessary prerequisite.

The impala gingerly made its way to the edge of the bank and set one cloven foot just into the gently flowing current, as if to test the water. She bent her graceful neck, lowering her head to drink. At the same time, the crocodile gathered its muscles as he prepared to surge forward.

Slowly, imperceptibly, Gordon's index finger squeezed the trigger, dropping the hammer on the metal cartridge which encased 100 grains of cordite and a 750-grain full metal jacketed slug. The explosion burst out upon the river like thunder.

The slug whistled across 182 meters, spinning from seven grooves in the barrel, and struck the crocodile flush behind its ear with a sound like someone striking a large wooden oar on the side of a boat. At the same time, the impala leaped back from the river's edge, and a flight of startled flamingos rose from the river, creating an angled pink brush stroke across the aquamarine sky and a cacophony of beating wings.

Struck by searing pain, the crocodile instinctively began to spin, its tail thrashing and its gaping jaws gnashing at the empty air. As it turned in its violent throes of death, the other crocodiles upon the river immediately sensed the commotion and instinctively moved forward to the feast.

A large female struck him on his back right leg and sunk her teeth to the bone. In an instant, he was surrounded, and he felt the jaws of his kin ripping into his heavily-muscled frame as they devoured their own. Then merciful shock set in, and he was vaguely aware of the river foaming as darkness enveloped him.

"Not the ending he planned, was it mate?" Gordon said softly.

He exhaled, moved by the frenzy before him, awed at the spectacle and his own power to create it. He lit a cigarette and inhaled deeply. He sat back on the canvas stool on the wooden deck of the steamer, rested the rifle against the railing that lined the vessel, and surveyed his surroundings.

"Damn fine shot," Romolo Gessi said with honesty. "Damn fine shot." The handsome, compact Italian Army officer took a sip of whiskey from his glass. He was Gordon's second-in-command. He too lit a cigarette and inhaled deeply. The smoke warmed his lungs.

"Too bad there was no one around to witness such majesty," Gessi poked fun. He gestured around them. The shoreline of the river was rimmed with reeds and thick clumps of grass that rose up past a man's waist. Desolate by any man's standards, black or white, the view grew even sparser as his eyes traveled away from the Nile, towards the northern horizon.

"I see no one," he said with his clipped Italian accent.

Gordon ignored him and stared out onto the shore. The two men had traveled far together. They were starting to get to know one another. That was good. They had a lot of work to do.

The land blended from green to brown and from brown to gray as the riverbank gave way to hard-packed clay, stone, and drifting seas of sand. It was over a thousand miles from the lush green foliage of the delta region surrounding Cairo to the barren wasteland that surrounded Khartoum. It was a journey that Gordon had taken so that he could bring law and order to the Sudan. His orders came from the prime minister.

Make order out of chaos.

Chapter Four

MONTEREY, 1874

Thomas Oliver Larkin II was in a horrible mood. As he drove his carriage towards the waterfront, his whaling ships sat idle in the harbor because the chicken-shit Chinese coolies were threatening to strike.

"Fucking slant-eyed heathen," he cursed as he cracked the whip over his horse's ears.

Larkin was nothing like his father.

His father had come to California in 1832, long before the American takeover from Mexico in 1847. He had become a prominent businessman and loyal agent to the American government. He had been negotiating with the Mexican Army before the arrival of the American army. A true patriot and statesman, he consolidated his various businesses into a small empire, with substantial holdings in San Francisco and New York. He built a large mansion on a hill that looked down on the harbor

His only son, Thomas Oliver Larkin II, now lived in the mansion, with his Mexican wife Lucinda, and their three children. Unlike his father, he had a mean streak as wide as his own insecurities. His employees derisively referred to him as "Junior" behind his back. Where his father had built an empire with his even-temper and diplomacy, his son seemed bent to destroy it with bad judgment, a vicious temper, and boorish manners. It was well-known within the town that he had hired killers on his payroll. He was not a man to be crossed. Some folks said he owned the town. Others said he was killing it.

As he grew older, Larkin came to favor dressing all in black, like an undertaker. His pale face was framed by a thin beard that ran down a crooked jaw, with thin, snarling lips, and narrow, hooded brown eyes.

Larkin pulled alongside a group of wooden shacks that lined the pier. He did not acknowledge the coolie that took the reins, and he walked briskly towards Chow Lin's shack.

"Chow Lin," he yelled. "Get your lazy ass out here now. You've got some explaining to do." God damn heathen, he thought to himself. The Portuguese were a hell of a lot better to deal with than these Oriental bastards. Two Chinese men in their early twenties sat hunkered around a small fire, smoking pipes, looking silently in his direction.

"What the hell are you looking at?" Larkin growled. The men quickly averted their eyes.

At the same time, Chow Lin emerged from his wooden shack. He dropped his head, his eyes downcast. He wore the traditional Chinese ponytail underneath a tight-fitting cap. His cotton shirt was buttoned at the throat, and his skin was rough from the sun and the sea. Chow Lin was the leader of the Chinese village.

Before the Gold Rush, Monterey was home to a large community of Portuguese fishermen and sailors. But they, like the rest of the country, had swarmed north to the foothills of the Sierras in search of gold. The Chinese from the village on the outskirts of the town took their place in the fishing fleets. And as a result, so did the talk of their curious customs and dress.

"Mr. Larkin," he began.

"Shut up, Chow Lin," Larkin ordered. "I don't want to hear your crap. I just want you and your coolies to get your butts back out and catch some goddamn whales." Larkin was a large man and he towered over the smaller Chow Lin.

"Begging your pardon, Mr. Larkin," Chow Lin said softly.

"Begging your pardon." He bowed several times, his bare feet slipping in the mud. He remained silent, head bowed.

"Did you hear what I said, you little heathen?" Larkin was both enraged and puzzled by the lack of response." He reached out and grabbed Chow Lin's shirt at the shoulder and shook him. "Did you hear what I said?"

"Begging your pardon, please do not touch," Chow Lin said. "Men no can work now. Not safe."

"I'll tell you what's not safe, you little bastard," Larkin hissed. "If your coolies don't get back to work, none of your little yellow asses will be safe."

Chow Lin shook his head. "Not safe. You make it safe, men work. Not safe, men not work."

"Get your men back to work. Now!"

Larkin let go of Chow Lin's shirt and spun away. In his fury, he kicked over the small cooking pot that sat on the fire by the two men. Scalding hot, it splashed onto the two men. They cried out in pain, jumping to their feet. The smaller of the two men held the other back from Larkin, his face contorted with rage.

"Anytime, boy." Larkin challenged. His hand went to his side, to the pistol that rested on his hip.

The man looked away and allowed himself to be pushed back towards the wooden shacks.

Larkin cleared his throat deeply and spat into the earth. "Get your men back to work, Chow Lin, or I'll burn down your fuckin' village and every one of you rotten little slanty eyed bastards with it." He got back into his carriage and rode off.

Chow Lin stood by the fire, staring at the glowing coals. The fire inside my heart burns brighter, he thought to himself. And hotter. He felt the bile rise up in the back of his throat, and he fought down his rancor. Now was not the time to lose his temper. A solution had to be found so that his people could go back to work. But what had transpired on the last voyage of the Rachel H. could not be ignored.

Chow Lin's men told him that Rodriguez had sent them out in a small dinghy in rough seas to hunt a large gray whale as punishment for missing their target with their harpoon cannon.

Enraged that they had wasted three harpoons on one whale, the Portuguese sea captain sent them out with a single lance to harpoon the whale by hand. He wanted to teach them a lesson. It was the way it had been done for centuries, before the advent of the steam engine and harpoon cannon. Unskilled and untrained, they were crushed by one swipe of the whale's mighty fluke.

Rodriguez only laughed when their bodies and the smashed dinghy were recovered from the sea.

The men would not work; no, could not work, under such dangerous and demeaning conditions. Chow Lin shook his head in amazement. The world was full of cruelty. The white man was no less evil than the rest.

Baun Li, one of the two young men standing by the fire came up to Chow Lin, shaking his head.

"That is a very dangerous man," Chow Lin said to Baun Li.

Baun Li spat into the dirt, his dark eyes flashing with anger. "That man is a coward."

"That is what makes him so dangerous," Chow Lin replied. "That makes him very dangerous. Go sit down and drink your tea," he said.

Chow Lin went back to his shack and sat down on the floor. Several months earlier a white man had come to speak with him. The man said he was from Washington, and wanted answers. They talked for over an hour, and then the man left. Chow Lin had heard nothing since. The men needed to work. They were running out of time.

CHAPTER FIVE

LONDON, 1874

From the moment of his birth, Winston's childhood was one of structured British wealth. It was programmed from the very beginning to ensure discipline and order, and to maximize the free time for the social requirements of his parents, members of Britain's upper class.

They were members of a very important inner circle, the "Marlborough House Set." It was a group of close friends of the Crown Prince and his wife. Grandiose dinners and fancy masquerade balls were never ending.

One night, when Winston was just two, Lady Churchill stopped by the nursery to say goodnight to her son. She and Randolph were going to a dinner party. A *very important* dinner party. The prince was attending. Dinner with the future King of England was an honor only bestowed upon Britain's upper class.

Winston toddled up to his mother, howling in fear, his chubby little legs beating across the hardwood floor. He wrapped his stout little arms around her legs with all his might and begged her not to leave him.

"There there, Winnie," his mother said gently. Jenny gently pried him away and guided him into the arms of his nanny, the ever-present Mrs. Everest. Then she paused as she carefully straightened out her satin dress.

"Don't cry," she soothed him. "Mommy's going out to dinner with daddy and the prince. One day your father will be his prime minister, and mommy has to help make sure that happens," she purred.

She looked down at the troubled, pallid eyes that stared up at her in loving adoration, great tears welling forth as his nanny swept him up in her arms.

"Mama," he cried.

"Mama has to go now, my dear child."

She kissed him on the forehead, and turned and left the room the same way she entered, smoothly, gracefully, and as always, completely aware of herself.

At age twenty-two, Lady Churchill was stunning. Her large, brown eyes were deep-set; her cheekbones were high and defined. Rich, dark -hued hair tumbled down in abundance over her shoulders. Her figure, even after her first child, was a perfect hourglass, her breast full and peaked. She was a young American beauty adrift in a sea of luxury and power, and she was determined to indulge. The young American girl had been described by many as a leopardess of enchanting beauty.

Jennie adored her husband, but she did not love him. Randy was funny, sweet and kind. His wit was sharp, and in social circles, he held his own. He was a favorite of His Royal Highness (HRH), the Prince of Wales, the future King of England. He was a member of Parliament, and on the short list, rumored by many, to be a future prime minister of England. When Winston was born, no less than the queen herself sent a note of congratulations, welcoming his arrival into the world. A male Churchill was guaranteed a place among his peers, regardless of ability.

But Randolph wasn't the prince, and he wasn't royalty. There was something about royal blood that appealed to both his wife and the masses alike. Jennie adored the attention and reveled in the gay life of high society. It was an endless stream of parties, balls and expensive dinners often attended by an orchestra for entertainment. And often, during the evenings attended by royalty, she felt the eye of the prince, and it warmed her deep within.

He was the life of the party. He set the tone for high society. He was the cock of the roost. In high society, it was all about bloodlines. It was in your blood. You either had it, or you didn't.

If you had the royal blood, the next most important factor was whether you were first born. Like a colony of hens, the pecking order of the royal family began with the cock of the roost. Of course, it all made perfect sense. After all, it was their tribal culture.

After the purest of blood came mixed blood. Dukes and duchesses, lords and ladies, earls and their wives. They had a mix of royal blood and money.

If you had the right bloodlines and money, you were in. And if you had a modicum of intelligence, which was often lacking given the immense amount of inbreeding, you were guaranteed a ride to the top. How far you rose up the ladder of fame and fortune was up to how well you played the game of power.

Randolph was already waiting in the stately brougham carriage when Lady Randolph came down the stairs from their brownstone apartment.

"Damn it, Jenny," he snapped, as the driver opened the carriage door and his wife stepped in. She could smell the fresh varnish on the carriage woodwork.

"Damn it, yourself, Randy," she chirped. "I had to finish powdering my nose. You do want me looking good for the crown prince, don't you?" she teased.

"Of course I do my dear, but I don't want to be late either," he scolded her. The reason one did not show up late for an evening such as this was because that right belonged to the prince. The party did not start until HRH turned up. And the party did not end until he left.

Randolph Churchill did not have royal blood, but he was a Churchill. He had ambition and ability. And he had more than a modicum of intelligence. Incredibly articulate and quick witted, the game of power was very much his game. His blood ran hot with ambition. Dinner that night was a crucial affair.

Jennie patted his leg. "Don't worry. We won't be late, dear. I promise," she soothed.

Randolph rapped on the side of the carriage, and the driver pulled them out onto the cobblestone streets of London.

"Tonight is the night," Randolph said.

"I thought we agreed that was not a good idea," Jenny replied.

"Fuck the Earl of Aylesford," Randy cursed. "I hate that bastard."

Dinner that night was at the palatial London home of Lord Heneage, the Earl of Aylesford. The earl was close friends with the prince. Very close friends. His wife, Edith, the Countess of Aylesford was close friends with the prince's wife, Alexandra, the Princess of Wales. The earl and his wife were a power couple.

Randolph and Jenny were jealous of the earl and the countess, which made that evening even more important to both of them. Obsessed with the game of power, they were like hungry jackals waiting for the first sign of weakness before they closed in for the feast.

"Tonight," Randolph growled. Jenny just turned away and looked out the window. The feast was going to turn into a slaughter. Men. If only Randolph would listen to her. She would have to hope for the best and be prepared to *handle* the worst.

It was a feast. The enormous dining room sparkled with light from the crystal chandeliers. Electricity was not for the common people. But it was all the rage in the upper class, and it lit up the room. An orchestra played the latest tunes and the women paraded and preened in the latest fashions.

The common people of London would have been aghast at the sumptuous meal planned for the evening. The opulence of the bill of fare was staggering. At each place setting was a menu, painted on silk. There were eight courses to the dinner, and each course offered each guest an astonishing array of choices. The Earl of Aylesford was determined that the prince would be impressed. Everyone knew the prince's appetite was insatiable. Whether it was women, wine or food, he could not get enough.

On the menu that night were some of HRH's favorite dishes prepared by the best chefs in London. Tartlets with crayfish in cream sauce, salmon trout, baron of lamb, grouse sautéed in sherry, ducklings, foie gras with brandy, truffles, and asparagus in cream sauce. Then there was the more standard fare, hors d'oeuvres, soup, leg of lamb, roast beef, vegetables and puddings. And of course, half way through the feast, orange liqueur sorbet to aid digestion and make room for the rest of the meal.

For drink, anything and everything one could imagine. Wine coursed like a giant river across the banquet tables. And with the wine and food came the chatter. The ballroom was filled with chatter. The women discussed the latest fashion and fad of the day. The men talked politics. And after the meal, the men would retire to the parlor for brandy, tobacco and deal-making. The women slipped away at that point. The men couldn't be bothered.

The royalty and wealthy upper class believed in one common principle. The laws were made to ensure they kept their riches and their power. Everyone and everything else came a distant second.

Randolph had a very clear objective that night. He was in a bit of a political pickle. He had quickly risen to power and prominence as a member of the conservative party, riding the coat tails of Robert Cecil, the 3d Marquess of Salisbury. Salisbury's conservatives had won the election, and he became the prime minister. He appointed Randolph as the Secretary of State for India. Randolph quickly made his mark, ordering the third Anglo-Burmese War, which resulted in the annexation of Burma. The crown was pleased, but the public was not impressed.

Timing is everything, in both love and war. Even more so in politics. And the political hot button of the day was Ireland, not India. A year later, Salisbury was voted out of office, and Randolph lost his job.

It just so happened that the Earl of Aylesford was his replacement.

All of this was not lost on the upper class of British society. Whispers and rumors were spread about the next election, who would win and who would lose.

So dinner that night held a special air of excitement as the guests filled the ballroom of the earl. It was to be a night of intellectual combat. And like all combat, there would be both the victorious and the vanquished. Randolph was planning to be victorious.

"I say, Randolph, have you read the India Times today?" the earl asked as they crossed paths.

Randolph wanted to choke him.

"No," he answered without emotion.

"It appears that there is a local protest against the queen. Some of her loyal subjects are not happy with her new title as the Empress of India," the earl baited. They made their way to the main dining hall. Randolph ignored him and escorted Jenny to their dining table.

The main table was reserved for the prince, the host, and whoever the prince wanted to eat with. That night, he chose Randolph and his father, the Duke of Marlborough. Of course, Randolph's wife, Lady Churchill, would be seated at the head table as well.

Although Cromwell had robbed the throne of any real power, the prince loved to get his rather stubby fingers around the issues of the day as well as the wives of his closest friends. It gave him an enormous sense of self-worth and satisfaction to believe that he was anything more than what he was: an overweight, rich, spoiled rotten philanderer who had been born with a silver spoon in his mouth and up his ass. The only power he wielded was at events like that very evening. He controlled England's social scene.

The next day, in back rooms of Parliament, amidst the smoke and brandy, HRH would be mocked while the politicians schemed and carried on with the business of the empire.

But that particular evening, the prince was feeling rather, well, royal. His long blonde curly locks flowed down over his shoulders. They had been brushed and oiled for hours to make them not appear quite so prickly. As always, his cloak and doublet were impeccable. That evening they were a light maroon satin embroidered with gold. This nicely contrasted with his black felt hat with a large white feather glued inside the headband. He wore his sword and his steel spurs, his medals and the ever present Order of the Garter hanging around his neck.

Randolph eyed the royal attire with both envy and disgust. His father the duke and his rival the earl were also in costume suited to their rank. So was Randolph. But he wore a business suit instead of the trappings of a peacock. His bowtie was very conservative. He was a member of Parliament, and he wore his costume with pride.

Dinner was served, and the prince dug in with his usual voracious appetite. He consumed more food and drink than an average family of four would eat in a week. When he was done, he grew bored and looked around the table for something else to make him happy. Time to have a little fun, he decided.

"And of course," the prince said in his booming voice, "there is the Irish problem," he intoned wisely. The table was set once again by the prince.

The table grew quiet. Only a fool would pick up that crumb.

The Earl of Aylesford couldn't resist. He was one of the prince's closest friends. He decided to have fun with the crumb, and throw it into Randolph's lap.

"Well, as we all know," the earl intoned wisely, "Mr. Churchill has had plenty to say about that particular problem, I believe. Haven't you Randolph?" he smiled wickedly. Lady Churchill began to choke on her food.

"You gave such an impassioned plea for Irish justice last week in your speech before Parliament," the earl continued. The earl was out to embarrass Randolph publicly. It would weaken him.

Randolph however, was quite prepared. He had done his homework. His arsenal was stocked, and he was ready for war.

"I'd rather talk about hunting," Randolph said cheerfully. "I say, old chap, how was your hunting trip in India? Did you bag a tiger?" he baited.

The earl and the prince had just returned from a hunting trip to India. It had been the earl's idea. He and the prince had a grand time. They had an especially good time as they had left their wives at home.

"Of course we did!" beamed the prince. He loved to tell stories about his heroic exploits.

"That's very good," said Randolph. "Because my brother, George, bagged the earl's wife while you were away," Randolph said gleefully to the prince.

Jenny spit out the piece of prime rib in her mouth.

Lady Aylesford turned crimson red.

The earl sat there, opening and closing his mouth, but no sound came out.

The duke looked as if he would murder his son right there at the table. His other son, the oldest and the future Duke of Marlborough, George, was seated two tables away. He had no idea his cat was out of the bag.

"More wine, Jenny?" Randolph said cheerfully.

The prince frowned. He hadn't yet decided how this would play out.

"Is that true?" the earl finally stammered, looking at his wife.

Tears burst from her face, and she fled the room. George saw her leaving, and quickly leaped to his feet and followed her out of the grand dining room.

"Apparently so," mused the prince.

Randolph could only smile.

"I will defend my honor," the earl proclaimed, rising to his feet.

He turned to the duke. "I challenge your son George to a duel," he demanded. He turned towards Randolph. "And I challenge you to be his second," he hissed.

"Of course, old man," Randolph said cheerfully. "Charmed, I'm sure."

Had this occurred at any other dining table in the cavernous hall, few would have noticed. But in between bites of food, all eyes were riveted on the royal table. The room was filled with silence. It was a very long and awkward silence.

But the prince did not feel awkward. He never did. The world revolved around him, and quite frankly, he was enjoying the drama. Then suddenly, his eyes began to tear, and his chubby cheeks shook. He threw hands up into the air, tilted his head back and roared with laughter.

"Randolph, you are such a prick," he chortled. He raised his glass. "To Dandy Randy, always quick with the rapier!"

"And with the dagger as well," Lady Randolph beamed. She raised her glass and clinked glasses with the prince, using her left hand. The prince sat to her right.

The earl just stood there at the table, unsure what to do next. His world had just collapsed around him.

"Oh for Christ sakes, man, sit down and eat," the prince ordered. The earl slumped to his chair. The large room broke into applause. They loved a good show. It was better than the theater.

Randolph Churchill could only smile. There was more where that came from.

Lady Randolph Churchill could only smile too. Underneath the table, she was stroking the prince's rather corpulent member with her right hand. The prince was positively beaming.

CHAPTER SIX

KHARTOUM, 1874

"Do you really think we can pull this off?" Gessi asked.

Gordon lit another cigarette. "I know we can. But first, we will have to organize our forces. That will take at least three months," Gordon replied.

"What forces?" Gessi chortled. "The Egyptian army is all but dead."

Gessi was right. The Egyptian army, a thousand miles from home, had eight outposts to cover over seven thousand square miles of harsh, unforgiving terrain. Morale was low, and life was miserable. Their outpost sat in squalid, fly infested villages that dotted the Sudan wherever water could be found.

Mud and straw huts with thatched roofs baked under the unforgiving sun. Children sat in the shade under the eaves, naked and dirty, coated with flies. Human waste and excrement built up around the villages, and along the dirt trails. What crops could be grown in the hard-packed soil was barely enough to avoid starvation. The men maintained small herds of camels, and the women grew corn and barley.

Where water was more abundant, palm trees rose over the village, providing shade as well as dates for food and husk for weaving into coarse cloth. At night, the women bent over small fires of dried manure to cook the evening meal, and the men drank the home brewed beer and chewed chat, the root of a plant that grew in the scrub lands that gave them a narcotic high. The night air was a mixture of heat rising from the soil and the sweet stench from the cooking fires.

"And those that aren't dead wish they were," Gessi added. He watched the reeds and grass pass as they steamed up the Nile. In the distance lay the unforgiving and endless sea of sand.

Disease was rampant. Malaria and dysentery were killing off most of the remaining Egyptians. The reports had been grim. Dysentery wracked their bowels for months at a time. Malaria ran unchecked. Those that did not die of fever died of dehydration. Take your pick. Either disease resulted in death.

"We will consolidate the outpost," Gordon countered calmly. "That will cut the number from eight to four. For these four, you will establish a supply line by camel caravan with Khartoum. Food and supplies can be moved along the trails to the outpost," Gordon ordered.

"I hate camels," Gessi said. He spit into the river. "Filthy, stinking, ill-tempered sons of bitches with bad teeth."

"Your teeth could use a little work as well," Gordon noted dryly. "And speaking of work, we'll need labor. We will set an encampment along the banks of the Nile. The black Sudanese slaves will be given their freedom, and then be trained and drilled in the best tradition of the British soldier. We will feed them, clothe them, and bring them order. And they will love us for that."

"Or slit our throats in the middle of the night," Gessi laughed.

Gordon ignored him. "And finally, we will build a fortress."

Typical Brit, Gessi thought. Nothing symbolized the power of the Englishman more than an impenetrable and imposing structure looming overhead. Gessi preferred marble statutes.

It was a grand adventure for both men. They knew it. They craved it. They both needed danger and excitement. They had fought countless wars together. Both men knew the challenge they were facing and relished it. Both had killed many a man in battle.

"Together, we will launch our expeditionary forces, find Zubehr and kill him and his henchmen. That will be the end of the slave traders. I dare say you'll see plenty of action," Gordon smiled. He knew the Italian mercenary loved a good war.

"You make it sound simple," Gessi said.

"It won't be easy," Gordon replied.

Gessi studied his commander. To his superiors, Gordon was a reclusive figure. They found him a bit odd. He rarely socialized with the very social British upper class.

Gessi thought he was a military genius. The man had proved himself countless times. He admired his strength and his courage. They had served together in the Crimean War. Both had distinguished themselves, displaying tactical cunning and daring in actions against the Russians in the Balkans.

But the truth was that Gordon's' was a very troubled soul. He had been born with a strong sense of both religion and self. He now feared he had lost both. Somewhere through the combat and the killing he both witnessed and committed, he had lost his faith and began to question that which he had always accepted for granted. He shared his torment with no one.

He was appalled by the vulgarities of Victorian England. The parties and the promiscuity of the ruling class disgusted him. Everyone was sleeping with everyone. Marriages were a sham. It was all about style and money. Especially money.

The upper class of English society was drunk with the technology of the industrial revolution. Electric lights replaced gas lamps. Steam engines and locomotives replaced the horse and wagon. Mighty ships made of steel roamed the seas. The empire was at its zenith. And it disgusted him.

But his loathing for the excesses of the empire paled in comparison to his loathing for Zubehr Rahamna, the blood thirsty slave king who had established his empire in the Southern Sudan.

"I need another drink," Gordon said.

"Likewise," Gessi said. The two men went into the dining room of the river boat. Gordon poured scotch into a glass and lit another cigarette. In his mind, the plan was always evolving.

"How will we find people to build a fortress when they can't even build a mud hut?" Gessi wondered as he followed Gordon into his cabin.

"We will teach them," Gordon replied confidently.

"That should prove interesting," Gessi replied. He rolled his eyes and poured himself a scotch. "I don't know why I drink this shit," he said.

"Because you're a drunk," Gordon replied. "Like me."

"True," the Italian mercenary replied cheerfully. "As we say in Italy, wine, woman, and song make a man grow strong. Here's to strength," he toasted. He downed the whiskey and poured himself another.

They docked at the wooden pier of Khartoum one week later. Their arrival caused quite the commotion. Word traveled fast through the town. A large crowd gathered on the shore when the two men disembarked the steamer. One white man alone would cause a crowd. Two could start a riot. Gordon moved among them easily; a handsome Englishman with brilliant, piercing sapphire eyes set beneath his broad, intelligent forehead. He wore a thick, well-maintained mustache, which along with his chiseled jaw gave him an aura of strength.

Gessi, resplendent in his Italian Army uniform with a chest full of medals and challenging dark brown eyes looked down on the crowd with his typical arrogance.

An Egyptian officer came through the mass and approached them. He wore his traditional uniform of the Egyptian Army. It looked rumpled and worn.

"General Gordon I assume?"

"Captain Mahmüd Husní, no doubt," Gordon replied. "Educated in Cairo at the school of engineering and a graduate of the Academy of the Cavalry, just recently commissioned a Mulazim II, correct?"

The young officer's dark brown eyes showed surprise.

"You know who I am?" Mahmüd could barely contain his excitement. The great British general knew who he was. This was a very proud day for him indeed. It validated everything his father had taught him, including his advice to join the army. Wait until my wife hears of this he thought. And my mistress.

"Yes. This is my second in command, Romolo Gessi," Gordon said, motioning to Gessi.

"Romolo, this is Mahmüd Husní. He is the commander of the Egyptian garrison in Khartoum."

"A pleasure," Gessi purred. "You have a hotel, yes?"

"Ah yes, of course," Mahmüd answered in precise English. "I have a carriage to take you both to your quarters. I'm afraid it's not much, a room in the hotel."

"Not necessary," Gordon interrupted. We will stay on the ship until our camp is pitched by the river. "Have you have staked out the area for the fortress?"

Gessi looked annoyed but kept silent. He wanted off this bucket of bolts they called a steamship. The women were ashore, not on the boat. It had been a long journey, and he hungered for the touch of a woman.

"Yes," Mahmüd replied. We have a thousand acres cleared. I assume that will be enough?"

"We'll see," Gordon answered. The crowd stared at the uniform officers standing on the pier. Some were pointing at them, their voices raised in anger.

"Let's go back on the boat and talk there until the crowd disperses," Gordon suggested.

"Agreed," Gessi said quickly. Maybe they would be better off on the vessel after all. They walked up the gangway and went inside the steamer into the general's cabin.

"Scotch?" Gordon asked Gessi. The endless ritual continued. They could live off whiskey and tobacco.

"I'd be honored," Gessi replied sarcastically. Gordon poured them both a measure of whiskey.

"No doubt there were spies in the crowd?" Gordon said to Mahmüd.

Mahmüd nodded. "Zubehr is all powerful. He has spies everywhere." He ignored the alcohol.

"Let them watch," Gordon said. He drained his glass and stood up briskly. "We have much work to do. We'll give the crowd another fifteen minutes or so to lose interest, and then we will require a tour."

"My pleasure," Mahmüd replied. "I am excited to begin this great adventure."

Gordon nodded in agreement. He wore his confidence like a medal. He had done it before. He knew why Prime Minister Disraeli had picked him for the job.

The world had never seen peace in Gordon's lifetime. His amazing and some would say incredibly stellar ascension from a second lieutenant in the Royal Engineers to a great general had one single defining truth. He was without fear. He was brutal. He made decisions, and if you stood in his way, he would have you killed or kill you himself.

His selfless courage did not pass unnoticed. When war broke out between the British and the opium lords in China, they knew he was the man for the job. He did not disappoint them. But he did shock them with a side of his character, previously unknown, which awed and mystified both his superiors and subordinates alike. The story was legendary.

After the war with the Russians in Crimea, his superiors sent him to the Far East, where he found himself at war with the opium lords, attempting to quell the civil war which raged in China. He was assigned the task of pulling together a group of ex-soldiers and mercenaries to lead a group of Chinese peasants to put down the rebellion against the Emperor of China. Gordon, then a colonel, led his army of peasants and mercenaries against the brutal and savage war lord, Lar Wang, the lord of the opium lords.

Lar Wang, firmly entrenched in his fortress city of Nanking, surrounded by a thousand warriors, and a large contingent of servants, slaves, and concubines sneered when he heard that the British colonel was approaching. Tall for an oriental, Lar Wang stood with one hand on his hip, the other caressing the handle of his sword as he watched Gordon's troops approach the city.

"They shall be dead by nightfall," he told his trusted lieutenant, Won Sung, "And I shall be asleep in the arms of five of my beautiful wives while Gordon rots on a trash heap."

It came as some surprise to both Lar Wang and his lieutenant when by nightfall they were prisoners of Colonel Gordon. Won Sung was even more surprised when, the day after their capture, Gordon had Lar Wang beheaded.

England sent Sir Halliday Macartney, a British diplomat, to negotiate a truce between what was left of the rebellious warlord's troops and the empire. When asked if the rumor of the beheading was true, Gordon reached under his bed and pulled Lar Wang's head out of a vat and waived the dripping trophy about, spouting obscenities about Lar Wang's atrocities upon his people. A sneer was still upon Lar Wang's wrinkled, lifeless face.

A shaken and subdued Macartney reported back to London that perhaps it was best to return Gordon to England for a "spot of rest and recuperation" before his next assignment. But before Gordon departed, the grateful Chinese emperor appointed him a Mandarin of the First Class, a fact not lost upon his superiors in London. They valued the ability of a British soldier to impose his will upon the enemy and gain favor with his allies.

And thus, in 1874, when North Africa was gripped by the merciless hand of the slave traders, Ismail Pasha, the Khedive of Egypt, turned to the new owners of the Suez Canal, the British, for help. Gordon's name was on everyone's lips.

And so Gordon began his quest to rid the Sudan of slavery. Sometimes encouraging, at times belittling, but always very much in control, he slowly built up a small contingent of well-trained black Sudanese soldiers, who unlike their Arab masters, could thrive under the intense heat, given the right conditions. He also spent a great deal of time mentoring the young Egyptian officer, Mahmüd. His goal was to put Mahmüd in charge of his Sudanese soldiers.

Gradually a small store of arms and ammunition was built, and Gordon put into action his plan to build a fort where his encampment stood. An engineer from England, Derrick Morgan, came at Gordon's incessant urging and set about drawing plans and gathering laborers. He set them to collect the tall grass that grew along the river, and, when dried, mixed in with the clay from the riverbanks to make bricks.

The bricks became bungalows, and eventually, a cantonment while the fortress was constructed. But the fortress was made of stone.

During the construction, Gordon and Gessi lived in richly furbished tents on the banks of the Nile. At night, they could be seen pacing the shoreline, smoking one cigarette after another, sipping at a glass of whiskey, always arguing. The stoic British officer and the flamboyant Italian mercenary talked politics, constantly traded ideas, and played devil's advocate with each other late into the night.

Months passed. While Gordon slowly built up his forces and the fortress to house them, Gessi began to develop an intelligence network to learn more about the whereabouts of Rahamna and the slave traders. Gessi was often seen retiring to his tent in the company of a young black Sudanese woman. He said he was gathering intelligence.

Gordon kept to himself. But he too found himself distracted by the pleasures of the flesh. He prayed for God to give him strength.

THREE YEARS LATER

CHAPTER SEVEN

BAHR EL GHAZAL, 1877

Zubehr Rahamna strode confidently into the village square. His entourage followed behind him. The women began to chirp their tongues, and the crowd grew excited. Zubehr always put on a good show. His entourage this week included two lions with thick leather collars, led by a chain attached to each. Two of his men held tight to the chain around each lion's neck. The lions were a symbol of Zubehr's strength and power. They signified his conquest over man and beast.

He was now at the height of his power. Under his leadership, and with the money earned from the burgeoning slave trade, Bahr el Ghazel had grown into the wealthiest province in Central Africa. Zubehr ruled over it with an iron fist, ruthlessly administering the law according to his well-settled principals and sometimes sheer caprice.

For three hundred miles in all directions, Zubehr ruled supreme. The slave caravans set out east for Suakin on the Red Sea and to the west, Dakar on the Gulf of Guinea. There they would barter with the white men in human flesh.

A caravan left the city once a week carrying its human cargo of suffering and misery to an even more horrible fate. Drawn by oxen, the carts carried large metal cages. Human cargo sorted by age and sex. Each caravan was led by one of Zubehr's trusted lieutenants. The round trip journey typically took six months, at which time the lieutenant would return with the proceeds of the sale.

Today was the day to publicly examine the week's capture, and to ensure the public's obedience to Zubehr. A hundred men, women, and children were in cages standing in the center of the square. The week's "catch" was on display for the slave king's pleasure and profits. As he walked to his wooden throne set on a stage above the crowd, he turned to his second in command, Rabih az-Zubayr, and grinned.

"This week was a good week," Zubehr said, eyeing the captured slaves.

"Yes, my Pasha," Rabih acknowledged. "But we will do better next week," he promised.

The crowd grew silent as Zubehr took his throne. His lions were chained to two wooden posts set solidly in the earth. The rest of his entourage formed a line around the stage. Zubehr calmly eyed the cages. The men were in separate cages from the women. All were stripped naked.

Slaves came to Bar el Ghazel from all over of Africa. His was a well-organized enterprise. Zubehr had organized his private army into four separate prongs.

The first, led by his son, Sulaimān, was a small but loyal group of Arab mercenaries loyal to him alone. They were skilled fighters and deadly assassins. Zubehr took care to treat them well, and they lived well.

The second group was his hunters. They were the best trackers in the Sudan. They fanned central Africa : from Abyssinia to the East, to the Congo to the west, and to Kenya in the south. They set up surveillance on the local villages and waited. In the morning, as the villagers set out on their various errands, they were tracked. Once they broke into smaller groups, they were ambushed. The hunters, armed with muskets and pistols, had little difficulty in terrorizing the black natives into submission. Once captured, the hunters inspected them for quality. Those who did not appear as if they would survive the journey back, or fetch a decent profit were killed on the spot, usually by slitting their throats.

Capturing women required different tactics. The easiest was to wait by the rivers or watering holes where the women were likely to come to gather water or to do laundry. Their shrieks of horror, when confronted by a group of armed slaver hunters, were quickly silenced with sharp blows from lead weighted socks. The women, repeatedly raped by the hunters, were often pregnant when they arrived. Zubehr tried to discourage the practice. Pregnant slaves did not fare well on the long, hot, dusty trails of the caravan routes.

Zubehr turned to his lieutenant. "Which of the women are pregnant?"

"They are marked green," Rabih az-Zubayr answered.

Zubehr nodded his head. Those showing signs of fertility were quarantined and imprisoned until they gave birth. Once they had given up their young, they were shipped off in the caravans. Their newborns were usually slaughtered and wound up on the trash heap outside the village. No one had the time or the interest to raise them. Their carcasses were quickly devoured by the hyenas that came in with the night. But every so often a woman would show such beauty or spirit that Zubehr would spare her and her child, and give them to one of his trusted inner circle.

Such gifts were necessary to maintain order, and to ensure each team functioned as designed. Occasionally, a man would challenge his authority or the laws. Earlier in his rule, one of his trusted men, Usama Bin, decided to take the money he received from the sale of his cargo in Dakar and convert it to his own use. Usama took the money and purchased a ticket on a steamer to Egypt, where he attempted to set up a small business. It took six months, but Zubehr got word of his location and sent several of his best men to bring Usama back to Bahr el Ghazal.

Eighteen months after he had left with the caravan, Usama came home in a box. His rotting corpse was dumped on the trash heap on the outskirts of the town. The hyenas fed on his flesh, and his bones were picked clean by the vultures that spied it while circling overhead. Usama's gleaming white bones stood testament to those who would betray Zubehr Rahamna. A wooden stake protruded from the backside of the corpse, and one from each ear. The rictus of terror demonstrated by the wildly grimacing jawbones, mouth agape, suggested that his death was not pleasant. But the torturing of traitors was child's play compared to the horrors of Zubehr's enterprise.

The third group of men in his empire was his caravan teams. They transported the slaves along the various routes to the distant slave markets for sale. These men possessed the finest survival skills in all of Africa. They could live off any land, any terrain, in any climate. And they could keep their cargo alive as well. These men were treasured, because of their skills, and the need for their return. They too were treated well by Zubehr, to ensure their loyalty and their return. Traitors like Usama Bin were a rarity. But he now took the added precaution of having an arrival team at each destination, to take charge of the cargo when the caravans arrived. The men on these teams were former leaders of the caravans, who no longer wished to travel, but were eager to remain employees of the slave king.

The fourth and final group of his forces was his standing army, entrusted with protecting the borders of Bahr el Ghazel from all enemies. They had families and children in Bahr el Ghazal. It was their home, and they would die to defend their way of life.

Zubehr turned to his son, Sulaimān, who sat to his left on the stage. "Does anyone suit you?" he asked.

"No father. Not this week," he replied. He already had over four hundred women in his harem.

"Very well," the slave king said. His face showed no emotion. He turned to Rabih. "And the trouble makers?" he asked.

"They have been marked with blood," Rabih answered.

Zubehr nodded. There were no women marked with blood, but three men who had been marked stood trembling in a cage, separated from the rest.

"This is what happens to anyone who dares to challenge me," Zubehr stood up and called out to the crowd in Arabic. Several translators echoed his words to the masses. He gestured towards his entourage. Then he sat back on his throne.

The lions were led to the cage with the marked men. The cage door opened, and the lions, excited by the red blood smeared on the men went inside. The door to the cage closed behind them. One of the lions immediately pounced on a slave, pinning him to the ground. The man screamed and then was silenced as the big cat bit down on his neck. Blood flowed out from his neck as the cat began to eat him alive. Zubehr threw his head back and laughed at the sight.

The other two men tried to climb out of the top of the cage, but several men with whips and torches turned them away. They fell back to the dirt, and the second cat lashed out with one paw, taking off the slave's head. It leaped on the other man, and its claws tore deep into his flesh. He screamed in pain.

The crowd cheered with excitement as the lions set upon their feast. There was laughter and pointing of fingers at the slaughter. It was good not to be in that cage.

CHAPTER EIGHT

LONDON, 1877

Prime Minister Benjamin Disraeli stared across his desk scowling. His bushy eyebrows furled so much they met in the middle. The object of his displeasure was the Duke of Marlborough.

"I have many important matters on my desk," the Prime Minister growled. "The opposition wants me drawn and quartered. Russia has the Ottoman Empire on the run and may be making a play for Constantinople. If Constantinople falls to the Russians, there is nothing to prevent the Russians from marching into Egypt and taking over the Suez Canal. That is the same Suez Canal that was owned and operated by the Khedive of Egypt. The same Khedive of Egypt who is such a blundering idiot that he wanted to sell it to the French for 100,000,000 francs. Instead, we bought it for four million pounds," the prime minister raged.

"Forget the fact that eighty percent of the ships going through the Suez are British," Disraeli continued. He had a stern look of displeasure on his face. He needed to vent. "Ignore the fact my emissary to the Constantinople Conference completely ignored my instructions to spread word of our intentions to occupy Bulgaria and Bosnia and take control of the Turkish army. Oh and by the way the only country remotely capable of stopping the Russians should they advance is Britain, so we may be facing a frightfully horrible war," Disraeli continued to rant.

The 7th Duke of Marlborough could only sit there and listen.

"Do you understand how complicated my job is?" Disraeli continued.

The Duke didn't like the fact that the prime minister's face was getting redder every second.

"And yet, despite these and other pressing matters, such as the ongoing problems in Ireland, I sit here at my desk, dealing with the most important issue facing the empire today," the prime minister paused for effect.

"Your son George can't keep his meat in his pants and your other idiot son, Randolph, has so pissed off the queen that she is ready to have him and his entire family shipped to a leper colony somewhere deep in Africa," the prime minister roared.

"I thought Randolph merely exposed the affair to the prince," the duke fumbled.

"Really now," the prime minister was turning crimson now. "Only an idiot would embarrass a noble in front of the prince. As it turns out, your idiot son Randolph also threatened to reveal that HRH is also shagging the Earl's wife. In fact, Randolph has somehow managed to come into possession of somewhat passionate, shall we say personal letters the prince wrote to Lady Aylesford and has threatened to make them public unless the prince quits shagging Lady Churchill as well!"

"The prince is shagging Lady Churchill?" the duke sputtered.

"The prince is shagging anything that wears a dress," the prime minister replied. "And perhaps some who are not wearing a dress," he added thoughtfully.

"Oh my," the duke could only say. "But then Randolph has a right to seek redress," he argued.

"Oh Jesus, Charles," the prime minister exclaimed. He was so exasperated he couldn't help but call his old friend the duke by his given name.

"Everyone, including you, knows that Randolph is sleeping with everyone not wearing a dress, and he couldn't care less if his wife sleeps with the entire fucking Royal Guard so long as they don't rub his face in it and jeopardize his political future."

"It's not right," the duke lamented. "That's not fair," he sputtered indignantly.

"It's not about what's right or wrong, old chap. You know that just as well as I do. It doesn't bloody well matter," Disraeli hissed. "Take your family, and get them out of London before they wind up in the Tower! Your son has blackmailed the future King of England, and his mother the queen is out for his blood."

"Oh my," wailed the duke. "Where ever shall we go?"

"If the queen has her way, Siberia. You don't mess with the 'chosen one'. But since we are trying to avoid a war with Russia, the next best place comes to mind." He paused for effect.

"Ireland," the prime minister instructed. "You shall be appointed the next Lord Lieutenant of Ireland. Take your idiot offspring and make them unpaid secretaries in your service."

The thought of leaving his opulent palace in Blenheim for the dingy Vice Regal Apartments in Dublin Castle made the duke shudder. Ireland was the armpit of the empire. Instead of living in the opulence of his palace he would be forced to live in squalor.

"But," he pleaded. "Ireland is not exactly my cup of tea. It's full of primitive and uncivilized ruffians."

"Yes, it is," Disraeli agreed cheerfully. "So your family should blend in nicely. No one will even notice them." Disraeli grinned wickedly.

"Benjamin, old friend," the duke sighed. "Please don't do this to me."

Disraeli scowled at his old friend. "Tell your son not to blackmail the prince."

"Do as I say and lay low. For at least a year. You know the Queen as well as I do. A year from now all will be forgiven. Lady Churchill is the most beautiful woman in the prince's s harem. He'll miss his favorite private piece of ass and will forgive Randolph as well just to get her back. Just give me time to make things right," Disraeli demanded.

The duke let out a deep sigh. "Yes, you are right."

"Of course I'm right," Disraeli looked offended. "Now if you will excuse me, Charles, I have some grave and confidential matters of state to attend to," Disraeli said stiffly. He rose and led the duke towards the door and opened it.

The duke left the prime minister's office in shock.

Disraeli walked back into his office and sat down. On his desk was a pamphlet. He had been avoiding reading it all day. He knew the author, William Gladstone. The same William Gladstone that Disraeli had run out of office and replaced. Now Gladstone was looking to return the favor. Elections were coming. Again. The never-ending drama of politics was rewritten daily.

"Today's drama appears to be the Arabs," Disraeli mused. "But then again, that seems always to be the drama," he added to himself. Throughout time, all great civilizations had perished. They had risen, only to fall under the weight of their human weaknesses. Borders and boundaries changed every year. Kings and queens changed power as often as they did beds. All had worn what they perceived to be their magician cloaks to keep power.

But one thing never changed.

Six hundred and twenty-nine years after the death of Christ, the prophet Muhammad conquered the pagan city of Mecca. Islam was born, and the tribes of Muhammad and Christ had been at war ever since. Technology had changed, but man had not. The endless battle between religions continued.

The latest clash was on the northern borders of the Ottoman Empire. The Christians were revolting against the Arab tribes, and the Arabs were not happy.

Disraeli thumbed through the pamphlet, occasionally letting out a grunt of disapproval. It told him nothing new. The problem was that the voting public was going to read the damn thing.

The voting youth of his nation would view the problem as new. Because they perceived it as new, it was, therefore, newsworthy, exciting, and for this group, very important. Disraeli harkened back to his studies at Higham Hill in Walthamstow. Greek history had been one of his favorite topics. Aristotle had been his favorite philosopher.

"Young people are not proper students of morals and politics. They are too inexperienced in the practical side of living. Young people are ruled by their emotions, their study will be vain and profitless, for the ultimate object of the study is not knowing but doing."

"How true," Disraeli said out loud. But the problem was the youthful vote of England had a vote and would be easily swayed by the rhetoric of the day. And the rhetoric of the day was dictated by the press.

Disraeli continued to read Gladstone's pamphlet. Eugene Schuyler of the Daily News, the same Daily News founded by Charles Dickens, was reporting that fifteen thousand Christians had been slaughtered by their Muslim oppressors in Bulgaria during the "April Uprising."

And if you couldn't trust Charles Dickens' newspaper, who could you trust, Disraeli wondered? Hell, if I were young, I'd be thinking the same thing. The reporter's words jumped out at him from the print:

> "...On every side were human bones, skulls, ribs, and even complete skeletons, heads of girls still adorned with braids of long hair, bones of children, skeletons still encased in clothing. Here was a house the floor of which was white with the ashes and charred bones of thirty persons burned alive there. Here was the spot where the village notable Trendafil was spitted on a pike and then roasted, and where he is now buried; there was a foul hole full of decomposing bodies; here a mill dam filled with swollen corpses; here the school house, where 200 women and children had taken refuge there were burned alive, and here the church and churchyard, where fully a thousand half-decayed forms were still to be seen, filling the enclosure in a heap several feet high, arms, feet, and heads protruding from the stones which had vainly been thrown there to hide them, and poisoning all the air.

> "Since my visit, by orders of the Mutessarif, the Kaimakam of Tatar Bazardjik was sent to Batak, with some lime to aid in the decomposition of the bodies, and to prevent a pestilence.

"Ahmed Aga, who commanded at the massacre, has
been decorated and promoted to the rank of Yuz-bashi..."

Disraeli sat back in his chair. Born a Jew, whom later converted to
Christianity, he had steadfastly and publicly backed the Arabs and the
Ottoman Empire. The same Ottoman Empire that had just massacred
fifteen thousand Christians. Gladstone, the man who wanted his job,
was urging England to disband the alliance with the Arabs. They were
slaughtering innocent Christian men, women, and children.

Disraeli scanned over the reporter's story again. Damn, I'm not sure
I want to be in bed with them anymore either, he thought. But to admit
that would be political suicide.

Marlborough can kiss my ass, the prime minister decided. I've more
important things to worry about than where the prince puts his peter.

CHAPTER NINE

MONTEREY, 1877

David Jacks pulled his carriage up to the hitching post in front of the Boston General Store and sprang blithely onto the raised wooden sidewalk without setting foot onto the packed clay on Alvarado Street. Jacks had just turned sixty, but he still had a spry step about him.

A soft breeze blew across the bay, and he inhaled the smell of the sea deeply into his lungs. He was wearing a white cotton dress shirt underneath a black leather vest and denim pants. He felt relaxed and refreshed in the morning air. He loved Monterey. It reminded him of home. He had left Scotland as a young boy to immigrate with his parents to America. But he still remembered the green hills of Loch Levin on the coast of his beloved Scotland.

The door to Boston's General Store was propped open to bring in the sea breeze, and Jacks could see Joseph Boston Jr. rearranging merchandise in the glass display case. It held all the latest bobbles and trinkets shipped from San Francisco.

"Morning, Joseph," he greeted his friend.

"Good morning, Mr. Jacks," Boston replied. He studiously dusted off the top of the glass display case, and rearranged the necklaces from San Francisco on a wooden tray. "I got these in from Frisco last week."

"Joseph, we need to talk," Jacks said.

Boston nervously ran his hand through his already thinning hair. "What about, sir?" he replied.

Boston knew where the conversation was headed. David Jacks was one of the most powerful and influential men in Monterey. Jacks owned over 60,000 acres of Monterey proper, and he also owned and operated the First Monterey Bank, which coincidently, owned the land upon which the general store had been built.

"Joseph, it's been two years since you've turned a profit in your store. The interest payment on your loan is going to come due next month, and you haven't even paid last month's payment, to say nothing of the principle on your loan, laddie," Jacks said.

He gestured around the small store with his arms.

"You're selling trinkets and baubles from Frisco. You have no customers, and your inventory is overstocked."

"People like jewelry," Boston stammered. He nervously rearranged the glasses on the end of his nose. "I like jewelry," he added softly. He sat down on the stool behind the counter.

When Jacks had first arrived at Monterey, Boston's father had given him his first job working in the general store. He allowed Jacks to live in his home. Jacks had never forgotten the favor shown him by the elder man. After his death, Jacks was determined to see that his son, Joseph Jr., would live a safe and prosperous life in Monterey. In fact, the dying Boston had practically wrung his wrist off as he clutched his hand, evoking a promise to look after his son.

It was a promise that Jacks was determined to keep, no matter how difficult. And it was difficult. The younger Boston, who inherited the general store from his father, had failed to inherit the business wits of his father. In fact, Boston had few if any wits about him. Thus the fervent prayer of a dying man.

David Jacks looked at the forlorn figure sitting in the corner of his dusty little store and felt pity. He also felt contempt, but tempered that emotion with his pledge to Boston's father. He wondered if Joseph's father had regarded him with pity when he gave Jacks his first job in the dusty little store.

"Come see me at the end of the week, and we'll talk. I have some ideas if you're interested," Jacks offered.

Joseph nodded his head gratefully. "I will," he said. "I will."

Jacks smiled, and walked out onto the raised wooden sidewalk, and gazed about. His town was growing, and so were his profits. Monterey had been good to David Jacks. For thirty-five years, he spent every waking moment trying to build it into the vision he had when he first arrived from San Francisco, running a load of pistols from New York. My god, he had been young and oh so reckless. But fortune had smiled upon him, and he made a good profit from selling those pistols. He took those funds and started a small loan business on the side. Before long, he quickly built that into another profitable enterprise. He put those profits toward buying land, building a small holding company that purchased small parcels of real estate and resold them at a profit later.

But David Jacks was not content just to make money off loans. He wanted power, and power came from owning land. In 1859, David Jacks executed a stroke of genius that brought him both fame and fortune.

At that time, Monterey was a small and impoverished town. The only industry was whaling. And in those days, whaling was even more challenging and dangerous. Unlike whalers like the Rachel H., crewed by men like Dirk McDuran, the whalers in the early days launched their long boats from the beach just below the Custom House. They went out to hunt with nothing more than the muscles behind the oars and the skill and aim of the man throwing the harpoons and lances. Their quarry—the massive humpback and gray whales that migrated up and down the coast.

But revenue from the whaling industry and the surrounding lands were not enough to support the debts of the City of Monterey, and one of the town fathers suggested that they put some of the lands up for sale at an auction. That suggestion came from James McKinley, a fellow Scotsman and close friend of David Jacks.

No one was sure exactly what happened next, but by the time the dust had settled, over 60,000 acres of land was auctioned off to the highest bidder, of which there was only one. David Jacks. He owned the town.

He also earned the hatred of Thomas Larkin Jr. Junior thought the town should belong to him because his father had been a rich and powerful man. What his father did not pass down to him was the intelligence to make that a reality, or the compassion to even understand how.

There was also a new project in the works. The railroad baron Charles Crocker was planning to extend the railroad from San Francisco to Monterey. He was also planning to build a new hotel on land that Jacks had sold him. The Del Monte was going to be the jewel of Monterey, a tony new place for the wealthy upper class to come and vacation.

Business was booming, Jacks thought happily. His thoughts were interrupted by footsteps coming up from his right. He turned and saw a rugged looking man smiling at him as he approached the store. Jacks grinned. It was Dirk McDuran.

Jacks stuck out his hand. "Always good to see a fellow Scotsman," he beamed.

The two men shook hands.

"How's business?" Dirk asked.

Jacks could only smile. "Better than ever," he said. "And you? How is that new son of yours?"

"Growing bigger every day," Dirk replied proudly.

"When do you go out to sea again?" Jacks asked. He saw Dirk's face darken.

"I'm not sure. It depends on whether the Chinese are going to end the strike."

Jacks scowled. "They're lucky to have jobs in the first place," he growled. He didn't like the Chinese. Their long pony tails and funny way of dressing annoyed him. Their food stunk, and so did their village. He knew that most white people in Monterey felt the same way.

"They're hard workers, Mr. Jacks," Dirk said evenly. "They don't deserve to be treated the way they are. Larkin treats them like slaves."

"I'm no fan of Larkin," Jacks said. "But on this issue, he may have a point."

"They're immigrants, just like you and me," Dirk said. "We're no better than they are."

Jacks just shook his head. "Bloody hell man. You best not be heard talking like that. It could get you into trouble with your boss," Jacks warned. "Clear your stubborn Scottish brain of such foolish thoughts."

Dirk looked away.

"I'm not made that way," he resisted.

"You've got a wife and a new child to support," Jacks said. "And Larkin's not a man to mess with." Jacks could see the look of concern on Dirk's face.

"Stay out of it, laddie," he advised without being asked.

"Too late," Dirk replied.

Jacks looked Dirk in the eye. "What did you do man?"

"I spoke with an investigator who works for Senator McDonald," he answered. "I know I shouldn't have, but I can't stand the way Larkin and Rodriguez treat these men. I thought our country just fought a war to end that kind of thing."

"Jesus Mary, mother of God," Jacks sputtered. "I know the Senator. Do you realize the can of worms you've just opened? Senator McDonald was close friends with Larkin's father. You are going to be stuck smack dab in the middle. The Senator may be a fellow Scotsman, but there are a lot of folks in Washington that don't like the Chinese either. I'm not sure I know which side of the fence McDonald falls on."

"Then why would he send an investigator out?" Dirk asked.

"To cover his ass," Jacks replied. "He's playing both sides of the fence just like all good politicians do. He can say he looked into the matter and found nothing." Jacks looked up and down the street. No one was watching the two men talk.

"I've got meetings to go to, Dirk. I'm going to pretend we didn't have this conversation, and you'd better shut the hell up and watch your back."

"Aye, I'll watch my back," Dirk replied. "I've got a few things to pick up in the store." He paused. "And thanks for the warning."

"You're kin. A fellow Scot. It's the least I can do." Jacks got in his carriage and pulled away from the store. He was troubled. Very troubled.

Chapter Ten

IRELAND 1877

Randolph sipped his tea and read the front page of the Irish-American newspaper with great interest. Colonel John O'Mahony, one of the founding fathers of the Irish Republican Brotherhood, had passed away.

"What a shame," Randolph mused. Randolph had quickly made the transition from an up-and-coming politician in London to an up-and-coming politician in Ireland. It was in his blood. He was delighted to find that everyone in Dublin knew his name.

"What's a shame?" Lady Churchill asked. She didn't look up, completely immersed in the latest edition of Punch magazine.

Randolph looked annoyed. "I'll read it to you," he said.

"One of the prominent members of the Fenian movement has been laid to rest. Thousands lined the streets for a chance to view the body and pay respects to Colonel John O'Mahony as he lay in state in the armory of the 69th Regiment."

"And why do I care?" she asked without looking up.

Now Randolph was annoyed. He looked across the table at his wife. Her long black hair flowed over her shoulders. He admired her jaw line, the curves of her throat, and the swell of her breast. She really was exquisite. Randolph couldn't explain why she didn't move him sexually. She just didn't. But she was a wonderful friend and companion, and he loved her deeply.

"Because if the Fenian's had their way, they would no longer be part of the empire. They want their independence," he added. "Home Rule."

Lady Churchill looked up from her magazine.

"And what is wrong with that?"

"You bloody Americans are all alike," Randolph laughed. "Liberty, liberty," he chanted. "Give me liberty or give me death," he quipped.

"We gave your ancestors lots of death and won our independence," Lady Randolph said smugly.

"Yes you did," Randolph agreed cheerfully. "And if every colony of the crown were to achieve their independence, England would no longer be the greatest country on earth."

"Pity," she smirked.

"A pity indeed!" Randolph exclaimed happily. "Because then you would be deprived of the upper-class social life that you adore."

Jenny yawned, feigning boredom. "No. I would go back to America," she said.

Randolph laughed. Ah, his wife was not only beautiful, but she was also very witty. He adored her.

"Bitch," he teased.

"Yes, I think so," she said playfully. She resumed reading her magazine.

Randolph looked back at the headline. It gave the names of members of the Irish Republican Brotherhood who attended the funeral. Randolph noted with interest that one significant name was missing. The rising star of Ireland and the newest member of Parliament, Charles Parnell.

The crown and the English upper class were very concerned about "the Irish problem," as the prince had put it. And it occurred to Randolph that he could kill two birds with one stone. End his banishment to Ireland and build his bridge back to the prime minister's office. Seize the moment, he thought. It just might be enough to put him back in the good graces of HRH and back on track for the one thing that mattered most to Randolph, his political career.

Ever since arriving in Dublin, Randolph and Jenny had been very busy with the surprisingly upbeat social circle. In fact, Lady Churchill was having a blast, riding horses through the potato fields by day and going to balls, theaters and dinner parties at night. While she was busy steeple chasing and fox hunting, Randolph was busy building contacts with influential politicians, on both sides of the aisle.

Always on the lookout for political leverage, Randolph believed he had stumbled upon a golden nugget. The rising star of Irish politics had an Achilles' heel. Parnell was literally in bed with the lovely Katherine O'Shea. The buxom red-head was married to another up-and-coming Irish politician, Captain William O'Shea of the 18th Hussars of the British Army.

The very same Captain William O'Shea who represented his government in talks with the political brain of the Fenian movement, Charles Parnell. Parnell was shagging his opponents wife and the British. Randolph could only rub his hands together with glee when informed of this valuable information by one of his many confidential informants. Parnell was the *undeclared* leader of the Fenian movement because he was also a member of Parliament.

"The plot thickens," he muttered happily.

"What thickens?" his wife asked.

Randolph could barely contain himself as he told his dearest friend his latest gossip. Like all politicians, blackmail was one of his favorite games.

Smoke filled the pub. So did the noise. The Irish like to talk when they drink, and the air was full of it. The pub was a place to relax and unwind, and the Bull and the Bear was no different. Charles Parnell settled into his seat on the wooden bench in the booth and perused the menu.

"I say old chap," Randolph Churchill said cheerfully. "Mind if I join you?" He didn't wait for the answer. He removed his top hat and top coat and set them on the other side of the table.

"I thought that was the plan," Parnell said casually. He put down his pint and smiled. He looked over Churchill's meticulous attire. Strictly upper-class House of Lords stuff. The silver stick pin and the cravat tie defined the parameters of the icy encounter between British upper class and the Fenians. In contrast, Parnell wore a casual tweed jacket and his collar was open.

"A splendid plan indeed," Randolph said, beaming. He brushed a piece of lint off the lapel of his silk jacket. "I greatly admire the manner in which you have championed the Irish cause," he continued smoothly. "And I wish to assure you that I have always favored Home Rule," he promised.

"Thank you," Parnell said. "I have your word?"

"As a gentleman. Yes, of course."

"And what do you want in return?" Parnell asked honestly.

"Nothing, at the moment," Randolph smiled. "It's good to have friends in high places. Ireland is critical to the crown. I'd like to see everyone happy."

Parnell looked at the intense eyes above the dark handlebar mustache. Could he trust him? A favor offered equals a favor owed. What game was Churchill playing?

As fate would have it, it was a very deep game.

CHAPTER ELEVEN

SUDAN, 1877

It took Gordon and Gessi months to build up an intelligence network to infiltrate Zubehr's organization. Gordon was growing impatient. Three years had passed since his arrival, but he still felt he needed more information. He decided to travel south to assess the situation himself. As was his custom, he traveled alone, by horse. Gordon also brought along two camels for his supplies. When he went in the desert, he only used camels. But when he traveled south, toward the more arid regions of the Sudan, he liked the extra speed and control that a horse provided him.

Gordon had no fear of traveling alone. His ability to live off the land, to ward off danger and to survive behind the lines was legendary. He wore the clothes of an Arab trader but carried the weapons of a British officer.

Legend had it that Gordon traveled unarmed. Legend was very, very wrong. No one survives in Africa unarmed. He carried a revolver underneath his robe. Strapped to the side of his horse in a leather harness was a gift from an American general he had met in London, a .30-30 Winchester repeater rifle. It allowed him to fire off seven rounds as fast as he could eject the shells. It carried a telescope, mounted on the side, which allowed him to aim at distant targets over three hundred yards away. It gave him an excellent tactical advantage. Arabs and Africans alike rarely carried firearms, and if they did, they were usually old, powder-fed muskets.

Strapped to the horse was his saber in a leather scabbard. An expert swordsman, it was his first weapon of choice. In his left boot was a dagger, in his right, a derringer. His camels carried water, food, sleeping gear, extra ammunition and his Farquharson rifle for big game.

Gordon's intended to get as close as he could to the borders of Bahr el Ghazal and probe the limits of Zubehr Rahamna's empire. Fluent in Arabic, Gordon had the accent of an upper-class merchant from Khartoum. His face was burned mahogany by the sun. He was frequently mistaken for an Arab trader. He wore a black turban, his face protected from the dust by a black shroud that covered his mouth and nose. Only his fierce sapphire blue eyes gave away his European descent. But by the time anyone was close enough to see his eyes, Gordon had already determined if they were friend or foe.

On this foray, he was now over four hundred miles south of Khartoum, northwest of the village of Fashoda. This southern area of the Sudan was higher, cooler and lush with vegetation. His navigation skills told him he was just south of the Nuba Mountains.

He broke camp at dawn and was riding towards the boundaries of Bahr el Ghazal when he heard a woman screaming. He urged his horse forward at a gallop and rounded the edge of a mountain ridge into an open area by a small stream. He saw a black woman stumbling as she ran from a group of men hotly in pursuit through the high savanna grass. She was pulling a younger black woman by the hand. They kept looking backward, eyes wide with fear. The men, on foot, closed the gap.

Slavers, Gordon thought. A hunting party?

There were five of them, armed with swords and spears. Their sandals clattered on the earth as they gave chase, their eyes wide with excitement, cloth robes flapping in the wind.

Underneath one of the robes, Gordon caught a glimpse of a pistol, and he knew that he had encountered some of Rahamna's hunters. They were too close to Bahr el Ghazal and too few to be hunting for new slaves. That could only mean that they were hunting escaped slaves. When slaves escaped, an example had to be made. And it was an ugly sight.

His horse now at a gallop, Gordon cut off the hunters from their prey and rode towards them without breaking his stride. Before they could react, he was among them. The closest attacker on his left went for his pistol, but his arm was severed from his body by one downward swipe of Gordon's saber. Gordon reined back his horse with his left hand, and another swipe to his right took off the head of the hunter on his right who had just begun to raise his sword.

Instinctively, Gordon backed his horse away from the three remaining men, to create space, and to determine his next move. They made theirs, and came at him from three directions, rushing his front and the sides. Mouths agape, screaming wildly, they came at him.

He smoothly switched his saber to his left hand, drew his revolver, and shot the man in front directly between the eyes. He backed up his horse, using pressure from his knees, further creating a gap, and calmly aimed for the temple of the man on the left, who was closest. Now there were two.

Suddenly, he felt his horse stumble as its right rear hoof struck a boulder. The horse felt itself losing its balance and pivoted left to keep its footing. The pivot tossed Gordon to his right side, and he hit the ground.

As he landed, he kept rolling, which proved to be a good idea, as the nearest hunter's sword hit the ground with a mighty thud a fraction of a second after Gordon rolled.

Gordon stopped rolling and brought his revolver to bear on his closest adversary. At the same time, his foe wrenched his blade from the ground, and the next blow took the pistol from Gordon's hand.

"Sweet Jesus!" he exclaimed. He rolled to his feet, pulling his dagger from his boot at the same time. The hunter swung from the hip. Gordon ducked, and plunged the six-inch blade to the hilt, twisting the blade inside the man's chest to sever as many blood vessels as he could, and then tore the knife out.

At the same time, he spun away, expecting the onslaught of his final adversary. It came, as the young Arab hunter plowed headlong into Gordon, knocking them both to the ground and their weapons from their grasp. Gordon went down on his back, the Arab on top of him. He could smell his fetid breath on his face and felt his fingers closing on his throat. Their eyes locked, and Gordon could see triumph in the hunter's eyes. His eyes said it was just a matter of time. He leaned forward increase the pressure.

With his eyes bulging from their sockets, Gordon reached into his boot, pulled his derringer, put it up to his assailant's head, and pulled the trigger. The recoil knocked the derringer from his hand and blew the man's brains out sideways onto the dirt. His eyes grew wide, and he fell off Gordon to the side, blood spurting like a fountain from the gaping hole in the side of his skull.

Gordon exhaled deeply and lay still on his back. That was five. He prayed that his count had been right. He was out of weapons and exhausted.

As he lay there, gasping for breath, he heard footsteps approaching from his right.

"Oh my lord," he exclaimed. He rolled his head to the right and saw the two women approaching him.

"Stay back," he warned them in Arabic.

They seemed to understand. The older woman squatted down on her haunches and waited. The younger one smiled. Her teeth were like ivory pearls, laid across lips of ebony silk. Huge brown doe shaped eyes, framed by high, polished cheekbones. Her black hair was long and braided. The image was imprinted in his brain, even while he pondered the absurdity of the moment, and his own ability to find beauty while surrounded by the blood and guts of five men he had just killed. Order out of chaos.

He slowly rose to his feet. The younger woman started to back away, but she still held his gaze. The older woman made a clucking sound with her tongue, and she surveyed the destruction around them.

"You are a mighty warrior," the old woman said in Arabic.

"A damn lucky one," Gordon responded. He picked up his derringer and stuck it back in his boot. He took the turban off one of the dead hunters and let the head hit the ground with a thud. He slowly wiped the blood off his dagger.

He looked around the foliage where his horse had lost its footing and found his revolver. His motions were smooth and deliberate as he ejected the old shells and reloaded.

"Why were they chasing you?" he asked as he slid the revolver back into his holster.

"We escaped from Fashoda," the older women said.

"You escaped from Bahr el Ghazal," Gordon corrected her.

"We escaped from Bahr el Ghazal," the younger one replied. "From that pig Zubehr Rahamna." She spit into the dirt.

The older woman shook her head in disapproval. "Do not trust the blue-eyed devil."

Gordon threw his head back and laughed.

"The devil indeed." He surveyed the landscape. "How far to the mountains?"

"Two, maybe three hours ride," said the young one. She was tall, very tall for a woman. She had a way of holding her chin upright and held his gaze. The foothills were close, only a few miles away.

"We'll make camp in the hills," Gordon said. "I don't want our fire in plain view." He rounded up his camels grazing quietly nearby. Gordon had a way with animals. They trusted him and seemed content to remain near him.

"We'll walk," he said. "Gather up whatever you can use from them," he said, motioning towards the five corpses.

"Water and food first. I plan on eating dinner."

They made the foothills just as the sun began to set over the plains to the west. Gordon found a small meadow nestled near a stand of trees and let his horse and the camels graze in the grass. A herd of oryx grazed on the flat savanna at the base of the foothills. Gordon briefly considered shooting one for dinner, but decided against it. He didn't want more company for dinner.

He eyed the two women who were gathering wood for a fire. The younger one laid out a small ring of stones. They had retrieved a copper pot, and the older one had found water in a nearby spring. She boiled water and mixed it with dried grain that she had taken off one of the hunters. Gordon opened a tin of bully beef from his saddlebag, and they ate quietly, watching the sun set on the plains. Gordon heard the bark of a lion in the near distance, and younger woman shivered.

"Why did you leave Bahr el Ghazal?" he asked. "It's two hundred miles to Fashoda."

"When I was eleven, I was raped by Zubehr Rahamna," the older women said quietly. "Now his son Sulaimān would like to do the same to my daughter." She clucked her tongue.

"Your daughter does not look like she is part Arab."

"Zubehr did not father her. She is the child of my husband, Zeda Teganemba. He was a Dinka warrior, who chose to fight to his death rather than be enslaved. Rahamna cut off his head when his hunters tracked us down. I was brought back to be his whore once again. My daughter will not share that fate."

Gordon leaned back on his bed roll and lit a cigarette. "My people want to do away with slavery. That's why I am here."

"How does a white man travel alone?" asked the young woman.

"I am a soldier. I have been trained to do this."

"You blend in well. At first, I thought you were a mercenary or a trader. It wasn't until I saw your eyes that I knew you were a white man," said the young woman, smiling at him. "My name is Sindella."

Gordon exhaled a ring of smoke. Of course it was. "My name is Gordon."

The older woman shook her head. "Not that anyone cares, but I am Mindau," she said. She watched her daughter, and she knew that she liked the Englishman.

"Mindau, I have never been to Bahr el Ghazal. What is it like?" Gordon asked.

"It is a great city. It has a giant wall around it. Rahamna has many soldiers in the city just to protect him. He has his own body guard." She paused.

"But you are just one man," she continued. "Instead of five you will find five thousand. You are a great warrior, but even you cannot slay a horde."

"I do not intend to try. I am here just to learn." I will slay them later, he thought to himself.

"Then you should know that Rahamna is planning to attack Darfur," blurted out Sindella. "After the rains."

"How do you know this?" Gordon lit another cigarette.

"Sulaimān was bragging to me, to impress me. He is to lead the army," Sindella replied.

Gordon's mind went through the permutations. The list was exhaustive. But if the source of information and the circumstance that led him to it matched, he would have to give it serious thought. If Rahamna's main fighting force were to go to Darfur, Bahr el Ghazal would be vulnerable to attack.

"We will leave at dawn," he said.

He lay down on his bedroll and blew a smoke ring into the air. The stars were brilliant in the African sky, and he heard the distant bark of hyena and the grunt of a lion. He was so far away from home. His comfortable manor, his servants, all seemed distant and unimportant. Here in the vast wilds of Africa, he felt at home. At one with nature, but at war with his enemy. He was finally getting close to striking his enemy a mortal blow.

CHAPTER TWELVE

MONTEREY, 1877

Larkin sat at a table in Cooper's general store across the street from his house. He tapped his fingers impatiently on the wooden table. He hated waiting for anyone. Finally, the dark face of Captain Francisco Rodriguez gazed at him intently as the sea captain made his way down the aisle lined with barrels of dry goods.

"About time you got here," Larkin groused.

Rodriguez sat down at the table. They were alone in the back of the store.

"The strike is over," Larkin announced smugly.

The barrel-chested seaman stared back at Larkin. His smoldering black eyes were deep set above a thick black beard. He was smart, ambitious, and meaner than a snake. Perfect for the job, Larkin thought.

"And what did it cost you?" Rodriguez asked.

"A promise from you," Larkin said firmly.

The bushy eyebrows went up.

"What promise?"

Larkin glared over his hooked nose. He looks like a vulture, Rodriguez thought to himself.

"You will guarantee the safety of the Chinamen on your boat," Larkin said.

Rodriquez threw back his head and roared with laughter. Larkin looked annoyed.

"I don't see the humor in that."

Rodriguez's whole body shook. He looked at the pale skinned, balding man sitting across from him.

"I can't even promise my own safety," he laughed. "Whaling is a dangerous business."

"You know what I mean," Larkin hissed.

The sea captain stopped laughing, and his eyes fixed on Larkin's. His right hand dropped to his right side where he wore a large dagger. No man called him out without paying the price.

"What are you suggesting, Mr. Larkin?" he growled. His fingers curled around the handle of the knife.

Larkin smiled back. His right hand was below the table and had been the moment Rodriguez walked in the door.

"Take your hand off your blade, Captain," Larkin said. "Unless you want me to pull the trigger on the .45 caliber Colt revolver pointed at your gut."

Rodriguez slowly brought his right hand up and rested it on top of the table.

"Good man," Larkin said. "No need to take offense. I simply mean that you will make an effort to show the slanty-eyed bastards that you won't take unnecessary risks with their lives."

"Define unnecessary," Rodriguez asked. His blood was still coursing.

"I'll leave that up to you," Larkin said. "I can't stand them any more than you can, but I need cheap labor, and I can't afford another strike anytime soon. So do your best to keep them alive. I'm not saying you have to sit around and drink tea with them at night. You're still the captain. But I've heard rumors that some people from Washington have been snooping around asking questions. So that's another good reason to keep the chinks alive."

"I'll run the ship as I see fit," the captain growled.

"As long as I keep you Captain, I would expect nothing else," Larkin said smoothly. "Who is going to be your first mate this time out?"

"That Scottish fella. McDuran. He's a good sailor. He also gets along good with the chinks, so I don't have to deal with them," Rodriguez said.

Larkin nodded. "Maybe too good." He brought his right hand up above the table. It was empty. Rodriguez glared at him.

"I was just bluffing, Captain," Larkin said easily. "I didn't want you to stick me with that blade." He held out his hand. "No hard feelings? We'll get rid of the chinks when we don't need them anymore."

They shook hands. Rodriguez never took his gaze off Larkin's face.

CHAPTER THIRTEEN

LONDON, 1877

"The General is here," Disraeli's secretary said.

Disraeli set down the copy of the New York Herald. Things were going from bad to worse. Januarius MacGahan, a reporter for the Herald, had interviewed Eugene Schuyler, fresh from his travels in Bulgaria. The print screamed up at him like the voices of the dead and the damned. The nightmare continued.

"My father in law went to meet the Bashi-Bazouk when the village was surrounded by the men of Ahmet Aga, who said that he wanted all the arms laid down. Trendafil went to collect them from the villagers. When he surrendered the arms, they shot him with a gun and the bullet scratched his eye. Then I heard Ahmet Aga command with his own mouth for Trendafil to be impaled and burnt. The words he used were "Shishak aor" which is Turkish for "to put on a skewer" (as a shish kebab). After that, they took all the money he had, undressed him, gouged his eyes, pulled out his teeth and impaled him slowly on a stake, until it came out of his mouth. Then they roasted him while he was still alive. He lived for half-an-hour during this terrible scene. At the time, I was near Ahmet Aga with other Bulgarian women. We were surrounded by Bashi-Bozouk, who had us surrounded, and forced us to watch what was happening

to Trendafil. One of her children, Vladimir, who was still a baby at his mother's breast, was impaled on a sword in front of her eyes. *At the time this was happening, Ahmet Aga's son took my child from my back and cut him to pieces, there in front of me. The burnt bones of Trendafil stood there for one month and only then they were buried."*

"So much for supporting the Arabs," Disraeli sighed. The cat was out of the bag again, and it bore the face of his rival Gladstone, grinning like a Cheshire cat. Disraeli had backed the wrong horse, and both Parliament and the public wanted an answer. They also wanted change.

"Send him in," the prime minister said. Gordon walked into the office. The general's skin, baked by the sun, was darker than most Arabs.

"General Gordon, thank you so much for coming on such short notice," the career politician said politely.

"My pleasure," Gordon replied. In truth, he was furious. He had just returned to Khartoum to find a summons from the prime minister. It had been a two-month journey. He had better things to do, such as catch Rahamna with his pants down.

"Whiskey?"

"Why yes, thank you," Gordon feigned politeness.

The prime minister poured them both a stout measure of Scotch from a crystal decanter. Gordon smiled at the starched cuffs and collar of the politician's shirt and the expensive jewel pin placed carefully in the cravat. He waited for the leader of the Conservative Party to begin. All the starch in the world and the *man still looked rumpled.*

"How was your journey?" Disraeli asked.

"Long, hot and boring," Gordon said honestly.

"Well thank you for coming," the prime minister said sincerely. "I need to speak with you privately about this slave king, Super Ramna," he said.

"*Zubehr Rahamna.* Who is proving himself to be a very worthy adversary," Gordon corrected politely.

"So much so, that I'm afraid he has the Khedive of Egypt rather in a tizzy," Disraeli said.

"An understatement," Gordon agreed. "When the Khedive sent his troops down to punish Zubehr for not paying taxes, Zubehr's army wiped them clean. Rather humorous that he apologized to the Khedive for defeating his soldiers."

"A bit cheeky, I agree," Disraeli said. "And now he has eyes on Darfur?"

"Yes. That was in my last dispatch. And when his army goes to Darfur I will take Bahr el Ghazal. He will be forced to retake it. I'll be waiting, and he and his army will be surrounded and cut to pieces."

Disraeli nodded his head. "That's an excellent plan."

"It's taken three bloody years, but by god, I swore to myself when I took this job I was going to bloody well finish that bastard off," Gordon growled.

Disraeli tried not to grimace.

"General, there's been a change of plans," the prime minister announced.

Gordon looked at him quizzically. "What?"

"The Khedive has cut a deal with Rahamna," Disraeli said. "He is going to appoint him pasha."

Gordon tried not to show his surprise.

"I would not expect you to know that," Disraeli soothed. "Our agents in Cairo uncovered the plan. We like it."

"Why the bloody hell would the Khedive want to give Rahamna a deal?" Gordon asked. "That's not going to change a thing."

"To accept his appointment, Zubehr will have to travel to Cairo," Disraeli said calmly. "He *will not* be allowed to return. It's not optional. And of course, they won't tell him until he's already there."

"He can always escape," Gordon countered.

"He'll be watched day and night by his own staff. It's the safest route. The Khedive feels threatened. He has not forgotten what happened the last time he used military force against Rahamna. He would rather have an ally than an enemy."

"I'm ready to cut the bastard to ribbons," Gordon said, his voice rising. "I was sent to destroy the slave king, not to get in bed with him," Gordon snarled. He felt his blood begin to boil.

"I say old chap, you know how the world works," the prime minister said. He needed to calm Gordon down. He was still the governor of the Sudan, and he was going to have to send him back anyway. Gordon was right. The Khedive had no qualms about using Gordon to defeat his enemy. Cornered, the Khedive was feeling threatened and would willingly sacrifice Gordon and his work to make a deal with the devil to keep power.

"Normally, England wouldn't give a rat's ass. But now there is a larger, more long-term problem to deal with," the life-long politician began.

"Enlighten me," Gordon said. He was trying very hard to not to come across the desk and throttle the prime minister. He had spent three years of his life in that godforsaken shit hole setting Rahamna up for the kill, and now the politicians were going to promote his sworn enemy.

"The truth of the matter is the empire is feeling threatened as well. Due to the mismanagement of his empire, the Khedive is broke. He's threatening to nationalize the Suez Canal and sell it to the highest bidder. With the Russians on the move in the east, the French are eyeing Africa as the next logical step in their plans to rule the world."

"Let me finish off Rahamna, and the threat will be gone," Gordon suggested. He was trying very hard to keep the sarcasm out of his voice.

"We are looking for a political way to end the rule of the slave king," Disraeli explained.

"That's not why you sent me there."

"No disrespect man, but not everyone is convinced you can pull this off. If it backfires, we have blood on our hands and mud on our face. It's a risk we can't afford."

"Then why did you send me there in the first place?" Gordon pressed. Technology had changed, but man had not.

Disraeli frowned. He did not like being questioned by his subordinates. The general might be all powerful on the field of battle, but the truth was Gordon was nothing more than a pawn in the game of politics. It was a shame, Disraeli thought. He seemed an outstanding officer. Very loyal to his country. Rather than dismiss him outright, he was determined to keep him onboard. He still had value.

"Gordon, you're a general. You defeat your enemy on the field of battle," Disraeli explained. "I'm a politician. My field of battle is public opinion. And right now, my opponent Gladstone has me by the balls for supporting the Arabs. As a result of the massacre of innocent Christians during the April Uprising in the Balkans, the public wants nothing to do with the Ottoman Empire or any Arab. The support for a military intervention in the Sudan on behalf of the Khedive is no longer present. There is another way of propping him up."

"How?"

"Can I trust you?" Disraeli asked. His dark brown eyes glared into Gordon's eyes like a sentry squinting through the fog for the slightest hint of danger.

"Yes. I obey orders and am a loyal subject to the Queen," Gordon replied. Bastards, he thought to himself. Seek power, find power, keep power. Some things never change. Not since the beginning of time.

"The leaders of my party, the banks and the queen are determined to hold the winning hand. We give the Khedive money and power, and he will keep paying his debts."

"With our money?" Gordon asked, incredulous. "That makes no sense."

"It's a short-term solution to a long-term problem. We are in a position right now to do something the French are not yet able to do. We are going to buy some time."

"For what?" Gordon said.

"The Arabs are very good at deceit. They consider it an art form to outwit their enemy," Disraeli continued, annoyed by the incessant questions. The man was damn near insubordinate.

"So what would you have me do?" Gordon asked, cutting to the point.

"Same as always," Disraeli replied. "Your orders are to return to

Khartoum, consolidate your forces, and be prepared to crush '*Zubehr Rahamna*' if he fails to play ball. If he does play ball, then be ready to welcome him," Disraeli grinned.

Gordon could only laugh.

"If I understand things correctly, we are making a deal with the devil in hopes that it will preserve the sale of the Suez Canal?" Gordon asked.

"Precisely," the prime minister answered. "And Zubehr Rahamna will travel to Cairo to be given the title of 'Pasha.' He will answer to the Khedive, and he will not be allowed to return home."

Gordon tossed down his whiskey and rose to his feet.

"Zubehr Rahamna has never answered to anyone. Nor will his son, Sulaimān. What makes you think he will now?" Gordon asked.

Disraeli looked at the steady blue eyes of the indignant general.

"General Gordon, if things go sideways, we shall revisit the future of Zubehr Rahamna's existence. But given the fact that the Khedive does not intend to let Rahamna return to the Sudan anyway, I suspect something must be done about his son. You just be ready to move on him when your orders come."

"Yes, sir." Gordon smiled wryly. What else could he say? With a smirk on his face, he left the office. They were going to give the slave king a promotion. It was always the same. The politicians liked to scheme their way out of a mess. Gordon would rather fight his way out.

CHAPTER FOURTEEN

SUDAN, 1878

When Gordon returned from London, he gave instructions for the two women he had rescued to be given quarters in the fortress. He wanted to learn more about his enemy. He pushed aside thoughts of the beautiful young Nubian woman. Focus on the mission. He wasn't here to seek the pleasures of the flesh.

He walked into his office and sat down at his desk. He was still filthy from his journey, but a bath would have to wait. He poured a tumbler of scotch and lit a cigarette. The game had changed. But even if they were successful in trapping Zubehr in Egypt, Gordon knew that Sulaimān would never accept his father's capture. He would have to be killed. Gordon was sure of that. He wasn't happy with his new orders but was compelled to follow them by his sense of duty and loyalty.

Much had changed since he had first arrived in the Sudan. The Egyptian army outposts were consolidated as planned. The fortress had been built and stood imposingly over the landscape. He stood on the balcony of his quarters and stared down at the city. Order had been restored to Khartoum. Trade flourished, and the people were no longer starving.

Gordon flicked the ash off of his cigarette, careful to ensure that it landed in the open-mouthed brass urn. Gordon was meticulously neat and orderly, in all things. So, he asked himself, why am I so damn so uncomfortable and uneasy at this moment?

He knew the answer. In the back of his mind it screamed at him, and his mind screamed back. It wasn't the damn politicians that were under his skin. Underneath that lacquered finish was a troubled soul.

After he had rescued Mindau and Sindella, he had decided to return to Khartoum. During the two-week journey he tried to ignore the supple figure of Sindella, but he found himself fantasizing about what it would be like to lay with her. One night, he dreamed that he had slept with her. Her breasts were full, black, and exotic. Her lips were equally full and demanded his mouth. Her long, powerful limbs entwined with his own as he felt himself burst inside her tight, muscular thighs.

Gordon was bothered by the dream. First, he was forty-four years old, and a very religious man. God would not look favorably upon his lust for a seventeen-year-old slave. Second, he was a white man; she was black as coal, and worse, the daughter of a slave. There was no place in his life for a black woman. And yet, he could think of nothing else. She haunted his every thought.

He was even more bothered by the fact that she was flirting with him the entire two weeks. She had a way of looking down, as if in subjugation, then her dark eyes would look up playfully, perhaps even invitingly, into his.

"Either she is possessed, or I am," he mused. His eyes widened as he cleared her image out of his brain. Time to focus on matters at hand. He turned to the sentry that stood quietly nearby.

"Find Mr. Gessi, and ask him to meet me in the conference room," he ordered.

The black soldier snapped to attention, nodded, executed an about face, and marched off down the corridors of the fortress. Gordon smiled. His confidence in his Sudanese soldiers grew ten-fold every day. Give them the tools and together we will rid this land of slavery once and for all. He walked the hallway to the conference room, and sat in his leather chair at the head of the large conference table. Gessi came in moments later, followed by Mahmüd Husní.

"I didn't send for you," he said to the young officer, smiling.

"You didn't 'send' for me either," Gessi admonished. "I invited him."

Gordon looked to Gessi. "What progress have you made towards building a strike force?"

Gessi sipped at his scotch. "We have obtained two hundred Martini-Henry rifles with triangular socket bayonets from England and another one hundred Martini-Henry carbines and sabers for the cavalry. We also received shipment of ten artillery pieces from Cairo, five seven-pounders and five Krupps. We have also added a hundred mules for hauling the artillery and supplies in rocky or hilly areas and another herd of camels for the desert." Gessi had been busy.

"Man power?"

"I can raise another two thousand Bazingers from Baggela. Their chief is tired of Rahamna."

"I am pleased," Gordon said. "But we must get to someone inside his circle."

"It will happen," Gessi promised. "Every man has a price. Someone will not be able to resist. What do we know about his intentions?" he asked.

"Our outside sources tell us he wants Darfur," Mahmüd answered. "If he conquers Darfur and its provinces, the Khedive of Egypt will have to acknowledge him as more than just a slave trader. Zubehr wants more power and a title. He fancies being a "pasha"."

"Arrogant ass," Gordon cursed. He didn't dare tell the Egyptian Army officer the truth. He was about to be betrayed by his commander, the Khedive. If Mahmüd knew the Khedive was going to promote Rahamna to pasha, Gordon would lose his services for sure.

"A very dangerous ass," Gessi added.

Gordon nodded in agreement. "Yes. But if he sends his army to Darfur, Bahr el Ghazal will be a sitting duck for us. We'll cut his legs out from under him. It's going to come down to timing. Can we build our expeditionary force in time to catch him with his britches down?" Gordon was planning his own end game. Besides, one way or another he was going to have to deal with Sulaimān.

"We must," Gessi replied. "Deprived of his fortress, Zubehr would have no means of keeping his army fed and watered in the field. They would be forced to scatter to survive. Once disbanded, we can hunt them down at our leisure. The hunters and caravan teams would be left with no city to return to. The slave king will be king no more."

"Yes," Gordon agreed. "There is only one concern I have."

"Which is?"

"Who will take his place," Gordon answered.

"What do you mean?" the mercenary asked.

"The people of the Sudan are used to being led. They need someone to follow. Egypt will continue to treat the Sudanese people as less than worthy. The only value the Sudan has to Egypt is to serve as a vast barren wasteland that protects its southern border. And that will suit England just fine, because they don't want anyone to sneak up on Egypt from the south. Egypt belongs to England and they will make damn sure it stays that way."

"I suspect that Sulaimān will take his place," Husní answered.

"And if we eliminate *him*?" Gordon asked. *Because I have seen what men do without laws. And I know what I can do.*

"Why do we care?" Gessi asked. "I only care about getting paid." He eyed Gordon carefully. "What's eating you?"

Gordon grimaced. "I care about these people. I truly do." He thought about the beautiful young woman that he had rescued from the slavers.

"Well then, we can't leave them at the mercy of the slave king can we?"

Gordon took a puff of his cigarette and blew the smoke out slowly.

"I have my orders," he finally said. "My concerns are my burden, no one else's." He rose to his feet and looked at his friend. "Make it happen," Gordon ordered. "Send message to our agent in Egypt. I want five hundred more rifles, and twenty more pieces of heavy artillery and more soldiers. We are running out of time."

"Yes, General," Gessi answered. He and Mahmüd both snapped to attention as Gordon rose and left the conference room. Let the fun begin, Gessi thought. And make no mistake, Gessi loved a good fight.

Gordon made his way up to his quarters. Business had been taken care of for the moment. Now another troubling matter had to be dealt with. He could wait no longer. He went to his office. His orderly stood guard.

"Bring the slave woman Mindau to me now," he ordered. He sat down at his desk and began updating his journal while he waited. Fifteen minutes later, he heard a knock on the door.

He sat up from his desk and saw Mindau at his doorway.

He motioned her to sit down on a camel stool. She shook her head, eyes downcast. She wore the traditional tob and hijab of the Sudanese women. "I will stand."

Gordon spoke to her in Arabic. "How are you and your daughter?"

Mindau smiled quickly. "You are too generous. We have our own room, food to eat, and freedom to move about your city."

"It is not my city," he said.

"But you are the governor," she replied.

Gordon nodded in agreement. "That I am." He pushed his chair back from the desk. "And as governor, I would like you and Sindella to remain with me, as members of my household staff. I will pay you."

"And what are my duties?" she asked.

"You and Sindella will be part of my house staff," he said. "Your duties will be whatever I determine them to be."

Mindau lowered her head. "A slave again," she said softly.

"No," Gordon replied, somewhat flustered. "Staff. Household staff. You will cook, clean, and keep my house in order."

"I do not know how to cook and clean an Englishman's house," she protested. "And Sindella doesn't know how to cook."

"God damn it, woman!" Gordon roared. "You will be trained by my present staff. You will have your own quarters in the palace. You will be fed, clothed, and cared for. What is wrong with that?" he challenged.

"I have seen you look at my daughter," she retorted. "We escaped Bahr el Ghazal so that she would not become a slave. She will not become your whore."

Gordon stood up and nervously paced his office. He lit a cigarette and inhaled deeply.

"I am a man of God and I do not need nor want a whore." Gordon was shaken by her directness. Have I been that obvious, he wondered? He had done many strange things in his life, but here he was, in this godforsaken hellhole, five thousand miles from England, probably destined to die in this fly-infested dung heap. But he was still a man, and he could do as he damned well pleased, because there was no one in five thousand square miles who could tell him what he could or could not do.

"My reasons are my own, and none of your bloody business," he said. He flicked his match into a copper urn next to his desk. He opened an ornately carved wooden cabinet next to the desk and took out a bottle of whiskey, pouring generously. The woman was becoming impertinent, and he was becoming annoyed.

"And what of Sindella?" Mindau asked. "Have you discussed this with her, or is she just to follow your orders like a slave?"

Gordon looked out the open window over the vast desert stretched as far as the eye could see. Why should he be compelled to ask for permission? Because, his conscience replied, you are not yet ready to become a tyrant. He turned to Mindau.

"Will you ask her if she will be my wife?" The words were out before his brain caught up with his mouth. The absurdity of the situation was almost overwhelming. She was a freed slave, and he felt shame for his lust. But he was master over his domain, and he knew he could do as he pleased. He knew he could make her his whore, but he was still in a struggle with God. If I marry her, how can I have sinned? If I marry her, she will be my wife, not my whore.

"Why should I?" Mindau asked. Eeeaye, she thought. The white man was possessed. She would have to consult with someone trained in dealing with the devil.

"I will give you your freedom."

She nodded her head.

"Speak with her now, and bring her to me," Gordon said. He walked to Mindau, and reached out and took her hands in his own.

"She can say no," Gordon said. "You will both still have your freedom." God forgive me, he thought. *Have I become some rich plantation owner enjoying his property?*

"She will not say no," the mother said honestly. "You are a brave warrior."

Sindella came to his office that afternoon. The Sudanese sentry dutifully looked away as he let her into Gordon's office.

"Thank you for coming," Gordon said.

Sindella looked down at the floor. Then her eyes lifted up to meet his. She felt his energy, his strength. She saw it in his eyes. His life force was overwhelming to her. Slowly she smiled. There was a twinkle in her eyes.

"My lord does me a great honor," she said. "But why does my lord want a slave?"

Gordon smiled. "Not a slave," he answered. "I want you to be my wife."

He went to her, and gently put his arms around her. She was strong. He felt her muscles beneath her tob.

"I have never wanted a woman as much as I want you," he said frankly. He lifted her chin, and their eyes met, then lips. She wanted him too.

The marriage took place in a secret ceremony. Gordon was a Christian, and he insisted on a Christian service. He swore his chaplain to secrecy, and the simple exchange of vows took place in candlelight, underneath a sky where the stars blazed like beacons against the backdrop of an impossibly black sky. The ring slid onto her finger, the chaplain left, and they fell into each other's arms. Her tob slid away, revealing her ebony skin, smooth, silken, supple and muscled. She tore at Gordon's shirt. Her breasts were large, taut, and they pushed against his bare chest. Gordon became lost in her passion, and their bodies became one.

Nine months later a child was born. Gordon named her Syrah. Her skin was mahogany. But she inherited the gene for her eyes from her father. They were sapphire blue.

CHAPTER FIFTEEN

CAIRO, 1878

Zubehr Rahamna, the soon to be pasha, resplendent in his lion skins and ostrich feathers, made his way into the conference room. The contrast between the native garb of the slave king and the richly furbished conference room was lost on no one save Zubehr himself. Zubehr Rahamna never felt out of place anywhere. And now that he would be appointed pasha, he truly was royalty. With a spear in his left hand and his sword in a leather scabbard fastened to his waist, he looked every bit the part of a slave king. His native Arab garb was topped off with a cheetah-skin hat tilted jauntily to one side.

The Khedive of Egypt, wearing his red fez with a gold tassel and the dark blue tunic of an Egyptian army general, felt a mixture of disdain and fear. He stroked his dark beard as the slave king made his way to the table. His heart was beating quickly, but he tried not to show his nerves. Little did he know that Zubehr too had a uniform with the same medals and trimmings. He chose not to wear it because he liked to frighten his enemy into submission. Sometimes it worked.

"Welcome," the Khedive said. He gestured to the table. "Please have a seat."

Zubehr looked at the upholstered leather chairs with their bright brass buttons and mahogany arm rests. They hardly appeared comfortable. They had no fur.

"I will stand," he said proudly.

The Khedive nodded as if he understood. He glanced nervously at his foreign minister who was also at the conference table. The minister could only shrug his shoulders.

"Very well," the Khedive answered. "I am honored you chose to accept my invitation," he said warmly. "And I welcome you as a friend."

"Thank you, Ismail the Magnificent," Zubehr replied. "I am honored by your invitation." He smiled. "Your emissary said you wanted to make peace with my kingdom."

The Khedive nodded. "Yes. I would like to name you Pasha of Darfur and Bahr el Ghazal."

Zubehr's eyebrows raised in surprise. "The Khedive does me a great honor. I accept." He felt goose bumps. He was now a pasha, a member of the Ottoman Empire. He did not know much about the Ottomans, but he was aware that the Khedive had received his power from them, so they must be all-powerful. He hoped that they would appoint him Governor General of the Sudan someday. Today was the first step. "How can I repay you?"

"You don't have to," the Khedive smiled. The trap had been set, and the rat had taken the bait. "Do you accept the title of Pasha?"

"Of course," Zubehr replied. He felt himself growing uncomfortable by the sudden look of satisfaction on the Khedive's face. He also noted that there were no less than fifteen armed sentries strategically placed around the large room. They were watching him intently.

"Excellent. We will establish your Excellency with a residence and office befitting your rank here in Cairo. I am sure you will be delighted here," the Khedive smiled wickedly.

Rahamna felt the hackles rising on the back of his neck. "I must return to Bahr el Ghazal," he insisted.

"I am afraid that will be impossible," the Khedive said. "Please turn over your weapons to the Sergeant at Arms," he ordered.

Zubehr knew going in that there were risks. Before leaving for Cairo, he had gathered his chiefs and his son, Sulaimān, under a tree between Shaka and Obeid. They questioned the wisdom of him going to Cairo.

"If my plan fails, and I do not return, then you are to take up arms and destroy the Egyptians and the infidel Gordon in Khartoum," he told them.

Chapter Sixteen

LONDON, 1879

The Prince of Wales pulled the bed sheets up over Lady Churchill's naked body. But he did so slowly, admiring the curve of her hips and the narrowness of her waist. He ran his hands through his messed-up hair and smoothed his beard.

"I missed you, Lady," he said. "How did you like Ireland?"

Lady Churchill smiled, her dark eyes smoldering. "It was horrible being away from you," she said truthfully. "But there were some fabulous parties and excellent hunts."

The prince laughed. "And you and Randolph were up to no good, as usual?" he asked. His eyes were twinkling.

"Of course, my prince," she said. "And you wouldn't believe the nuggets Randolph has uncovered."

The prince's eyes stopped twinkling and looked interested. He ran one hand underneath the sheets, caressing her firm breast, and then teasing her nipples. "Oh try me, my dear," he said. He was feeling stimulated in more ways than one.

"Well," she began coyly, "It has to do with 'The Irish' problem." She used the prince's phrase from the dinner party at the Earl of Aylesford's mansion.

The prince chuckled. "Your timing was excellent, Lady Randolph."

"My timing was deliberate," she purred.

The prince could only smile. Everything Lady Randolph did was deliberate. Including lying in his bed. What does she want this time, he wondered, as he traced the long curve of her back down to her leg.

"Randolph has become quite the expert on Ireland," she offered. "Perhaps it was just serendipity, but he worked hard while we were there. He has an excellent grasp on Irish politics and politicians."

"Ireland will never rule itself," the prince interjected. HRH wanted no part of "Home Rule." The Irish people were his subjects, and that was never going to change. Cromwell may have forced the throne out of Parliament, but not so with politics.

"That is something Mother and I both feel very strongly about," he added. He hated having to include his mother in his conversations. He was ready to take the throne but for her incredible longevity. How long must I wait to be King?

"Your highness, Randolph and I stand faithfully behind you and the Queen," she assured him.

"Mother was beginning to have her doubts," the prince advised her. "But she seems ready to forgive him and is willing to welcome him back into the fold. I think Randolph should have lunch with my mother."

This was music to Lady Randolph's ears. It was time to return the favor.

"Now what was that little nugget you wanted to share?" the prince asked. His face took on a little boy's mischievous smile. The prince loved gossip. His eyes grew wide as Lady Randolph whispered into and licked his ear at the same time.

"In bed with his counterpart's wife?" the prince was impressed. "Now that's a trick I have to work on."

Lady Churchill smiled. "You're such a pig," she teased.

"Oink," he admitted.

"Let me ask you about a little trick," she said. "How ever do you keep our affair secret?"

The prince smiled into her eyes.

"The first rule of power is not to let anyone know where you are at any given time. If they know where you are, and where you are going to be in advance, they can exploit that. So the trick is to stay unpredictable."

"How about a concrete example ?" she probed.

"Well, I suppose this is not exactly a state secret, but almost every day I travel by carriage to visit various places. In fact, I'm at one now," he added a hint of mystery to his voice.

Lady Randolph couldn't keep her impatience at bay.

"Tell me," she begged.

"It's all so very simple. My carriage predictably leaves the palace. A man who resembles me in appearance and is wearing my clothes sits in the back, and off they go. Voila. I'm not here with you. My carriage was seen leaving this morning."

Lady Churchill nodded her head. She was impressed.

"I'll have to remember that one," she said.

CHAPTER SEVENTEEN

SUDAN, 1879

Gordon looked up at the night sky. The moon was full, and it illuminated the valley that lay in front of him. It had taken almost five years to get to this point. Zubehr Rahamna was captive in Cairo, and his son Sulaimān was waiting in the valley beneath for his forces to return from Darfur. But they were not home yet, and Bahr el Ghazal lay exposed. Gordon lit a cigarette and inhaled deeply. It was time for a fight.

"Timing is everything," he said softly to Gessi.

The Italian mercenary smiled back, his white teeth flashing against his tanned face.

"My Bazingers are ready. They have the village surrounded."

Gordon nodded. "Hold the regular Sudanese force in reserve."

He looked up at the sky, waiting for the first hint of sunrise. "We attack at first light."

Gessi nodded. They waited patiently from their vantage spot. Finally, Gordon saw the first streak of red on the horizon.

"Begin the barrage," Gordon said calmly.

Gessi raised his whistle to his lips and blew loudly. The shriek of the whistle pierced the valley fog that was just rising from the damp earth, and suddenly four ten -pound mortars began dropping round after round into the village.

Gessi, watching through his telescope, saw figures darting out from their thatched huts as the mortar rounds exploded in their midst. The hot shrapnel cut down one man, nearly severing his body in two. Gessi shot a flare into the air, and 2,500 Bazinger riflemen opened fire on the village, aiming at anything that moved.

Screaming women ran from the huts with their children. Gessi had ordered his men not to shoot women and children, but no one obeyed. Metal-jacketed slugs tore into the ground and into flesh with equal abandon as explosions filled the air. The village began to look like an ant colony after an elephant stepped in the middle. Dark figures scurried for safety in the brush. Gordon had anticipated this and had a line of soldiers hiding in the scrub. The escaping villagers scrambled for the safety of the forest only to be met by a wall of lead that cut them down like kindling.

Gordon stood up and looked down upon the carnage he had created. A huge cloud of black smoke twisted up into the morning air as the village, and the villagers, burned in a hellish red glow. Sparks danced into the morning sky as the screams subsided.

"Mop it up," he ordered. Gessi gave the signal, and the bugle rang out. The riflemen rose up from their positions and advanced on the town. The mortars ceased firing lest they hit the advancing infantry.

An hour later, Gordon and Gessi stood in the village center, where Zubehr Rahamna had once held court. This time, it was his son Sulaimān that knelt in the dirt in a cage, along with six of his lieutenants.

"I sent you a letter asking for your surrender last month," Gordon said in Arabic. "Did you not receive it?"

Sulaimān looked up, his eyes flashing hatred. He spit into the dirt.

"I used it to wipe my ass," the Arab slave trader said defiantly.

Gordon nodded and smiled.

"It appears you didn't do a good enough job," he said to Sulaimān in Arabic. Gordon turned to Gessi.

"Take them outside the town and execute them by firing squad," he said in English.

Gessi nodded and motioned for the guards to take the prisoners out of their cage.

"You should have surrendered while you had the chance," Gordon yelled out in Arabic as Sulaimān and his men were led away. He walked away, uninterested in watching the execution. He had seen enough bloodshed.

It was time for a change. He had a child now. And from the moment she came into Gordon's life, he was a different man. He adored his daughter, and he wanted to assure her the finest education available. She was reading and speaking both English and Arabic by the time she was four -years-old.

It was also time for a change in scenery. Disraeli was so pleased by the outcome in the Sudan that he sent Gordon a telegram offering him any position in the realm. Gordon was deluged with offers. King Leopold II of Belgium begged him to take charge of the Congo. The Cape Colony offered him a position as commandant of their local forces. He turned down those offers to accept an assignment to serve as the private secretary to the Marquess of Ripon, the Governor General of India.

Gordon believed that his wife and child would be better off in a non-white country. Their presence would raise few eyebrows in India. Interracial relationships were accepted there. However, he was certain their presence would raise more than a few eyebrows and "highbrows" back in London.

He could also assure Syrah's education would flourish under the tutelage of a master. She was already showing a gift for languages.

FIVE YEARS LATER

CHAPTER EIGHTEEN

CAPE FOULWEATHER, 1884

Dirk stood at the helm of the Rachel H., his course set towards the hunting grounds off the coast of Oregon. Humpback whales were plentiful this time of year. Dirk felt at peace with the wind in his face, and the sea stretched out in front of him. He felt at home on the sea.

"Six months off Cape Foulweather doesn't sound good to me," Chow Lin said. He pulled his hat tight as a white cap struck him in the face. Dirk could only smile at his friend's discomfort. He had been on deck when they hit a giant wave.

"Relax Chinaman. And next time remember to duck," he teased.

"You no tell me to relax, round eye," Chow Lin said. Water dripped down his neck inside his shirt. "You steer boat into wave on purpose." He wiped the sea spray off his face.

Dirk threw his head back and laughed. He had grown to like the man. Chow Lin was very smart but didn't let you know it. Dirk had grown to trust him.

"Yes, I did. And there's more where that came from, so you'd better be alert," Dirk said smiling.

"It's not the waves that make me miserable," Chow Lin said. Dirk saw a look of concern on the Chinaman's face. "Larkin promised to make changes. Everything still the same."

Dirk shook his head. "No," he said honestly. "Now that I'm the first mate, things are changing," he assured his worried friend. "That last voyage wasn't so terrible with me along, was it?"

"That's what worries me," Chow Lin said. "What happens if you not the first mate?"

"You worry too much, Chow Lin," Dirk replied. "Nothing's going to happen to me."

"Whale!" barked out the watch from the crow's nest at the top of the mainsail.

Dirk scanned the horizon and saw the blow from an enormous humpback.

"See, things are getting better already," Dirk said happily. The crews manned the boats and were lowered into the water. "Sharpen your lances, boys," Dirk called out. "There's whale to be taken."

Rodriguez came out of his cabin and onto the deck. The crew looked lively, and there was whale off the bow. It still irked him that he was using slant eyes instead of white men trained for the sea. He was about to call out to them to hurry up but thought better of it. His first mate had lived up to his job so far. He decided to let him run the hunt without interference. He couldn't care less about Dirk. He'd kill him in a heartbeat and probably enjoy it. Before they shipped out, Larkin told him that he had information that Dirk was the rat that sent the government sniffing around. But Rodriguez did care about his profits. A good hunt would line his pockets with cash. He would deal with the Scotsman when he felt like it.

Dirk watched as the four boats left the safety of the hull and launched out onto the ocean. The swell was manageable, maybe four-foot waves, he thought. They should be ok as long as they headed into the wind on their approach. Baun Li helmed the first boat. His crew put their backs into the oars, and the whaleboat surged forward.

Dirk noticed that the sky had darkened. They were just off Cape Foulweather. Ah, she wants to live up to her name. He knew the weather could change in seconds. He looked into the approaching gale. Five miles to the north the sky was blacked out as the rain cascaded down into the slate gray sea. They've got time, he decided. The storm was big, but it was also slow.

Suddenly, the second boat veered off course. The harpoon man had stood up and turned to one side, searching for the whale. He lost his balance as a wave hit and fell into the helmsman's lap. The helmsman cursed as the boat lurched away from him, sideways to the approaching waves. He tried desperately to turn the nose to the swell, but it caught them sideways and rolled them.

"Man overboard," Dirk called out. It was time to stop the hunt and save the men. "Rig for rescue, man overboard!" The men in the water were drifting away from the whale. "Set course directly for the men in the water," he yelled. He began to bring the ship around.

"Belay that," barked Captain Rodriguez. He had watched the mishap unfold right before his eyes. Stupid coolies were not going to ruin his hunt. "Those chinks need to learn how to steer a boat," he cursed.

"Captain, we can do one or the other, but I don't know how to do both," Dirk said. He had a look of despair on his face.

"Maintain course, continue the hunt" he ordered. "We'll pluck them out *after* we kill our share of whales."

"Sir, with all due respect, they won't last that long," Dirk said. Chow Lin was standing nearby and heard the concern in Dirk's voice. "They can't swim!" Dirk added.

"Stay the course, Mr. McDuran. *And if you ever question my command again I'll have you killed*," Rodriguez warned. His face was as harsh as his words. "If you trained them right they will find a way."

Dirk held the bow on the whale's path. The drowning Chinamen tried to tread water but were flailing badly. They would tire soon and succumb to hypothermia.

"Throw them a rope," he yelled to Chow Lin who had instinctively moved to the windward side of the Rachel H. Rodriguez be damned, Dirk thought.

"Belay that!" the Captain roared.

"Captain, we have to try to save them," Dirk pleaded desperately.

Rodriguez sneered at him as he pulled a pistol from his waistband.

"I warned you," the captain said calmly.

CHAPTER NINETEEN

PHOENIX PARK, 1884

Joe Brady had started drinking at three o'clock in the afternoon at Wren's Public House, and the whiskey was starting to burn a hole in his stomach.

"Give me another, langer," Brady ordered the barkeeper. "And one for my friend here," he said, gesturing to John Smith.

"Joey, it might be best to give it a rest," Smith replied. He started to giggle.

"What's so funny lad?" asked Brady.

"That rhymed," Smith sputtered. He had also been drinking steadily for two hours, and his face was as bright red as his hair. "I'm a fuckin' poet," he announced.

"That you are, my friend. That you are," Brady agreed, pretending to play along. "So how long have you known the under-secretary?" he asked.

Smith furrowed his brow. "I still don't understand why you are so interested in him," he stated. "I just work in Dublin Castle. I've never spoken with the man; I just know his face."

"That's good enough," Brady answered. "No big matter. I just want to talk to him about a grave political question, but I'm afraid he won't speak to me if he knows I'm coming. I thought maybe I could run into him on his way home."

"You're not going to make him angry?" Smith queried.

"No, I don't want to make him angry," Brady assured him. "Here, drink up, laddie," he urged. He took the glass of whiskey and set it in front of Smith.

"You're not going to do anything to him, are you?" Smith asked.

"Talk to him, that's all. I promise. You'll help me out then? Help an old friend?"

"I just met you today."

"See, we've been friends for hours, mate. Drink up," Brady ordered.

Smith raised the shot glass to his lips. "To old friends," he agreed. He tilted his head back and tossed down the whiskey, and then slammed the glass back down onto the bar.

"Woof!" Smith exclaimed. "I'm two sheets to the wind."

"Woof indeed," Brady agreed. "Barkeep er, another whiskey." He pulled his watch out of his vest pocket. It was five o'clock. Time to go.

"Drink this one fast, Smith," he ordered. "We've got to go meet your friend at Phoenix Park on his way home from work."

Thomas Henry Burke tapped his cane nervously as he waited for Lord Spencer to finish speaking. Lord Spencer finally finished his speech, in which he had just sworn in the new Lord Lieutenant of Ireland, Lord Frederick Cavendish. The small group of people assembled in the main dining room of Dublin Castle broke into a polite round of applause. Lord Spencer raised his hands, bid everyone a pleasant evening, and departed the room. It was a signal that everyone else who had attended the ceremony had permission to leave.

Burke was the permanent under-secretary to the Irish office, and as such, was the chief civil servant of the British government in Ireland. Burke was an anomaly. He was an Irish Catholic, but he worked for the British government. The Church of England was Protestant, and so was the majority of the British Parliament which ruled over Catholic Ireland. Irish Catholics despised Burke and considered him a traitor. Burke considered himself a conduit between the two. He walked a fine line, and he knew it. He needed to talk to Lord Cavendish, and he needed to speak with him soon. He walked up to the newly-appointed chief secretary and motioned him aside.

"We have some information from our agent in America," Burke began. "There is genuine concern that the Fenian's have sent a great deal of money to Belfast. The informant said the Irish Americans are unhappy with the cause and want more violent action. They want unrest, and they mean to create it by assassinating several key figures in the British government."

Lord Cavendish looked Burke in the eye and could tell he was concerned. Burke was a good man, loyal to the English, sympathetic to the Irish. He motioned to his aid, Lieutenant Marksby.

"Tell Lord Spencer, with my deepest apologies, that I won't be able to accept his generous offer of a ride home in his carriage. I'll walk as usual. Please convey to him that I must attend to urgent government business and that I will give him a full briefing tomorrow morning."

The aid saluted smartly and turned away.

"I'll walk you home," suggested Lord Cavendish. "We can talk along the way. There should be a polo match in Phoenix Park; we can take in a bit of the game if you like."

"Outstanding," replied Burke.

Michael Kavanagh stopped the carriage in front of Wren's Pub and waited patiently. It was five o'clock. The man next to him, a dour looking individual with cropped salt and pepper hair, also watched the entrance to Wren's. James Carey was a builder and a slumlord in Dublin. He was also one of the leaders and founding fathers of the Irish National Invincibles.

"If Brady's not out of there in five minutes, you go in and fetch him," Carey ordered.

Kavanagh nodded. Knowing Brady, he was probably passed out on a bar stool. "Aye, Captain, I'll fetch him," he said. Kavanagh didn't like taking orders from Carey, but he didn't have a choice.

Carey blew out a cloud of smoke from his cigar. "There they are," he said, pointing towards the two drunken Irishmen stumbling out of the tavern door.

Kavanagh jumped down off the driver's seat, went around, and opened up the side door of the coach.

"This way, gentlemen," he said politely.

Brady guided Smith into the coach, and Kavanagh climbed back up to the driver's seat and flicked the reins. "Phoenix Park, lad," whispered Carey. He tipped his hat to the woman standing on the edge of the street as the horses pulled away from the curb. Act like everything is normal, he thought to himself. Do nothing out of the ordinary, nothing that anyone will remember.

Assassination was a delicate business.

The repercussions for killing Thomas Henry Burke, the British under-secretary, would be enormous. Reprisals would follow, and heads would roll. But eventually things would calm down, and order would be restored. More important, a somber message would be sent to the British and anyone like Burke who sympathized with them. And perhaps most important of all, a message would be sent to Parliament that as long as Ireland remained subservient to the British empire, there would never be peace.

It was still light as they approached the spacious grounds of Phoenix Park. A polo match was underway on one of the grass fields. Lathered ponies galloped about the field, ridden by wealthy aristocrats. Carey shook his head in disgust. It was the epitome of British arrogance. They took their lifestyle with them to their colonies and expected everyone to enjoy the same customs. Carey couldn't give a damn about polo. A waste of time and money.

"Pull up to the sidewalk and park," Carey said. Kavanagh nodded and halted the horses next to the curb near the park entrance. Neither man had ever seen Thomas Henry Burke in the flesh. But they knew that Phoenix Park lay directly between Dublin Castle and his residence at the Vice Regal Lodge and that Burke walked home every day after work. That was why they needed Smith. Smith worked in Dublin Castle and would be able to identify Burke as he walked through the park.

There were five other members of the squad, entering the park from the other side in order to not attract too much attention. Dan Curley was leading them. The plan was to position themselves on the other end of the park, just outside the Vice Regal Lodge, so that Burke would have to pass their location.

The two groups moved into position, loitering casually on the lawn, pretending to be interested in the polo match that was finishing on the green. Kavanagh nudged Carey, who tapped Brady on the shoulder. Two men were approaching the lodge, deep in conversation.

"Smith," said Brady. "Is that my friend Burke?" he asked.

Smith rubbed his bloodshot eyes, trying to remove the whiskey's mist. "Yes, that's 'em alright. Going to talk to him, are ya ?"

Brady's right arm swung silently, and the blackjack struck Smith behind his left ear. Kavanagh caught him as he fell, and eased him into a sitting position against the stone wall that ran around the park's perimeter. In the meantime, the two groups closed in on the two men.

"Who is that with him?" Carey hissed.

"I don't know," Kavanagh said, worried.

We'll have to take them both," Carey ordered. "No witnesses."

Lord Cavendish saw a group of men running towards them and assumed they were in a hurry to get to the other side of the polo fields. He eyed them as they approached, and never saw Dan Curley, who came up from behind him. The surgical knife cut through his throat to the bone, and a great fountain of blood spilled out onto the stone pathway.

Burke turned in horror, his mouth agape. Carey stabbed him in the side, and Kavanagh quickly slit his throat. The others fell upon the two men like hungry animals, cursing, stabbing and kicking, caught up in their bloodlust. It was Brady who came out of it first.

"Right lads, they're done. Now let's be off before we're seen."

"He's right," Carey said, blood dripping from the knife he still clutched in his right hand. "Make your way home, as we agreed. We'll meet again as planned."

The men scattered in different directions, leaving the two corpses lying on the stone path now slippery with their blood. Across the green, a cheer went up as the final point was scored in the polo match.

A black crow hopped across the lawn and stopped next to Lord Cavendish's head. It cocked its head to the side and pecked at the flecks of flesh on his cheek. It was an hour before anyone discovered the bodies.

CHAPTER TWENTY

ENGLAND, 1884

The Reverend H. W. Sneyd-Kynnersley looked out over the classroom of tousled-haired boys, searching for a transgression. Nothing noted, he bent his head back down towards the large, heavily-bound Bible on the desk in front of him. The Reverend was the headmaster of the school and its religious leader.

St. George's School for Boys. The wealthy and powerful of English society sent their young boys to his school because of its reputation of a harsh regiment of academics and sports mixed with equal measures of discipline and religious study.

After dinner, when the women went away to do whatever it was that women did after dinner, the men settled in for brandy and cigars. The conversation would run from politics to war, and eventually, someone would bring up family.

"I say, old boy, where is that young man of yours?"

A proud father would take a deep breath but announce modestly, "St. George of course. Hopefully an athlete and a scholar in the making, with a strong, solid faith in the Lord."

"Quite, quite," would be the envious reply.

The truth was the Reverend H.W. Sneyd-Kynnersley was a mean-spirited, bitter man, jealous of the wealthy young sons he squired. He took great pleasure in beating the bejesus out his charges for the slightest infraction. The hell and brimstone lecture that accompanied the beating was punctuated by the sting of birch across bare bottoms.

He squinted peevishly through one monocle like a vulture looking for his next meal. He found it, where he usually did. The small, fair-skinned, red-headed little boy whose father was rumored to one day be the next prime minister of England. Winston Churchill was the Reverend's favorite whipping boy, and today, he was earning a beauty.

Winston, unaware that by age nine, he was already a marked man, had just managed to insert a baby newt into the ear of the boy sitting next to him. Nicholas Hogby had enormous ears, and it had occurred to Winston that the newt could find a home there. Hogby shrieked, the lizard dove for cover, which just happened to be dark caverns of Hogby's inner ear, and Sneyd-Kynnersley leaped from his chair, all at the same time.

"You!" he roared. "Master Churchill, come forward." But he didn't wait for Churchill to get out of his seat, for he was already out of his, striding down the aisle. The Reverend Sneyd-Kynnersley was six-foot-three, and his strides covered a lot of ground. Too much ground to allow for a strategic retreat, Winston decided. It was time to go on the offensive.

"I say, Hogby, are you alright?" Winston inquired. He turned to face the charging Reverend and realized from the fleck of spittle at the corner of Sneyd-Kynnersley's mouth that he was not facing an angry headmaster but rather was being charged by an irate water buffalo. He dove for cover under his desk, just as the outstretched claw-like fingers grasped the collar of his tunic. Suddenly he was airborne, snatched from his warren like a rabbit in the clutches of an eagle.

"You will not interrupt my class again!"

The Reverend shook the dangling boy in his right hand, while the index finger of his left hand jabbed at the red-faced boy. "That will be twenty lashes, Master Churchill. *And*," he paused for emphasis, "no dinner. Go to my office, and fetch my rod," he ordered. "Wait for me there."

Winston's classmates cringed. All had felt the headmaster's rod on their backside. Corporal punishment was the rule in the nineteenth-century classroom. Forty-three heads bowed over their desk, waiting for the Reverend's stern lecture which would undoubtedly follow.

"Oooh," yelped Hogby, his index finger stuck inside his ear. "It's wiggling!" He got up from his desk and began to jump up and down, his head cocked to the side as he tried to dislodge the terrified reptile.

"Look mates, he's dancing a jig," chortled Kenneth Sothby, whose father was a peer in the House of Lords. Sothby was big for a nine-year-old, and he had his father's long arms and legs. He also had his father's belief that he was superior to those around him, and took great pleasure in being the school bully. His classmates roared in laughter as Hogby continued to bounce up and down, all the while shaking his head. Suddenly the poor newt, no longer able to find purchase inside the waxy crevices, became dislodged, and hit the hard-wooden floor with a soggy "splat."

"Eeeuuww," Hogby's classmates gasped. Then more laughter burst out.

"Silence!" roared Sneyd-Kynnersley. "Get that blasted thing off the floor man," he ordered. He glared about the room and heads ducked back down. "You will continue reading, and the next boy who lets out a sound will get thirty lashes," he threatened.

He turned around, just in time to see Winston, with his thumbs stuck in his ears, wiggling his fingers at him, tongue extended. The room burst into laughter.

"Get to my office, Churchill. Now!" Sneyd-Kynnersley strode forward, grabbing Winston's ear. He threw the classroom door open, and with Winston in tow, walked quickly towards his office

Later that evening Winston was washing up in the lavatory running hot water into a basin. His best friend, Archibald Sinclair, came up beside Winston

"Did it hurt?" Archie inquired.

"Like a hive of bees, all trying to get at my arse at once," Winston replied with a tight grimace. "Actually, it was more like a great big bear, ripping through a hive, and my backside was the hive."

"Searching for honey, was he?" Archie giggled. "Did he find any?"

"I should have blown a big, nasty cloud right into his ugly face," Winston snarled. "I mean, look at my bloody arse!" He pulled down his britches and bared his buttocks. Archie's eyes grew wide. The skin was slashed and bleeding, the wounds surrounded by large purple welts.

"Oh, that's not a beating," Archie said seriously. "That's a massacre."

Winston nodded thoughtfully. He was determined not to show his pain. In fact, he was ready to burst into tears from the agony. It took all his strength not to. Instead, he finished his wash and waddled down the polished wooden floor towards his room. Portraits of famous Englishmen lined the hallway, and he wondered if they had ever gotten such a beating when they were in private school.

"Good night Sinclair," he said.

"Goodnight Churchill," Archie replied. He walked away very much in awe of his small but incredibly brave classmate.

Later that evening, Churchill sat at his desk, pen and ink bottle at hand, the paper lit softly by a kerosene lantern. Winston kept the flame turned down low. He was writing to his father. Winston Churchill idolized his father. As with all small children, his father seemed larger than life. The fact that Randolph Churchill was, in fact, larger in life than most Englishmen was not lost on his son. Although he was only nine, he was already becoming aware of the very special status his father had in the world.

He scratched out the beginning of a letter to his father, furled his brow, and then let out a sigh of disgust at his effort. He crumpled the parchment and threw it in the woven straw basket next to his desk. It landed on top of twenty other equally crumpled pieces of paper. When he was in his father's presence, he trembled, and never knew what to say. Now, pen in hand, he was equally at a loss for words. The lantern's glow flickered against the window pane. Winston stared out into the darkness. Words escaped him.

The following morning found Winston in an equally somber mood as he sat at the breakfast table with three other boys. Fine linen tablecloths rested on long tables adorned with fine china and silver. The tables were placed in perfect formation inside the massive eating hall. St. George's School for Boys catered to the wealthy of English society. The Reverend knew the parents expected their children to become accustomed to finery.

Winston, oblivious to the finery, was plotting the downfall of Sneyd-Kynnersley. He imagined a coup d'état, with the students rising up much like the French in their revolution. Of course, he was at the center of the plot, delivering an impassioned, fiery speech to the student body. Amidst the roars of his fellow students, he led the charge down the long marble hallway towards the Reverend's office. With cricket bats and fencing sabers they had ransacked from the gymnasium, they burst into the Reverend's office and found him cowering. Winston raised his saber high, prepared to deliver the killing blow.

"I say mate," intoned Sothby, sitting to his left. "You planning to cut someone with that butter knife?" he giggled.

Winston, startled back to reality, found himself clutching his butter knife in an iron grip.

"Oh back off Sothby," he growled. "You are a fearsome bore."

Sothby's eyebrows raised in astonishment. One did not challenge the school boxing champion. And certainly not in such a direct fashion. His upper lip curled back menacingly, his teeth clenched, and he glared at Churchill.

"For a little shrimp, you are awfully cheeky, boy," he hissed.

"For a little turd, you have an enormous stench," answered Churchill.

Archibald, sitting next to Winston, gasped at Churchill's frontal assault on the school bully. It was an audacious attack. Sothby also found it reckless and looked around at the other tables to see if anyone else heard the exchange. The boys at the tables on either side of theirs had set down their forks and were watching. Sothby knew he had been called out. An example would have to be made.

"After Latin, I will meet you in the courtyard. Bring your second," Sothby challenged.

"Agreed," Churchill replied. Oh bloody hell, he thought. He's going to kick my arse. And it's still bleeding from the whipping from the Reverend. His lower jaw clenched, he spent the rest of breakfast glowering. Archie thought he looked courageous.

"Can I be your second?" Archie whispered after they left the dining hall and walked across the small grassy courtyard to their first class of the day.

"You may have to fight," Churchill warned him.

"I can fight," Archie said bravely. They took their seats at their desks. Neither boy heard a word that was said the rest of the morning. All they could think about was the impending doom that enveloped them, and Sothby's menacing scowl.

Latin came and went quickly, and before Winston knew it, he found himself standing in the courtyard, Archie at his side. A crowd of boys had gathered around them. There was nowhere to run.

Winston looked around at the throng of boys, their faces flushed with excitement. "Fight, fight, fight," they chanted. He felt sick to his stomach, but at the same time, a sudden flame seemed to ignite inside his body.

Sothby pushed through the circle, followed by his friend, Reginald Malby. Malby was like Sothby, but bigger. He looked like he was at least thirteen. His lips were thick, and he had heavy eyebrows. Archie felt his knees go weak. He looks like a gorilla, he thought.

Sothby reached out with his left hand and shoved Churchill's shoulder.

"So Churchill," he said loudly, "let's see how you box." He raised his fist up high in the classic fighting pose of the English gentleman.

"Fight, fight, fight, fight," the boys chanted again. The circle closed around them.

"Box?" Winston asked quizzically, one eyebrow raised. "You want to box?" he said, louder, his voice strong, his tone incredulous. "What kind of challenge is that?"

"The kind where I kick your arse," Sothby replied.

"Oh no, no, no, no. You've got it all wrong old chap," Winston said confidently. His hands were still down at his side.

Sothby kept moving his fist, but a slight hint of puzzlement broke out on his brow. He didn't want to hit Churchill while his hands were at his side.

"Coward," he said. "Put your hands up and fight like a man."

Churchill dropped his head and looked at the ground. Then he looked up and shook his head side to side, smiling. He felt himself go cold.

"No Sothby, we're not going to box," he said. "We're going to duel," he grinned.

"Duel?" gasped Archie.

"Duel," Winston said. "Swords, actually. I prefer sabers."

"Sabers?" Malby exclaimed. "What in bloody hell are you talking about?"

"In the gym. Where we have fencing class. Reverend Sneyd-Kynnersley has a pair of sabers in the closet where he keeps the fencing gear."

"What the hell are you saying, Winston?" Archie implored.

"I'm going to cut his head off," Winston said calmly.

"You're going to what?" Archie cried.

Churchill glared with disdain at Sothby's raised fist. "Boys box," he paused for emphasis. "Men kill. Come on Sothby," he ordered. "To the gym."

He shoved Sothby's hand down and turned his back on the startled boy and started towards the gym.

Sothby stood his ground, unsure what had just transpired, or what to do next. One thought stood out in his mind. He was the school boxing champion. But Churchill was the school fencing champion. Sothby was right with his fist, not with his rapier. And he had never held a saber. Besides, sabers could kill. Winston could kill him!

"Are you mad, Churchill?" he cried.

Churchill wheeled about and came up to Sothby, nose to nose.

"Yes. I bloody well am. And I intend to cut you to shreds," Churchill declared. "So if you want to challenge me, Sothby, then you'd best be prepared to defend your honor."

The circle of boys grew silent.

"Sothby," Winston hissed, "Accept the challenge with honor or surrender with dignity." Churchill lowered his head, and his lower jaw thrust forward. He resembled a bulldog pup, glowering at a bone. His eyes bored through Sothby.

Sothby burst into tears. "I don't want to die, Winston," he sobbed.

The other boys stood stunned. They knew they were witnessing something, but they were too young to comprehend anything other than the fact that Winston had stood up to the school bully and reduced him to tears without lifting a finger. Now that was something.

Magnanimity struck young Churchill. Now that he had conquered his foe, he would befriend him.

"Very well Sothby, I won't kill you after all," Winston said. He stuck out his hand. "Shake," he declared solemnly.

Sothby wiped his nose, and then stuck out his hand.

"Thanks, Churchill," he said softly as Winston shook the proffered hand.

Archie was just beside himself. He was certain that Sothby was going to pound his dear friend like a chef flattening a chicken breast with a mallet, with the same result. Instead, Winston stood victorious, granting pardon to his enemy. He could contain himself no longer.

"Three cheers for Winston!" Archie whooped.

"Hip hip, hurray!" The boys responded. "Hip hip hurray, hip hip hurray!" They gathered around Winston and patted him on the back.

"Great job old chap," one exclaimed.

"Winston for class president!" shouted another.

"Yes, Churchill for class president!" yelled Archie, eager to promote his best friend into a position of power that would eventually rub off on him. "Speech, speech," he chanted.

"Speech, speech," the other boys joined in. Now there were at least thirty boys gathered in the courtyard. Someone grabbed a fruit crate that lay next to the building and set it at Winston's feet.

"Come on man," Archie urged. "Get up there and give a speech for class president."

Winston looked around at the excited faces and felt a flush of excitement. He wished his father could see him at this moment. He was certain that he would be proud of him. He stepped up on the soapbox and thrust his hands into his pockets.

"My dear friends," he began. They grew silent as they listened intently.

"My dear friends," he repeated while thinking to himself, whatever do I say?

He paused for a moment and stared at the ground. He had read many of his father's speeches in Parliament. His father always attacked his enemies in his speeches, and look what a great man his father had become. There was talk that he would be prime minister some day. If it worked for his father, it would work for him.

"My dear, dear friends," he began, looking about at their faces. "Too long have we suffered under the cruel and wretched curse of a man not fit to walk in the company of civilized men... or boys," he added.

He looked about at the young boys that had gathered around him. They looked back intently. Blimey, he thought, they're listening. Emboldened, he continued, his voice louder, more confident.

"Too long have we endured the whippings and the bullying. Too long have we put up with this," he paused for the right word, "madman!" he bellowed. "The Reverend Sneyd-Kynnersley is an evil...evil man!" He shook his head in disdain, overwhelmed by his own sagacity.

"He is the devil incarnate," he pronounced boldly. "He is ..." Winston paused. Something was amiss. It was in their eyes. It was fear. But why should they be afraid of him? They should be afraid of Sneyd-Kynnersley, his arch foe. He needed to bring his audience back.

"Let me give you an example of just what a madman he is," he began. "Last week, he slaughtered a pig. He could have let the cook do it, but he wanted to do it himself, with a machete," he continued. He was in deep now and getting deeper by the moment. But they looked so scared. Obviously, they were captivated by his story. So was he.

The Reverend Sneyd-Kynnersley however was not. He towered over Winston, still perched upon his soap box. The young boys gathered around the soap box stood paralyzed by what they were witnessing.

Sneyd-Kynnersley appeared out of nowhere. No one dared speak. It was as if they were in the jungle, and a massive, horrible beast had come upon an unsuspecting animal. Winston was dead, that they were sure of.

Winston felt the hairs on the back of his neck begin to stand up. Some primordial instinct told him that he was in danger, but he couldn't understand why. He had no idea the headmaster was behind him, but he felt fear.

"He cut its throat, and drank its blood!" he blurted out in desperation. He had lost control of his audience, and himself.

"I'm going to drink your blood," the Reverend thundered. Winston Churchill was a precocious, spoiled rotten, arrogant little shit who had an affinity for getting under his skin. To hell with his "prime minister"-in-waiting father and his whore of a wife.

"To my office, Churchill. Now!" he roared, his head thrown back, his eyes rolling back so that only the whites were visible. Hogsby shrieked, and the other children panicked. They ran from the courtyard, crying. Winston stood still upon his soapbox, white as a ghost, unable to move. As quickly as the Reverend Sneyd-Kynnersley had approached, they were now alone.

The Reverend Sneyd-Kynnersley felt his blood pressure begin to drop, and his anger abate. In front of him, standing forlornly upon a wooden box, stood a small boy with a mop of red hair and a face full of freckles, his skin flushed scarlet with fear.

"What is it with you, Churchill?" inquired the Reverend. He dropped the pretenses, dropped the role playing. He was just a man speaking to a boy. "Why are you always such a bloody pain in my arse?"

The young boy ruefully rubbed his buttocks. "Begging your pardon sir, but it would seem that the pain in the arse has been all mine."

The Reverend felt his face start to flush. The boy stared up at him. The little bugger's not afraid of me, he thought to himself. Cheeky little bastard. I'll show him.

"My boy, you've earned every whipping I've given you and the next two at least," he hissed.

"You lay a hand on me again, and my father will see that you are fired from this miserable dung heap," Winston bluffed. "I've already written him about the last whipping, and when he finds out, he'll have *your* arse."

The Reverend's hand came up to strike down the boy, but he checked himself at the last second. The boy's father was rumored to be the next prime minister of England. And although it appeared from the lack of correspondence that he couldn't give a damn about his runt of a son, perhaps a bit of caution was prudent. He wouldn't strike the boy, but a good whipping was well within the rules of any English gentlemen.

"My office, boy," he ordered. "And make sure you have my bamboo cane down off the wall."

Chapter Twenty-One

MONTEREY, 1884

The wooden school house stood shaded by a grove of burr oaks. Children's feet bounced happily down the wooden steps to the dirt path leading to freedom from the day's lessons. Kip McDuran's feet barely touched the ground as he flew down the street, leather satchel flapping on his shoulder. It was the third Friday of June, and that meant two very special things.

First, no school for three months. Second, and more important, it meant that Dirk would be coming home from sea. Kip missed his father and the safety and security he brought to the home.

His father spent most of the last three years chasing the gray and humpback whales up and down the coast in its migratory path, with only a rare visit to Monterey. The Rachel H. would have finished her final hunt and would be coming home. Perhaps he would already be home, Kip thought as he raced down the tree-lined dirt road that led to their cabin on the outskirts of town.

He turned the corner, dust ripping up from his heels, and bolted towards their small cabin. As he closed in, he slowed, puzzled by the black carriage drawn by a single horse that was tied up to the hitching post. A rather tall man, dressed in black, was leaving the front door of the cabin, walking to the carriage.

Kip felt the man's eyes, and he slowed to a stop and looked into the man's face. It was framed by a thin beard that ran down a crooked jaw, with thin, snarling lips, and narrow, hooded brown eyes. The man tipped his hat and smiled grimly. He untied the horse and took a seat in the carriage. The man gave a command and the horse began to trot down the road.

Kip felt both a sense of fear and loathing as the carriage drove off in a cloud of dust. The man looked over his shoulder as he rode off. Kip met his gaze. The man smiled and then turned away.

Kip went to the door and inside his home. He saw his mother sitting at the table by the window, her head lying on the table, buried in her arms. She was crying softly, and her shoulders were shaking.

"Momma!" Kip cried out. "Momma, what's wrong?" He ran to her side, dropping his satchel. He put his arms around her shoulders and hugged her tightly.

She continued to cry, shaking her head slowly from side to side. "Oh God, Oh God," she cried. "Kip, oh God, Kip. Sweet Jesus, I don't think I can stand this."

Kip felt something in the pit of his stomach. A rising wave of fear gripped him.

"It's your father, Kip. He's dead," she cried. She lifted her face from her arms. Tears rimmed her green eyes. "He was killed at sea. Larkin said it was an accident. He drowned, and they never found his body," she whispered. "I don't believe him. Oh Kip," she said. "We're alone. We're all alone, and your father is never going to be back."

Kip looked into his mother's eyes, saw the panic, the pain, the fear. A coldness washed over him. He felt something snap in his head. There was no feeling, nothing. He looked into her eyes and reached out to wipe her tears.

"It's alright Momma," he said. He took off his cap and set it on the table. He sat down and took her hands into his. He was ten-years-old, but he remembered his father's voice, his face the last time he left for sea. And what his father had said to him. "Kip my boy, you be lookin' after your mother while I'm at sea." Dirk had patted his cheek with his rough, calloused hand.

"You're the man of the house till I come home. Be strong and be brave, lad. And never forget how much I love you and your mother."

It was time for him to become a man. His father would have wanted that.

Several weeks passed while Mary mourned. She could barely get out of bed and spent most of the day in the small bedroom of their cabin. The wives of several of the other fishermen brought food and firewood. The closest neighbor, Mrs. Patterson, came one night, took away their dirty laundry, and brought it back clean the next day. Kip spent most of that time in a haze, trying to accept the loss and fear.

One afternoon, he walked down to the dock whether his father's boat lay tethered. He saw several men around the Rachel H., scrubbing down her sides and varnishing the deck rails. Two Orientals stood by her stern on the dock, talking quietly. One of them looked up and saw Dirk. He said something to the other man, who nodded, and then he walked towards Dirk.

"You Dirk McDuran's boy. I Chow Lin," he said, smiling. Kip liked the way his eyes crinkled when he smiled. He had a warm smile.

"Yes," Kip replied. "I remember Father introduced us once."

Chow Lin laughed. "Owwe, you remember good. You little boy then." He held out his hand above the ground. "Maybe this tall." His voice was sing-song, soothing.

"I want to know what happened to my father," Kip said. "I want to know how he died."

Chow Lin's smiling face darkened. His coal black eyes gazed into Kip's. He clucked his tongue several times making a popping sound, and he shook his head. He looked down at the ground, thinking to himself.

"You know where my village is at, north of the harbor?" he asked.

Kip nodded. Everyone knew where the Chinese village was. Most white people wouldn't set foot near it.

"Come to the village tonight. Ask for me. They will bring you to my home, and we will talk there. Not safe here," Chow Lin said. "No one see you come tonight, boy. No one, you understand?"

"Yes. I understand."

That night, after his mother cried herself to sleep, Kip snuck out into the night and made his way down towards the Chinese village. He followed the contour of the bay, staying in the shadows as he passed the gas lamps by the cannery, staying clear of adults who walked along the street. At the north end of town, he found the road that led towards the village. No more gas light, but the moon was three quarters full, and he easily made his way.

Soon he heard laughter and smelled smoke from cooking fires. It had a very different smell to it, sharp, almost pungent. It smelled delicious and his mouth watered. Kip came to a stand of trees and saw the village. Rows of wooden shacks were set out neatly on dirt paths. Pigs, goats and chickens grazed in a pen nearby. Clothing lines hung between the shacks, and paper lanterns glowed, hanging from the lines.

"Hey, you lost boy," asked a rather tall Oriental. He didn't have the usual ponytail that Kip saw on most of them. "You don't belong here," he said.

Kip took off his hat and clutched it in front of him.

"No sir," he said. "I came to talk to Chow Lin. He told me to meet him here." Kip was both fascinated and scared by the village. It seemed mystical.

"You come with me," the man said. He led Kip behind the row of shacks, and down towards the ocean. There was a bluff in front of the bay. Three wooden shacks stood among the tall grass, overlooking the sea. The man called out in his native tongue, and Chow Lin emerged from the middle shack. He smiled at Kip.

"How is your mother?" Chow Lin asked.

"Not good. All she does is sleep," Kip replied.

Chow Lin nodded his head and sighed.

"You father a good man," he said. "He tried to help us." He motioned for Kip to sit on a small wooden bench next to a small cooking fire. He lifted a small brass pot off a stone set near the rim of the fire and poured a steaming liquid into a clay mug.

"Drink this," he urged. "It will warm you."

Kip realized that his hands were shaking as he reached for the mug. It was cold down by the sea at night. A stiff breeze was blowing in from the sea, bringing in a layer of fog. He sipped at the mug, slowly at first, then with more relish. It was tea, but it also had a taste of orange and cinnamon.

"What happened to my father?" Kip asked.

Chow Lin took a seat on the ground, his legs wrapped underneath him, his palms in his lap. He sighed. Kip waited patiently, staring at the blue and yellow flames that danced atop the glowing embers of the fire.

"You are very young to learn about these things, these ways of men," Chow Lin began. "But now your father is dead, and you have no one to teach you. Sometimes I think your father, Dirk, did not understand the ways of men. If he did, he would not be dead." He picked up a slender stick and gently poked at some pieces of wood to keep them burning.

"There is a man, Larkin," Chow Lin continued. "He owns the fishing fleet, the boats, everything. He wants us to work his boats but will not pay very much. Conditions are very bad but there is no other work. We tried to get him to give us better pay, make boats safer. He told us it cost too much," he said. He spit into the ground.

"Your father wrote a letter to a very important man in Washington, a Senator named McDonald. He was a friend of your grandfather in Scotland. Dirk tell him about how bad things are here, how bad Larkin treat the Chinese, treat everyone bad. A man from Washington came to Monterey, asking questions. When he left, Larkin very worried, very angry. He threaten your father. He said some day he would pay for that letter." Chow Lin paused and poured both of them more tea.

"My mother says we have no money. She said that Larkin told her Dad was reckless, got himself killed, and cost him money," Kip said. "She doesn't know how we are going to get by."

"Your father was murdered," Chow Lin stated.

Kip was only ten-years-old, but the impact of what Chow Lin was telling him began to sink in, and it made sense. His father had been a kind and generous man. A tough, good looking Scotsman who would give the shirt off his back to a friend and a ready hand to a vanquished foe. If Chow Lin said that Dirk had died trying to help the Chinese, Kip believed him. Besides, he liked Chow Lin. He could see how his father would as well. Kip looked up at the carbon black sky. A million stars shone brightly. Somewhere up there was his father. Kip could feel him looking down at him.

"I will find the man who is responsible," Kip said in a matter of fact voice. "And I will kill him."

Chow Lin shook his head and sighed. "No boy. That is not what your father would want you to do." He stirred the embers again, and Kip felt the warm glow of the fire and the tea inside him.

"Your father would want you to take care of your mother and take care of yourself. Life is a precious gift, not to be wasted. We are poor people, the Chinese. But we love our lives. Buddha gives us our meaning, our vision. We live for each day and love each day. You are poor too, but your life is meant to be lived and loved."

Kip shook his head. "My father died helping you. I want you to help me find out who killed him."

"I will help you, but it will take time. You must promise me that you will not kill this person," Chow Lin urged.

Kip thought about what was being asked of him. It didn't take long, even for a ten-year-old boy. "No, I can't make that promise," he said.

Chow Lin stood up and put his hands together, as if in prayer, and touched his fingertips to his lips and held them there, his thumbs tucked under his chin. He took a deep breath and looked into the bright blue eyes of the boy who looked back at him. He recognized that look. It was one that the boy's father had given him more than once.

"Go home now, before it is late. We will talk more later. Go home. Take care of your mother. But do not stop going to school. Knowledge is power. You must learn all that you can about this world if you are to survive," he instructed.

"When will we talk again ?"

"Next week. Come again at the same time."

Kip stood up and held out his hand to Chow Lin. "Thank you," he said.

Chow Lin took the boy's hand in his. "Your father a very good man. You good man too," he said. He bowed slightly. "Now go home, boy, and tell no one that you were here. The white man does not like to see his children with the yellow man. Go!"

Kip smiled. "Next week," he said. Then he turned and walked away from the village, his small figure disappearing into the evening fog which had settled around the village.

Chow Lin shook his head sadly. If I tell him Rodriguez murdered his father, he will grow up waiting for revenge against him. Not that revenge was a bad thing. But the life before and the life after would leave little life left to the boys' soul.

CHAPTER TWENTY-TWO

ENGLAND, 1884

Prime Minister William Gladstone took his seat at the conference table and motioned for his cabinet to take their places. This was William Gladstone's second administration. He had learned the hard way about the issues the British people care about most. He was a careful and cautious man and did not make the same mistakes twice. He had run Disraeli out of office, again. This time it was for good. He nodded his head to the officer at the podium.

"Begin the briefing," the prime minister said.

The young major cleared his throat and walked over to a large map of Egypt and the Sudan.

"Sir, we all know about the teachings of the prophet Muhammad. He is to Islam what Christ is to Christianity. And much like the predictions of the second coming of Christ, Muslims in the Sudan have always believed that the prophet would return. Now they believe he has." The young officer paused as he gathered his thoughts.

"Who is this false prophet?" Gladstone asked.

"Muhammad Ahmad bin Abd Allah, who has proclaimed himself the 'Mahdi,' is the son of a Muslim priest, born on the banks of the Nile in the province of Dongola. Raised from early childhood to follow his father's footsteps, his life took a sudden turn when his father died while he was just a child. Muhammad Ahmad was, if anything, a very resilient soul, and he continued in his training, learning the Koran, its principles, its message, and eventually, he found his way to Khartoum, where he became a disciple of Sheikh Muhammad Sharif. The sheikh was an influential religious leader in the city."

The major paused for a moment to get a sip of water. Briefing the prime minister made him very nervous.

"Go on," Gladstone said calmly.

"Muhammad lived with his two brothers, who were both boat builders. And while they built their boats for the Nile, Muhammad built both his faith in Islam and his reputation."

"So the new prophet is a boat builder?" Gladstone asked.

"No," replied the young major. "The people of the Sudan, particularly the Muslims, are devout in their faith. Muhammad Ahmad is not devout. He is a fanatic. While his brothers lived in a hut of packed clay and stone, he lived on the banks of the Nile in a cave he had carved out for himself in the banks that lined the river."

"So he is both boat builder and cave dweller?" quipped the Secretary of State for War, Hugh Childers.

"Sir, it gets better," the major continued. "Muhammad Sharif, being the leading Muslim sheik in the area, declared a feast to celebrate the circumcision of his sons. Sharif temporary lifted the ban against dancing and singing and gave a free pass for any other sins that came to pass. That did not sit well with Ahmad. After all, he was living a life of celibacy, wearing holes on his knees praying to the east, while the Sheikh was wearing holes in his knees, and not while in prayer. Ahmad let his feelings be known. In fact, in his fervor, he made his feelings known in the village square, to anyone who cared to listen. And he completely let loose his scorn and contempt for the hypocrisy of the Sheikh. Word quickly spread of his discontent."

"That can get you killed," Gladstone noted dryly.

"Word spread to the Sheikh, who was outraged. He immediately dismissed Ahmad from the brethren and ordered him back to his province of Dongola. In short, he was banished."

"Nice town," cracked Childers. "He went back to the mud caves?"

"Not at first, sir. Ahmad realized that he had overstepped his bounds. He covered himself with dirt and ash and locked a large wooden collar about his neck. He went to see the Sheikh, seeking forgiveness, sure in his soul that such a display of humility would place him back in the good graces of his master," answered the major. "Predictably, the Sheikh was not impressed, and still sent him packing. Muhammad Ahmad returned to the mud cave, simmering and festering at both the breach of Islam and the subsequent cruelty of his dismissal."

"So what became of this malcontent?" Gladstone asked.

"He immediately began to plan his revenge on the Sheikh. The indignation of his plight coupled with the audacious trampling of his religion by the hypocritical Sheikh gave him energy to a new and just cause. Like a scorned lover, he took his affections elsewhere, to the camp of the religious rival of his foe, Sheikh el Koreishi, who lived in Mesalamia. Like all rivals, Koreishi was acutely aware of the value of a turncoat. So when he received a letter of introduction from the priest from Dongola, the former disciple of his rival, he was quick to invite the simmering soul of Muhammad Ahmad to his presence," the major went on.

"This is all very fascinating, but why do we care?" Lord Carlingford, the lord privy seal asked wearily. He was hoping to get out of the meeting and to the New London Club for a drink.

"Word got back to Sheikh Muhammad Sharif. He was concerned. He had heard rumor and gossip among the villagers about the pious priest from Dongola, who had stood up to the powerful, rich, and apparently corrupt Sheikh. He also knew that underneath the poverty and oppression born by the people of the Sudan laid a religious fervor that would someday be unleashed against their oppressors."

"There may be some truth to that," Lord Carlingford agreed. Gladstone looked at him, annoyed.

"I want to hear this, Lord Carlingford," he said politely. "There is concern about this growing radical, religious movement. The Khedive of Egypt is very alarmed."

"And with good reason, sir," the major continued. "Sheikh Muhammad's spies told him people were in the streets proclaiming that the Mahdi had indeed come to the Sudan. The Sheikh wanted to quash the rumors, so he sent word that he would welcome Muhammad Ahmad back as his disciple and that he would accept his apology."

"How did that work for him?" Gladstone asked.

"It didn't sir. Muhammad Ahmad no longer desired a return to servitude under Sheikh Muhammad Sharif. Nor did he have any desire to apologize. He instead publicly rejected the offer and returned to the village of Aba where he had grown up as a child. The villagers heralded his return, and soon, word of his teachings, his faith, and his fanatical devotion to Allah spread throughout the Sudan. The 'Mahdi' had come. Muhammad Ahmad no longer existed. The next great prophet of the Arab world had come to the Sudan, and was ready to throw off the yoke of the Egyptian and English oppressors."

"Which is why I am concerned," Gladstone interjected. "The Mahdi has proclaimed a holy war against the Khedive, and traveled to all the regions of the Sudan, spreading his faith, his message, and his desire to expel the traitors from his lands. He is the expected one, the prophet. And the people, hungry, full of despair and misery, heard his calling. And they came." The images conjured up by the dispatches on his desk concerning the horrific brutality of the Arabs was alarming. They were savages.

The major continued his briefing where Gladstone left off. "The Mahdi formed an inner circle of advisors, led by his most trusted lieutenant, Abdullah. Abdullah is a gifted organizer and politician. Using the fervor and excitement created by the coming of the Mahdi, he channeled that energy into building an army to sustain the cause."

"Is this a revolution or a religious uprising?" the home secretary, Sir William Harcourt, asked.

"Both," the major said. "Like people of all tribes, religious fervor in and of itself is not enough to bring change. There has to be fuel for the fires of revolution to burn."

"That is a consistently recurring event in history," Gladstone said.

"Well sir, there is no shortage of fuel. The slave trade still exists. Hunger and famine have swept the countryside. Disease and pestilence are rampant. Hatred, anger, and helplessness fed the people's emotions.

The Mahdi has promised hope and change. He has laid the blame for their poverty at the feet of the Egyptians. His message is simple. The Egyptian government ruled them, and the British Empire ruled the Egyptians, who were responsible for their plight. Get rid of them, and replace them with the glory and endless bounty of Islam. The message is clear and very simple."

"Where does it stand now?" Prime Minister Gladstone asked.

"Blood has spilled," the major answered. "The Khedive sent two companies of infantry into the countryside to track down and arrest the Mahdi. They arrived in the province of Dongola, in the village of Aba where the Mahdi had his most devoted following, and attempted to locate and arrest the trouble maker. They had the town surrounded and moved in for the kill under cover of darkness," the major continued.

"It was dark, and there was little moonlight. The two companies, attacking from either side of the village, began firing upon each other, each company thinking that they had encountered resistance from hostile forces. It was a classic case of fratricide. Panic, confusion, the explosion of gun powder, the shrieks of the wounded and the misdirection of the officers turned the battle into a rout for the Mahdi's loyal followers. They watched and waited as the enemy devoured itself. When the enemy came to its senses, the Mahdi's forces quickly went after the panicked Egyptian soldiers and finished them off. The slaughter was quick. We have debriefed a few survivors. It was also quite bloody. Decapitation, mutilation, that sort of thing," the major added.

"So this man is for real, then," Gladstone said. "Sending the army into the Sudan to rout the Muslim hoard would not sit well with the public, nor would the expense sit well with Parliament. The public is sick of the Arabs. It seems to me that this fight is for the Egyptians, not for us," Gladstone stated. "Thank you, Major, you may leave now. We are going to confer. Please remain outside the room in case we have further questions."

The major saluted briskly, spun on his heels, and gratefully left the room.

"We've seen this before, and we'll see it again," Gladstone commented.

"Agreed," said the Earl of Granville, the foreign secretary. "I had hoped that after Gordon got rid of Rahamna and Sulaimān that things would stay quiet in the Sudan. It would appear that Africa is becoming a costly venture."

"Indeed. How large of a problem?" Childers asked.

"That is why I called this meeting," Gladstone interrupted. "What the major did not tell you was that I've just received word from the Egyptian government that the forces of the Mahdi had grown beyond anyone's wildest imagination. Every tribe in the Sudan has answered the call of Islam. Like a virus, the fever has spread. Rebellion has broken out in the Delta. Urabi Pasha, the leader of the Egyptian army in the Delta, has sworn his allegiance to the Mahdi".

"So the Egyptian Army is revolting against the Khedive?" Lord Carlington asked. He was all ears now.

"Yes," Gladstone answered succinctly. "And this is classified of course. Once this hits the press, they'll have a field day with it."

"Indeed, they'll make us out to look too incompetent to handle the empire," the foreign secretary warned.

There was silence in the room, almost as thick as the cigar smoke.

"Open rebellion against an important ally to the British government cannot be ignored. We must give the Egyptian government support. We cannot lose the crown jewel of the Nile or the Suez Canal to a religious fanatic," Childers argued. "Rebellion spreads like wildfire, and I for one do not want this to go any further."

"Agreed," Gladstone sighed reluctantly. He turned to the Secretary of State for War.

"I want a plan of action to put down the rebellion. Have it ready for my review tomorrow. That is all," he finished. The ministers stood as the prime minister left the room.

Chapter Twenty-Three

MONTEREY, 1884

Kip sat next to Mary as she lay dying on her bed. His mother had wasted into a skeleton, unable to eat or drink. Her skin was drawn tightly around her gaunt face. He held her as she wretched into a bedpan. It was a combination of blood and mucus. Her ribs were showing and although he tried not to look, he saw her breast. It was shriveled. He took the bedpan outside and emptied it in the compost pile.

He was ten-years-old and had no one to help. Since his father's death, the town of Monterey treated him and his mother like the plague. Word on the streets was that Larkin would kill anyone who aided them.

Mary's eyes opened for a moment as she gazed at her son. She felt the life draining out of her, and felt that instinctive human understanding that her time to die had come. She stroked his hair.

"Kip, I love you," she whispered.

"I love you too, mother," he whispered back.

"Kip, I will die any minute. I can feel it. Before I do, you must listen to me," she said.

"You are not dying, mother," Kip pleaded. But he knew she was.

"Kip McDuran, the world is not a very nice place. I am afraid for you. There are many dangers in this world, too many to warn you about. But I can only warn you about the evil that men do. Trust no one, Kip," she urged.

"Father was murdered," he told her.

Her eyes began to glaze over.

"Kip, leave it be. Live your life. Try to find joy in life. But beware of the evil men do," she repeated. Her breathing slowed. It took her three hours to die. Kip held her the whole time.

When she mercifully passed, he shut her eyelids and lay her back on her bed. He knew she would have to be buried, but had no idea how to make that happen. He ran out of the cabin and sprinted up the hill through the pine trees that lined the trail. He headed to the village to talk to Chow Lin.

Chapter Twenty-Four

IRELAND, 1884

Rain splashed down on the cobblestones as Randolph Churchill sprang from his carriage and bolted for the door of the tavern, leaving his driver shuddering in the rain. He cursed as mud splashed up on his black frock coat. He quickly pushed open the door to the pub and a blast of hot, sour air met him as he went inside. Kerosene lamps filled the air with a pungent, heavy odor.

"Godforsaken place," he swore under his breath. He looked about for an empty table. There were more empty seats than occupied, and he settled into a booth near the back of the tavern, facing the entrance. He took off his top hat and carefully peeled the gloves off his numb fingers. He was conscious of the looks he was getting from some of the customers. They were not accustomed to seeing a gentleman in their midst. Damn Parnell for getting me to meet him here, he thought. He understood the need for secrecy, but this was taking it too far.

"I say, Randolph, you look positively miserable," said a voice behind him.

Randolph turned, startled, and saw the smiling face of the leading Irish politician of the day, Charles Parnell. Though not dressed in the stylish clothing of an aristocrat, Parnell still looked neat and polished, his cuffs and collar were starched, his cravat fixed with a jeweled pin. He was moving up in the world.

"Quite miserable, actually," Randolph agreed. "This rain isn't helping my mood any, at all."

Parnell slid into the booth.

"It was good of you to meet me," Parnell began. "Look, I won't beat around the bush. There's been a genuine concern that you would be working behind the scenes to push through the Coercion Bill. You and I both know there's no way to limit that kind of power. It's sure to be abused, and my people will suffer. The British will be allowed to detain anyone in Ireland without probable cause. They can lock us up and throw away the key without justice. We're already being persecuted."

"I agree," Randolph assured him. "You have my word. I will not support that bill."

Parnell smiled. "I am relieved." He paused as the waitress brought them both a pint of lager. He waited until she walked away before he continued.

"And your position on Home Rule?" Parnell asked.

"Your people should be able to govern themselves."

"That's also reassuring."

"It should be. But I need something in return," Randolph advised.

"Name your price," Parnell said, but he was uneasy. Churchill had a reputation for being unreasonable.

"I need information," Churchill replied. "And I need a sacrifice."

"First born?" Parnell said, choking on his lager. It was meant to be sarcastic. He had no idea at that moment that it was instead prophetic.

"A minor political triumph," Randolph continued. "I want the murders at Phoenix Park solved and the murderous wretches dead."

Parnell leaned back in his seat. "Ahh," he said. "That might prove difficult."

"Difficult, yes, but essential," argued Randolph. "I have launched an official inquiry into the murder of Lord Cavendish. I intend to bring those bastards to justice."

Which would, Randolph knew, assure him of such an outpouring of public emotion and support that he would be swept to the front of the pack, and be all but virtually guaranteed of finding new quarters in Number 10 Downing Street, the official residence of the Prime Minister of Great Britain.

"And in return, you will defeat the Coercion Bill and support Home Rule?" Parnell asked.

Randolph Churchill held out his hand. "I want my son to grow up in a peaceful nation. Ireland should have her freedom. I give you my word as a gentleman."

Parnell was struck by the sentiment. He too had sons, and they were his life's blood. He grasped the politician's hand, his heart pounding. "Perhaps we have a chance," he said.

"Perhaps indeed," Randolph Churchill agreed happily. He had no intention of carrying through on the promise. It was an ambush. Once he had the widespread support of the voters, he would crush the Irish pricks. Home Rule my arse, he thought. You'll go home, and I'll rule.

CHAPTER TWENTY-FIVE

EL OBEID, 1884

"You are telling me we're lost?" General Hicks listened dumbfounded before he cut his junior officer off mid-sentence.

"What the hell is going on?" he demanded. He was incredulous. His face was turning red. They had marched two hundred and forty miles southwest from Khartoum. Hick's target was the Mahdi himself and his army camped at El Obeid. But now they had entered a densely wooded forest. Hicks didn't like the feel of it.

Captain Littledale looked at his map and then at their surroundings. "The guides say that this is a shortcut to El Obeid. It will save us three days." He wiped the sweat from his brow underneath his pith helmet.

Hicks grew impatient. "And have you asked them why this is not on the map?" he demanded. He shook his head in disgust.

"No fucking wonder Gordon had moved on to bigger and better assignments," Hicks cursed. "Bastard went to India to be the frigging Viceroy's right hand, and I'm in this hellhole. He's probably sipping tea and eating biscuits while I'm sweating my ass off."

Hicks paused. He hadn't seen a guide all morning. "Where the hell are the guides anyway?"

"They've deserted us, sir. They snuck out before dawn," Littledale answered. Hicks could hear the tension in his voice. Seven thousand men and nearly as many animals had traveled through the desert to get to this spot, and they were lost. This is not happening, Hicks thought.

"Order an about face. We'll go back out of this forest the way we came in. I want to pick up our trail at the Shirkala River," the general ordered tensely. "We need water."

"Very well sir," Littledale replied. He signaled to the sergeant major, and the bugle sounded. The signal corps raised their multi-colored signal flags, and directions were communicated. Seven thousand foot soldiers and 1,000 mercenary bashi-bazouk cavalry wearily did an about face.

"Well at least they got that right," Hicks said sarcastically. He was beginning to regret this assignment. He could be resting happily at home in retirement. But his restlessness and a generous salary had coaxed him into the service of the Khedive. And now he was leading the Khedive's army against the "chosen one." An army he was quickly learning was the worst he had ever commanded. They were unpaid, untrained and undisciplined. Many had participated in the rebellion against England two years earlier. Hick's doubted their loyalty.

The young captain was happy to hear any compliment, however.

"Thank you, sir," he said, just before his forehead exploded and a bullet exited the back of his head. Hicks froze for only a second, enough time for Littledale's body to pitch off backward from his saddle.

They were halfway out of the forest. The shot had come from the front. Hick's turned to his adjutant. "Sound the take cover alert," he commanded. He looked to Colonel Barrow of the 19th Hussars.

"Get those bloody horsemen out of here. Ride!" he screamed. He looked around him. The forest had come alive with movement. Thousands of screaming dervish warriors suddenly charged out from the trees amid a burst of gunfire, arrows, and spears. Hicks knew he was in trouble.

"Direct fire on that tree line!" he screamed. A volley of lead cut down the charging men.

"Lieutenant Baker, get those Nordenfeldts up and running and take out anyone advancing from the south!" Hicks ordered.

He wheeled his horse about, careful to keep the big animal under control. He galloped towards the head of the infantry line when suddenly his horse was cut out from underneath him. Hicks flew forward into the air and hit hard on his right shoulder. He tried to roll with it and quickly got to his feet. He stood up in the middle of hell.

His Egyptian soldiers were locked in hand-to-hand battle with forty thousand screaming warriors. Limbs were flying in the air, as were heads.

"Form the square!" Hick's screamed. "Form the square!"

The men fought for their lives, slashing with their swords and blasting with their pistols. Men with rifles on both sides took cover and began picking off anyone they could.

"Take out their riflemen!" Hicks ordered. Slowly a giant defensive square began to form, and the crackle of sniper fire subsided, giving way to the curses and groans of hand-to-hand combat. The battle raged through the night. By morning thousands of bodies lay dead upon the ground.

Hick's was now in the center of the square. They were running short of both ammunition and water. In addition to the dead and wounded, thousands had deserted during the night. They were surrounded and outgunned.

Wave after wave of screaming dervish came at them from all sides. The battle roared into its second day, the square growing smaller until finally, it was just Hick's and the man next to him.

"Fuck you bastards!" he screamed, as he fired his revolver into the advancing horde. He was dimly aware of a spear sticking out of his chest. He noted that the spear had two barbs. Funny he thought. I can't see the ends because they are stuck inside me. But I can feel them. He went down, and mercifully lost consciousness as he was beheaded. His executioner could have used a sharper blade.

Chapter Twenty-Six

England, 1884

"That went well," Gladstone said sarcastically. There was an uncomfortable silence in the cabinet room. Word of Hick's slaughter had made the rounds.

"Any other bright ideas?" He didn't expect an answer. He wanted to vent. The Mahdi had killed or captured eight thousand Egyptian soldiers and mercenaries, and quite a few English officers as well. The Khedive was in a panic as usual. The truth was Gladstone had lost all hope for the Sudan. It had been a foolish gesture in the first place. Who cared who ruled that shithole?

"I didn't think so," he added. The grand old man had never looked so defeated. His heavy jowls and mutton chop sideburns framed a sad face.

"I have sent word to the Khedive that the time for battle is over. We are pulling out of the Sudan. I have ordered the evacuation."

"There will be chaos," the foreign secretary warned.

"Oh *there will* be chaos and more, I assure you," Gladstone replied emphatically. He didn't want anyone to doubt his logic on this one.

"The British people have had enough of these Muslim butchers. They are sick and tired of hearing about women and children being raped, beaten and burned. They are sick and tired of hearing about thousands upon thousands of British trained and led Egyptian soldiers acting like amateur provocateurs. Let the Ottomans have it," he exclaimed. "It's time to pull out of the Sudan."

"With Hick's dead, who the hell do we send down there to make order out of chaos?" the foreign secretary asked out loud.

Silence hung over the room. One man's name was on every man's lips.

Gordon.

Chapter Twenty-Seven

SUDAN, 1884

Frank Powers was worried, and for a good reason. The international correspondent for the Times seriously began to wonder about the wisdom of his decision to accept this assignment to cover General Gordon's evacuation of Khartoum. They had been under siege by the Mahdi's forces for six months. Supplies were running low, and the last contact with England had been in April. It was now September 9, 1884, and there was no sign of help on the horizon. Powers was no stranger to the dangers of the world, but he had never experienced the mayhem and madness that accompanied this holy war.

It was indeed a battle between Christianity and Islam. No one in England ever even broached such an idea. But stuck in the middle of it, Powers no longer had doubt. The Mahdi was going to rid the Sudan, and then Egypt, of western civilization and the infidel. He would establish himself the leader of an Islamic holy land, ruled by his interpretation of the Koran.

Powers looked around General Gordon's office. It was their first meeting of the day, and he could see the strain on Gordon's face. He was amazed at Gordon's inner strength. He had maintained order and discipline in a city under siege for ten months. It would have killed a lesser man.

"I have received a message from the Mahdi," Gordon began. "He again has demanded our immediate surrender and assures that in return he will not harm anyone."

Gordon's chief of staff, Colonel J.D. Stewart, laughed. "Tell that to Hicks," he said sarcastically. Stewart volunteered to come to the Sudan in place of Gessi, and was Gordon's second-in-command. He was very loyal to Gordon.

"I'm not sure how much longer we can hold out," Gordon said. "We have had some success with our steamers attacking the Mahdi's forces at Berber. The Mahdi controls the banks of the Nile, but not the river itself."

"I don't think the population of Khartoum will fit on a few steamers," Powers joked.

"That's not what I have in mind," Gordon replied. He was not in a good mood.

"What are you thinking?" Stewart asked.

"I'm thinking that you could take the steamer Abbas and force your way up the river to Dongola, which is still under Egyptian control. From there, Powers can send his dispatches to England and we can get the plight of Khartoum to the press. I have every reason to believe that once England learns of our situation, Gladstone will be forced to act," Gordon said.

"What do you hope he will do?" Stewart inquired.

"Send a relief expedition," Gordon replied.

"Gladstone wants out of Sudan, not in," Powers reminded him.

"Yes, but he changed his mind once; perhaps he will again." Gordon puffed heavily on his cigarette.

"Given the present tactical situation, of which they are not aware, evacuation is no longer possible without relief," Gordon explained. "I'm not asking the British government to take on this religious fanatic. I'm simply saying that we can't get the people out unless we have an expeditionary force to protect them en route."

"I am not going to abandon you here and run for safety," Stewart stated calmly.

Gordon was touched by his loyalty.

"I would expect nothing less from you, J.D. However, I am ordering you to take the steamer Abbas to Dongola. I am ordering you to take Mr.

Powers with you, and also, the French consul, Mr. Herbin. In addition to the Abbas, we will send two other steamers as a backup. Stay on the river, and you should be okay. Whatever you do, *do not go ashore*. Except of course, to get around the fourth and fifth cataracts. You'll have no choice there."

There was silence in the room. Cataracts, fast moving rapids over boulders, could not be traversed by the steamers. At some point, they would be forced to proceed on foot.

"Sir, no disrespect, but will you put your orders in writing? Should something happen to you, I do not want people surmising that I am a coward," Stewart asked softly. "And have you given thought to leaving me in charge here so you can take your family to Dongola instead?"

"No, I must remain." Gordon knew he had to get his family out, but he didn't want to risk Sindella and Syrah in a mad dash for safety. "No offense, but I must hold down the fort. You must go for help." He turned to the correspondent.

"Will you help us?" Gordon asked.

Powers couldn't believe his luck. He was getting the hell off this sinking ship and would be able to tell the entire story. His editors would love him, and certainly, a good reward would come his way. Perhaps an assignment to Paris? But he did not let his emotions show.

"Yes. I will do my best," Powers agreed somberly.

"It's done then," Gordon instructed. "The ships are ready; you leave at dawn tomorrow. I have all the dispatches for you to take with you. You will have fifteen Greek body guards from their outpost. They can be trusted. They will be paid well. I will give you a small amount of gold bullion in case you have to buy your way out of a tight situation. Any questions?"

"No," both men replied.

"Good luck then," Gordon said.

"Sir," Stewart said.

"Save it, John," Gordon said. "I'll be seeing you in London when this is over."

"Yes sir," he said. He saluted smartly, and the two men left Gordon's office.

"Well now," Gordon said to himself, pouring another Scotch. "All we can do now is batten down the hatches and hope to bloody hell this ship doesn't sink before help arrives."

Of course, on the other hand, Gladstone may decide to do nothing, Gordon thought to himself. He could say I disobeyed orders and refused to evacuate and come home with the others.

Technically, Gordon *had* disobeyed orders. Gladstone had been very clear. Arrange safe passage for those individuals deemed worthy of rescue. But Gordon couldn't stomach the idea of playing God. So he opted for a different plan. He knew that if England summoned her might she could defeat the dervish. But whether England could summon the will to do so was a different matter. He was determined to force Gladstone's hand.

Sending Powers and Stewart back to Cairo was the last card in Gordon's hand. He could only hope and pray that he had not played it too late.

It was an enormous gamble, with horrific personal consequences if it failed. Both Sindella and Syrah had accompanied him to Khartoum. He could not return to England with an African wife and child.

Syrah had just turned seven. She was a whirlwind of energy. Gordon was amazed at her gift for language. She was already fluent in English and Arabic, and could read and write both at a level far above children twice her age. Her mother had taught her the language of the Dinka as well, and mother and daughter often engaged in a debate that Gordon could barely follow. Syrah was strong-willed and stubborn, like her father.

She was a beautiful child. Her dark mahogany skin and high, proud cheekbones framed her brilliant sapphire eyes, enhancing her already intelligent face. But Gordon knew that she, like her ebony-skinned mother, would never be accepted by English society.

Gordon lit another cigarette and let out of stream of smoke. He silently prayed to God to deliver them from this evil. He loved his wife and child more than life itself.

Ten days later, Colonel Stewart sat on the deck of the Abbas as she steamed down the Nile towards Dongola. He was sitting on a rattan chair smoking a cigarette, watching for any signs of trouble. They passed Berber without incident and were approaching the fifth cataract. Stewart was beginning to think they might pull it off. Just maybe the Mahdi's forces were so busy attacking every Egyptian outpost in the Sudan that they weren't watching the river.

The ship's captain, Abiz, was an Arab. Stewart hoped he could be trusted. So far, so good. The Greek bodyguards were alert and armed, watching the crew.

Powers remained secluded in his cabin, even taking his meals there.

The French counsel however, turned out to be a pleasant companion. Stewart was beginning to warm to him and felt Herbin liked him as well. They had an interesting conversation about their two countries one night, and laughed at the number of times their countries had tried and failed to conquer the other. England and France had been at war with each other at least once every century for the past thousand years.

The pulse of the steam engine was comforting. Stewart was enjoying the sun on his face when a voice called out from the river bank. His body instantly went cold.

"Hello" the voice called out in English. "I am Achmet, the son of Sheikh el Obeid. I am coming to speak with you, don't shoot!"

Sheikh el Obeid's son? Could it be? The sheikh had sworn loyalty to Gordon, which had put him in great peril.

The Frenchman, Herbin, came up on the deck.

"Do you think it is a trap?" he said to the Stewart.

"Perhaps, but we can stay in the river and parley. If it is safe to put ashore here, we could replenish our stores. We are running low on wood," Stewart replied. "And fresh meat would be a nice change." He motioned to the ship's captain. "Abiz, bring us to a stop in the middle of the river, lay anchor while the boat approaches. I want to talk to this man."

"Yes, sir" Abiz replied.

A small boat rowed out to them. One of the crew tossed a rope and they pulled the boat up against the steamer. The anchor held against the current. They were at a full stop now in the middle of the Nile. The shoreline was fifty-yards away on either side of the steamer. They were in the range of both rifle and artillery fire.

Achmet came aboard the steamer. He was about twenty years old and dressed in a white flowing caftan and traditional Arab headdress.

"You are from Khartoum?" he asked.

Herbin and Stewart looked at each other. Neither had to say a word. They both knew that advance word had been sent through secret channels to try to ensure their safety with some of the tribes on the Nile.

"Let's just say we are traveling," Stewart said, putting on a smile.

"My father has guaranteed your safety," Achmet said. "We have been expecting you."

"Sheikh el Obeid is a friend," Stewart agreed. "Where is he?"

Achmet winced. His dark eyes looked frightened.

"Hiding right now. The Mahdi has spies everywhere. I can take you to him, but you must guarantee you will not divulge his location to anyone. Even General Gordon."

"I have no reason or desire to put the Sheikh in jeopardy," Stewart assured him.

It was a gamble, but they were fifty miles from Abu Hamed, where the Nile turned west, towards Dongola.

"Curse the Mahdi," Achmet assured him. "He has brought death everywhere. You will be safe. No doubt you need food and wood? We have both," he assured them. "We also have beef."

"Very well," Stewart decided. "We will pull closer to the shore and anchor. We will send our ketch ashore to gather supplies and to meet with the Sheikh."

"Okay, I will go back to shore and tell him you are coming." Achmet climbed down the rope ladder to his boat and pushed off towards shore.

"Abiz, bring us as close to the shore without grounding the anchor or us. We will send the ketch ashore for food and wood. I will go ashore with five Greeks."

"I will go with you," Herbin said.

"As will I," Powers said from behind them. He had emerged from his small cabin when he heard Achmet call out. "I want to get off this wretched boat."

"We are not staying," said Stewart. "We will gather supplies, meet with the Sheikh, and then get the hell back out into the middle of the river."

"Can we trust them?" Powers asked.

"About as far as I can spit, but we still have a long way to reach Dongola, and we knew we would have to put ashore somewhere to resupply. This seems to be our best opportunity," Stewart said.

"Gordon said not to go ashore," Powers noted.

Stewart was torn. But if it was safe, they could get fuel. To make steam, they needed wood for the boilers.

When they reached shore, Stewart cautiously looked for signs of Nile crocodiles on the muddy banks. He didn't see any fresh tracks. They came upon a clearing along the shoreline and walked across it, looking for Achmet. There was an outcropping of rocks facing them and Stewart was thinking about climbing to the top of the rocks when a shot rang out over their heads.

"Put down your weapons," a voice called out in English, "and you will not be killed."

"Merde," whispered the Frenchman. "Where are they?"

"Put down your weapons now or the next shot will be aimed at your head instead of over it," the voice warned. Stewart recognized Achmet's voice.

"I thought you said we were going to meet with the Sheikh," he argued.

Another shot rang out, and this time one of the Greek body guards dropped to the ground, blood spraying from a bullet wound to his head.

"The Sheikh is dead, and my name is not Achmet. I am Mustapha and I serve the Mahdi," he said. "You are now his prisoners."

Another shot rang out, and another Greek body guard dropped.

"I told you to put down your weapons," Mustapha ordered.

"Yeah," said Stewart. "Because you want to interrogate us. No doubt a little torture?"

"I have questions, but not torture," Mustapha assured them. "I have two hundred men behind these rocks, and they are going to kill you now if you do not drop your weapons."

Powers looked at Stewart in horror. "We must do as he says, quickly, drop your guns," he pleaded.

"No chance in hell," Stewart said. "They want information about the fortress in Khartoum and the fort at Omdurman," he said resolutely.

"This is it fellas, get ready for a fight."

Stewart knew his adversary. In Arab culture, trickery, guile, cunning, and lies were all fair play in a fight. If you were dumb enough to fall for it, shame on you.

"Take cover!" Stewart yelled, running towards the rocks.

"Shit!" screamed Powers. He ran for the boat.

"Merde!" exclaimed the Frenchman. He and the three remaining Greek bodyguards followed Stewart into the rocks, taking cover, rifles raised. Stewart had guessed right. He knew they wanted him alive, not dead. They could have dropped him in his tracks as he ran for cover.

Two shots rang out and Herbin and Powers were both dropped, shot in the legs. Suddenly three Arabs rushed out from behind the rocks sprinting towards the wounded men. Stewart and the Greeks opened fire, and all three were hit. Stewart heard a massive roar and looked up to see hundreds of dervish warriors coming down the rocks. He ducked behind a boulder as shots rang out over his head.

"God damn it!" Stewart yelled. His mind raced. He had guessed wrong. I'm not going out like this, he decided. He knew they would capture him and torture him. He did not want to betray Gordon. He thought of his wife and family back home and smiled as he saw their faces. He quickly drew his revolver and fired one .45 caliber slug into his brain.

The dervish warriors whooped and cut off his head. Then they gathered around the downed correspondent and the French diplomat.

Mustapha, formerly known as Achmet, walked up to them.

"We need to chat," he said calmly. His warriors picked up both men and dragged them over to the rocks.

Powers cried out in pain, his right leg pumping out blood. "I don't know anything. I'm just a reporter," he begged.

"Really," said Mustapha. "Then you have your dispatches on the boat?"

"Yes," Power's said, looking out at the steamer Abbas. He saw the remaining Greeks peering over the parapets, rifles at the ready. He saw the captain, Abiz, run to the helm of the ship, barking out orders to his crew to cast off.

Suddenly, the Arabs opened fire, and the Abbas was lit up like a Christmas tree, hammered by a fusillade of lead. Many of the slugs deflected off the armor causing sparks. Abiz was hit so many times he pitched over the side of the steamer.

The firing continued until everyone exposed aboard the Abbas was killed or wounded.

Mustapha raised his hand, and the firing stopped. He looked at Powers, still clutching his wounded leg.

"We will get the dispatches off the boat," Mustapha said calmly. "I noticed that the other two steamers that left Khartoum with you turned around before you reached Berber," he said. "Where are they?"

"I don't know what you are talking about," Powers begged.

"Yes you do. You will talk. Skin them alive," Mustapha ordered.

Their screams could be heard for hours.

Chapter Twenty-Eight

ENGLAND, 1884

Gladstone took his usual seat on the center floor of the House of Parliament. His ministers sat around a large table next to his position. The various members of Parliament took their seats. Gladstone rose to the podium and faced the vast hall.

"The right and honorable Sir Dilke has asked, and Lord Harrington concurs, that I give you an update on our situation in the Sudan," Gladstone began. "We have asked for an accounting from General Gordon on his situation. We have not yet received a reply."

This was true, because the message never reached Gordon. The lines of communications had been cut by the Mahdi when he took Berber.

"Yet I can assure each and every one of you the rumor that Khartoum is under siege is greatly exaggerated," Gladstone continued.

A groan of discontent filled the ancient hall.

"Perhaps the Minister can assure us that Gordon is indeed even able to receive or transmit dispatches at this moment," yelled out one young member.

"Yea," a rising tide of voices rose.

Gladstone held out his hands in a calming and conciliatory gesture.

"I realize that there is a great concern for General Gordon's well-being. And I too share that concern. I have been in frequent contact with the Queen, who also shares our concern. But I assure you, the information as we have it, is that there is no need to panic," he lied. Sir Baring's dispatches from Cairo were clear about Gordon's plight.

"I will report to you upon General Gordon's reply to Sir Baring's request for an accounting when it is received," the prime minister concluded.

Randolph Churchill rose from his seat on the Conservative side of the House of Commons. The chamber was packed; it was standing room only in the upper balcony overlooking the floor. One hand rested easily on the lapel of his jacket.

"We have been told by Mr. Gladstone that Khartoum is in no danger of falling. His government assures us that General Gordon is not presently in any danger. Apparently, Mr. Gladstone's government has decided to ignore fact and espouse fiction. It is a very dangerous fiction indeed," Randolph Churchill said, staring directly at the prime minister.

"Colonel Coetlogon has stated that Khartoum may be easily captured. He believes General Gordon is surrounded by hostile tribes and cut off from communications with Cairo and London," Randolph continued. He paused for dramatic effect.

"It is fair for the House, indeed it is the *right* of the House, to ask her majesty's government whether they are going to do anything to rescue Gordon? Is the government going to remain indifferent to the fate of the one man on whom they have counted upon numerous times in the past to extricate them from their dilemmas, to leave him behind to fend for himself, and not make a single effort on his behalf?" Randolph sat back down and folded his arms. Silence hung over the great room.

Lord Fitzmaurice, a retired Army general, looked at Gladstone, who in turn gave him the nod. The lord rose to his feet and cleared his throat.

"Her majesty's government is quite aware of the situation in the Sudan. The government is also quite aware that General Gordon ignored the orders of his government to evacuate the English and Egyptian subjects and instead has tried to defend the entire populace of Khartoum. Now he finds himself in the very situation the government instructed him to avoid. One man's stubbornness and another man's ignorance," he paused, looking at Randolph Churchill, "cannot drive the engine of the foreign ministry. We remain a free society."

Cheers came from Gladstone's supporters.

"The government is closely watching the situation in the Sudan. We are doing everything we can to correct Gordon's folly," Lord Fitzmaurice lied, sitting down.

The great room erupted into cheers and jeers, catcalls and whistles. Randolph smiled to himself. Gladstone's government was on the ropes.

Months had passed without word from Gordon, and only innuendo and rumor came by way of spies who briefed the British agent, Baring, in Cairo. Baring was aware that much of the intelligence he received was faulty, but it did appear as if the situation was degenerating quickly. He sent a letter to the queen stating that it was questionable if there was even enough time left to send a relief expedition. She sent word to the Secretary of State for War, Hugh Childers. She invited him to come to Buckingham Palace and have tea.

As they sat in the lavish garden in the palace, the queen sipped her cup of tea and then smiled at Childers.

"Mister Childers, I know I am just a figurehead of the government and not the prime minister. But if the government does not send an expedition now, I will have to speak my mind. And my mind is telling me the empire cannot allow the world to watch as it abandons one of its greatest soldiers and allows him to be slaughtered by an Islamic religious fanatic and his followers. I will be forced to publicly ask Mr. Gladstone to resign," she said.

Childers soaked in her words. The crown did not run the government. Cromwell made sure that royalty was no longer calling the shots. But that did not mean the queen was without power. Rarely had Queen Victoria allowed herself to be drawn into political discourse. She wasn't bluffing. Gladstone's position was precarious. A censorious word from her majesty would all but guarantee a vote of lack of confidence.

"I shall speak with the prime minister this evening, your majesty. I understand the throne's concerns." Childers stood up and bowed to his queen. "I shall take leave now ma'am."

The queen smiled and took another sip of tea.

Chapter Twenty-Nine

SUDAN, 1885

Gordon sent word to Sindella to keep to the servant's quarters and to stay away from him. The situation was beyond desperate. He had received word that a relief expedition was on its way, but he had little hope it would arrive in time. When it appeared the palace would fall, he would send Sindella and Syrah to the fort at Omdurman, a few miles up the river. From there, they were to make their way down the Nile to meet the relief expedition. Gordon had received word that Gladstone had given in. Help was on the way.

He gave Sindella a handwritten note to give to the British, explaining that she was his wife and Syrah was his daughter. The letter requested safe passage to England and for a trust account to be set up for their well-being from his estate.

The men were weakening. Food was scarce. They were eating dogs, rats, anything with flesh. Their supplies of grain, sorghum, and millet were depleted. Disease was rampant, and he feared a deadly outbreak of plague.

Gordon stood on the rampart of the palace looking out over the walls and to the perimeter. Every night shots were fired at the fortress. The lines of communication were cut.

He was completely isolated from the rest of the world. The last letter from the Mahdi had demanded his immediate surrender. The letter was written in English. No doubt by Slatin, the Austrian officer Gordon had entrusted to become governor of Darfur. He had been captured by the Mahdi and offered his life in exchange for his conversion to Islam, which Slatin had accepted. Now he was the Mahdi's translator. Traitor, Gordon thought to himself.

Suddenly Gordon heard a great roar in the distance, and he saw a sea of bodies moving towards the palace perimeter. The mines his men had so carefully laid began exploding, and bodies flew into the air.

"Sound the alarm!" Gordon yelled. A trumpet rang out to alert the palace guard.

"Oh, my," Gordon said out loud. Thousands of screaming dervishes were running amok in the streets of Khartoum. Thousands more were making their way to the palace. He walked back into his office and poured himself a very large Scotch. He threw it down and then lit a cigarette.

He could only pray that his wife and child would be safe. The further they stayed away from him the better. He knew they would be captured now, no chance of making for the fort. Their only hope for survival was to avoid being associated with him.

Gordon heard the roar of the advancing horde, musket fire and the chopping sounds of metal on flesh. He walked calmly back out to the rampart and saw a sea of faces staring up at him. Suddenly, silence fell over the advancing horde.

They watched in amazement as Gordon inhaled deeply on his cigarette and looked at them with disdain. He started down the stone steps toward the crowd, and they began to back away in awe. It is the instinct of every wild beast to pursue and kill a fleeing prey. It was also the instinct of every wild animal to stop and pause when faced by a prey that turns to fight.

In the slave quarters, Syrah hid behind a stone wall and watched her father calmly advance down the steps toward the thousands of men that now filled the court yard. Suddenly a spear flew through the air and impaled Gordon in the chest. Syrah opened her mouth to scream, but Sindella quickly covered her mouth and pulled her back inside the servant's quarters.

As Sindella pulled her back inside, Syrah saw the horde cut off her father's head and impale it on the end of a spear. They shook the spear madly in the air, and Syrah mercifully passed out as her mother carried her back into the servant's quarters.

The air filled with moans and screams as the slaughter commenced. The men were butchered, the women raped and slaughtered. Blood ran down the stones of the courtyard. Small rodents quickly ran to lap it up before it disappeared into the earth.

CHAPTER THIRTY

MONTEREY, 1885

David Jacks unleashed his carriage from the hitching post in front of the Customs House and drove down Lighthouse Road. He couldn't help but feel proud as he set course for the Del Monte Hotel that sat at the edge of the forest by the sea. It was partly his creation. The hotel featured the latest in modern amenities; hot and cold running water and gaslight. It even boasted a swimming pool. There were over four hundred rooms at the hotel. High society members of San Francisco walked through the formal gardens and took carriages down to the water's edge to take in the breathtaking views of the ocean.

Jacks owned a one-third stake in the hotel. He had contributed one hundred acres of prime land. His partners put up the capital to construct the hotel. They were raking in cash from their investment. It was an incredibly scenic and popular tourist attraction. But the tourists were beginning to complain about the unsightly Chinese fishing village that hung on the edge of the water. Unsightly if you were a white man.

"Damn those slanty-eyed little heathen," Jacks growled to himself as he mused over the problem. It was the reason for his trip to the Del Monte. Charles Crocker himself had come into town to discuss the effect the unsightly and somewhat odorous village was having on the tourist business. Normally, lunch with Crocker was an unsettling affair for Jacks to begin with. Jacks's land holdings and wealth were minuscule compared with that of the California railroad baron. Crocker was what Jacks had aspired to be but never became. He was also a ruthless asshole.

"Damn that fat bastard anyway," Jacks growled again. He grumbled and groused all the way along the bumpy road that paralleled the coast, an aging figure with a salt and pepper beard gripping the reins with hands gnarled by hard work and time.

Lunch at the Del Monte was always an elaborate affair, but even more so given the special luncheon being served in the Stanford Room. The founding partners of the Pacific Improvement Company, Leland Stanford and Charles Crocker, were in town for a private lunch with David Jacks.

Fresh seafood packed in ice had been brought in that morning on a train from San Francisco. Charles Crocker didn't like the local seafood and insisted on nothing but the finest in dining. He brought his own.

Leland Stanford, however, was a big fan of the local beef. The main course of his meal would be thick steaks cut from the finest cows raised in the Salinas Valley. The kitchen brimmed with activity as the staff readied for the elaborate affair.

One of the kitchen helpers set several freshly baked pies and loaves of bread on the oak counter next to the kitchen window. The window opened up into the lavish garden that surrounded the hotel. She shook her fingers to ease the pain from touching the hot metal pie pans and bread trays, and then turned and went back to tending the wood burning oven, completely unaware of the young boy that was hiding just beneath the ledge of the window.

Without a sound, a small hand quickly reached over the open window ledge and snatched a loaf of bread. A moment later, a hot rhubarb pie disappeared from view, quickly followed by another loaf of bread. The young boy, dressed in tattered clothes, quickly retreated into the dense foliage of the garden, and then into the edge of the forest that surrounded the hotel. He made his way to the base of a giant fir and set down his take. The loaves of bread went into a burlap bag. The pie he would have to carry with his free hand.

Kip McDuran was now eleven. It had been a year since his mother had died. The months leading up to her death had been brutal for Kip.

Every day after school he had set about trying to keep things together. He found odd jobs sweeping and cleaning various establishments to earn a small wage.

After his mother passed, Kip began roaming the streets at night. As he grew more adept in nighttime prowling, he soon learned to travel quickly through the game trails of the forest and the dirt roads that surrounded the community at night. His legs became robust and fast; necessary tools for any creature that survived by its wits, to say nothing of a young boy. He could run for miles in a steady, stealthy stride. When speed was necessary, he could accelerate to a sprint that left behind even the most determined pursuer.

There are many motivators in life. Hunger is one of them. And Kip was hungry. As his hunger grew, so did the frequency of his prowling. Eventually, he found the Del Monte Hotel. The scent of freshly baked pies and bread led him to the garden outside the kitchen.

Pie in one hand, burlap bag in the other, Kip began to lope away from the hotel through the woods, his feet falling softly on the pine needles that covered the floor of the forest. He broke through the trees, crossing a dirt road that led to the hotel from the town, right into the path of an oncoming carriage drawn by two horses.

"Jumpin' jehoshaphat !" Jacks yelled. His horses reared up on their hind legs as the small boy dodged their hoofs. The rhubarb pie went flying into the air as Kip threw up one arm to protect himself. The carriage smacked into the rear of one of the horses, causing its legs to buckle. Jacks, wearing a leather vest and denim pants came off his seat, and his head hit the rump of the horse in front of him.

"Holy Mary, mother of Jesus!" Jacks cried out as he bounced back onto his seat. "You there, don't move, laddie!" he barked. Kip had dodged the horse's hooves but had dropped his bag. He was already moving quickly to grab the bread and bolt.

Perhaps it was fear; perhaps it was the familiarity of the male Scottish brogue. But something made Kip stop in his tracks. He ran one hand nervously through his thick black hair.

"Yes sir, sorry sir," he said.

"You damn near killed us both, lad!" David Jacks roared, his face still beet red from the excitement of the moment. Jacks' heart was pounding. He looked down at the dirt covered urchin wearing torn and tattered rags. Lord, where does this child live ?

"What do you have in that bag there laddie, and what is that plate doin li'en there on the ground?" Jacks asked. "And what's your rush?"

"Just a couple of squirrels I trapped in the woods," Kip stammered.

Jacks climbed down from the carriage and walked over to the upside-down pie pan. It was still warm to the touch; its sweetened contents spilled onto the dirt. Kip gazed at the lost pie with anguish on his face.

"Rhubarb," Jacks said, tasting the tip of his finger that he had stuck into the pie. "You trap that too, laddie?" He stroked his salt and pepper beard and gazed sternly down at the boy. Caught with his hand in the cookie jar.

"No, sir, no I didn't," Kip admitted.

"What's your name, boy?" Jacks asked.

"Kip McDuran, sir."

Jacks brow wrinkled at the name. "I knew your father, boy." He raised his eyebrows as he gazed at the boy with more interest. "Fisherman, whaler, right?"

Kip nodded his head.

"Killed at sea awhile back, wasn't he?" Jacks said. The words hit home, and Kip stared down at the dirt and nodded again.

"Ah," Jacks thought. I should have checked on his family. He remembered the easygoing smile and devil-may-care attitude of his fellow Scotsman. He had been in San Francisco when Dirk had been killed at sea. I'm getting old, he thought. By the time he had come back to Monterey, it had completely slipped his mind.

"How's your mother, lad?" he asked.

Kip shook his head.

Jacks felt pity for the boy. "Nearest kitchen around here is the Del Monte," he said. "Reckon they gave you this pie, and whatever's in that bag." He picked up the burlap bag with the two loaves of bread and handed it to Kip.

"Where are you living, lad?" he asked softly.

"No offense sir, but I don't know you, and I don't know why you're asking," Kip replied bluntly.

"No, you don't. But I knew your father, and he was a fellow Scotsman. David Jacks is my name, lad. And I'm pleased to make your acquaintance," he added, holding out his hand.

"Kip McDuran," the boy replied. He shook the outstretched hand firmly.

"Humph," Jacks muttered. "So where are you and your mother living?" he asked again. "I never stopped by to pay my respects after your father's passing."

"She died," Kip said matter-of-factly.

"Where's your home now?" Jacks asked.

Kip was ashamed to answer.

"You got a home boy?" Jacks asked again.

"Yes," Kip finally answered. He did. A soft bed of pine needles and a roof made from a canvas tarp he had stolen. He had food, water, and shelter. He didn't need anything or anyone else.

"Where?"

"No offense sir, but my mother taught me not to speak with strangers," Kip said. He wanted to get away from there and back to the safety of the forest.

"Look, laddie, I'm a Scotsman, just like your father. You're not in trouble for filching a bloody pie. We look after our own. And you look like you could use some help," Jacks said. Something told him the child was in danger.

"Aye," Kip said. "That I could," he admitted. He felt small and foolish in the older man's presence. Jacks was well dressed. His carriage looked immaculate, trimmed with leather and thick, sturdy polished pine. Kip was embarrassed, aware of his own poverty, but he refused to be cowed.

"I'll manage fine, sir," he said. "Thank you, anyway."

Jacks pulled his watch out of the breast pocket of his vest. He needed to get moving.

"Suit yourself, boy," he said. "Remember, my name is David Jacks. And I am your friend," he said earnestly. He climbed back into the carriage.

"Yes, sir."

Jacks flipped the reins, and the horses began to canter down the road towards the Del Monte. Proud and stubborn little kipper, Jacks thought to himself. It reminded him of another boy he once knew, fifty years in the past. Kinda reminds me of me, he thought to himself, smiling. Shouldn't be too hard to find the little kipper. Jacks knew everyone in town. Hell, I own the town, he thought happily as he continued down the road.

Jacks handed over the reins of his carriage to the doorman at the Del Monte Hotel, kicked the dirt off his boots and strode through the lobby towards the dining room. There was a separate private dining room reserved for the owners and their guests. The walls were wood-paneled and the carpet was a dark forest green. The walls were lined with hunting trophies; lifeless heads of deer, bear and elk were mounted on the walls. A large glass-paned window looked out over the garden and the huge seven-foot high topiary, trimmed with cypress hedge, and onto the shimmering Pacific.

Crocker and Stanford were already seated at the main dining table. Crocker raised a hand in greeting. Crocker was a mountain of a man, with a full head of gray hair and a stout beard. His eyes were narrow set, but very focused.

"I thought perhaps you were not going to join us, David," Crocker said. He rose, and they shook hands. "Pull up a chair and have some lunch." He motioned to the plates of cracked lobster and crab.

Leland Stanford finished a mouthful of steak and shook Jacks hand also. "Sit down, David," he smiled. "Sit down."

"To prosperity, gentlemen. May she smile upon us all," Jacks said, raising his glass.

"She's not going to be smiling much longer if we don't do something about that damn village on the edge of your town," Stanford began, chewing on a piece of steak as he spoke.

"There's no need for Chinamen here," Crocker joined in.

Crocker had made his name and his fortune as the mastermind behind the Transcontinental Railroad. He had connected Sacramento with Omaha. The railroad had been built in haste, on the labor and the backs of the Chinese coolies. Poor working conditions, disease and reckless use of dynamite killed off hundreds. Crocker simply hired more. They were fungible and the railroad had to be built.

"What would you have me do?" Jacks asked.

"We could get an ordinance passed that would not allow settlers on that land," Stanford suggested.

"Who owns that land?" Crocker asked. "I thought you owned everything around here."

"Not that parcel. They do," Jacks said. "They bought it and settled there about fifteen years ago. It was outside city limits. Quite a few of them used to work on your railroad," he added.

"Buy it from them," Stanford said.

"They don't want to sell," Jacks answered. "That's their home."

"I don't give a damn if they think it's their home," Crocker fumed. "It's a godforsaken eyesore, and it stinks. We spent a million dollars to build this hotel. It's the finest establishment south of San Francisco, and it's got a goddamn wart on its face."

Stanford shoved a huge mouthful of beef into his mouth and some of the juice ran down his beard.

"We could run them out," Stanford suggested through his mouthful of food. "We've got men for that kind of work."

"That Larkin fellow," Crocker said. "What's he been up to lately? Didn't he have some problem with the Chinese a while back?"

"He tried to get them into his whaling business," Jacks answered. "But they didn't take to it very well."

"They didn't take to the railroad either," Crocker laughed. "But by the time I was done with those little yellow bastards, the railroad was built. They didn't have a choice," he said proudly.

"It would be a lot easier on the town folk if we went through the council instead of using your men," Jacks said. "This used to be a pretty rough town. But now folks are settling down. Some of the Methodists in Pacific Grove are hiring Chinese women for cleaning and laundry. Some of them even take in the New Year's celebration in the village."

"The goddamn place stinks and the smell is drifting on the wind. I took in a walk last night and I thought I was going to puke," Crocker stated. "I want that village gone, and I want it gone soon." He paused to crack open a crab shell.

"I second that," Stanford said. He belched and then shoveled another mouthful of steak into his mouth.

David Jacks nodded in understanding, but inside he was troubled. He had no love for the Chinese, but they were a cheap source of labor and were hard workers.

"I'll get on it," he promised.

"I know you will," answered Crocker. "You're a good man Jacks," he said. "No matter what they say," he added, laughing. Stanford snorted in agreement and forked in another load of beef. The topic turned to politics, and the remainder of the luncheon passed quietly.

CHAPTER THIRTY-ONE

IRELAND, 1885

Parnell felt his blood pressure boil as he read the daily news. Home Rule had been shot down in flames and the Coercion Bill had passed. His life's works had been reduced to shambles by one man. A photograph next to the article showed Randolph Churchill with a grin plastered on his face. He was celebrating the victory and claiming it as his own doing.

Parnell set the paper down on the table. He sat in his kitchen, having dinner with his two sons, Benjamin and Issac. Ben was nineteen, Issac was seventeen. Both were members of the Fenian movement. Both were very proud and loyal to their father.

"I cannot believe that man has double-crossed me," Parnell stated.

"It will be alright, Father," Issac said, trying to soothe his father's rage.

"Randolph Churchill has no honor and no shame. And now, neither do I," Parnell cursed. "Daniel Curley has been arrested, and so have Joe Brady and the rest of his men." Parnell was overcome with despair.

"And what you don't know is that I gave them up to Lord Randolph for his assurances that he would not support the Coercion Bill. Those men will hang because I betrayed them."

Ben was shocked. Issac was confused.

"Father, are you telling me you informed on them?" Ben asked.

"Yes!" Parnell cried. "I made a deal with the devil because I thought it would bring peace. Instead I have brought death."

"Your intentions were good father," Ben reassured him. He reached out and took his father's hand. "You cannot blame yourself. Blame Randolph Churchill."

"I hope he rots in hell," Parnell fumed.

Ben looked at his watch. "Father, I have a meeting, I must go."

Issac jumped to his feet. "I'm going with you," he said.

"No Issac, you are not," Ben said to him. "Father, tell Issac to sit."

"Issac, sit," his father instructed.

Issac sat down, frowning.

"When will you be home, Ben?" Parnell asked.

"A little after midnight, maybe sooner if the meeting is short."

"Watch out for the police," Parnell warned. "They have spies everywhere. And they will be arresting everyone they suspect of any illegal activity now that damn bill passed Parliament."

"I'll be safe, father," Ben assured him. The confident young man left the house and went out into the cold, blustery evening air. He walked briskly to keep warm, his collar pulled up around his neck. Raindrops spilled off the brim of his hat.

"What's your hurry?" a voice said. Detective O'Malley stepped out from behind a building.

Ben felt fear, yet tried to appear nonchalant. "Looking for a pub and some ladies, sir," he replied.

"No ladies out on the streets at this time of night," said the detective. "Just prostitutes." O'Malley knew who Ben was. He also knew who his father was. And he wanted them both to go to prison in a very bad way.

"We arrested Kavanagh," O'Malley continued. "He talked. He said you were involved in the Phoenix Park murders."

Now Ben was very frightened but suppressed the urge to run.

"Sir, I was only sixteen when that happened. I had nothing to do with it, I swear," he pleaded.

O'Malley shook his head. "I wish I could believe you, but I've got to take you in for questioning. You may be right. But then again, you may be lying." He'll talk, O'Malley thought to himself. The British were well-adept when it came to getting people to talk. Just look at the Tower of London.

Parnell awoke to utter chaos. His wife was screaming, and Issac was calling him urgently.

"Father, father, come quickly," Issac called out.

Parnell ran down the stairs in his nightgown. Ben lay on the floor by the front door. He was bleeding badly, his teeth smashed out. He was coughing up blood and one eye was completely closed.

"Oh my God," Parnell gasped. He heard his wife wailing. "Be quiet woman, bring towels and warm water," he instructed.

"Ben, what happened?" He knelt next to his son and put his arms around him. He sat down on the floor and rested Ben's head against his chest. Ben's breathing was labored. His ribs were broken and so was his spleen. He was bleeding internally.

"I was arrested," Ben gasped. "O'Malley and his men. They accused me of being a lookout in Phoenix Park."

He coughed up more blood. His face was pale. Parnell held his oldest son tightly and ran one hand through his hair. It was covered in blood. His skull was fractured as well. Parnell looked down on the face of his son. He could see a glaze come over Ben's eyes.

"Ben, hang on," he pleaded. "We'll get the surgeon."

Ben saw his father's face and smiled. He knew he was dying.

"It's okay father, I told them nothing," Ben said. He laughed and more blood came out of his mouth.

"That's why they beat the shit out of me," he said. "I wouldn't talk. They said I was a tough little bastard, and I am. They sent me home as a message to you."

"Ben, don't talk. Lay still. We'll get the doctor," Parnell pleaded.

Issac stood at his father's side and looked down into his brother's face. "Ben, I love you," he whispered.

"You too, little brother," Ben gasped. "Father," he pleaded. "Look out for Issac. Do not let the government take him too." He began to choke on his blood, drowning in it. Parnell saw the fear in his son's eyes as he was now unable to speak. All Ben could do was gurgle.

"Oh God," Issac cried. He dropped to the floor, grabbing his brother. "Ben. Ben. Don't die, please don't die."

Slowly, the light in the room faded, and Ben saw his father and brother kneeling over him as his spirit left the room.

Parnell threw his head back and screamed. The whites of his eyes were the only thing showing. He clutched his dead son to his heaving chest, his heart breaking.

"I swear to you Issac; I swear to you on your dead brother's soul that I shall have my revenge," he sobbed. Issac put his arms around his father and cried.

"I will not rest until Randolph Churchill's firstborn son meets the same fate as Ben," Parnell swore. "On my oath, I shall have my revenge."

"I swear too, father," Issac said, tears streaming down his face. "He will die like my brother."

"You will stay out of it," Parnell ordered. "This is my burden."

"Not anymore, father," Issac said. He was now a man. "Not anymore."

CHAPTER THIRTY-TWO

MONTEREY, 1885

Kip had become a regular visitor at Chow Lin's hut in the Chinese village. The moon and stars illuminated his path as he ran along the trail to the village on the edge of the sea. Suddenly, he heard gunshots.

As he neared the village, he saw a group of men on horses riding towards him. He heard screaming coming from the Chinese fishing village. The night was lit by the glow of a fire coming from the village, but his instincts told him it could not be a cooking fire.

He ducked off the trail as the horses approached and watched through the thick brush. There were a dozen white men, and they were riding hard. Two held torches that were still burning. Kip's nose picked up the scent of kerosene.

"Ride," one man called out as they passed. "Ride before anyone knows we torched the heathen little slanty-eyed bastards."

The horses passed, and Kip ran back out onto the trail, towards the village. He recognized the face of the man who had spoken. It was framed by a thin beard than ran down a crooked jaw, with thin, snarling lips, and narrow, hooded brown eyes. It was Larkin.

As he got to the hill that looked down on the village, he stopped dead in his tracks and gazed down at the inferno before him. Every shack was ablaze with flames shooting high into the night sky. Every boat, every pier, everything was on fire. People were screaming, trying to throw buckets of sea water on their homes. Others just sat in the dirt wailing. There were dead bodies on the ground, some of them still on fire.

"Chow Lin!" Kip screamed as he ran towards the burning village. He fought his way through the flames, covering his eyes from the smoke. Tears ran down his face, and he began to cough as the smoke seared his lungs.

He found Chow Lin's small hut, ablaze. Chow Lin's wife sat outside in the dirt, wailing, holding her dead husband.

"Oh my God!" Kip cried out. Chow Lin's body was badly burned and shot in the chest.

"Who did this?" Kip cried out. "It was Larkin and his men, wasn't it ? Who else was with him?"

Chow Lin's wife's back heaved as she sobbed, holding her dead husband in her arms. She did not speak English.

Kip looked around him. The village was completely ablaze, and everyone was standing back from the flames, hopeless. He grabbed Chow Lin's wife and pulled her away from her husband and the approaching flames. She pushed him away, but Kip reached out again. The brush around them was now on fire, and they were in a firestorm. He had to get her to let go of Chow Lin, but she was strong, and wouldn't move.

Kip felt the sting of the fire and saw the flames now only a few feet away. The grass was on fire, and the underbrush and pine needles only added fuel. He felt a wall of heat drive him backward. At the same time, Chow Lin and his wife ignited, their bodies quickly consumed by the flames.

Kip gasped and ran from the fire, towards the hills. He ran up the trail, absolutely beside himself, his heart pounding and his mind racing. He was alone. Completely alone. He ran until his legs gave out and he fell in a clump of brush, now miles from the village. He gazed up at the sky; the fog was red from the distant fire.

I am in hell, he thought. Absolutely in hell. He passed out from exhaustion.

EIGHT YEARS LATER

CHAPTER THIRTY-THREE

WEST POINT – ANNAPOLIS, 1893

"There's no way they can bust our wedge," Billy intoned seriously. "Last year, ok, we had our problems. But this year, we drop twenty-four on their fat butts."

Kip McDuran turned away from the window of the passenger car and looked over at his friend. There was just enough light from the full moon shining through the windows of the coach to make out his smirk. Billy was a short, stocky fireplug with a crop of thick brown hair parted in the middle.

"Aye, we'll whip 'em for sure," Kip replied confidently. He looked back out the window. Trees rushed by. The steam locomotive pulled them past the blurred landscape as the cars wound their way through the forest like a giant snake.

Kip looked at his time piece.

"It's late, Billy. You need to sleep. It's the big one tomorrow, Army versus Navy. And we're Army, playing at Navy. You know what that means?"

"Lots of squid?"

Kip laughed. "Aye, and lots of mucky mucks from Washington will be watching the game, and maybe a few ladies."

"Admirals and generals, no doubt?" Billy gasped sarcastically.

"More than a few bets will be laid down, I imagine."

"I'd like to get laid," Billy said wistfully.

Kip shook his head and stretched his six-foot frame in the narrow space between the wooden benches in the coach. The gangly, dirty urchin who had run from one end of the peninsula of Monterey to the other along the dirt roads and game trails had matured into a sturdy young Scotsman, just like his father.

"Keep your mind on football, mate," Kip advised. "That's why we're here. The commandant has his heart set on us winning, and he'll be there too."

"I just hope P.T. remembers to call the right plays this time," Billy said.

"He was calling the right plays the last game. It was you that couldn't remember them," Kip teased. P.T. was the quarterback. No one knew what P.T. stood for.

"How would you know, you were knocked out silly on the sidelines," Billy teased back.

Kip ruefully ran his hand through his dark hair. "Just once," he said. "And I did come back into the game," he reminded his friend.

"That's you, Kip. Never out of the game," Billy answered happily.

Kip was already a legend at West Point. When he first arrived from California during summer camp, Billy thought that the upperclassmen were going to kill him for sure.

Hazing had become a rite of passage at the Academy, and Kip had been an early target of the upperclassmen. Cadet Kip McDuran still had the Scottish accent of his parents, which the southern upperclassmen, still smarting from the Civil War, took as a challenge to their own.

Kip endured many a sleepless night and quite often found himself snatched out of his bed and tossed into a drainage ditch behind the barracks, or thrashing on the ground as he "swam to Newburgh" at the orders of upperclassmen. The harassment was relentless. But Kip and the rest of the "plebes" not only took it; they were also determined to show no ill effects. Many a plebe was found unconscious on the ground after a particularly grueling session. But "Kip" McDuran never, ever gave in, and eventually, the upperclassmen grew bored and turned to easier prey.

But it was late one winter night that Kip truly made his name at West Point.

It was one of many rough traditions at the Academy, but next to football, the most entertaining. Fistfights organized by the upper-class "scrapping" committee. The unfortunate plebe was ordered to take on his opponent, handpicked by the upperclassmen. The school surgeon became adept at stitching up lacerated cheeks and brows. But no one ever said from where the injuries had come.

Third Classman Frank "Bull" Keller had no love for the sturdy Scotsman and was determined to make sure that McDuran went down and stayed down. Keller was easily three inches taller than Kip and outweighed him by thirty pounds. His nickname was "Bull," and since he was the largest cadet at West Point, no one ever tried to call him anything else.

"Eight o'clock, on the high ground by Fort Putnam," Bull declared at the secret meeting held in the upperclassmen's barracks. "Otto, you keep time. Two-minute rounds, no limit, last man standing."

"What about seconds?" Cadet Oscar Lyle inquired.

"He can pick his own," growled Bull. "You're mine. We need lookouts to make sure no one from the faculty wanders over."

"No problem there," said Otto. "They can't stand the guy anyway."

Which was all too true. Cadet McDuran was a "rogue." He had no pedigree. He came from a dirt-poor family, both parents dead at an early age. Admissions to West Point were normally reserved for the sons of the wealthy and upper class. "Rogues" had no power, no influence and thus nothing to offer. Only the insistence of David Jacks and his friend in the United States Senate, Daniel McDonald, of California, forced the admission's committee's hands. The same David Jacks who took in a small orphan that reminded him of a kipper, and adopted him as his son.

"Good. Because when I'm done with him, he won't have a brain left in his head nor a chance in hell of staying at West Point," Bull swore.

"Bull, you can't be serious," Oscar said.

"Why not?" Bull shot back. "It will be a fair fight."

Bull saw the worried look on his classmate's faces. "Don't worry, mates. I'm just getting psyched. But he's going to get a whipping for sure."

They broke into easy laughter. Otto kept silent. He knew Bull.

There were more than a "few" cadets gathered on the high ground that night. A good fifty upperclassmen huddled in a circle holding torches. Someone had already chalked out a circle on the ground. Kip looked at the crowd of excited faces, red-faced and full of anticipation.

"Christ almighty, Billy. There's close to fifty or more of the buggers," he said softly.

Billy looked at the torchlight, the crowd, the circle. He felt sick.

"Just keep your eyes on the big fellow, Kip."

"Jesus," whispered Kip. "How can you miss him?"

Bull stepped into the circle, wearing a pair of boots and field pants. His upper torso was massive, especially his neck.

"Kip, you do know how to fight?" Billy asked.

Kip grinned at his friend.

"Guess we're gonna find out."

He eased out of his army sweatshirt and stripped off his undershirt. He let his arms hang, and shook them slightly to loosen up. No one in the crowd missed his bulging biceps and triceps and his sleek, well-muscled frame. They also noticed his confidence.

The truth was Kip grew up fighting. Sometimes for his life. The docks and pubs of Monterey were full of drunken sailors and adventurers looking for sport. Or victims. There was a four-inch scar on Kip's left upper shoulder. His assailant had slashed his shoulder, pulling out a knife when he realized the young Scot was going to get the better of him in a fistfight. Kip took the knife away and left the drunken sailor laying face down on the hardwood floor of the run-down pub. The surgeon had been unable to reset the man's nose properly, and someone gave him the nickname "Pug," which was fitting.

"Ready?" Otto asked Bull.

Bull snorted, nodding his head.

"Ready?" Otto asked Kip.

Kip nodded his head and mimicked Bull's snort. There was a titter in the crowd. Bull didn't like that.

"Step in," Otto instructed.

Both men stepped into the circle.

"Fight!"

Bull rushed Kip and threw a right hand that would have knocked a hole in a two-inch board. Instead, it found air, and the momentum carried Bull forward. His eyes bulged as he received a powerful kick to his left butt cheek, adding to his energy. He landed face first in the dirt, mouth open. The crowd grew deathly silent.

Bull jumped to his feet and turned to face Kip.

"You're dead, bitch!" Bull yelled. He charged again, this time arms out, legs driving, as he sought to pile-drive his opponent deep into the earth.

Kip rolled backward, grabbing the outstretched hands. He pulled the charging Bull over him as his back hit the ground and then placed his feet underneath Bull's chest. He continued to roll backward on the ground, and at the last second kicked up with his feet and let go. Bull flipped over Kip, now wholly airborne, arms flailing. He landed on his back, and the air came out of his diaphragm like a locomotive belching smoke. He rolled over, gasping, and got back to his feet. His face was full of fury.

"Aaaaaarrrrrrrrrhhhhhhhhhhhhhhhhh!!!!!!!!!!!!!!!!!!!!!" Bull screamed as he charged again, eyes bugging out of his now lowered head.

"Arrggh yourself, mate," Kip said. He grabbed the outstretched left hand of the charging Bull and stepped to his left. As Bull passed him, still hurtling forward, Kip jerked back on Bull's left arm. The pop of the bone, wrenched from its socket, drew a groan from more than a few upperclassmen. One retched.

What happened next was the subject of many a debate for years to come. Kip grabbed the back of Bull's pants and threw him forward. It didn't require much effort. Bull was going in that direction anyway. The fact that he ran headfirst into a two-foot thick fir tree could not be conclusively attributed to accident or good aim.

The loud clap of his head striking solid wood drew a "Jesus" from the crowd. Bull fell to the ground like a sack of potatoes, unconscious, blood pouring from his nose.

Kip walked over to the unconscious body and rolled him on his side.

"Don't want him to choke to death on his own blood," he said to no one in particular. He felt Bull's neck for signs of fracture and then raised his eyelids, checking the pupils. He felt for a pulse and listened for respiration.

"He'll live," Kip said, getting back up to his feet. "But he needs to see the surgeon." Kip picked up his sweatshirt and pulled it back on. "Better hop to it," he instructed the upperclassmen. His gaze was steady. No one challenged the lower classman's instruction.

They silently gathered up the Bull and carried him off to the surgeon's office.

"Well Billy, let's hope Bull can still play next year against Navy," Kip said softly.

Billy had nothing to say.

The train continued through the night, but Kip couldn't sleep. His friend snored softly. The rattle of the tracks seemed soothing, but Kip's mind was racing. The commandant of West Point was indeed going to be at the game, as was the commodore from the Naval Academy. Senator McDonald had written Kip a letter before the big game, warning him that the annual match had turned into a political and military spectacle in Washington. Football was growing popular in the nation, and the rivalry between Army and Navy was reaching new heights. Many a "gentleman's wager" had been placed. Politicians and the press would be there as well.

Kip felt his stomach getting tight. Butterflies be damned, he thought. These are more like menstrual cramps! Kip was no stranger to pressure. His entire life was one challenge after another just to survive. Adding to the pressure was his sense of self-worth. Or lack thereof.

After his father's murder, and six months after his mother's death, he was nothing more than a wounded animal, living in the forest of

Monterey. He stole to survive. He vanished from the school and no one noticed.

Until David Jacks finally found him in the forest. It had taken Jack's months to track him. By then, the boy had become legendary. Not a clothing line was safe, nor were pantries or kitchens. And of course, neither was the Del Monte Hotel. They assigned a Brinks detective to catch the thief who routinely raided their kitchen, and who also pilfered a large brown goose down comforter and a pillow from one of the Bridal Suites. Kip's mind drifted back in time. Back to when his life took a sudden turn for the better.

The sun was just beginning to set on the western horizon; purple and magenta brush strokes on a sky-blue canvas. Jacks sat frustrated in the seat of the carriage. No one had seen the McDuran boy after his mother passed. The last time Jacks saw him was on the trail. That had been a year earlier. That's not right, he decided.

David Jacks went to find the young boy.

The light was dimming in the forest, but he smelled the fire and followed his nose. He had left the game trail a hundred yards behind when he came upon the twelve-year-old Kip, whose back was turned as he tried to pry off the top of a tin of fruit from the Del Monte kitchen.

"Hungry laddie?"

The boy spun to face him. His face was caked with dirt; his pants had holes, and his shirt was too large, hanging to his knees. He recognized Jacks from the trail. He said nothing, and sat on his haunches, watching the older man. He continued to try and get the top of the tin.

"It works best with a key," Jacks said softly.

"I don't have the key," Kip replied, his eyes now fixed on Jacks.

The piercing blue eyes set above the smooth, high cheekbones smudged with dirt stared deeply into his eyes. Much like a hawk, Jacks mused silently. Or maybe, better yet, a young puma cub. Jack's eyes softened. Jesus, he looks just like his old man.

"I do," Jacks said. "So you'd best come with me."

And so, Kip did. His instincts told him he needed a better shelter than his lean-to. At age twelve, Kip McDuran became the adopted son of the wealthiest man in Monterey. A fact not unnoticed by many, including both the enemies of his father and David Jacks.

But along with the notoriety came something else; a steady hand, guidance and a chance to grow. Kip went back to the schoolhouse and his education. But David Jacks taught him so much more. Every night they would sit by the massive stone fireplace in Jack's home. Jacks would talk, and Kip would listen.

His father's murder went unsolved and all but Kip forgot his mother's death.

"Next stop Baltimore!" the conductor called out. Kip snapped out of his daydream and grinned. The Navy would be sending carriages to take them to Annapolis. They would have a good meal and sleep in the gymnasium on their bedrolls. And then the next morning, the "game."

Chapter Thirty-Four

SANDHURST, 1893

The weather was glorious. A warm autumn sun bathed the carefully mowed lawns and the gray brick and stone buildings of the Royal Military College. The hoof beats of the horses drawing his carriage along the road kept time with the humming of the driver. It was Churchill's first day at Sandhurst, and it could and should have been a glorious arrival for an 18-year-old that was setting out to find his place in the world.

For Winston Churchill, however, it was hell. He clutched at the left breast pocket of his tweed jacket. The letter and the watch were still there.

The letter.

For a young boy who had spent his entire life trying to win his father's favor, the letter was his ultimate defeat. For the young man who now was arriving at one of the most famous and storied military academies in the world, it represented a dark shadow cast upon his life, blocking out the daylight forever. The die was cast, and his fortunes, or better put, misfortunes, were set in stone. By his father.

Those who knew Randolph Churchill the best in his later years would describe him as "cruel." He had risen to power on his family name and his gifted public speaking. His speeches before Parliament were often barbed, even incising.

But even his most ardent admirers would describe the letter he wrote to his son on August 9, 1893, upon learning of his acceptance to the

Royal Military Academy at Sandhurst, as just plain mean. And if the letter was meant to strike home, it succeeded with utter ruthlessness.

> "The first extremely discreditable feature of your performance is missing the infantry, for in that failure is demonstrated beyond refutation your slovenly happy-go-lucky harum-scarum style of work for which you have always been distinguished at your different schools….."

Winston's hands shook as he took out a cigarette from his expensive silver case and lit the end, inhaling deeply. He could cite the letter line by line. It was an intrusive thought that would not leave his brain alone.

> "With all the advantages you had, with all the abilities which you foolishly think yourself to possess & which some of your relations claim for you….."

That would be "mother" Winston thought to himself.

> "You may find some consolation in the fact that you have failed to get into the '60th Rifles' one of the finest regiments in the army. There is also another satisfaction for you that by accomplishing the prodigious effort of getting into the Calvary, you imposed on me an extra charge of some £200 a year. Not that I shall allow you to remain in the Cavalry. As soon as possible I shall arrange your exchange into an infantry regiment of the line…"

That will be miserable, he thought to himself. He had visions of himself going in the opposite direction on this very same road three months hence.

> "I shall not write again on these matters & you need not trouble to write any answer to this part of my letter, because I no longer attach the slightest weight

to anything you may say about your own acquirements and exploits. Make this position indelibly impressed on your mind, that if your conduct and action at Sandhurst is similar to what it has been in the other establishments in which it has sought vainly to impart to you some education, then my responsibility for you is over......"

Indelibly impressed ? I can't sleep or eat thanks to you.

"I shall leave you to depend on yourself giving you merely such assistance as may be necessary to permit of a respectable life........"

How much would that be, Winston wondered to himself?

"Because I am certain that if you cannot prevent yourself from leading the idle useless unprofitable life you have had during your schooldays & later months, you will become a mere social wastrel one of the hundreds of the public school failures, and you will degenerate into a shabby unhappy & futile existence. If that is so you will have to bear all the blame for such misfortunes yourself...."

What do you mean "will" degenerate into a shabby and futile existence? I'm already there, Churchill thought despondently. With a cigarette carefully hanging from his lip, he reached into his other pocket for his flask of whiskey. The cigarette came out of his mouth only long enough for the whiskey to enter.

Adolescence had not been kind to Winston. He stood five feet six inches tall, weighed 120 pounds and had already developed a smoker's cough, which he regularly tried to extinguish with an excellent scotch.

As he rode past the bower and arbors of the polished landscape, all he could think about was what a miserable failure he had become. No matter what, in his father's eyes, he was a failure. A miscreant. A.........

he didn't even want to think the word, but there.....it jumped into his head again, "*wastrel.*"

He had looked it up in the dictionary. The definitions were still indelibly etched into his brain. "Scoundrel." He liked that. "Rogue." Most certainly his favorite, "degenerate failure."

"Ouch," he said out loud. No doubt father had the same dictionary.

The carriage came to a stop in front of the two-story "Old College" building that loomed over the parade grounds. Eight fluted columns framed the grand entrance. Carefully polished brass cannons, used at Waterloo, lined the roadway and stood testament to the school's tradition and greatness. As if to further impress its institutional power and importance upon the unwary newcomer, a high wall rose up, with figures of English lore cut into the stone. Mingled of course with the Roman god of war, Mars, and Minerva, the roman goddess of wisdom.

Winston couldn't help but think that it paled in comparison to his uncle's palace at Blenheim, but he appreciated its splendid message. No doubt about it. The British Empire was at its zenith. A brilliant light to guide the rest of the planet.

And I am nothing but a degenerate wastrel, destined to crawl in its shadows, he thought.

He got out of the carriage, his eyes squinting in the sunlight. He saw the gymnasium off in the distance, the large windows set amidst the brick and mortar. He walked up the steps of the Old College and smelled stale smoke and old wood as he entered its hallowed halls.

A young cadet sat at a desk, his single-breasted frock coat and blue serge trousers were immaculate. Portraits of famous British generals loomed behind him on the walls. He gave Churchill a studied glance.

"Your name, sir?"

"Winston Churchill."

Ah, of course, the young cadet thought to himself. The son of the legendary Randolph Churchill. The nephew of the Duke of Marlborough. He's not much to look at, and not very big. And he doesn't seem too bright, the cadet noticed.

"Of course, sir. Let me show you to your room."

The cadet handed Churchill a large manila envelope.

"Your schedules, the rules, your courses, and a map," he said in perfect, clipped English.

"Right," Winston replied in his best Cockney accent.

The cadet eyed him momentarily. "Smart ass," he thought, but outwardly chose to ignore the obviously feigned accent. Instead, he led the way up the stairs to the second floor.

Winston was moderately impressed with the smoking room, pleased but not surprised at the worn felt on the billiard tables in the game room, and relieved to see that his quarters, which he shared with two others, was divided by a partition. He already knew that there was a company butler at his disposal to shine shoes and the like. Unlike his American counterparts, he had no desire to waste time shining buckles or rifles. That's what servants were for.

The fact that slavery had just been outlawed in England three weeks earlier did not diminish his sense of entitlement. The fact of the matter was that at age eighteen, Winston Churchill had never cooked a meal for himself, never done his own laundry, never shined his own shoes or picked up his room. And he certainly did not intend to start now.

He reached for the watch in his breast pocket. It was silver and had his father's name etched on the back. He had given it to Winston on his tenth birthday. It was a happier time. His father had patted him on the back and gave his shoulders a good squeeze. It was the only physical affection he could remember from his father. He held the watch in his hand and thought about the letter in his pocket.

> "Because I am certain that if you cannot prevent yourself
> from leading the idle useless unprofitable life you have
> had during your schooldays…"

Winston furrowed his brow, and stared out the large open window onto the vast expanse of the military academy, past the stables and the firing range, past the sports fields and the golf links, past the tennis courts and the parade grounds gaily decorated with various brightly colored flags.

"Because I am certain *if...*" he said to himself. *"If"* was a very interesting word. The conditional tense of his father's message was not lost on him. There was hope.

He patted the tight wool green blanket that covered his bed. He opened up the curriculum and read the outlines of his first session. Fortification, tactics, topography, military law and military administration. The schedule listed his other tasks; drill, gymnastics, riding, marksmanship.

"God, they're out to make me a bloody soldier," he whispered. "I can't do this." He shook his head, tears streaming down his face. "There is no way I can do this." Hope slowly slid into despair.

Chapter Thirty-Five

BAHR EL GHAZAL, 1893

With its shiny black shell and sturdy legs, the dung beetle worked a ball of feces into a sphere twice the size of its body. Syrah sat in the dirt just outside the entrance to her grass hut. I am just like that insect, she thought. Destined to roll up balls of feces for food and condemned to live out my days in the hot humid swamps of Bahr el Ghazal.

She looked around the zeriba, the small area around her hut was surrounded by thorns from acacia trees. She was an *abid*, a slave to Kauūk 'Alī.

Despite her father's best efforts, slavery was still alive and well in the Sudan. And now his daughter, Syrah was the property of the Arab Kauūk 'Alī, who had bought her at an auction in Fashoda.

Syrah, now fifteen, tried to block out the images of the Mahdi's soldiers raping and then killing her mother.

She was better in the day. She could focus on the creatures of the Sudan, like the dung beetle. She could commiserate with its misery.

It was different at night. The dreams were always the same.

The head of her father impaled on a spear. Her mother, sobbing, then gasping under the weight of the bodies of a wild horde of Arabs who raped her until she bled from her vagina. In their frenzy, they mistook the bucking of her hips from the pain as ecstasy, and they were only more encouraged to continue. Finally, she hemorrhaged, and as the blood coursed out from her body, the attacking horde stood back, then roared its approval. Another man entered the now lifeless and bloody body of her mother.

When the lifeless body no longer amused them, they looked at the seven-year-old girl standing in the corner of the slave quarters. She had passed out when her father was slaughtered, but came to as her mother took her inside the stone walls of the servant's quarters. She remembered the look of sadness on her mothers' face as the dervish horde kicked in the wooden doors. She remembered the way the men looked at her, hungry with blood lust.

As they approached her, an emir came into the doorway and barked out an order. The men backed away.

"She is a virgin," he said. "Do not touch her. She is mine now," he ordered.

And I will sell her for great profit as I take her south to Fashoda, he thought to himself. The emir himself did not fancy children for sex. He had his own harem of beautiful young women. But he knew she would fetch a handsome profit. Her skin was not as dark as most Sudanese, and her nose was more aquiline than broad. She was more mahogany than ebony. But her sapphire eyes were piercing, just like her father's.

And so Syrah was taken south, to the town of Fashoda, where she was sold to Kauūk 'Alī.

He took an instant fascination to the seven-year-old with blue eyes. She reminded him more of the slaves from the Nubian Desert to the north. He had a small hut built for her on his zeriba, and he regularly visited her shelter.

And so I am a slave, she thought, shaking her head from her memories. And no doubt, Kauūk 'Alī will be returning home again soon, with his foul breath and long grey beard, and I will be his, she thought. Just like the beetle. I live and eat shit, she thought. She could only wonder why she had not yet become pregnant. Perhaps it's me, she thought. I am good for nothing anyway, why would I be able to bear a child?

Not that she wanted to bear a child of the putrid Turk. To carry his seed was one of many of her worries. Most of all, she worried about staying alive. There was little safety in the swampland along the river Bahr el Ghazal. Small zeriba like Kauūk 'Alī's were a community unto themselves, rarely interacting with anyone.

The Mahdi had died of an illness six months after slaughtering her father. But his trusted lieutenant, and now leader of the jihad, the Khalifa Abdulla, was very much in control of most of the dervish movement, and the Khalifa was determined to build his caliphate in the desert.

The Khalifa's attention had now turned south, towards Bahr el Ghazal. The Khalifa was acutely aware of the natural resources of the woodland and the savanna of the southern Sudan that could help sustain his army.

Syrah was stirred out of her thoughts by vibrations she felt on the ground. A horse was approaching. Her ears fixed on the sound. It was approaching fast. She stood up. She was a tall woman, with sturdy muscular legs. She was dressed in the traditional dark cotton tob and hijab of a Sudanese woman. Only her eyes showed through the slits in the cloth.

Her eyes and ears told her that a horseman was approaching the zeriba at great speed. She could see the outline of his body, and suddenly she could make out his garb. He was dervish, a soldier of the Khalifa. She could make out the multi-colored patches sewn into his white cotton tunic.

The terror of her childhood flooded every nerve in her body and her adrenaline kicked in. She felt the impulse to flee. Fight or flight, the natural reaction to fear, be it beast or man, coursed through her blood.

She chose flight. The area around the zeriba was cleared and it was a thousand yards to the Sudd, the swampland surrounding the river. If she could reach the Sudd, she could hide. The horse would have a hard time navigating the swamps.

Syrah broke into a sprint. She was fast and she was young.

The horse too was fast, and as she clawed through the tall grass of the swamp she could hear the horses heaving breath close behind. The grass tore at the skin on her face. She ran up a small island in the Sudd and then slid down the muddy bank. She drove forward into the thick reeds and sharp grass that flayed skin off her flesh. She was too afraid to feel pain.

Muhammad Khair smiled to himself as he watched the fleeing Nubian slave. He had seen her hands. She was too light-skinned to be Danaqla or Dinka. Someone had paid a pretty price for this slave. She was soon to be his. He was a scout for the Khalifa, but scouting also had its personal rewards.

He drove his horse forward into the Sudd and could feel the thick mud pulling at the legs of his horse. Allah, he prayed, give my horse strength. Suddenly, he broke into a clearing as he approached the banks of the river. He saw the girl sliding down the muddy banks. She was only a hundred yards away.

He pulled up his horse, slowing to a walk. She had nowhere to go. She was his.

He smiled as he watched her heaving body continue forward into the swamp, fighting the reeds and the saw grass. She lost her footing and fell hard, only to leap back to her feet and continue fighting forward.

She would bring me much pleasure, he thought. After I have broken her spirit and taken her body.

Suddenly, it was his turn to be startled by the sound of approaching hoofs. He turned, just in time to make eye contact with Kauūk ʿAlī, approaching from his right side, sword drawn. He reached for his own sword, but it was too late. The Turk swung a mighty blow that Muhammad Khair could only try to duck.

Their horses collided and both men were knocked to the ground. Muhammad Khair felt satisfaction as his sword found its way into his hand. The Turk and the Arab engaged in a vicious exchange of blows. Kauūk ʿAlī made a quick parry to Khair's thrust and felt exhilaration as the sword flew out of the dervish's hand. He drove his own sword deep into the chest of his opponent, noting with satisfaction that Khair's eyes bulged from their sockets. But the religious zealot was not finished. He drew a dagger from his waist and plunged it into Kauūk ʿAlī's right shoulder. He had hoped for a more lethal strike, but it was all he could manage.

Kauūk ʻAlī screamed in pain and dropped his sword. He charged forward, and knocked his opponent into the swamp. With his uninjured arm, he grabbed Muhammad Khair and held him under the water, thrashing about. But the blade had severed the arteries in Muhammad Khair's chest, and he slowly stopped moving.

Kauūk ʻAlī threw his head back and roared. His whole being was focused upon the destruction of Muhammad Khair, the man who had dared to enter his zeriba to steal his abid.

He was so focused he failed to see the sturdy, muscular young woman behind him, holding his sword. Syrah screamed as she swung with all her might. Kauūk ʻAlī's roaring head was silenced and severed from his body.

Syrah, driven by an insane rage, began hacking both men to pieces. It wasn't until she saw the approaching crocodiles that she backed off. She watched in satisfaction as they feasted upon the flesh of both men. The swamp turned red with their blood, and Syrah could only smile.

"Yes!" she exclaimed. She felt joy as she watched the spinning bodies of the crocodiles as they tore Kauūk ʻAlī and Muhammad Khair into a thousand pieces of meat, gulping down arms and legs. It sent a shiver up her spine. I was not the prey this time, and I will never be the prey of men again, she vowed to herself.

She sat at the edge of the river until dusk, until the giant lizards had finished every last piece of Arab flesh. I too am one with nature, Syrah thought. And I too can become a predator. I too can avenge my parents' death, she decided.

It would be a long journey to Khartoum, through the swampland of the south, and then across the savannah, and then the desert. But it was her land, and she knew the dangers and where to find safety. So long as she could avoid man she would be fine. She had no fear of beasts.

Chapter Thirty-Six

ANNAPOLIS, 1893

Kip stood on the sidelines in absolute awe. The growing rivalry between Army and Navy had filled the sidelines with spectators. He saw generals and admirals huddled together. Officers of all ranks and all services filled the crowd, medals carefully polished. Wooden bleachers surrounded the field, filled with a raucous crowd. Tobacco smoke hung in the air.

"Holy shit," Kip said to Bull. "I've never seen this many people in one place in my life."

Bull looked around at the crowd. "No worries mate," he said. "I've got your back." And he meant it. Bull had grown to respect and admire the sturdy, fast young Scot. Kip held no grudge in his heart. Bull was now his boy. And he was going to need him today.

"That's great, Bull," quipped Billy. "And who's got your back," he teased.

"You, you little bastard," Bull said affectionately. He reached out and tousled the hair of the smaller man.

"P.T.," roared Otto. "You better be quick today, my friend. Those squids are looking mighty riled."

P.T. was the quarterback. "I've got this," he said confidently.

Kip looked over at the Navy sidelines. They were jumping up and down, pounding each other on the backs, screaming.

"Piece of cake," Kip said. The whistle blew, and he found himself ready to receive the kick from Navy.

He let out a deep breath. Here we go, he thought. Just like stealing vegetables out of old man Larkin's garden. He smiled at the memory as the ball was launched into the air. Kip took two steps to his right, caught the ball perfectly with his hands, tucked it under his arm, and looked for the broad back of Bull in front of him.

Bull delivered a crushing blow to the plebe in front of him, and Kip danced to his left. Suddenly he was hit by a ton of bricks named Navy cadet Owen Wilson. Wilson drove Kip into the dirt and then jumped up screaming.

First and ten at the twenty, thought Kip as he got to his feet. That hurt.

P.T. called them into the huddle. He looked at Kip.

"You alright?"

"Just dandy," Kip replied. "Let's kick some ass. Bull, next time block both those guys."

"Sorry," Bull said. He spit out some blood. He was missing a tooth.

"Wedge right," P.T. said. "Kip, climb inside Bull's ass."

"Already been there," Kip quipped.

They all laughed. It was football, and it was fun. They broke the huddle and set up their formation. Bull took a bead on Cadet Wilson in the secondary. On the snap, he slapped the lineman in front of him in the head, knocking him to the ground. Bull charged towards Wilson, who was focused on Kip, who took the handoff from P.T. Bull hit Cadet Wilson low, chopping out his legs.

Wilson screamed and dropped to the turf. Bull rolled out of the way and Kip sprinted down the right side of the field, all the way in for a touchdown.

Navy fans screamed for a penalty flag. Army fans just screamed. Kip dropped the ball in the end zone and nonchalantly ran back to his team. They slapped and hugged him. Bull grabbed him in a bear hug, smearing blood on Kip's jersey.

"Jesus, Bull," Kip gasped. "Can you wait until we get a room?"

The rest of the team burst into laughter.

On the other side of the field, Admiral Dougherty was not amused.

He felt that the Army cadets were laughing at the Navy cadets. The admiral did not like being made a fool of, and even more so, his cadets. He took a deep sip of whiskey from his flask and started to make his way to the West Point side of the field.

"Listen up," Navy coach Jerod Smith barked. He grabbed Cadet Wilson by the hair and shook his head. "No sissies allowed here, sailor," he hissed.

"No sissies here, coach," Wilson replied. His right knee felt like pudding.

"Get that fuckin' McDuran off the goddamn field first chance you get," he ordered his team. A growl arose from the midshipmen. They had been called out by their coach. Their honor was at stake.

"He's mine," stated Cadet Jones. Jones was a tall, muscular lineman. "I'll break him in two," he announced.

"Break him into pieces!" ordered Coach Smith.

On the other sideline, West Point's coach, Dennis Michie, gathered his team on the sideline.

"Gentlemen, we have scored, but we have a long battle ahead of us," he warned.

"Army!" the team roared back in unison.

"Go Navy, beat Army!" the crowd roared.

Admiral Dougherty, now behind the end zone, continued his stride towards the Army sidelines.

After the kickoff, Navy had the ball at its own twenty-yard line. Their quarterback barked out his cadence, and the nation's future officers and leaders collided in a frenzied pile of muscle, sinew, and sweat. Cadet Wilson had the ball and followed the wedge. He powered straight towards Kip, following the enormously broad buttocks of Cadet Jones.

Jones mowed over Billy like he was a daisy and aimed at Kip. Kip watched Wilson switch the ball from his right side to his left. He's going to cut right, Kip thought. At the same time Bull hit Jones in the head with his forearms and Jones dropped unconscious to the turf, clearing Kip's path to the runner.

A howl broke out from the Navy sideline as Kip drove his shoulder deep into Wilson's chest, knocking him backward five yards.

"Oh my God!" burst Admiral Dougherty. He was now at the West Point sideline. He strode over to Coach Michie and grabbed him by the collar.

"You better play fair, or I'll have your balls cut off!" he yelled into the coach's face.

Major General Thomas Smith watched in horror as the admiral grabbed the coach. He briskly walked up to the admiral.

"I say, old man, you need to get a grip and let go of the coach," he growled. General Smith was a combat veteran from the Civil War and was not about to let this arrogant, angry swabbie grab his coach.

"Fuck off," the admiral roared. "Your men are cheating," he accused.

General Smith felt his blood boil. Accusations of dishonesty were grounds for a duel. The admiral had called him out.

"Listen you cock!" he yelled. "Don't accuse us of cheating," he warned.

"Don't call me a cock, you bastard!" Admiral Dougherty bellowed. He threw a right hand at the general, who deftly dodged the punch. General Smith countered with his own right hand, deep into the solar plexus of the admiral.

"Ooof," the air hissed out of the admiral's lungs.

"Fight!" roared the crowd. Chaos enveloped the field. Fists and blood flew. It took twenty minutes to restore order. The referees called an end to the game and both teams retreated.

Bull wiped the blood from his mouth and smiled. "I knocked the shit out of that guy," he bragged.

Kip reached out and touched the profusely sweating lineman who had once been his adversary.

"Aye, that you did Bull," he said smiling. "You saved my ass, and I will never forget it."

After the game, as both teams went back to their academies, President Grover Cleveland rode the train back to Washington. He was troubled by the violence he had just witnessed in the stands. The game was supposed to celebrate the finest young cadets the nation had. It so troubled him that he ordered a cabinet meeting. At the meeting, he ordered the Secretary of the Navy, Hilary Herbert, and Secretary of War, Daniel S. Lamont, to suspend any further matches between Army and Navy. They could continue to play, but just not against each other.

But something else he had noticed stuck in his mind. The determination of the young Scotsman who was leading his team to victory. The president liked winners, and he knew the value of brave leaders. He wrote to the commandant of West Point, and confidentially requested updates of Cadet McDuran's progress. The young man had a future.

Chapter Thirty-Seven

SANDHURST, 1893

After the first three days, Winston was encouraged. They had been relatively painless. He learned his way around the academy grounds, attended lectures on what to do and what *not* to do while attending the Royal Military Academy. They were issued uniforms and gear, which delighted him to no end. He proudly wore his day uniform and cocked his field cap to one side as the upperclassmen did.

The morning of his fourth day, however, had him a tad bit uneasy. Instead of wearing his jaunty field cap, he was wearing a full helmet. He wore the day uniform, but this time he also carried a pack that weighed ten kilos. In addition, he was carrying a Lee-Medford rifle, a bandolier of ammunition, and a canteen. He was in the third row of his company of sixty cadets, and he felt like a racehorse at the gate just before the start.

It was a one-mile formation run, and each man had to hold his position. Winston was so nervous that he smoked two cigarettes after breakfast.

Somewhat pale in the face, Winston looked out from under his campaign helmet and into the ever-watchful eyes of Staff Sergeant Girling; the noncommissioned officer in charge of Company E. Girling was also the company drill sergeant.

"Gentlemen," the drill sergeant addressed his men. "We will shortly begin a formation run in full combat gear. Sergeant McCrystal will lead the run and set the pace. I have instructed him to not run at the level he is accustomed to because quite frankly, it would kill most of you," Sergeant Girling added dryly.

"However, I did encourage him to make you work hard, and you will. If you find yourself feeling faint, you are to drop to the side of the formation *without causing a commotion* and sit on the field until help arrives. Any questions?" He looked out over the sixty young men.

Girling was not a sadistic soldier. But this was his favorite part of breaking in a new class. He and his senior NCO's had taken bets on who would drop out first, who would be the first to puke, and who would have to go to the infirmary. Winston didn't know it, but all the bets favored him for a perfect "trifecta." No one had ever had the distinction of accomplishing all three on the first run.

"Aye," McCrystal had growled. "My money's on Churchill to win the Triple Crown," he predicted.

The Triple Crown was a difficult feat. Usually, the first one to drop out was so out of shape that they didn't have it in them to push their body to the point where they puked.

The pukers, once they got some water in them and had time to recover, could live to march another day.

The last man to finish the course was usually a rabbit at the beginning. But by the time the finish line approached, the rabbit discovered to his horror that he had pushed his body far too hard and collapsed from heat exhaustion. That meant a trip to the infirmary, where they were observed for twenty-four hours and were commended for their effort.

"Formation, double time haaaarrrrrrch!" barked McCrystal as he broke into a sturdy trot.

Winston was feeling queasy just from his nerves. As the row in front of him broke into a trot, he took his first stride forward. His field helmet, which he adjusted too loose, fell forward and cut the skin on the bridge of his nose. Now unable to see, he veered sideways.

"Damn it, man," Cadet Francis Parsons hissed from behind.

Parsons pulled Churchill's helmet back and shoved him back on course. Winston staggered forward, trying to find his stride. After the first hundred yards, he was gasping for breath. His legs felt like they were on fire, which they were. He should have ensured he was hydrated with water. Instead, he consumed a great deal of alcohol the night before.

Breakfast now felt like a brick in his stomach and he felt sweeping pangs of nausea. Which of course, only heightened his anxiety. He was laboring for breath and they still had almost a mile to go. The Lee-Medford rifle weighed over eight pounds, and it flopped up and down on his back. He had also forgotten to tighten the strap.

"Churchill, pick it up," Cadet Parsons whispered. He knew Churchill was not going to make it. He was worried that he would trip over him if he fell.

Staff Sergeant Girling ran alongside the formation at a steady trot. He could keep this pace for miles. Only McCrystal could give him a real run for his money. He let his eyes glance over the formation, and then looked back at Churchill.

Winston Churchill, he thought. Many said his father would be the next prime minister. Born with a silver spoon in his mouth and it showed. He had everything. And he was nothing more than a ninety-pound weakling with a big mouth. An obnoxious blend of "noblesse oblige" and an air of entitlement.

Sweat poured down Churchill's face as he gamely passed the halfway marker. His rifle and helmet bounced up and down in contrast to the rest of the formation. The rest of the formation had made sure to arrive at the parade ground early *and* adequately geared up. Churchill, as his custom, was last to show up.

And, from the looks of it, thought Girling, with a wry smile, first to dropout.

And there he goes, he thought.

Churchill tripped and sprawled head first. Girling noted with admiration the carefully timed leap of Cadet Parsons over the prone cadet. The rest of the formation split around him and then closed ranks, leaving Churchill still lying motionless in a cloud of dust.

Staff Sergeant Girling chuckled, but stayed with the formation. First to drop. One of the enlisted medics stationed at the field ran over to the fallen cadet to render first aid.

Pussy, thought Sergeant Girling. I bet he pukes next. "Carry on men," he ordered as he stopped to examine the fallen cadet.

"Steady men," barked McCrystal. "Close the ranks," he ordered. The formation adjusted to Churchill's empty spot with McCrystal in the lead.

Now a hundred yards behind, Churchill finally moved. His hands were scraped and bloody, and the elbows of his blue serge tunic had torn fabric. He felt dizzy and hot.

"I say, Cadet Churchill," the enlisted aide said gently. "You okay, sir?"

"Water," Churchill gasped. He grabbed his canteen and gulped greedily.

"You may want to slow down a tad there, sir," Corporal Backus urged.

Churchill tilted his head back and let the rest of the cooling water rush down his parched throat. It felt so good, he thought.

He staggered to his feet, but started to collapse again. The corporal gave him support and Churchill fought to keep his balance. Suddenly, the water hit his stomach. The two were not meant to be combined at that moment.

"Buuuuuuuuuu," Churchill puked. Projectile vomit shot forward out of his mouth. The corporal jumped away, and Churchill fell to the ground. He lay there on his side, retching. Last night's scotch, the morning breakfast porridge, the entire contents of his canteen and stomach emptied onto the parade field.

"Yuck," said the corporal, who failed to notice the heaving shoulders of the drill instructor looking over his shoulder. Tears of mirth ran down Girling's face. Bloody hell, I think he's going for the Trifecta. That bastard McCrystal is going to win the bet. Girling could only watch. It was time for the assistant surgeon to take over now. He saw him come running, with a stretcher crew behind him.

Churchill continued to vomit, now just dry heaves. Foam and saliva flew out of his mouth.

"I'm dying," he retched. He was sure of it. He was on his knees.

The assistant surgeon trotted up.

"Dehydration and too much food and water don't mix on a formation run, cadet," he instructed the fallen cadet.

"Corporal, a wet towel for the cadet. Let him wipe his face." He motioned to the stretcher crew standing by, who were trying hard not to laugh. "To the infirmary for 24 hours rest and observation," he ordered. "Monitor for heat stroke."

"Aye aye, sir," the stretcher bearers answered smartly. They loaded the still retching cadet onto the stretcher and made their way towards the infirmary.

"Hah!" McCrystal chortled from the other side of the parade field. He had won the bet. Sergeant Girling gave him a dirty look. There were others who fell out of the formation that day, but only Churchill had won the Triple Crown.

That evening, a cleaned up and bathed Churchill rested comfortably in his bed in the infirmary. He no longer felt sick, just embarrassed. He knew he was not the finest physical specimen, frail in the shoulders and very skinny. He was reading his father's last letter again.

> "Because I am certain that if you cannot prevent yourself from leading the idle useless unprofitable life you have had during your schooldays & later months, you will become a mere social wastrel one of the hundreds of the public school failures, and you will degenerate into a shabby unhappy & futile existence. If that is so you will have to bear all the blame for such misfortunes yourself...."

Tears began to run down his face. He was failing miserably. And this all seemed very futile indeed.

"Ah hem," the voice cleared.

Churchill looked up, and saw his Company Commander, Major Oswald James Henry Ball standing at the foot of his bed. Major Ball's uniform was starched and creased, every ribbon in perfect order. His mustache was carefully clipped, his tie perfectly knotted.

"Mind if I sit for minute, Cadet Churchill?" he asked.

Churchill put the letter aside and sat up in his bed. "Of course sir, please, have a seat." Oh my god, Churchill thought to himself. Prepare to receive a full broadside.

The major sat on the wooden stool next to the bed.

"Probably not the way you had hoped to begin your military career," the major stated.

"No sir," Churchill replied.

"Well, let me give you some advice," the company commander continued. "You have hit bottom, and now you have nowhere to go but up. You will face some good-natured teasing, of which you richly deserve. You will also be the subject of a great deal of scrutiny, again, of which you richly deserve, to see whether or not you can deal with this day's misfortune."

The major paused, and then leaned forward.

"What happened to you today has happened every first formation run in the history of Sandhurst," the major said. "You are not the first, nor are you the last," he added. Of course, he thought to himself, you are the first to win the Triple Crown, but now was not the time to add to the poor cadet's misery.

Major Ball's mission was to take young men, especially young aristocrats like Churchill, and turn them into weapons of war. That was the essence, the very reason for the existence of a military academy. To build the minds and bodies of young men and turn them into officers who could lead other men into the chaos and horror of the battlefield. Men who could maintain their calm under fire and lead their men to victory.

It was a mission that would take time and patience. He had no desire to see young Churchill fail. Many a nobleman's son had come to Sandhurst, and the major bore them no malice. He considered it a challenge. The major was not yet a combat veteran, but he knew when the time came he would serve with distinction. It was his job now to ensure that this young cadet and the rest of the young men under his command were trained to do the same.

"Churchill," the major continued. "Let me give you some very straight talk. You are the son of a very famous man. And no doubt, you have grown up with the wealth and splendor that most young men can only read about. Our country has a fine tradition of respecting and maintaining the upper class and nobility. It is our tradition, indeed, our heritage and way of life. I'm not here to be your enemy. Rather, I am here to be your friend and your mentor. Do as I say and you will not only graduate but will do so with distinction and honor," he said.

Churchill wiped away the remainder of a tear. He listened intently.

"You must train your body and mind to be a soldier," the major continued. "No one can do it for you. You have to want it so bad that failure is unacceptable to you." The major patted his heart. "Never quit, never give up. When you are down, get back up on your feet. And when you are going through hell, keep moving," he added.

Churchill liked the sound of that line. "When you are going through hell, keep moving," he repeated. "Yes sir, I can do that," he said.

"Your mother, Lady Randolph, wrote me a letter," the officer continued. "She told me much about you, and what to expect of you. I know it is your desire to be assigned to the cavalry after graduation. She also told me that your father wants you in the infantry."

In fact, Lord Randolph had already written a letter to the Duke of Cambridge requesting reassignment. His father wanted him to join the 60th Rifles when he graduated.

Winston grimaced. "Yes, that would be father. But I want to join the cavalry," Winston said sincerely.

"Then work hard," the major urged. "Work harder than the rest. I know you like to read," he said. He handed Churchill a sheet of paper. It was a list of books and their authors.

"You will find these in the academy library. Read them, digest them. Learn how to do things by the book first. It is a tried and tested way to win. That does not mean you are not to use your intellect. Learn how to do it by the book first, and then one day, after a great deal of experience, you will be the one writing the book. A lot of good men have died learning these lessons," he added. "It's silly to make the same mistakes over and over again. Learn from their mistakes and you will live longer."

Churchill looked at the list; *Operations of War by Hamley, Prince Kraft's Letters on Infantry, Cavalry and Artillery, Maine's Infantry Fire Tactics, On War by Clausewitz. Winston stopped reading the titles. It was making him dizzy.* There were ten books in all.

"I know that's a lot of reading," the major continued, "but it will help prepare your mind for your curriculum next term. Two are two other things I recommend. First, I want you to spend an extra hour a day in the gymnasium, getting into shape. And second, during the winter holiday, you must take riding lessons. I know an excellent horseman and instructor, Captain Charles Henry Burt. He is stationed at the Hyde Park Barracks. He is the riding master of the 2nd Life Guards. He will prepare you for the rigors of next term. If you want to be a cavalry officer, you must know how to ride," the major said firmly.

"Yes sir," Winston said, trying to absorb all the advice.

"Keep your marks up."

"Yes sir."

"And Churchill," the major added. "Try to learn to be on time," he added firmly.

Churchill's cheeks flushed red. It was true. He was always late. For everything.

"Yes sir, thank you, sir."

"You are welcome, Cadet Churchill. I will be watching you closely."

Winston recuperated, and after twenty-four hours found himself back in the smoking lounge down the hallway from his room. He was reading *Operations of War* and found it fascinating. The 500-page book sat on his lap. It weighed nearly five pounds.

"Good stuff?" asked Cadet Parsons, as he sat in an easy chair next to Churchill.

"I've been jumping around a bit, getting the lay of the terrain, so to speak," Churchill replied. "However, I must admit the Union's retreat from Chickahominy, chased all the way by Stonewall Jackson, is a fascinating tactical operation," he added.

"And a desperate one," Parsons agreed.

"Churchill," Parsons began, "About the other day."

Churchill waved him off.

"My apologies Francis. I not only almost knocked you out of formation, but I also almost puked all over your tunic," he admitted smiling. "Not exactly my finest hour," Winston said. "But rest assured, I will do better. I do apologize."

Cadet Parsons was impressed. Self-deprecating humor from the spoiled rotten son of Randolph Churchill.

"No apology necessary," Parsons said.

"Good," Churchill agreed. "I believe I have set the school record for the most dry heaves on the parade ground."

Other cadets had gathered around to listen in to the conversation.

"I dare say it is one record that will never be broken," Winston added proudly. "Cheers!" he said gamely, a smile on his face as he looked around the room.

"Records were made to be broken," Parsons teased good-naturedly. There were murmurs of approval in the room. It was nice to see that Churchill had some humility after all.

CHAPTER THIRTY-EIGHT

SUDAN, 1893

No one noticed Kauūk ʿAlī was missing the first few weeks. After his gruesome demise, Syrah made her way back to the zeriba to gather her belongings. The sense of rage was replaced by uncertainty. She had no idea where to go. She had no idea what to do. She was in complete shock. All she knew was that she wanted to run as far away as she could.

Instead, paralyzed by fear, she lay in her hut, hiding under a blanket. It took her several days to process what she had just been party to; but finally she admitted to herself that she liked herself better now. She had learned to taste real power. And she liked the way it tasted.

Three days later, as she made her way back to her zeriba after drawing water at the river, she heard voices ahead. She exited the thick scrub along the waterway.

In front of her were thirty men, all wearing multi-colored tunics with bright colored patches. They were staring at her. The leader trotted his horse over to her.

He saw a very tall, muscular young woman of astounding beauty. Her hair fell in long black braids down her muscular back. Her skin was rich and dark brown. Her tob was torn, and he could see a glimpse of cleavage from her large, full breast. Her brilliant blue sapphire eyes were on fire with an energy that made him shiver. And she carried the sword of the recently dispatched Muhammad Khair.

Khalifa Abdullah, the successor to the Mahdi, looked down at the beautiful young woman and tried to guess her race. She was too light to be Dinka or from some of the other southern tribes. She was too dark to be Arab. She almost appeared to him to be a blend. Of what, he was not sure. There were no white men in the Sudan still alive, except for his European translator, Slatin. However, it was not uncommon for Arabs to father children with the Sudanese. The leader took note in his mind. But most Arabs did not have blue eyes.

What he was certain of was that she would be a needless distraction to his men. He looked at the sword in her hand.

"That sword belonged to my trusted officer, Muhammad Khair," the Khalifa commented.

"He lies inside the bellies of the crocodiles," Syrah said proudly in Arabic. "I put him there," she added, her voice full of disdain.

Khalifa Abdullah was impressed by her lack of fear, but he had no time for games.

"Ibrahim, take back Muhammad Khair's sword from this woman and put her to death," he said matter-of-factly.

Ibrahim grinned. The Khalifa did him great honor, singling him out to retrieve the sword of his fallen comrade. He took out his long sword and advanced towards the beautiful tall woman in the tattered robe covered with specks of blood. What a waste.

He let out a mighty roar and brought his sword up over his head, preparing to bring it down on her head and clove her in half. He knew if he caught her just right he would sever her torso completely. His blade would sever her vagina as the sharp metal cut through her body and exited between her spread legs.

Syrah's legs were spread, with her weight evenly distributed. She gripped the hilt of her sword with both hands, watching the grinning Arab as he approached her. As he brought his arms up over his head and let out a mighty roar, Syrah saw him lunge forward with his right leg exposed.

The speed of her strike left the Khalifa greatly surprised. Ibrahim was even more surprised. She was quicker than Ibrahim and she cut his right leg off completely. Ibrahim's eyes were wide with horror as he collapsed face first into the ground. Syrah quickly sidestepped his sword, which continued downward into the hard clay soil. She raised her own sword and promptly cut off his head as he let out a scream, which turned into a gurgle and a fountain of blood.

Syrah stepped back, her sword at the ready. She was in no mood to live a slave, to be raped, or to be a dung beetle.

"Take that you piece of shit!" she screamed in English. She waited for the next man to come.

The Khalifa raised his hand. "Stop," he commanded. His men stood still. This was truly an oddity, the Khalifa thought. The woman speaks English, the language of his sworn enemy. He himself did not speak English. But he recognized the expletive. He had heard his translator, Slatin, use it when he was upset.

"Can you read English as well as you speak it?" he asked in Arabic.

"Yes," she said defiantly in Arabic.

"Very well then," the Khalifa said. "Put down your sword. We will not harm you. I need a translator." She could give him verification of what Slatin translated. He didn't trust the European. He had been the Khalifa's captive for years. But he could not bring himself to trust a white man. He would play the two against each other.

Syrah stood defiantly. "I am no one's slave, and I would rather die now than let you or your men take me like a whore," she said.

"I give you my word," the Khalifa said. "And I believe you would rather die first. However, today I need a translator and interpreter more than I need a dead, raped slave. I am the Khalifa, the Mahdi's successor. My word is law," he said. He turned to his men.

"This woman now works for me. She is not to be touched. If any man tries, I give orders that he is to be castrated and to feed on his own flesh before he dies," the Khalifa ordered.

"Is that sufficient?" he said politely.

Syrah thought quickly. As a child, her father had made sure she was receiving a traditional British education. She could read and write English as well as speak it. She had every intention of avenging the death of her parents, but she doubted she could kill all thirty of the men around her to get to the Khalifa himself. He was the successor to the man who had killed her father.

She smiled up at him. Her teeth were as white as ivory, her lips full. "I accept," she said.

"Then put down your sword," the Khalifa asked politely.

She looked down at the blood on her hands.

"Of course," she said politely, joining in the game of cat and mouse. She dropped the sword. But she was ready to pick it up if this turned out to be a trick.

"Mohammed, give her the reins to Ibrahim's horse. She is to have his tent and gear as well. And Mohammed, you will be her body guard. She is valuable to me. Do not let anything or anyone touch her. If she tries to kill you, run," he ordered, laughing at the end.

Mohammed bowed to the Khalifa, and eyed the corpse of Ibrahim on the ground. He had no desire to fight with this woman. She was possessed. Women were supposed to be dumb animals, like cows, goats and lamb. They did not kill warriors with a sword.

"Yes, master," he said. Still, he kept far out of her reach as he handed her the reins, extending them out with one hand.

CHAPTER THIRTY-NINE

SANDHURST, 1893

Winston was feeling a little better about things. He was now two months into the junior term, and before long, the winter holiday would be coming. At some point he would make plans on where to spend it, but at the moment he was crossing the footbridge over the stream near the parade ground. He leaned over to look at what appeared to flecks of gold in the stream. To his horror, the watch his father had given him slipped out of his pocket and fell into the water below.

"Oh my god!" Winston cried out. It disappeared into the rushing water. "Oh my God!" he cried out again, this time with real panic in his voice. It was his only real gift from his beloved father.

He ran down to the end of the footbridge and dashed down to the stream. He quickly stripped off his tunic and pants and jumped into the stream, splashing out to where the watch had fallen, searching wildly.

"I say," Staff Sergeant Girling said to Major Ball as they rode their horses around the perimeter of the parade field. "Isn't that Churchill?"

They saw Winston, clad only in his undergarments, thrashing wilding about in the stream underneath the footbridge.

"That's an odd place to bath," Major Ball stated dryly.

"Doing his laundry perhaps?" quipped Sergeant Girling.

"Hmm, I'm not sure," replied the major. "Perhaps we should ask."

They briskly rode their horses onto the footbridge, now looking down on Winston, who was still madly searching for his father's watch.

He was completely unaware that his commanding officer and chief noncommissioned officer were directly above him.

"Ahem" Major Ball cleared his throat politely.

Winston was oblivious. He was in an utter state of panic.

"I say old chap!" the major shouted. "Have you lost your mind?"

Winston heard voices above him talking, but he was too busy to listen.

"Cadet Churchill!" Sergeant Girling roared. "Come to attention at once! Your commanding officer wishes to speak with you!"

Winston looked up and saw Sergeant Girling and Major Ball on horseback above him. He immediately snapped to attention, water dripping off his underwear. It was all Major Ball could do to keep from laughing but instead, he looked calmly down at the young cadet.

"I say again, have you lost your mind?" Major Ball asked.

"No sir," Winston said dejectedly. "I've lost my father's watch. It was a gift, a keepsake."

Major Ball nodded. "I see," he said. Now he understood the panic. He noticed that Churchill's lips were turning blue and he was beginning to shiver.

"I am ordering you to return to your quarters, take a warm bath, and then meet me in my office," the major ordered.

"But…….." Winston blurted.

"Yes sir," Sergeant Girling advised, cutting him off for his own good.

"Yes sir," Winston agreed. He was standing in a stream, soaked, in only his undergarments. This does not look good, he thought to himself. He looked wistfully into the stream. Father's watch. How will I ever explain it to him? He climbed out of the stream, got dressed, and did as he was told.

An hour later he stood outside his company commander's door at attention and rapped on the frame.

"Sir, Cadet Churchill requests permission to enter," he said briskly. He had bathed, groomed, and changed into a fresh uniform.

"You may enter," the major said.

Sir," Winston snapped a salute. "Cadet Churchill reporting as ordered," he said smartly.

Major Ball returned the salute. "Take a seat, Cadet, at ease."

Winston took a chair facing the major's desk.

"Churchill," the major began. "I'm going to speak frankly. You are a very smart young man, and you have a great deal of respect for authority. That's all good. It's commendable. But you are always late for class, late for formation, and late for drill. You have folded like a deck of cards on the parade field in front of your fellow cadets, retched your guts out on a routine training exercise, and now I find you nearly naked, thrashing about in an icy creek as winter approaches."

The major paused as he collected himself. "I don't think you are going to make it," he said.

Churchill sat there in stunned silence.

"Son, what in god's name were you doing in that creek?" Major Ball asked.

"Sir, that watch means everything to me," Churchill said honestly. Tears ran down his face.

"I have loved my father with all of my heart, and tried so hard to earn his love. There is always this great distance between us that I cannot bridge," he sobbed.

"That watch was given to me on the only day in my life when I felt his love." Winston shook his head. "I know that sounds pathetic, but it means everything to me, and I don't know how I will ever explain to him that I lost it. He already thinks I'm a 'miscreant,' a failure," Winston added.

"I see," said Major Ball. "But son, I'm afraid the watch is lost," he added.

"No sir, I have a plan," Winston said.

Major Ball looked at him in amusement.

"A plan?"

"Yes sir. In our military fortifications class we learned how to divert streams for tactical necessity. We could use the classroom instruction and put it into a practical application. It would be a good exercise. A practical application of lessons learned, sort of a hands-on approach. We could damn up the stream, divert the flow, and I'm certain we could recover the watch," he pleaded.

"That would take at least 30 cadets, and several days," the major replied.

"It would be a good field exercise of our classroom teachings," Winston argued.

"Come see me this time tomorrow," the major ordered. "That will be all, cadet."

"But......."

"That will be all, cadet. Same time tomorrow. Dismissed."

"Yes sir," Churchill gave in. He came to attention smartly, saluted, and left his commander's office.

Major Ball leaned back in his padded leather chair, and let out a sigh. The nephew of the Duke of Marlborough, the son of one of Britain's leading statesmen, whose mother was on very close terms with the heir to the throne, was presenting quite a challenge. Major Ball believed in his heart he could make an officer out of him, if only Churchill would just quit getting in his own way.

Perhaps I should let him try to recover the watch, he mused to himself. Would it help him to develop his leadership skills and serve a practical application of problem-solving? Major Ball knew he couldn't authorize a change in fortifications curriculum without the commandant's approval.

"I must be daft," he said out loud, as he made his way down the hallway to the commandant's office.

The commandant, however, was intrigued. He was accustomed to giving particular attention to the sons of prominent men. It might not be fair, but it was in his best interest to make powerful friends as opposed to powerful enemies. Besides, he was curious to see how the young cadet handled himself. He approved the "exercise."

Major Ball briefed the company, and told them that they had three days to accomplish the mission. Cadet Churchill was placed in command of the three-day exercise. Whatever equipment they decided they needed would be provided if possible.

After that, he and Sergeant Girling sat back and watched.

They were impressed. Winston organized the company into four groups, dividing up their tasks and appointing leaders of each squad. Plans were drawn up in the classroom, and meetings were held to discuss how to best approach the work. They decided to divert the water first.

The first squad began building an earthen damn to block the stream. A second squad dug a bypass to reroute the water around the search area. The third squad was assigned the task of borrowing one of the academy's fire pumps and enlisted the aid of a fireman to show them how to run it. They were to transport the massive steam-driven pump to the stream bed and stand ready to pump out any remaining water once the diversion was complete. The fourth squad would dredge through the remaining water to find the watch.

Throughout the entire exercise, Churchill gave his all. And something interesting began to take place. The pale, frail, incompetent young man, given a challenge that he cared about deeply, took charge, encouraging his men, digging the trench with them, up to his knees in mud. When the time came to change the flow of the water, he gave the order, and the dam was put in place, the water shifted down its new course, and the machine began pumping out the pool of water remaining under the bridge.

And on schedule, on the third day, Churchill found the watch wedged under a river rock and held it up in triumph. A cheer came from the men, and they were instructed to leave the diverted stream in place. The next class would be responsible for returning it to its original state. The commandant found the whole exercise useful in team-building and problem-solving. From then on, it was written into the curriculum.

A grateful Winston sent the watch to London to be fixed by a reputable watchmaker. As the end of the term approached, he found himself thinking of all that his commander had said to him.

The next term would involve a great deal of training on horseback, and Winston so wished to join the cavalry. He would take up the major's advice and take riding lessons over the holiday. He had no desire to make a fool of himself again.

CHAPTER FORTY

WEST POINT, 1893

Kip sat at his desk looking at the grizzled face of Professor Emeritus Wilfred P. Jones as he lectured the class. All the cadets knew that Professor Jones had fought for the South during the Civil War, and it amused them to no end when he would launch into a diatribe about how the South could have won the war.

"You all were provided with a copy of Clausewitz's 'On War,' and by now I expect that you have read it. I do not expect, however," the professor paused dramatically, "that you are remotely capable, at this point at least, of understanding it."

There was an uneasy shift in the lecture hall. Wilfred was getting ready to sucker someone into "intellectual discourse," as he liked to call it. The cadets sarcastically referred to it as "intellectual intercourse." Some unsuspecting cadet was about to get it. Some of the cadets slouched down in their seats. Clausewitz's book had become *the* standard read at all military colleges and academies worldwide. It was also very, very dry, unless you were one of those individuals who truly enjoyed deep thought and theory.

Realizing that Cadet "Bull" Keller did not enjoy deep thought or theory, the professor decided to pick on him.

"What is war?" the professor asked rhetorically as he stood on the wooden lecture stage. He smiled at the silence that greeted his question. It was designed to be open-ended.

He looked at the cadets in the audience. His gaze fell on Bull.

"Cadet Keller?"

Bull shifted uneasily in his seat. He hated military history and theory.

"War is hell," Bull answered with a straight face. The lecture hall erupted in laughter. Professor Wilfred P. Jones was not amused and scowled down at Bull.

"Let me refine my question, Cadet. How would Clausewitz, the famous German expert on warfare, answer that question?" He couldn't keep the sarcasm out of his voice.

"It is a means by which the government is able to survive an attack by the enemy by using force," Bull answered. He wiped the smirk off his face. Wilfred P. Jones was not amused.

"But that presumes an attack in the first place, doesn't it?" the Professor baited. "What justifies the application of force in the first place? In other words, what moral right is there to strike your enemy before he strikes you?"

Bingo, Kip thought. Who gets to decide when war breaks out? He understood the theory, and it was troubling. Time to rescue Bull, he thought. After all, he saved my bacon in that last game.

Kip raised his hand. Professor Jones looked at the chiseled jaw and the high, intelligent forehead of the young cadet with his hand raised. Cadet McDuran had engaged him in debate on more than one occasion and usually distinguished himself on the field of intellectual combat. The professor felt a twinge of excitement. He loved a good debate.

"Cadet McDuran?" he inquired.

"War is an instrument of national power," Kip replied. "Clausewitz would define it as an expression of national policy. I find it more a blunt instrument than an expression of will."

"Let's put your own opinion aside, cadet, and focus on the former, rather than the latter, part of your answer," the professor said sternly. "I disagree. It is an instrument of national policy, not power. Would Clausewitz not refer to it as policy rather than power?"

"Of course," Kip agreed. "But your question to Cadet Keller was what justifies the initiation of an attack in the first place. The lust for power is antecedent to the actual initiation of hostilities," Kip stated. "Not policy."

"Lust for power?" asked the professor. Here we go, he thought happily. He loved to teach. He loved to see young men ask questions that they could not answer.

"A lust for power," Kip repeated. "Power is the current by which humanity flows. The lust for power is always present in every situation; sibling rivalry, domestic dispute, family argument. No one wants to be the loser. And certainly, no one who has found any power will be willing to give it up."

Professor Jones raised a brow.

"Why should they give up the fruits of their hard labor?" he asked innocently. "Doesn't Clausewitz teach that the political objective *is* the goal. War is simply a means to reach that goal."

"If the government is competent in how it determines its goals, maybe. There is a distinction to be made when the government is not a competent manager of the use of force." Kip answered.

"You are not suggesting the government of the United States is incompetent, are you?" baited the professor.

"At times," Kip said. A gasp rose up from the other cadets. Kip was challenging authority. They had not yet come to grips with the fact that Kip respected no one. Not even the government. The government was merely a group of men. And Kip knew the evil that men do.

"Can you cite me an example?" the professor challenged.

"Chivington's Raid," Kip replied without hesitation.

It was as if a balloon let the air out. There was an audible sigh from Kip's classmates. Another epic argument between Kip and the professor. And Kip was going to use the massacre at Sand Creek as his foil to drive the point home. Billy looked longingly towards the exit. They all did.

"Chivington acted within his individual capacity, without express authority," Professor Jones argued. "It was initiated by an individual, not a government."

"It was the initiation of hostilities against a peaceful people by a government officer acting within the scope of his authority," Kip countered. "He launched a preemptive strike on his enemy."

"Which was investigated by the government, was it not?" queried the professor.

"After the fact, with no consequence. Chivington was never held responsible for his actions. He testified that he was using current intelligence from the battlefield, and in his tactical point of view, it was necessary. But the real reason he was never held accountable was that would have meant tarnishing the legacy of President Lincoln." Kip's voice never wavered. He was simply being honest.

More than one cadet shifted uneasily in his seat. Kip was calling out his own government at a military academy. The "Massacre at Sand Creek," was not one of America's finest hours. Billy leaned over to bend P.T.'s ear.

"I can't believe we're going here," Billy whispered into P.T.'s ear.

"I think maybe Kip has lost his mind," P.T. agreed with a grimace.

"Refresh us all on the facts, Cadet McDuran," Professor Jones suggested. He ignored Cadet Keller who was nodding his head in agreement in the back row of the lecture hall. Bull had forgotten the facts and now Bull was interested, too.

"In 1851, America had an Indian problem. They were in the way. So the government 'repositioned' them. The United States signed a peace treaty with the Cheyenne and moved them to Colorado. At the time it seemed a convenient solution to the Indian problem." Kip maintained his steady, even tone. No emotion.

"Was it?" the professor asked.

"No. As it turned out, seven years after the Cheyenne moved into their new land, gold was discovered. The Indians had no use for gold. But the white man did, and a mass of people began rushing in. The Indians were in the way again. So, logically, the government decided the Indians had to move once more," Kip said.

He was having a problem keeping the sarcasm out of his voice. The massacre at Sand Creek evoked a powerful memory for Kip. He could see the charred bodies and the burned-out village in Monterey. He remembered Chow Lin's wife disappearing into a burst of flames.

"They offered the Cheyenne a new deal. They told their chief, Black Kettle, to make camp at Sand Creek. Black Kettle decided to appease the white man. They were outgunned, and the Indians knew it. They didn't want to fight anymore," Kip continued.

"So, Black Kettle took his people to Sand Creek. He was assured by the U.S. government at Fort Lyon that they would be safe. They were even instructed to fly the American flag over their village," Kip said, "along with a white flag, which *they did*. The U.S. government assured Black Kettle that no U.S. soldiers would attack."

"I'll take it from here, Cadet," the professor cut in. "We're running short on time. And so our brave Colonel Chivington, military commander of the Colorado home guard and representative of the American government, by his own deeds and actions in negotiating with Black Kettle, led 800 soldiers, with artillery, to Black Kettle's village," he recited.

"That night, they had a pre-victory party where they consumed an enormous amount of alcohol. At the first light of dawn, they launched their attack. Many, nay, perhaps most of the men, were drunk when they began the massacre," Professor Jones lectured.

"And what was the outcome, Cadet Keller?" he asked.

Bull froze in his seat. He had fallen asleep somewhere between the Rocky Mountains and the Gold Rush. He heard his name called and realized the entire lecture hall was now watching him breathlessly. He was caught like a rat in a trap.

P.T., sitting directly behind his star lineman, could not help himself. "They signed the peace treaty," he whispered to Bull.

"They signed a peace treaty," Bull said confidently. He loved P.T.

The entire lecture hall broke into laughter. P.T. slapped his leg so hard it hurt. Tears of mirth began to flow down his face. Professor Jones kept a poker face, but inside he too was roaring with laughter. But the older and wiser man was not going to let the lesson pass. Like a good comedian, he waited for the laughter to die.

"Cadet Keller, you couldn't be more wrong if you tried," the Professor stated calmly. Again, the lecture hall burst into laughter. All the cadets were howling and slapping each other on their backs at Bull's expense.

"And what was the outcome, Cadet McDuran," Professor Jones asked, turning his gaze to the young Scotsman. Show me what you've got, son, the professor thought. Are you a real leader, as the commandant keeps telling me?

Kip thought about Chow Lin. He thought about his father. He thought about that night on the trail when he saw the men on horseback riding away from the burning village. He could see their faces in his mind. He would never forget those faces.

"It was rightly named the massacre at Sand Creek," Kip said softly. The hallowed halls grew silent as they strained to hear his answer.

"Louder please," instructed the professor.

"The men had left the village to hunt," Kip continued. "Major Chivington knew that. There were nothing but old men, women and children in the village." His voice grew louder as he struggled with the emotions of his own nightmares.

"They launched an artillery attack first, using four pounders set up on the south bank of the river. Then they opened fire with muskets and moved in for the kill. The few braves that were still there tried to fight back, but they were cut down immediately. Chivington had told his men to take no prisoners. So they turned on the women and children and old men. The body of Black Kettle was found in the creek, mutilated. The soldiers had scalped him, cut off his nose, ears, and his balls. They executed his children at point blank in the head."

Kip paused to take a breath.

"They took the body parts that they severed from the women and children and wore them as trophies on their hats and their gear. They rode proudly back to town to display the more than one hundred scalps of the women and children, along with the various male and female genitalia they cut from their victims. Then they held a post-victory party at the Apollo Theater where they proudly displayed their trophies and got drunk to celebrate their victory. They called it an 'American victory'," Kip concluded.

Dead silence in the lecture hall.

Couldn't have said it better myself, thought the old professor. And now the test. Was this kid the real deal, a military genius?

"And so, how do we reconcile the massacre at Sand Creek, with the teachings of Clausewitz?" the professor asked politely.

"The military is subordinate to the political authority. Politicians make war, not the other way around. They had an Indian problem, and Chivington took care of it for them on behalf of his government," Kip answered.

"But certainly, Clausewitz would not condone a slaughter?" the Professor asked.

"Clausewitz wrote that real war is the composite of three elements: violence and passion; uncertainty, chance and probability; and political purpose and effect. The massacre was a preemptive strike against an enemy Chivington knew didn't exist. But the violence and the passion had been building for years. Both sides had already engaged in atrocities. There is uncertainty in every war, but Chivington had political aspirations. He hoped to win a congressional seat, and his hopes rested upon his actions at that moment in time. Chivington knew that by leading his raid on the Cherokee, he would build his reputation. His motives were purely political. As the military commander, he held power, and he used that power to try to further his fortunes at the expense of the hapless Cheyenne. He wanted to be famous."

"And so in closing, how would *you* analyze Chivington's raid?" Professor Wilfred P. Jones pressed the young cadet.

"War is an instrument of national power that is frequently abused to obtain and keep power, much like religion," Kip concluded. "Be it priest or politician, they are both searching for control of your soul."

"I couldn't have said it any better," the professor admitted. "However, you might be wise to keep your thoughts on religion to yourself." He pulled out his watch.

"Class dismissed."

As the cadets filed out of the lecture hall, Professor Jones motioned for Kip to wait behind. He had long since concluded Cadet McDuran was a brilliant young officer. But he was also a little bit reckless. As the room emptied, he looked quizzically at the young cadet.

"War and religion?" he asked. "Are you at war with religion? There is nothing in Clausewitz that includes the interaction of religion and war."

"We both know that religion has been the catalyst for countless wars and atrocities, as well as acts of extreme depravity," Kip replied.

"You would be well advised not to publicly attack religion," the professor warned him.

"You will be branded a heretic. I do not disagree with your premise that man has often bastardized religion to obtain power. But today's lesson was on Clausewitz, and the definition of war, not religion. You will have to keep your views on religion to yourself, or you will lose everything. Do you understand? There are very important people interested in your career. But if they hear blasphemy from your mouth, you will lose all credibility and become an outcast," the professor warned.

"What about the separation of church and state?" Kip asked.

"Religion, like war, is also a balance of violence, chance, and politics. Those were your own words. Keep your views on religion to yourself. Please," the professor asked.

"Yes sir," Kip answered.

"None-the-less," the professor concluded, "you have learned well. You knew where I was going, didn't you?"

"Yes sir," Kip answered honestly. "Even before you did."

Chapter Forty-One

England, 1893

Lady Churchill wrapped her naked body around the heaving muscular torso of Colonel John Brabazon and met the thrust of his loins with her own. She matched his rhythm as he came closer and closer to climax.

She began sucking his nipples and was pleased to hear him groan in ecstasy. She felt his hot semen shooting deep inside her vagina and she arched her back as she felt the flooding of her own fluids inside her body.

"Oh my God," the colonel gasped. "You are so wet and so warm."

Lady Churchill kissed him deeply on the mouth and then whispered in his ear.

"You make it so," she complimented him. She held him close, feeling his beating heart against her breast.

"You are an incredible lover," he said. He ran his hands through his hair. "I am putty in your paws," he purred.

She purred too. Lady Randolph loved making love. It was something that she and her husband never did. She was insatiable, and she craved the hard bodies of the military officers the most. They were her best lovers.

They also happened to be the movers and shakers of the upper class of England. She continued her secret rendezvous with the future King of England. His majesty was so enamored by her beauty and charm that he had a private entrance to his castle built just for her.

Jenny Churchill's affair with Colonel Brabazon had ancillary benefits as well. He was the commanding officer of the 4th Hussars cavalry regiment, the Queen's Own. Their history and bravery in combat was legend. It just so happened that her son Winston had made it very clear to her that he wanted to join the cavalry. What Winston wants, Winston gets.

"Father wants me to join the 60th Infantry. I have no desire to carry a rifle and be cannon fodder," Winston had complained to her.

"John," she said, pausing to light a cigarette. "I need to talk to you about something." She knew he wouldn't say no.

Chapter Forty-Two

SANDHURST, 1894

Winston sat on his horse, eyeing the other cadets of Company E as they attempted to keep their horses at attention. He was grateful for Major Ball's advice. Over the holiday, he had taken at least a dozen lessons from the famed riding master Captain Burt while he was in London. In fact, the holiday had been one of the best times in his life. His father seemed to be different in a number of ways now. He appeared distracted by politics rather than engaged. But even more curious, he paid attention to his son.

Winston had been stunned and amazed when his father invited him to the race track. He introduced Winston to many of his influential friends. They went to the homes of some of the most famous and wealthiest men in England.

As he sat on his horse, watching the riding master, Major Hodgins, he told himself to focus on the matter at hand. He could reflect on his father's attention later. Indeed, it sat inside his stomach like a warm, comforting fire. As he watched the cadets struggling to control their horses, he thought about his lessons over the summer.

"The echelon is ever changing," Captain Burt had explained to him during one of their many lessons.

"The column of horses must be kept in formation, and able to turn on a single command so as to always be able to present the front to the enemy. Whether it is a company, a regiment or a brigade, the entire force must be able to shift directions upon command. That requires the strictest discipline of both the rider and his horse. They must learn to stay in control despite the gunshots and artillery explosions of the battlefield. You will have a practical demonstration of that in your riding classes at Sandhurst next term," he warned.

Winston was snapped out of his lessons and back to the present as Major Hodgins barked out an order to the cadets.

"Form the echelon, standard ranks," he ordered. The cadets tried to move their steeds into formation on the large drill grounds. There was a great deal of jostling and disorder.

"It takes a great deal of time and training for a group of men and horses to form as one," Captain Burk had warned him. "Expect chaos before order."

The red-faced riding master surveyed his company of cadets with disgust. Horses kicked up their hooves; cadets gripped the reins with white knuckles. One young cadet had dismounted his horse and was trying to put him in formation, leading him by the reigns. Confusion spread.

"What a clusterfuck," fumed Major Hodgins. He pulled out his horsewhip in one hand and pistol in the other. Steering his horse with his legs, he quickly came up to the dismounted cadet. He snapped his whip into the buttocks of the wayward horse and then fired a round from his pistol into the dirt beneath it.

Horses and cadets went flying in all directions away from the loud explosion. It turned from utter confusion into a bolt of horses stampeding away from the center of the riding ring with their riders holding on for their lives. Several cadets were thrown off their horses and landed awkwardly on the dirt. The major sat upon his horse in the center of the ring, now surrounded by sixty horses that had nowhere else to go. The cadets fought to calm their steeds, and eventually, they formed a giant circle around the grinning riding master.

"Well now," he said. "Anyone think it's possible that someone might actually shoot at you while you are on your horse? Moreover, that was not the correct way to form an echelon. Each one of you knows your position in the echelon. You have been instructed in the proper way to form the echelon. It must be an orderly process," he admonished them.

It had not passed his notice that young Churchill actually had no difficulties with his horse, before and after the gunshot.

Winston felt a swell of pride in his chest. He had not been caught off guard by the chaos and had firmly held his horse in check with his knees. The horse, sensing the rider's calm, had not joined in the confusion.

"Form the echelon," ordered the riding master. "Mr. Churchill, take the lead," he barked.

"Yes sir," Churchill replied. By god, he was getting the hang of this after all.

"You there, Parsons, on my left, you there Smythe, on my right, fall in by the numbers," Winston yelled at the top of his voice.

Major Hodgins noted that the formation that the cadets formed would have brought laughter to the face of any experienced cavalry officer, but at least it was an improvement. He also noted that Cadet Churchill could hold his own on horseback.

CHAPTER FORTY-THREE

WEST POINT - MONTEREY, 1894

Commencement at West Point had been an experience Kip would never forget. The grandeur, the tradition, and the vast crowd gathered to pay tribute to the nation's finest warriors was an impressive event.

Now it was time to go home and see his benefactor before he reported for duty. As he crossed the country by train, he was in awe as usual by the sheer grandeur of his young nation. Endless mountain ranges and lush forest rolled by, only to give way to the prairies and plains. Then the enormous Rocky Mountains stood imposingly, as if daring them to pass. Finally they crossed the desert and then began the long climb through the high Pacific Coast range and the Donner Pass.

Kip had spent countless hours studying engineering at West Point. He knew all too well the human toll it had exacted to connect to the two coasts together. He thought of his friend, Chow Lin, and he shuddered as he remembered the night the village burned. He could still see the faces of the men as they rode away.

One of those men had been Larkin.

It was the same dark figure he had seen leaving his mother's cottage the day he learned of his father's death. And once he was living with David Jacks, Larkin was a person he had encountered on more than one occasion in Monterey. As he rode the train from Salinas to Monterey, Kip wondered if he would see him.

Kip had come to spend the holiday with his mentor, David Jacks, who was getting older and in ill health. In fact, in his letters, Jacks had sounded as if his days were numbered. Kip wasn't sure what to expect, but he wanted to see the man who had changed his life forever once more. The love he felt for the old Scotsman was much like the love he had felt for his father.

The train pulled into the Monterey station. Kip was amazed at how much the town had grown. The melting pots of blubber had been replaced by a large port, with several piers leading out into the harbor. There were still a few whaling ships, but there were more merchant vessels and even a few naval ships.

With the arrival of the railroad and the rich from San Francisco, and the shipping of produce from the Valley, Monterey was a boom town. Pacific Grove had blossomed into a community of its own, and construction was underway everywhere.

Kip stepped onto the station, his one suitcase in hand, and saw the smiling face of David Jacks. Kip waved happily and walked over and embraced the old man. He couldn't help but notice that Jacks seemed frail and used a cane.

"Hey laddie," Jacks said happily. He reached out and grabbed Kip's hand.

"You are looking like a fine young Scotsman," Jacks said. And he meant it. The young man had grown. He was a touch over six feet and must weigh around two hundred pounds. And muscular at that. Not an ounce of fat on him.

"Jesus lad, what the hell have they been feeding you at that place?" Jacks teased. "Buffalo meat?"

"Sometimes," Kip laughed. "They make sure we don't go hungry," he added.

"My carriage is outside, let's go home," Jacks said happily.

They walked out of the station into the sunlight. It was a beautiful day. Kip smelled the sea. He had missed it. As they rode up Alvarado Street to Jack's mansion, Kip was pleased to see gas lights on the street corners. Modern technology had come to his hometown.

They sat across each other at the dinner table. Maria, the cook, worked her usual magic, and Kip was delighted to find all his favorite dishes set in front of him. The candles flickered warmly on the table.

"Thank you so much, David, for everything you have done for me," Kip said gratefully. "I don't know that I would have survived in this world without you."

The old man raised his hand.

"Nonsense boy, you were doing just fine without me," he laughed. "It was the neighbors I was tryin to protect. There wasn't a garden or a wash line in Monterey safe from your thieving hands," he added.

Kip smiled ruefully. "I was getting pretty good at it," he agreed. "I didn't know how else to survive." He started laughing himself now. "I was especially good at stealing from the back of Larkin's house," he chuckled. "I could climb over that stone wall and filch his vegetables like a wolf. He never knew I was there."

"Aye, good thing too, because he would've shot ya," Jacks added. Kip's smile turned into a frown.

"Aye, he would have," Kip agreed. "How is the mean old bastard?" he asked. He had never repeated what Chow Lin had told him to anyone. Not even David Jacks.

"Same. Mean as a snake, just older. No wiser, that's for sure," Jacks added. "Still lives in the same place you used to sneak into every night."

"I only snuck *into the house* twice," Kip feigned indignation. "And then only into the kitchen. I was hungry," he smiled at the memory. "Well, that was not completely true," Kip added with a mischievous grin. "Larkin had a teenage daughter who liked to sleep with the window open."

Jacks laughed. He sipped his glass of red wine.

"So how did they treat you at West Point?" Jacks asked. "How was commencement? I'm sorry I could not travel."

"Very well, sir," Kip said sincerely. "I loved it there. And I love the army," he added. "Don't worry about not being there."

"You'll do well," Jacks predicted. "What is your first assignment?"

Kip paused while he finished the last of his plate.

"Some pretty influential generals have talked about a career in the military intelligence branch," Kip said. "They don't say much, but I may be going to Washington for a bit," he added.

"Washington," said Jacks. "My, you are doing well," he added, pleased.

"We'll see," Kip said. He looked across the table at the white-haired gentleman with his wire-rimmed spectacles and knitted shawl around his shoulders. David Jacks was a good man. Kip hadn't always liked the way he talked, especially about the Chinese, but he understood that Jacks bore them no personal malice. He knew in his heart that Jacks had nothing to do with murder of Chow Lin or his father.

Unlike Larkin, he mused to himself. That snake still lives in the same house up the road. "What about that Rodriguez fellow, the one that used to skipper one of his whaling boats?" Kip asked innocently.

"Doesn't sail much anymore," Jacks said. "He lives over on the west end of town," Jacks added.

Kip nodded. "Town sure has grown," he said. But his mind was very much elsewhere. "I'll probably take a walk after dinner and look around," Kip said.

"Aye, you should. Don't stay out too late, and don't be going to those bars on Lighthouse Road," Jacks warned.

"They're still there?" Kip asked with feigned innocence.

"If I remember correctly, that's where you learned to fight and drink," Jacks said.

"Not me," Kip laughed. "I'm a lover, not a fighter." He got up from the table and hugged the old man. He put on his navy pea coat.

"I won't be out late, and no fighting or drinking," he promised. "I have two weeks to spend here before I take the train back to Washington," he said. "I've got lots of time to find trouble."

Jacks laughed. He thought Kip was kidding, of course. Jacks had no idea that trouble was precisely what Kip was looking for. In fact, Kip had already made a cold and calculated decision. He had been given many years to think about it.

Chapter Forty-Four

SUDAN, 1894

The dervish warrior led Syrah to the entrance of the Khalifa's tent. He pushed aside the tapestry and she followed him inside. She saw the Khalifa seated on his cheetah skin wooden throne. A white man sat next to him. His skin was bronzed and wrinkled by the sun. He wore the multi-colored cotton tunic of the dervish and he wore a turban. He was small in stature, but appeared both confident and assured. Syrah had been held prisoner by the Khalifa since her capture. She had never seen a white man in the camp. She could feel real fear welling up inside, and she fought to keep her composure.

The Khalifa Abdullah, the man who had inherited his mantle of power through his faithful servitude to the Mahdi, was no fool. Something bothered him about the slave woman. He motioned to her to sit down on a wooden stool.

"Abd al Qadir, this is the woman I spoke with you about," the Khalifa said.

The man nodded without expression.

"My master has asked me to speak with you," al Qadir began, speaking in Arabic. "I am Abd al Qadir, faithful servant and translator for the Khalifa. The Khalifa is the chosen one to take the place of the Mahdi. As I speak both English and Arabic, the Khalifa has asked me to inquire as to your family history."

Syrah felt a knot in her stomach. She was to be interrogated.

"Ask me anything you wish," she said confidently in Arabic. "I have nothing to hide. But I am nothing but a stupid cow, so I do not understand your master's interest."

The Khalifa liked what she had said so far. He waved his hand for her to continue.

Abd al Qadir switched to English.

"He does not speak English, so listen carefully to what I say. I am Austrian by birth. I was captured by the Khalifa, like you, *eleven* years ago. I was sent to Darfur by General Gordon. I was his tax collector. The Mahdi's men captured me at El Obeid. When the Mahdi died, I became the Khalifa's interpreter. I have been in his service ever since, and I am desperate to escape," he said calmly.

Syrah could only nod. She was stunned. He had known her father.

"The Khalifa is impressed by your courage and your ability to speak English. He wants to know how you learned to speak English, and why. He also wants to know why your eyes are blue instead of brown. He thinks you are the child of a white man and may be a spy. If he believes you are, he will have you killed immediately, so choose your words wisely."

The Khalifa jumped up to his feet and screamed at Abd al Qadir.

"Enough English, speak Arabic only from now on! Who is she and why are her eyes blue? Why does she speak English?" he demanded.

Al Qadir kept his calm. He knew his speaking in English would infuriate the Khalifa, but he wanted to earn her trust. "I was simply ascertaining her knowledge of English," he lied. "She speaks it fluently."

The Khalifa nodded in satisfaction. "Ask her why her eyes are blue."

"Why are your eyes blue?" al Qadir confronted her in Arabic.

Syrah ignored the white man and focused her gaze on the Khalifa.

"I am a slave. I was sold to my master at birth. My master was a rich merchant and I was taught to read and write English so that he could use me as an interpreter. He was too lazy to learn English himself, but he was fascinated by the white man. So he made me read English newspapers and books. As to why my eyes are blue, I have no answer. I didn't get to pick my parents. I am a slave. No one has explained to me why my eyes are blue, so I don't know and I don't care. What else do you expect from a slave?" she asked. "Do you think anyone ever cared enough about me to find out?"

The Khalifa sat back down on his throne. It was true that anyone raised since birth as a slave would not necessarily be educated as to their past. But her eyes were blue.

He looked up at the heavens, exasperated. The Khalifa had used al Qadir as his interpreter for many years now, but he did not like having to trust him for his word. Now with two interpreters, he could play one off the other. Curse the infidels, he thought. I need her but I don't trust either one of them. They both have ties to the white devil, he decided. I will use them to help me defeat the infidel, then I will kill them both.

"Take her to her tent," the Khalifa said as he stood up.

Al Qadir nodded.

"You are to return to your tent," he said in Arabic. He led her out of the Khalifa's tent into the darkness. As they walked to her tent, he whispered to her in English.

"I know everything there is to know about the Khalifa, his army, his formations, his tactics. I have spent eleven years his slave. I must escape and pass this information on to the British. Will you help me?" he asked in English.

Syrah nodded.

"How can I trust you?"

"Because I am General Gordon's daughter," she said. She nearly collapsed. Her secret was out.

Al Qadir stopped dead in his tracks. He had heard rumors. So it was true. Obviously, the Khalifa heard the same rumors.

"And now, how do I trust you?" she asked.

"My name is Rudolf Anton Carl Freiherr von Slatin. Your father brought me to this place," he explained. "He was my friend and they murdered him. I want revenge."

"Then we have much in common," Syrah answered as she lifted the flap to her tent and disappeared inside.

Chapter Forty-Five

MONTEREY, 1894

Summer break was nearly over. Kip had enjoyed spending time with David Jacks. He also enjoyed getting to know Monterey. He walked along the docks and went inside the Whale's Eye Tavern. It was crowded, but he found a seat at the bar. There was a warm fire on one side of the tavern reflecting its heat off the large stone hearth.

"What will you have, mate?" the barkeeper asked.

"Whiskey," Kip said. He had many a fight in this place as a young man. He noticed that no one seemed too interested in picking on him now. He looked around the tavern. In one corner, he saw a familiar face. He remembered his father pointing the man out to him when he was little. His hair was white now, but he still had the same pushed in nose and overpowering brow. The mouth was thin lipped and wrinkled, but it was him. The man was none other than Captain Rodriguez.

Larkin Jr., and Rodriguez still in Monterey. His father's mortal enemies. Perfect, he thought.

The cadet from West Point slammed down his whiskey and ordered another. A slow fury rose within him. He was troubled by it.

He thought about his philosophy class. What was it Aristotle had written? "Young in years or young in character makes no difference: the weakness is not in the time lived, but in living by emotions and choosing pursuits accordingly. For such people, knowledge is useless, just as it is for those without self-control."

He looked across the tavern. He was now twenty years old. A

full-grown man. And the shriveled Portuguese sailor was no longer the man who had murdered his father.

Or was he?

Kip watched as the grizzled sea captain sat at his table, drinking his rum. His hands were gnarled by the sea, but they still had strength. The dark eyes still seemed cruel.

Living by my emotions, thought Kip. Or pursuing knowledge?

He got up from the bar and walked over to the old man's table.

"Excuse me," Kip said.

The old sea captain looked up at the young man. Another dumb ass looking for work, he thought to himself.

"Get lost boy, I'm not hiring," he muttered. He looked back down at his glass; the young man was forgotten.

Kip sat down at the table. The older man looked up in surprise.

"I told you, I'm not hiring," he said. "Now get lost."

Kip smiled. "I'm not looking for work. I have a job," he said.

"Great, get lost," Rodriguez said gruffly.

"I knew one of your sailors, a man named Chow Lin," Kip said. "I've been gone for many years. Do you know if he still lives here?" he asked innocently.

Captain Rodriguez took a newfound interest in the young man. He was asking about a topic that was dead and buried. Rodriguez may have already consumed a great deal of rum, but he could drink a lot more and still maintain his wits about him.

"I haven't heard that name in a long time," Rodriguez said. He turned his head and spat on the floor. Fuck this kid looking for his chink friend.

"Haven't seen him either. Not since his goddamn village burned down," Rodriguez said. "Why are you asking fuckin' questions mate ?" he asked, looking directly into Kip's eyes. "And why do you look so damn familiar?" he added.

"I grew up here as a kid," Kip answered calmly. "You've probably seen me around. That's why I was asking you about Chow Lin. I remembered he used to work for you. Sorry to bother you," Kip added, standing up. Kip went back to his stool at the bar and continued sipping his whiskey.

An hour passed. Rodriguez was on his second bottle of rum. Kip was still nursing his second glass of whiskey.

"Drink up or leave," the barkeep said roughly.

Kip tossed it down. "Bring me another," he said.

Come on you drunk old bastard, Kip thought. The drunker you get, the more curious you are going to become, so just come over here and start drooling. Five minutes passed, and Kip decided to up the ante. He looked over at the old man and stared at him.

That worked. The red-faced old man had enough of the bastard. He got up from his table and walked over to the bar.

"What are you staring at, you little prick," he hissed. Kip saw the knife in his belt. No doubt he had a gun on him too. A derringer, Kip thought.

"I wasn't staring," Kip answered.

"Yes, you were."

Kip smiled.

"As I said, I think I remember you from growing up. You used to hang out with that McDuran guy, that asshole that lived in that cabin outside of town with his slut wife," Kip said laughing. "He was such a prick," Kip added.

The old man felt a little of the steam come out. "He was no friend of mine," Rodriguez agreed. "He worked for me."

"That's right," Kip said easily. "He was on that ship, the Rachel H., that my old friend Larkin used to own."

"You know Larkin?" Rodriguez asked. He looked at Kip with new found interest.

"Lives right up the street," Kip said. "Been into his home many a time. Big old fireplace in the corner, just around from the kitchen. Big old chandelier over that table in the dining room. Nice garden too, out back. Big stone walls." Kip hadn't been entirely truthful with Jacks. He even had made his way up the staircase, to the long hallway that ran down the second floor, and into the bed of Larkin's teenage daughter. Kip could still remember the layout of the mansion.

"Aye, that's the place," Rodriguez agreed. "Didn't know you were a friend of Larkin," he said.

"Larkin Jr.," Kip corrected him. "Very good friend of my father. They both hated that McDuran guy," Kip said.

"Me too," said the sea captain. "Had a big mouth. Ran it too much. Tried to rat out Larkin to the government. Big mistake."

"Yep," Kip agreed. "Larkin is not a man to cross. I heard he had McDuran killed," he added. "Don't know if it's true, but if it is, the bastard had it coming to him. That's why I was looking for Chow Lin. I figured he might know."

"Why do you care, mate?" Rodriguez asked suspiciously.

"Because the cocksucker McDuran was fucking around with my Mom," Kip said. "He even beat her once. I thought maybe I'd track him down and kick his ass."

"You're too late," Rodriguez laughed. "Years too late. We took care of him a long time ago."

"Oh," Kip said. "Like I said, I've been out of town a long time. Just came back to visit some family, then up to San Francisco for business," he said lightly. "Too bad, because I would have loved to rip him a new one."

"Don't worry laddie, he didn't die easy," the old man laughed reassuringly. "When Larkin wants a problem solved, I don't fuck around. I'm his problem solver."

Aristotle was right, Kip thought. He looked around the tavern. He suddenly felt very cold. He finished off his whiskey and slapped Rodriguez on the shoulder.

"Thanks for the chat, mate," he said. "Always good to run into a friend of Larkin. I'll be stopping by later this week. I'll make sure I tell him I ran into you."

"Do that," Rodriguez said. The kid wasn't so bad after all. He took another shot of rum. He was too drunk to notice that he forgot to get the kid's name.

Self-control, Kip thought as he left the tavern. Self control.

He made his way back to Jack's mansion.

There are moments that define all of us, who we are, who we chose to be.

The next day Kip sat on the rocks by the harbor, looking out over the vast bay. As Kip struggled with his hatred and anger, he tried to calm himself.

Larkin and Rodriguez would be easy prey. Both had murdered not only his father but also his friends and innocents. Kip had every right to retaliate. He thought about Professor Jones at West Point.

Despite the horrendous atrocities Chivington and his men had had committed, no one had been held accountable. Kip remembered the quote taken from Chivington to justify his actions. "Damn any man who sympathizes with the Indians! I have come to kill Indians, and believe it is right and honorable to use any means under God's heaven to kill Indians."

Interesting choice of words, Kip mused. Chivington had been a Methodist minister before joining the military. His invocation of God to justify the slaughter of innocents didn't sit right with Kip. Neither did the fact that Larkin and Rodriguez got away with murder.

Men had been invoking the name of God for thousands of years to justify the slaughter and persecution of innocents. The first crusade had been the grand idea of no less than the Pope himself, who urged the conquest of the Middle East to restore Christianity. That had been around 1097 B.C. Four hundred years later, Mehmet II had conquered the Christian empire in Constantinople, and established himself the leader of Islam. Thousands perished.

And yet here I sit, powerless to act, Kip thought. Powerless to avenge the death of my father, the death of Chow Lin, and the death of Chow Lin's village. The world is one big killing field, and I am a soldier. When the time comes, will I be able to kill, he wondered.

He pondered further. If I kill for the government, my acts are moral. If I kill for myself, my acts are immoral. What rules do I live by? Or do rules exist only for those who are willing to obey them in the first place? Who gets to say what the rules are? The pope? A Methodist minister? A religious fanatic? Certainly Chivington was a religious fanatic. No doubt he went to his grave believing he was a great man. A righteous man of God.

The Civil War had left a million men dead and wounded. Now cadets from North and South trained and served together. Just like they had before the war. What was the point? Will heaven open up for those who killed in the name of their country? Will I go to hell if I take revenge on my father's murderers?

Kip got up off his perch on the bay and walked back to Jacks' mansion. David Jacks had several boats in the harbor.

It was time.

A noise in the garden startled Larkin out of his slumber. It sounded like some kind of creature was in his fruit trees. Damn raccoons, he cursed. He got out bed. His wife was snoring. Wearing his sleeping gown and cap, Larkin went down the hallway, down the stairs and the kitchen toward the garden. He grabbed a club from behind the door and went out to confront the offending creature. He looked around the garden and heard a rustle behind him just before he lost consciousness.

Captain Rodriguez awoke to a rolling sea. I must be dreaming, he thought. Because I remember going to bed. Now I am at sea. He could feel the rolling of the waves. He tried to sit up, but he couldn't. His hands and feet were bound. He tried to speak, but he couldn't. He was gagged and blindfolded. He could smell the ocean and could hear the wind hitting the canvas of a sail.

Larkin came to just as the sun was starting to toss sunlight over the mountains. Not that he could see the dawn coming. He too was blindfolded. He too was gagged and bound. He too smelled the sea and heard the wind hitting a sail.

Both men lay in the bottom of the small sailing vessel as it made its way out of the harbor to the open ocean. Larkin was cold. Rodriguez was afraid. Other than the wind and the waves, there was no sound.

After an hour, Rodriguez felt himself in the grip of powerful hands and was shocked as he was lifted and placed on a wooden board, sitting upright. Grateful to be off the bottom of the boat, he sat there, wondering what was going to happen next.

He heard muffled groaning and then a thud. He felt someone sitting next to him.

A hand removed his blindfold. Rodriguez squinted into the fog, trying to figure out his location. He saw Larkin sitting next to him, also bound. Someone had removed his blindfold as well. Their eyes met. It took a few seconds for them to focus.

They turned away from each other and to the front of the boat.

Kip looked at them both matter-of-factly. He felt no emotion. They were his prisoners now. A thick rope ran through a grommet on the boat and led out to the ocean. Thirty feet from the ship, the bloody carcass of a goat floated on the top of the sea.

"That's one of yours," Kip nodded to Larkin.

Larkin looked out at the animal tied to the rope. It bobbed up and down in the water. It had been slit open and its entrails were hanging out. A small float was attached to the carcass to keep it from sinking. Larkin looked around. He saw nothing but ocean. There was a fog layer on one side of the boat. He had no idea which direction land was.

Larkin looked at the man sitting in front of him. He looked familiar. He was young, in his twenties, with dark blue eyes and dark wavy hair. The man reached out and untied the gag from Larkin's mouth.

Larkin coughed and spit ran down his face. He tried to swallow, but his throat was dry. The young man poured some water out a canteen into his mouth. Larkin choked at first, but then was able to drink.

"Who are you?" Larkin gasped. "And what do you want of me?"

"Kip McDuran. I believe you knew my father, Dirk McDuran. He was first mate on the Rachel H."

Kips eyes locked on Larkin. "Remember?"

Larkin was stunned. "I don't know anything," he sputtered. "Let me go."

Kip removed the gag from Rodriguez's mouth. He too choked as he took sips of water from the canteen held above him.

"I thought you were Larkin's friend," he whispered.

The wooden boat rolled gently from side to side. Larkin felt himself getting seasick.

"I believe the two of you know each other," Kip said.

Both men sat silently. Neither one answered.

"Let me explain how this is going to work," Kip continued. "We are several miles off the coast. Your billy goat there has been bleeding for a good hour. It has attracted some interest." Kip looked out at the floating carcass. Several large fins appeared in the water, circling the carcass.

"Sharks," Kip observed. "Big ones, too. Probably white shark."

Larkin began to tremble uncontrollably.

Kip pulled out a pistol from his waistband.

"You are both going for a swim," he announced. "The lucky one will be dead when he hits the water. The unlucky one will still be alive." He set the pistol down and drew out a large knife. He sliced open Larkin's leg clean to the bone.

Larkin screamed. Kip lunged toward Rodriguez. Rodriguez tried to kick him, but his legs were bound fast. They were also going numb. He too screamed in agony as Kip's knife plunged into his skin.

"What do you want?!" the old sea captain shrieked.

"Last night, you told me that you and Larkin had my father killed," Kip growled through gritted teeth. "The one who tells me what happened will get the bullet. The one who doesn't will be conscious while he is devoured alive."

Larkin saw the fin close in on the goat. Massive jaws struck the animal solidly, shaking the carcass until a chunk of flesh broke off. Larkin started to cry.

"You had my father killed and burned the Chinese village," Kip said coldly. "Why?"

Then he spun toward the old sea captain.

"And you killed my father," Kip glared at Rodriguez. "Why?"

"I was a different man then," Larkin interrupted. "Please, don't kill me."

"I'm not going to kill you," Kip said. "But they will if you don't talk," he pointed towards the fins. The sea was red as the ravenous sharks tore the carcass apart.

"Why?" Kip demanded.

"Because he went to the government," Larkin confessed. "Rodriguez killed him. I didn't."

"Shut up, you bastard," Rodriguez hissed.

"And why the village?" Kip asked.

"We were just following orders," Larkin pleaded.

"Whose?"

"Crocker," Larkin said.

"The railroad man?" Kip asked.

"Yes."

"Why?" Kip asked.

"The village was blight. It stunk, and was going to keep away the tourists."

Kip froze. His eyes widened.

"You burned their village and killed them because you didn't like the smell?" he asked in amazement.

"I know it was wrong," Larkin pleaded. "They tried to get David Jacks involved," he added.

"And?"

"He wouldn't do it."

"Shut your damn mouth, Larkin!" Rodriguez bellowed.

A single pistol shot exploded neatly into Larkin's forehead and he toppled into the sea.

"You knew the rules," Kip said quickly. He kicked Rodriguez overboard.

Kip turned the boat around and headed back to the harbor. He could hear the shrill screams from behind him, but he ignored them. He heard the thud as jaws struck flesh, howling, crunching limbs, groans, and then silence. He took a bucket and rinsed the blood off the bottom of the boat. He untied the rope and let it float on the sea. He set out several fishing lines as he sailed back to shore.

Kip had a nice catch by the time he pulled up to the pier. He took his fish up to Jack's mansion and dropped them in a large tub of water in the backyard. Maria would clean them.

The old man walked out into the yard.

"Were the fish biting?" David Jacks asked his adopted son.

"You might say that," Kip smiled.

Two weeks later Kip took the train back to West Point. By then, Monterey was abuzz about the disappearance of Larkin and Rodriguez. They had vanished without a trace. There were suspects, but they were all enemies, past and present. No one suspected the once small boy that the town had forgotten. Even David Jacks failed to make the connection, because Kip had never told him about Chow Lin, or what he saw that night.

CHAPTER FORTY-SIX

SANDHURST, 1894

As graduation approached, Winston had arrived, brimming with confidence. He had put on some weight, some muscle, and was no longer the runt that had come to Sandhurst coughing and wheezing two years before. He had the look of a devil may care, young, elite officer from the ruling upper class. He was feeling cocky and arrogant, and ready to take his place in society.

He was twenty years old and convinced he was invulnerable.

He also fancied himself as a future member of Parliament, like his father. He felt a need to make an impact on society. To be more precise, to impact the world with his presence.

The status of a cadet in his senior term allowed a great deal of freedom. On weekends, he regularly hired a carriage into London to visit the Promenade by the Empire Theater, where a gentleman could have a drink sitting at a table on the sidewalk and watch the ladies of the evening stroll by.

Now, sitting in the smoking room of his dormitory, reading the daily paper, he was confronted with an article reporting the closing of the promenade.

"Damn," he said to no one in particular. "They can't do that."

"I say, old boy, damnation so early in the morning?" his friend Cadet Parsons said dryly.

"They're closing the Promenade," Winston said with indignation.

Parsons stretched out his legs and sipped his tea. His uniform was immaculate, his brass shining, his shoes freshly polished. The company butlers made sure that the young officers looked very much the part.

"They can't do that," Parsons said, a frown on his face.

"It appears that Ms. Purity's campaign has vanquished her foe," Winston continued.

"From here on out, a canvas curtain shall be erected between the bars and the Promenade," Winston read the article out loud in horror. "Ms. Purity has been assured that young men shall no longer be tempted by the flesh while they imbibe alcohol at the local bars."

Winston threw down the paper.

"That wretched bitch!" he exclaimed.

"Indeed," Parsons agreed. "Now where will we get horizontal refreshment?" he asked.

Churchill paced the smoking room, hands clenched behind his back. This was his chance to make his first impact on the society of London. Purity be damned, he thought. This is a time of enlightenment and virtue. Of freedom and great empires and noblemen! Who wants purity?

How dare they treat us like schoolboys, he decided. It was as if his old schoolmaster, the Reverend H. W. Sneyd-Kynnersley had suddenly taken over the mind of this woman. Shut down the Promenade? He thought about the carefree evenings he and his friends had spent, indulging in camaraderie and good spirits. It was quite pleasurable to have the ladies sit and join them at the sidewalk tables, attempting to entice the young nobles to the neighboring hotels.

"We are going to the Promenade this Saturday," Churchill announced to the room.

Parson's looked at him quizzically.

"We, as in you and me?" he asked. Parsons looked around the smoking room. It was just the two of them.

"We shall gather as many of the company that cares to make a statement, and go to the Promenade and have a civil disobedience," Churchill stated.

"A civil disobedience?" Parsons asked. "Are you daft?"

"No," Churchill stated firmly. "I am," he paused, "drunk."

That Saturday evening, Winston sat in his civilian clothes at a bar on the sidewalk next to the Empire Theater. He glowered at the canvas curtain that blocked the Promenade where the ladies of the evening strolled. Six of his classmates sat with him at the table, drinking their beer.

"This will never last," Churchill proclaimed loudly.

"Agreed!" yelled a young man at the table next to him.

Winston looked over at the young man at the next table. "Sothby?" he said in amazement. It was Kenneth Sothby, his schoolboy nemesis.

"Yes, old chap," Sothby said. "I'm at the University. What about you?"

"Sandhurst," Churchill said proudly.

"My mates and I think this is a terrible atrocity," Sothby stated, pointing to the canvas screen.

"So do I," Winston said.

"And so the hell do I!" a man at another table roared. He was extremely intoxicated and red-faced.

"This is an outrage!" Sothby yelled in encouragement.

"An injustice!" echoed Winston.

Soon, other voices joined in the protest. Winston felt the excitement. He had hoped for something like this. He quickly began to outline a speech in his head. He hoped to incite the crowd with his passionate plea.

The crowd, however, was already incited. The drunken gentleman at the table next to them picked up his umbrella and plunged it into the canvas.

A roar came up from the crowd and suddenly they turned on the offending screen and tore the canvas off the lumber. They piled the whole thing on the middle of the street.

This is my chance, Winston thought. He mounted the pile of wreckage and raised his hands to the crowd. Among the group were now the ladies of the evening, who eyed the young man with admiration.

"Ladies of the empire. I stand for liberty!" he cried.

"It's amazing that he can stand at all," Parsons said drolly to one of the other cadets. "How much has he had to drink?" he asked.

"I would estimate enough to make a complete ass out of himself," another cadet answered.

"Where does the Englishman in London always find a welcome?" Churchill continued to address the crowd. A growl of approval answered him.

"Where does a man first go when, battle-scarred and travel-worn, he reaches the safety of the Promenade?" he asked the crowd, impassioned. Another roar of encouragement. He felt a thrill. It was his second public speech, and it was met with approval. Much better than his first.

"Who is always there to greet the tired and weary warrior, home from battle? Who greets him with a smile and joins him with a drink?" he continued, emboldened by the crowd. "Who is ever faithful, ever true?" he paused.

"Why, the ladies of the Empire Promenade," he yelled, holding out his arms to the ladies standing on the street corner who began applauding him.

The crowd roared its approval and moved into the street happily tearing the remaining shreds of canvas to the ground.

"Three cheers for Winston!" Sothby called out.

"Hip hip, hurray!" the crowd roared. Winston found himself lifted onto their shoulders and carried down the street in celebration. Father will be proud, he thought to himself. Winston was very, very drunk, but happy. It failed to dawn on him in his drunken stupor that he had just incited a riot and given his first real speech in support of the prostitutes in London.

The next day, however, as he read the paper with concern, he was relieved to find no mention of his name.

Chapter Forty-Seven

WASHINGTON D.C., 1895

Kip took his seat at the table in the main briefing room of the army's Military Intelligence Division (MID). He was now a captain, recently promoted and assigned to MID. Kip noticed Andrew Drummond, the chief of the U.S. Secret Service, seated at the table. Drummond, along with General Hanson, the chief of the Army's Military Intelligence Division, were two of the president's primary policy advisors.

Kip felt a little out of place seated at a conference room with such high-ranking officers. But as always, he was determined not to show any fear. His new boss, General John "Bulldog" Hanson, had been thoroughly briefed by the commandant at West Point about Captain McDuran. During his education at West Point, Kip had demonstrated his military acumen, his physical toughness, his complete lack of fear. He was excellent in hand-to-hand combat and was deadly with any weapon. His professors raved about his intellect and ability to grasp complex theories. He was the "complete package," the commandant boasted. Perfect for military intelligence.

General Hanson nodded to the intelligence officer at the podium. "Begin the briefing," he ordered.

"Sir, as you know, a revolution has broken out in Cuba. The Cuban Revolutionary Party, the CRP, has called for a revolution to drive Spain out of Cuba. Their manifesto is land reform, racial equality, and redistribution of wealth. Jose Marti has come out of exile along with Maximo Gomez and Antonio Maceo. They have 25,000-45,000 rebels under their command. The Spanish government has approximately 20,000 troops.

Our intelligence sources are lacking in that region, but we believe Spain will be sending an additional 30,000 troops to put down the rebellion."

"What is our strategic interest in Cuba?" asked General Hanson.

"Sugar," the intelligence officer replied. "Edwin Atkins owns a massive plantation that exports sugar to the United States.

"He is also a partner with J.P. Morgan and Company," Drummond added. "The same J.P. Morgan who also happens to own General Electric."

"Exactly," said the young intelligence officer.

"Which brings us to why we are sitting here today in the first place," General Hanson said. He turned to Kip.

"The president is not pleased by the lack of intelligence we have on the situation. He wants us to send a military attaché to Cuba to obtain intelligence on the revolution and the likelihood of its success," the general said.

"Richard Olney is the president's leading expert on Cuban affairs, and right now he is not sure which direction the wind is blowing." General Hanson was not a happy man. Significant question marks concerning foreign policy were the bread and butter of intelligence. He knew the president would be demanding results.

"I don't know him," Kip spoke up.

"That would be Richard Olney, a close friend, and advisor to both J.P. Morgan and Edwin Atkins," Andrew Drummond said smiling. "But don't get the idea that corporate America is deciding our foreign policy," he joked. "Just who will be the next president."

Of course, Kip thought. Politics. Power. Greed. Some things never change.

"The president has assigned you to be the United States military attaché to Cuba. You will be working closely with the military staff of Marshal Martinez de Campos, the military general in charge of the Spanish Army in Cuba. The president will want weekly dispatches from you on the situation. You will be his eyes and ears in Cuba," General Hanson said.

"If I remember correctly, you learned Spanish as a young boy growing up in Monterey?" the general queried.

"Yes sir, I studied Spanish at West Point as well," he added. "I can get by," Kip assured him. Maria, the cook, had spoken a great deal of Spanish with him when he was growing up. As did her teenage daughter. He had spent many a long afternoon learning how to speak Spanish from her and how to kiss.

"Marshal de Campos has agreed to assign you an aide, fluent in both English and Spanish just in case. The aide will also know his way around Cuba."

"When am I leaving, sir?" Kip asked.

"Your ship sails out of Baltimore in three days," General Hanson replied.

"Pick up your gear from supply. Plan on staying in the hotel the first few days, but grab your field gear, because we want you to get to the front lines to obtain first-hand intelligence," he instructed.

"They know you will arrive armed, so take whatever gear and weapons you think you'll need to survive in the field. We don't expect you to engage the rebels yourself, but you are entitled to defend yourself," the general added.

"Very well sir," Kip said.

The general slid a portfolio across the table.

"Here are your orders, letters of introduction, letters of credit at the Bank of Havana, and your authorization to draw supplies," General Hanson said.

"And Kip," he added. "Be careful. This is a perilous assignment. The rebels are extremely aggressive, using hit-and-run tactics that the Spanish are not accustomed to."

"Kind of like we did with the British in the Revolutionary War," Kip added with a smile.

"Exactly. That will be all."

Kip came to attention, saluted smartly, put the portfolio under his arm, and left the room.

"He's young," the head of the Secret Service observed.

"He'll need that. But he's the best man we have," General Hanson said. "The president still remembers him from the Army-Navy game," he added with a laugh.

"Let's not go there," the other man said.

CHAPTER FORTY-EIGHT

ENGLAND, 1895

Lieutenant Churchill sat at the table in the mess hall at Aldershot. It was his first assignment since graduating from Sandhurst.

"I'm bored," he announced to his good friend, Reginald Barnes.

"How so, old chap?" asked Reggie.

"Well," Churchill explained between bites of food, "we've spent five months drilling, playing polo, drinking heavily and in general, doing nothing."

"I'm not complaining," said Reggie. "Especially about the drinking," he added.

"But we can drink anywhere, we're British cavalry," Winston pointed out.

"Where are you going with this, Churchill?" Reggie knew his friend was up to something.

"Cuba," he replied proudly.

"Winston, there's a revolution in Cuba. People are dying. Why do we want to drink where people are fighting and dying?" Barnes questioned.

"We could get killed there," he added.

"Nonsense," Churchill replied. "We'll be fine. That's the sport of it."

"Sport?" asked Reggie incredulously.

"Yes, of course," Churchill answered quickly.

"That and the chance to gain combat experience," he added. "Just think of it. Of all the soldiers here at Aldershot, how many can say they have seen combat?" Winston challenged his friend. Combat experience went hand-in-hand with politics.

"I don't want to get shot; I want to stay here," Reggie retorted. "Besides, what are you going to do, enlist in the Spanish Army? Last time I checked, that was an act of treason punishable by death."

"No," Churchill said, exasperated that Reggie wasn't grasping his plan. "We'll go as observers and report back to the government," he added.

"Churchill, we are lieutenants in the cavalry. Why on earth would the army send us to Cuba to spy?"

"We're not going to spy," Churchill said. "We will be stationed with the Spanish as liaison officers and report back on our observations. I am sure the Spanish government would be appreciative of our presence.

"Besides, I want to be a foreign correspondent," he added. "I could get some great publicity out of this. I can run dispatches for the papers. I've already got one interested!"

"Churchill," Reggie said, now agitated by his friend. "Have you taken leave of your senses? What are you going to do, just go ask the commander-in-chief of the army to send us to Cuba ?"

"Yes," Churchill replied matter-of-factly.

"You know him?" Reggie asked in disbelief.

"Reggie my friend, just stick with me. Yes, I know him. He wrote a two-volume biography about John Churchill, the First Duke of Marlborough, one of my ancestors," Churchill said. "He also knows my mother," he added. "I also know the Queen, I know the prince, I know the prime minister, I know just about everyone," Winston concluded. "It will be a piece of cake and a grand adventure."

Reggie just shook his head. He knew Churchill's family was famous, but he had never known how famous.

"You're daft," he said.

Churchill wasn't daft. He knew what he wanted. And now that he had come of age, he knew how to go about getting it.

His first foray was with Colonel Brabazon. He explained his plan to Brabazon at his office. Brabazon was immediately impressed.

"Splendid," the colonel said approvingly. He had fond memories of Lady Churchill and was all too happy to help.

Winston next wrote a letter to an old friend of his father, who also happened to be the British Ambassador to Spain, Sir Henry Wolff. Sir Wolff, in turn, contacted the Spanish Foreign Minister, who in turn wrote a letter of introduction to the commander of the Spanish forces in Cuba, Marshal Martinez de Campos. Finally, Churchill sold his plan to Lord Wolseley, the commander -in-chief of the British Army.

Lord Wolseley not only supported the plan, but he also contacted General Chapman, the Director of Intelligence. He was intrigued. He provided Churchill with maps, intelligence briefings, and a private request for some Cuban cigars. He also wanted information about the battlefield, weapons, and strategies.

Lieutenant Reggie Barnes could only watch in amazement as the "mission" unfolded in front of him. The fact that young Churchill had been the driving force behind all of this was astounding to him. *It's all about who you know*, he thought. Just the luck of the draw in British society. It's all about the bloodlines.

Two weeks later, they sat in the officers' mess, sipping brandy and making plans. Churchill was animated.

"We'll need gear," he said, pulling out a piece of paper and a pen. "Anti-termite matting, mosquito netting, thorn-proof linen, canvas baths, quinine..."

"Jesus man, are we going on a safari?" Reggie asked.

"An adventure, old chap. We'll need pistols, rifles, bandoliers," Winston continued.

"Booze," added Reggie.

"Of course," Churchill looked at him with feigned indignation. "We'll even have our own butler," he added. "And, the best part is, I signed an agreement with the Daily Graphic. They will pay me five guineas for each dispatch I write to them from Cuba. Reggie, we're going to be famous," he added excitedly.

"Or dead," Reggie sighed.

"We leave Liverpool on November 2. A week to cross the Atlantic, then some red-carpet treatment in New York," Churchill continued.

"New York, red-carpet?" Reggie asked.

"Mother was born in Brooklyn. She has lots of friends there, including a congressman. We'll get a tour of West Point while we are in New York," he added. "And from there, train to Tampa, Florida, where we'll catch a steamer to Havana, where we will stay at the Grand Hotel Inglaterra," he finished with a flourish.

"I'm impressed," Reggie said.

"So am I," Churchill said proudly. He sat back in his chair and sipped his brandy. "So am I." He was up and coming.

Two days later, Winston received a telegram. His father had passed away. He sat in a leather chair in the smoking room all night long, trying to make sense of it all. He had been expecting it, but no one is ever ready for it.

He attended the service and went with his mother to the family plot in St Martin's Church in Bladen. He sat through the burial silently, then sat on a bench next to his father's grave and wept. Lady Churchill came over and sat next to him. She put her arm around her son's shoulder.

"Winston, your father has been ill for a long time. He was suffering a great deal. This is the best he could hope for," Lady Churchill said.

Winston was silent. There was a question weighing heavily on his mind and his heart. He looked at his mother.

"Did he love me?"

"Yes," she answered immediately. "Your father was a very unique man. In many ways, he was very eccentric. But he loved you. He just didn't know how to show it."

"I wanted to follow in his footsteps," Winston said sadly.

"What's stopping you?" Lady Churchill asked. She looked into his eyes. "The only person that can come between you and your dreams is you."

A week later he was off to Cuba. On his new mission. His father would have been proud.

Chapter Forty-Nine

SUDAN, 1895

Syrah sat in her tent, frightened. She could hear the Khalifa screaming at his men. Something had gone wrong.

"Find him and bring him to me at once," he screamed. He burst into her tent.

"What did he say to you ?" the Khalifa threatened.

Syrah saw the whites of his eyes.

"Who?" she asked.

"Slatin," he yelled. "Abd al Qadir!"

He grabbed her by her collar and yanked her to her feet.

"He has escaped," the Khalifa hissed. He put a knife to her throat. "Tell me everything you know," he ordered.

Syrah could only look at him dumbfounded.

"Why would I know anything," she said defiantly. "I sit in my tent all day long guarded by your men. Kill me and put me out of my misery," she challenged.

"If you didn't speak and write English, you would have died a long time ago," the Khalifa swore. She could smell his breath. He let go of her collar and shoved her backward. She fell to the ground. "If I find you aided in this treachery, you will die a slow death."

"I'll take any death I can get," Syrah spit back.

The Khalifa suppressed the urge to kill her on the spot. She was too valuable. And true, her tent was guarded around the clock. He threw open the tent flap and stepped back out into the camp.

"Bring me the European, now!" he screamed at his men.

One week after Slatin escaped, an Egyptian soldier watched a camel approach the outskirts of the camp. It was limping and carried a small man dressed in a jibbah, the white cloth covering that Arab men wore in the desert heat. The man's face was burned from the sun, wind, and sand. He was filthy, thirsty and starving.

"Halt," said the sentry. "Who are you?" he asked, "and what business brings you here?"

The man looked up at him.

"Where am I?" he asked the sentry, his voice raspy and dry.

"You are at the camp of the Egyptian Army," the sentry replied.

The man began to laugh.

"Tell your commander that the Governor of Darfur wishes to speak with him. Tell him I bring him tidings from the Khalifa. I have much to tell him."

Chapter Fifty

CUBA, 1895

Kip rested his feet on a railing on the wooden veranda of the Grand Hotel Inglaterra. His Spanish aide, Manuel, sat next to him. They both were drinking beer. It was exquisite; especially after a rigorous week-long patrol in the jungle.

Kip saw a large carriage approaching the hotel drawn by four horses. It was a big carriage, loaded with bags and gear. It came to a stop in front of the hotel. Kip watched two men in uniform get out. They are British officers, Kip thought. What the hell are they doing here?

He watched in amusement as one of them, a short young man with sandy hair, rosy cheeks, and pouty lips barked out orders to his coachman and what appeared to be an aide. The other British officer was looking up and down the street as if he was expecting an attack.

Manuel started laughing. "They look so lost," he said.

"I think they are. The Brits have no dog in this fight," Kip observed. "The little guy sure likes to act like he is in command," Kip noted.

He sipped his glass of beer and watched the two British officers supervising the unloading of their carriage. Two porters from the hotel came outside and began to take their bags and gear into the lobby of the hotel. The two British officers followed them up the stairs and onto the verandah outside the lobby.

The smaller of the two British officers noticed Kip and stopped. "American?" he asked.

Kip eyed the young soldier. He was about the same age as Kip, slightly built, very pale, had a baby face, and spoke with a bit of a lisp. Apparently, this was an upper-class British officer. Kip eyed the freshly polished black boots, the smartly decorated patrol jacket edged with black astrakhan and black mohair braids. Kip took an instant dislike. He despised the Victorian upper class of England.

"Captain Kip McDuran, United States Military Attaché," he introduced himself. "And this is my fellow officer, Captain Manuel Gonzales, Spanish Army."

"Hola muchachos," Manuel said.

"Lieutenant Winston Churchill," Winston said, "and this is Lieutenant Reggie Barnes. We are both British cavalry, 4th Hussars," he added proudly.

"The cavalry has arrived, Manuel," Kip said sarcastically. "We are saved."

Winston felt his face turn red. He did not like being teased, especially by an American army officer. He looked away from Kip for a moment, composing himself, and looked down the broad street lined with palm trees.

"Well, you certainly don't look like you need rescuing," Winston said diplomatically. He decided to leave this encounter for another day. Besides, the American looked a bit edgy. He was a powerful looking character with a chiseled jaw line and piercing blue eyes.

"Well if you will excuse us, we need to check in," Winston said.

"Cheerio," Kip smiled.

The two British officers went into the lobby and were met by several Spanish soldiers and the hotel manager.

"They seem important," Manuel said.

"They certainly think they are important," Kip said.

"You no like them?" Manuel asked.

"Nope," Kip said. "I no like them. The British officer is born with a silver spoon in his mouth, coddled from the day he was born, and then sent off to boarding school and then a military academy. After that, a guaranteed career with plenty of promotions, regardless of merit," he added.

"Hmm, you no like them," Manuel agreed.

"Hey!" Kip exclaimed. "That guy said his name was Churchill. That's a pretty famous name."

Kip watched all the attention the two officers were receiving inside the lobby. *I wonder? Washington would be interested to hear that a British officer from a very influential family was in Havana, hobnobbing with the Spanish. Just what are they up to?*

During the next few days, Kip met with his Spanish counterparts in the army and got a briefing on the upcoming mission. During a break, he asked one of his colleagues about the British officers. It was indeed Winston Churchill, the son of the famous British politician, the recently deceased Randolph Churchill. The Spanish officers told Kip that they were just observers and that the Spanish government was indulging them as they did not want to insult such a famous person. It was almost as if they were here on holiday.

They described Churchill as boyishly exuberant, eager to see action, and very immature. Their biggest concern was to accommodate his wishes to go to the front and yet somehow keep him alive. Marshal Campos had no desire to send a dead British officer back to England. Diplomatic relations between England and Spain were good right now, and his government wanted to keep it that way.

As far as Kip was concerned, that was the end of his interest. He had more important things to worry about than some spoiled brat seeking glory. He knew Washington wanted his assessment of the fighting and the likelihood of the revolution succeeding.

Two days later, Kip set out to meet Marshal Campos at his headquarters in Santa Clara. He and Manuel traveled by train. It was an uneventful journey save for a torrential rainfall that darkened the skies and cooled the air. He could smell the lingering scent of the lush green rainforest and tropical jungle.

When he arrived at Santa Clara he was met by a Spanish officer with a very interesting name.

"Colonel Juan O'Donnell, at your service," the handsome Spanish officer said in perfect English.

"Captain Kip McDuran, United States military attaché to Cuba," Kip said. He shook the colonel's hand warmly. "O'Donnell?" he asked.

"My father is the Duke of Tutan," the Spanish officer said sheepishly. "Somewhere in the past I am afraid one of my ancestors must have fallen in love with a Scotsman," he teased.

"Thank you for meeting us," Kip said. "How's the fight going?" he asked.

"Right now, quiet. We are anticipating a strike at the rebel stronghold near the town of Arroyo. We have received intelligence that Maximo Gomez has 4,000 rebels there. We will crush them and the revolution by the spring," he said confidently.

"Mind if I tag along?" Kip asked. "I'd like to be able to report back to Washington on your successful counter-insurgency," he said.

"That would be good," O'Donnell agreed. "I want the Americans to know that the sugar fields are not in danger of falling into rebel hands," he replied. "However, I'm afraid I won't be able to devote too much time to you during our journey," O'Donnell said apologetically. "The marshal has me babysitting two visiting British officers," he grimaced. "Nobility, I'm afraid. They asked for two horses so they could ride to the front lines. They wouldn't last two minutes alone."

"No worries, sir, I have Manuel with me. You tend to your guests."

"Good, I will introduce you to General Valdez's aide-de-camp, Major Tampa. He is your liaison officer during the mission. Now if you will excuse me, there is a British officer inquiring if we have ice for his gin and tonic," O'Donnell said with a forced smile.

Kip looked around the camp, set in a clearing in the middle of a jungle.

"Of course," he smiled.

They boarded a train that would take them to the small town of Sancti Spiritus. The railway was heavily fortified, like the roadways. The army had cleared wide dirt roads in the jungle and lined them with barbed wire, searchlights and sentry towers. Every few miles there was a small fort. The roads were designed to allow constant travel of supplies and troops to the fight. But it also made them a sitting duck for guerrilla raids. They would hit and run. Kill a few Spanish soldiers, blow up a blockhouse or fort, and then disappear back into the jungle.

When they arrived at Sancti Spiritus, Kip was appalled at the conditions. Yellow fever and smallpox had taken its toll on the people of the town. They were wary of the Spanish troops. Manuel told him that the army controlled the village, but the rebels owned the jungle.

"We will leave for Arroyo tomorrow," Major Tampa told them when they checked in. "On horseback at dawn. You'd better get some sleep."

Kip nodded his head in agreement. "I will."

He went over to the mess tent where he found Manuel. They ate a meal of beans and rice and salted pork. Their food was simple but tasty.

"What did you learn today?" Kip asked. He trusted Manuel. He was a Spanish army officer, but he was an honest man. They had become good friends over the last three months.

"To be honest, Kip, I think my government is fighting a losing battle," Manuel said, looking around to make sure they were alone. "The army controls the towns; the rebels control the countryside. This is their home, and they view us as occupiers of their country. They are willing to fight to the bitter end to send us home," he said. "Much like you Americans did with the British. Don't you repeat that to anyone," he urged.

"Don't worry, I don't have to. I've been watching for three months now, and I agree with your assessment," Kip assured his friend. He punched Manuel in the shoulder playfully. "So now you don't have to worry about being a traitor."

What he didn't tell Manuel was that he had a source inside the Western Union Telegraph office in Havana. Kip was reading the same dispatches sent back and forth between Field Marshal Campos and the Spanish Army in Madrid. The source was being richly rewarded. His family was in Florida and they were well taken care of. The chief of the secret service, Andrew Drummond, could be resourceful when he wanted to. Kip's dispatches were sent in code. He had spent three months in Washington learning how to make it work.

They woke early the next morning, before daybreak. The large column of Spanish soldiers set out on the march to Arroyo. There were approximately 2,500 infantrymen, dressed in white cotton uniforms and wearing straw hats. They were heavily-laden with ammunition and weapons. The officers were on horseback, along with about 300 cavalry troops. The rear of the column consisted of an artillery battery pulled along by mules, and of course, the supply column, which included nearly three hundred civilian wagons.

Kip and Manuel rode on horseback at the side of the infantry column. Kip saw Lieutenant Churchill at the front of the column, riding alongside General Valdez.

"Ass-kisser," he said to Manuel.

"Indeed," Manuel agreed. "Jealous?"

"Disgusted," Kip replied. "I don't like the way the world works."

"Si mon," Manuel agreed with a grin. "On a more important note, there are 20,000 rebels in that jungle," he warned. "Yesterday I learned that they hit a blockhouse on the railroad. They captured fifty Spanish soldiers and their weapons."

Kip looked at the rifles the infantrymen were carrying. German Mausers. They were heavy and held a five-round box magazine. It was a breech-loading rifle and fired a 7.92 mm round. In other words, slow and bulky.

The rebels, on the other hand, had obtained an ample supply of Remington rifles which fired a .45 caliber round up to 1000 yards. It was a deadly accurate weapon, useful for ambush. The rebels also carried machetes for close-up hand-to-hand fighting,

It was a two-week journey to Arroyo, through dense jungle foliage full of chattering monkeys and loud chirping birds. It was hot, humid, and full of snakes and insects. Water dripped off the thick leaves of the trees onto the jungle floor. Kip was surprised the first morning of the march when they stopped after about eight miles and set up camp.

Some of the troops were setting up picnic tables. Kip smelled coffee brewing. He walked over to the officer's area and saw Lieutenant Churchill busily engaged in a deep conversation with General Valdez.

Churchill was smoking a Cuban cigar, which he waived with one hand while sipping from a cocktail glass with the other.

Jesus, thought Kip. This guy knows how to work it.

Manuel walked up beside Kip.

"Siesta time. The cocktails are called 'roncotelle.' It is rum and pineapple juice," Manuel explained. "It's very delicious."

Kip watched Churchill down his cocktail and happily accept a refill. His face was already flushed. The cooks brought out several pots of stew, and the officers ate a leisurely meal. After eating, they brought out bedrolls and hung hammocks in the shade.

"Nap time," Manuel told him.

Kip couldn't believe it. But sure enough, the troops bedded down for a four-hour nap in the shade. They had even taken the saddles off the horses so they could rest. Sentries were posted on the perimeter while the column slept.

Half these guys are plastered, Kip thought as he lay in his own hammock. We're sitting ducks. I wonder if the rebels are sleeping too, or are they sneaking up through the jungle ready to cut our throats?

He heard Churchill snoring from a nearby hammock. That guy is plastered too, Kip observed. Cuban cigars and roncotelles. Drunk by noon, sleeping it off. Kip lay in the shade. He wasn't about to sleep. He got up and walked over to the mess tent to get a cup of coffee. It was becoming clear to him that the Spanish army was not going to defeat the rebels. Their tactics were archaic and ill-suited for unconventional warfare.

After their siesta, the column reformed and returned to the trail. They marched another ten miles, then made camp. More cigars, more roncotelles for the officers. Kip noted that the enlisted soldiers were drinking rum straight from the bottle.

They set out again at dawn the next day. As the sun lit up the jungle, Kip noted signs of combat. They passed several burned-out buildings. They were in rebel territory now.

Suddenly, Kip heard shots fired from the front of the column. An infantryman dropped, hit in the chest. Several of the Spanish soldiers fired into a clearing that opened into a large meadow. Kip saw several rebel scouts riding away, back into the jungle. That sniper is long gone, Kip thought to himself.

After they crossed the clearing, the jungle closed back in around them. Dense foliage blocked the road. The men at the front of the column pulled out machetes and chopped a clearing.

Kip was relieved when they finally reached Arroyo. He needed a bath. It was a small town, with about twenty houses. There was a garrison of 200 Spanish soldiers, heavily fortified with barbed wire and more sentry towers and searchlights. The town folk eyed the column of soldiers cautiously. Women held babies on their hips as they watched the soldiers march in. A large well stood in the center of the town next to an adobe mission with a large wooden cross affixed to the side.

They set up camp on the edge of the town, just inside the perimeter. Kip sat in on a briefing inside the general's large tent. His Spanish was good enough that he understood most of the presentation.

After the briefing, he went to his tent and sat on his cot. He pulled out his journal and wrote down his thoughts for the day, planning his dispatch back to Washington when they returned to Havana. He was certain to recommend that the United States withdraw its support of Spain and to support the rebels. They were going to win. Or at least, they would never lose, and there was no way Spain could afford to keep 200,000 men on an island across the Atlantic Ocean.

As he lay on his cot, he wondered about the next day. They would undoubtedly come under attack. The rebels had spies in Arroyo. They knew they were here. There would be more hit-and-run attacks and sniper fire. Some firefights, but he predicted that the rebels would be content just to jab away.

Winston Churchill sat in front of his own tent, smoking a cigar and drinking his fifth roncotelle of the evening. Reggie was trying to keep pace. He felt buzzed.

"Finally, we are going to see some action," Churchill slurred.

The air reeked of cigar smoke.

"I am excited," he announced. "Something tells me that we will see combat. Just think about the stories we can tell the others back at Aldershot," Churchill continued presumptuously. "As soon as we get back to Havana I'll send my letters to the paper. By the time we get home, we'll be famous," he predicted.

Or dead, Reggie thought. He felt ill. He went outside the tent and wretched.

Churchill could hear him puking. "Sissy !" he laughed.

They were up again before dawn and on the trail before the sun came up. Kip rode in his usual spot in the column, with Manuel. The lush green jungle forced them into a single file, and Kip was acutely aware of the dangers of taking sniper fire. He took note of the Spanish army's willingness to accept the risk in hopes of ambushing the rebels. The hunter may soon become the hunted, he thought to himself.

They finally stopped in the small village of Las Grullas, which lay in a bend in the river. It was a sweltering afternoon and Winston Churchill felt unclean.

"I say, Reggie," Winston said. "That river looks rather inviting. We could bathe and get some of this sweat off," he suggested. "And you can rinse the puke off your face," he laughed.

Reggie looked at the river, then at the riverbank on the other side. Nothing but jungle.

"I think that is a little too close for comfort," Reggie replied. "Hard to say what's in that jungle."

"Nonsense my man, the only thing in that jungle is birds," Churchill opined. "The birds would scatter if rebels were moving about," he said, proud of his logic. Before long, he and Reggie were naked in the river, bathing, laughing and splashing about.

This does feel good, Reggie thought, as he felt the sweat and dirt melt off. The water was clear and warm.

Suddenly a shot rang out and water flew from where a bullet struck just three feet away. Another burst and more bullets whizzed over their heads.

"Shit, Winston!" Reggie yelped. He started wading towards the shore. "I didn't hear any birds, you fucking bastard!" he yelled, ducking more rifle fire.

He looked over his shoulder and saw the skinny pale frame of Winston Churchill, standing in waist deep water, glaring at the enemy snipers, as if to dare them to hit him. He looks very annoyed, Reggie noticed, as he scrambled up the bank and grabbed his uniform.

Kip was at the canteen tent getting a cup of coffee when he heard the shots. The deep booms of Remington rifles left little doubt in his mind who was doing the shooting. He grabbed his Winchester and ran towards the river bank. As he broke out onto the bank above the river, he saw Barnes, naked, scrambling up the bank, bullets slapping into the damp ground around him. He saw Churchill standing in the river, frozen.

"Churchill, get your ass out of the water now!" Kip roared. He threw himself to the ground and quickly put down covering fire into the jungle on the other side of the river. The deep boom of his own Remington .44 caliber was immediately followed by the metallic chatter of Spanish Mausers around him. Manuel, already at his side, also fired into the lush undergrowth.

Churchill finally seemed to snap out of his stupor and casually waded to shore. He picked up his clothing in disgust and sat down on a rock to get dressed.

"Jesus, take cover!" Kip yelled.

Suddenly at least fifty rifles opened fire from around him as Major Tampa lead his men down to the rescue. They lay down covering fire and eventually, the deep booms of the enemy rifles were gone. The enemy retreated into the jungle.

"Cease fire," the major called out to his men.

Kip got up and stomped over to the now dressed Churchill. Kip was furious.

"Jesus H. Christ, what the fuck do you think you were doing?" he demanded, his nose nearly touching Churchill's.

"Bathing," Churchill said curtly. "I say old chap, do you mind getting out of my face?" Churchill asked politely.

"Yes, I do. I ought to kick your fucking ass right now, you stupid shit. Bathing? You could have gotten someone killed. What the hell did you think was in that jungle?"

Reggie came over and pulled Kip away from the Englishman.

"Birds," Reggie said, trying to calm down the American military attaché.

"Birds?" Kip asked incredulously.

"Churchill said that if the rebels closed in on us the birds would give us warning," Reggie continued.

Kip ran his hand through his hair. "Jesus!" he exclaimed. He was completely exasperated now.

"Did it ever occur to you that they might have been watching us the last three fuckin' days, and maybe, just maybe, might have already set up an ambush? They were just waiting for something like that. I bet you didn't notice any birds flying until the shooting started," Kip continued.

"Steady on Captain, might I remind you that you are speaking to a British officer, and in particular, a Churchill?" Reggie pleaded.

"I don't give a damn if he's Teddy fucking Roosevelt," Kip continued hotly. The Scottish temper and brogue he inherited from his father and mother were now unchecked.

"That kind of stupidity could have gotten someone else killed," Kip added. "If you want to get your ass shot off, be my guest, Churchill. But I'm not going to stand by and keep my mouth shut just because your daddy was someone famous. Got that?" he said menacingly, his eyes ablaze. He loomed large over the smaller man.

Churchill eyed the American with interest. "A wee bit Scottish, are we?" he smiled.

"More than a wee bit," Kip shot back.

"My mistake, it won't happen again," Churchill said disarmingly. He held out his hand.

"I'm sorry," he said politely.

There was nothing else Kip could do. Kip shook it. His grip was firm. He was surprised to find that Churchill's grip was firm as well. They locked eyes.

"Why the hell did you just stand there?" Kip continued.

"I was pissed off at being wrong," Churchill said. "Besides, I knew if they were aiming at me they would miss."

"They are not bad shots," Kip warned.

"I didn't say they were," Churchill answered. He pulled cigarette out of his soggy tunic and coaxed it to flame. He exhaled a cloud of smoke. "I just knew that I wasn't going to get hit," he said matter-of-factly.

"Jesus," Kip snorted. He shook his head and walked back up the river bank to their bivouac. Manuel came up beside him as they walked back to camp.

"Un poco loco," he said.

"No shit," Kip said, still annoyed. "I wonder if he'd be so cocky if someone had been wounded or killed." Still, the guy had apologized. Give it a rest, Kip, give it a rest, he told himself. Not your problem, not your fight. They reached camp and settled in for the night.

Kip was sound asleep when he was suddenly awakened by more shots. From the sound of it, the rebels were still in the jungle. He rolled out of his cot and hit the dirt. He crawled for his Remington and then out of his tent. Cooking fires still burned from the evening meal. Seconds later, a bullet hit a Spanish officer standing by Churchill's tent. The man pirouetted, blood spurting from his neck.

Kip and the other officers again started firing into the jungle. The shooting stopped. Kip got up and looked at Churchill's tent. There was a bullet hole in its side.

"Damn," Kip cursed. He walked over and lifted up the tent flap. Churchill was snoring like a baby.

Kip snorted in disgust, dropped the flap, and went back to his own tent. He rested his rifle against a tree trunk and got inside. It was going to be a long night. He thought about the hole in Churchill's tent. He's either very stupid or very brave, Kip thought. Perhaps a little bit of both. Is that what being born rich does to you? Makes you believe you are so special you can't be touched?

They broke camp as usual before dawn. After several hours, they came into a clearing that looked out over a large meadow. Kip estimated the clearance to be at least five hundred yards wide. On the other side, they saw the first signs of the enemy camp. Wooden hitching posts stood off in the distance, along with several small buildings on a ridge line behind the meadow. Minus the horses, Kip noticed.

Kip could feel the column come alive as General Valdez organized his attack. If intelligence sources were right, they would soon be facing 4,000 determined rebels. He watched as the general, resplendent in his white uniform and gold lace, rode about his men, barking orders. Two columns of cavalry were sent forward, one on each side of the meadow. Behind the cavalry, was a column of infantrymen.

Then, to Kip's disbelief, General Valdez proceeded with his staff and artillery up the middle of the meadow, until they were within rifle range of the rebel camp. Winston Churchill was by his side. His boyish face flush with excitement.

Kip shook his head.

He looked over at Manuel, who sat on his horse next to him. Manuel smiled, a flash of white teeth in the still, dark morning.

"It seems we are going into the lion's den," Manuel said.

Kip nodded in agreement. He spurred his horse forward. He didn't express the disagreement he was thinking. If he were a betting man, that lion would take a few more shots, then slip back into the jungle, lying in wait for them to follow.

As dawn broke out upon the meadow, General Valdez and his staff were about three hundred yards from the rebel position when the rebels opened fire. By then Kip and Manuel had joined them.

"Open fire!" the general barked. The cavalry on each flank surged up the sides of the meadow, and the infantry began firing on the rebel position. At the same time, small artillery pieces dropped a string of explosives on the enemy's position.

Kip winced as several of the general's staff officers were shot off their horses. Nonetheless, the general and his staff scorned taking cover. They watched the unfolding battle with their binoculars. Kip would have preferred taking cover, but he stayed on his horse with the other officers. This is ridiculous, he thought.

With the cavalry closing in on each flank of the enemy position, the general gave the order to advance. The infantry moved forward in a rush, as did the general and his staff. By the time they reached the enemy camp, the firing had stopped.

The camp was empty. The enemy had slipped away into the jungle behind the ridgeline.

Kip watched the general's face. This was the moment of truth. Would he fall for it?

General Valdez shook his head in disgust. He looked to his staff. "Reform the column," he ordered. "We will return to Santa Clara, victorious," he announced. "Maximo Gomez is a coward and has fled the field of battle. Spain will be proud."

After they returned safely to Havana, Kip sent his final dispatch to General Hanson. His conclusion: Spain was dead in the water, mired in a hopeless effort to match the rebels' guerilla tactics with conventional tactics which would lead to nothing more than a protracted loss of men, time and money. Kip knew the financial burden the war placed on the Spanish. They would eventually have to downsize, and then finally leave. The rebels would wait them out.

The president and his staff agreed with General Hanson's final recommendations, based in part on Kip's own comments. The United States of America was about to have a shift in foreign policy towards Cuba. The natural resources and sugar plantations were too valuable to lose. They ordered Kip home.

Once back in Washington, Kip sat in the living room of his brick townhouse on G Street and propped his feet up by the massive hearth, enjoying the warmth of the fire. It had snowed that morning. He opened the paper, and read with amusement an article about Churchill's exploits in Cuba. He had been awarded the Cross of the Order of Military Merit, First Class, Red Ribbon. A grateful Churchill had even posted an article for the Saturday Review in London.

> **"The rebels neither fight bravely nor do they use their weapons effectively. A Cuban government would be corrupt, more capricious, and less stable. There would be frequent revolution and insurrection. If the rebels won, the government would be dominated by the 'negro element' among the insurgents who would create a renewed and even more bitter conflict of a racial kind."**

Kip threw another log onto the fire. So Churchill was racist. Figured. It was a common sentiment in America as well.

"Idiot," he said aloud.

Kip was grateful to be home. His first assignment was a success, and he would remain in Washington on General Hanson's staff until his next task. He didn't care where he went, as long as he didn't have to see Churchill again.

Chapter Fifty-One

ENGLAND, 1896

Gladstone was no longer prime minister. His liberal government had been replaced by Robert Arthur Talbot Gascoyne-Cecil, the 3rd Marquess of Salisbury. This was the third time that Lord Salisbury had been asked to form a government and sit as prime minister. He was a scholar and a career politician. Accordingly, he was able to learn from the past in order to not repeat the same mistakes. In his mind, there was no higher gauge of intellect.

And it was his keen eye for public opinion and politics that made him acutely aware that Britain's neighbors were attempting to chip away at the empire; attempting to erode both its prestige and power. In the past, Britain had found itself embroiled in endless European conflicts. France and Russia were still viewed with caution, as was Austria.

Lord Salisbury was an expert in foreign policy. In his view, the empire could no longer be involved in European intrigue. Instead, the government should focus its energy and efforts on its vast empire of dominions and territories.

Egypt, with its proximity to the Suez Canal, was without a doubt a vital asset. India, with its vast natural resources, was the crown jewel of the empire. Britain could not tolerate a threat to either.

He convened a meeting with his ministers. They needed to talk.

The ministers gathered around the huge conference table in the main conference room at Number 10 Downing Street in London. The prime minister had a matter of urgent importance he desired to discuss.

"The reason I've called you here today is that we still have an Arab problem in the Sudan," Lord Salisbury began. "The Mahdi's successor, Khalifa Abdullah, has expanded his empire to the very border of Egypt. We have received information that the Khalifa is looking to press north into Egypt, with designs to overthrow the Khedive himself." He paused for a moment to let the news sink in.

"I can't tell you how destructive that would be to the image and prestige of the empire. We cannot afford the loss of such a valuable territory. We also have information that the French are viewing us as extremely vulnerable and soft, especially after the fall of Khartoum and General Gordon's death," he added.

"In fact, British intelligence has learned that the French are sending an expedition to Fashoda from Brazzaville under the command of Major Jean-Babtiste Marchand with orders to make Fashoda a French protectorate. They will link up at Fashoda with two other expeditions coming through eastern Ethiopia. They are planning to establish a permanent presence there, including establishing a base for French gunboats. They want us out of the Sudan so that they can link up the west coast of Africa with French Somaliland and their outpost at Djibouti. They are planning to build a dam, cut off the water supply and force us out of Egypt."

The ministers sat quietly, soaking it all in. It was no secret that France had regretted its decision made in 1882 not to join the British in the Sudan. The French bitterly disputed the British hold on Egypt. Now it appeared they were taking action.

"Gentlemen, in short, we need to reassert ourselves as a military power, capable of projecting our power, and dealing quite sternly with those would present a challenge to our occupation of Egypt," Lord Salisbury concluded.

Arthur Balfour, leader of the House of Commons, cleared his throat. "The public will not support an expedition against the French. It could lead to war," he warned.

Lord Salisbury smiled. "I concur."

He paused and looked around the room at his cabinet. Their faces looked shocked. They were hanging on his every word, waiting for the prime minister's punch line.

"I can think of no greater challenge to the empire than the radical Islamic madman that is holding the Sudan hostage and threatening the borders of Egypt. The public still clamors for revenge for Gordon's death and for salve on the wound of British pride," he said. "They will support a war to exterminate the Khalifa and his men. They don't need to know about the French. Let's consider that an *ancillary* benefit. Quite simply put, gentlemen, *why not* kill two birds with one stone?"

Balfour frowned. "Prime Minister, I do not believe occupation of the Sudan is feasible," he said honestly. "The cataracts of the Nile and the vast expanse of desert make it impossible to sustain any long-term military operation without lines of communication. And we don't have any. And quite frankly, the Egyptian army is not up to the task of making such an effort."

"I agree," the prime minister said, much to Balfour's surprise.

"Then I must confess I am at a loss," said Balfour.

"My solution to the equation is that we build a sustained force in Cairo, with a significant number of British officers and soldiers. We train and equip the Egyptian army to assist us. We will build a railroad from Wady Halfa to Abu Hamed. We will no longer have to rely on the Nile as our primary line of communication between those two points, nor be burdened with transporting our equipment and forces at the upper cataracts. Once established in Abu Hamed, we can extend the rail south, and rely both on the rail and the river to reach our objective," he proposed.

The room was stunned. The plan was daring and bold. The prime minister was proposing a desert railroad deep into the heart of Africa.

"Our publicly stated objective?" inquired the secretary of state for war, Lord Lansdowne.

"Omdurman," the prime minister replied. "The final resting place of the Mahdi. And from there, Fashoda is just down river."

"Again, even with a railhead, how could we afford to occupy so vast a territory?" asked the leader of the House.

"We won't," Lord Salisbury said. "We'll crush these dervish fanatics once and for all. Then, we will pull out, leaving behind a group of advisors to ensure that this time the Egyptians get it right."

"Why?" asked Balfour.

"To demonstrate to the world, France in particular, the might of the British empire. Not just on the seas, but on land as well. We need to set an example, and quite frankly both the French and the Khalifa are a threat to our national interest. I'm not going to let them dam the Nile," he stated.

"Do the math," Lord Salisbury continued. "We build a desert railroad alongside the river through the desert. By land and by water, we can build, equip and supply the largest fighting force Africa has ever seen. When we are done, we can secure the borders of Egypt, and maintain and fortify bases along the railroad. The lines of communication will be uninterrupted. And, I might add, we can then look at Cecil Rhodes's long-standing desire to continue the railway all the way to Cape Town. We can finally realize the opportunity to draw a thin red line through the entire continent of Africa, all the way to South Africa. The rest of the Sudan will be left to the Egyptians to manage. We will leave behind a Sudanese army capable of defending itself, governed of course by our proxy with Egypt. They will serve a useful buffer as well as an alarm for any further French or Islamic mischief."

"Who will lead this expedition?" asked Lord Lansdowne.

"General Horatio Herbert Kitchener, the Sirdar of Egypt," Lord Salisbury replied. "He has already been briefed. In fact, he was instrumental in designing the plan," he added. "He is, after all, the commander-in-chief of the Egyptian army and a military genius."

He paused, looking around his conference table. Lord Lansdowne looked annoyed. The prime minister had not given him advanced notice of the plan. He had been left entirely in the dark. Lord Lansdowne *would* have been briefed before the meeting, but Salisbury was worried about leaks to the press. A leak on foreign policy before it gained approval by his ministers would be exploited by his enemies.

"Gentlemen, if her majesty's government supports this effort, Egypt will be secure for a hundred years and we will keep the French out of both the Sudan and Egypt," Lord Salisbury concluded.

The smoke-filled room broke out into an earnest debate of the proposal. Word leaked out and the discussion carried on into Parliament and the press. England was finally avenging Gordon's death, the tabloids blared.

Chapter Fifty-Two

MONTEREY, 1896

Kip sat at his desk in the War Department. A young orderly knocked on his door and handed him a telegram. Kip opened up the envelope. It was from David Jacks's attorney in Monterey. His adopted father had died. General Hanson granted him emergency leave and Kip was on the train the next day for Monterey.

The journey was bittersweet. As the train crossed the vast expanse of continental America, he thought about things that he had tucked away in the deep closets of his memory. As he mourned the loss of Jacks, he also remembered the terrible pain he felt when he lost his parents, and the depression that had overwhelmed him on more than one occasion. He grew up feeling alone in the world.

No one on the train would have guessed he came from such a humble and impoverished childhood. No one would have imagined that the handsome young Scotsman was battling depression again. David Jacks and Chow Lin had been his only positive role models growing up. He never had the quality time to spend with his father. Dirk had always been at sea and then had died so early in Kip's life.

The fact that he was suddenly a very wealthy young man about to gain the entire estate of David Jacks did nothing to make him feel better. Money and the pursuit of wealth meant little to Kip. His childhood and later the teachings of David Jacks made him all too aware of the games that men play to climb the ladder to fame and fortune. The modest values instilled in him by his parents instilled a scorn for those who spent their lives scheming and climbing up the backs of others.

He wanted no part of it. He had already decided that all of the old man's estates should be sold off. Kip would put the money in the bank and forget about it until he grew old. The only thing he wanted in life now was adventure. Travel the world and seek excitement. The fact that it might involve combat made it even more desirable. Kip liked danger. It heightened his senses and gave him an edgy satisfaction.

His tour as military attaché in Cuba confirmed his desire to continue in the army. The MID gave him the opportunity to travel and see the world. It had other perks as well; a decent salary, an excellent standard of living and an unending supply of young ladies eager to bed and wed such an upcoming, handsome young officer.

Acting on Kip's reports, the United States foreign policy towards Cuba swung 180 degrees. Edwin Atkins and J.P. Morgan were thrilled. Their investments in Cuba were safe. Kip's dispatches had also backed up the position of Richard Olney, who was now the Attorney General of the United States.

Kip had no shortage of admirers, yet he still felt alone.

Finally, they reached home. He stepped off the train and was met at the small station in Monterey by Jacks's attorney, Thomas Brown. He was a small, balding man with glasses and a crooked grin that Kip thought was appropriate for a lawyer. He grasped Kip's hand warmly as he introduced himself.

"I am Thomas Brown, your late father's lawyer," he said. "It is a pleasure to meet you. I was the one who prepared the papers when David adopted you," he added.

"Thank you," Kip said sincerely, shaking his hand. "If you don't mind, I would find it too painful to stay in the mansion. Any chance we could swing by the El Carmelo Hotel on Lighthouse?" Kip asked.

"Not a problem, I know the manager there very well," the lawyer said, steering the carriage towards the hotel.

"How long are you here for?" Brown asked.

"I can only stay a few days; then I have to get back to Washington,"

Kip answered. He smelled the fresh sea breeze blowing in from the bay. He could understand why his father had chosen to be a fisherman.

"I've drawn up all the documents you asked for to sell your father's holdings. You do realize it could be more lucrative to appoint a trustee to continue his business?" he added hopefully. That trustee, of course, would be the lawyer.

"No," Kip answered. "Sell it all for as much profit as you can, and then deposit it into my bank account at Wells Fargo," Kip said.

"They have a good reputation," Brown agreed. "We can be done with the documents in a few hours. How about tomorrow morning?" he asked.

"That would be fine," Kip said. "A bath and a good night's rest would be great. Business tomorrow." He was tired and depressed. He just wanted to go to bed.

"Oh, one other thing," Brown said. He looked worried. "Robert Johnson, the chief of police, would like to ask you a few questions."

"What about?" Kip asked.

"Several years ago, two men disappeared. One was Thomas Larkin, Jr. The other a Portuguese whaling captain named Rodriguez," the lawyer said. "They went missing two years ago. No one has seen or heard from them since. And their bodies have not been discovered," he added.

"What's that got to do with me?" Kip asked calmly.

"Your father worked for both of them when he died," Brown said. "I think they are still looking for people who had a motive to kill them."

Kip smiled. "Well, at least that leaves out my father. He's been dead for a long time," Kip said sarcastically. "I'm afraid I can't be any help."

The next day Kip spent two hours in Brown's conference room signing the necessary documents to inherit and then sell off his adopted father's estate. They had finished the document review when Brown's secretary poked her head into the lawyer's conference room.

"Chief Johnson is here," she said. Kip noticed she was a pretty red head with high cheekbones. She blushed whenever she saw him. Memo to self, Kip thought.

"Send him in," Brown said.

Chief Johnson was a pleasant looking man, large mouth with white teeth that lit up the room when he smiled, a large nose, and brilliant light blue eyes under a mop of brown hair. Kip guessed him to be around thirty. He shook the policeman's beefy hand.

"Major Kip McDuran," he introduced himself. "United States Army."

"Rob Johnson," the chief said back. "Damn glad to meet you. Mind if I sit down?" he asked.

"By all means," Kip said. He sat down too. "My attorney said you wanted to talk to me?"

Johnson smiled broadly. "I do." He slid two photographs across the table to Kip. Kip picked them up and looked at them.

"Do you know either of those two men?" Johnson asked. "They went missing two years ago, and quite frankly, I need all the help I can get. I've talked to anyone and everyone who might have known them, and I still don't know squat," he said.

Kip nodded. "Thomas Larkin, Jr., and Captain Rodriguez," he said. He gave the photos back to the police chief.

"When is the last time you saw either of them?" Johnson asked.

"I saw Rodriguez at the Whale's Eye a while back when I was last in town," Kip said truthfully. "Larkin, geez, I don't know. When I was a kid, I guess."

"Some folks said they saw you talking to Rodriguez the night before he disappeared," Johnson said.

"I saw him at the Whale's Eye," Kip agreed. "Yep. The crusty old bastard was drinking that night. But then, so was I," Kip said.

"Some witnesses also saw you with him the next day," Johnson lied.

Kip smiled. The first rule of interrogation is to listen to the question. The cop didn't say *where* the witnesses saw Kip. He's bluffing.

"No they didn't," Kip said. "And you said I was talking to him the night before he disappeared, not me. I remember seeing him at the tavern, that's it."

Johnson looked at him, puzzled. "Why would they lie?" he asked innocently.

"I didn't say they lied," Kip said. "You did. I wasn't with Captain Rodriguez the next day. That means you are making this up."

Johnson looked like he had been slapped.

"Kip," Brown started to say.

Kip raised his hand to silence his attorney. "Chief, I'm not trying to be rude. But as a member of the Military Intelligence Division in Washington, I know a thing or two about interrogation techniques," Kip said firmly. "I'm happy to answer any questions that can help you with your investigation, but I'm not going to let you go down that path with me."

Johnson was annoyed. The wise guy was talking back to a cop.

"There was talk that Larkin had your father killed," he said.

"I grew up with that talk," Kip said. "I heard Rodriguez might have been involved too," he added helpfully.

"Which could give you a motive," Johnson suggested, eyeing the young officer.

Kip smiled.

"Indeed it could. Or, it could give you a lead as to who murdered my father, not that you or anyone else ever investigated it. And to tell you the truth, I'm not that heartbroken to hear that they are missing," Kip added.

He was careful *not* to say dead. At worst, their half-eaten bodies could have washed up ashore. By then they would be so severely decomposed there would have been nothing recognizable left of them. The gun had gone overboard just after Larkin. There had been a very dense fog that morning. No one saw anything. He knew the trail was cold, and Johnson was just testing him, looking for leads.

Not going to give you any, Kip thought. Bastards killed my father, Chow Lin, and burned the village. Good riddance. He had enjoyed shooting Larkin, and kicking Rodriguez overboard still gave him satisfaction.

"So you don't deny animosity towards them?"

Kip smiled again. "No. But then they had both had a lot of enemies. I doubt I'm the only person that didn't like either of them," he added.

"What do you do for military intelligence?" Johnson asked, shifting the topic.

"If I told you I'd have to kill you. Whatever the government orders me to do," Kip said.

"Anything else, Chief?" Brown interrupted.

Johnson eyed the young man. Some help you were, he thought.

"No, thanks for your time, Major," Johnson said. They shook hands, and the cop left the room.

Brown let out a sigh. "You handled yourself well," he said. Indeed, he was impressed with the way the young officer called the cop's bluff without appearing scared.

"There was nothing to handle," Kip said. "I never liked those two blokes, and I couldn't care less what happened to them. Not my problem," he continued. "What's next?"

"The bank," Brown said.

"Let's go," Kip said. He grabbed his top coat off the chair and they went out to Brown's carriage. Suddenly he was feeling more energetic. His adrenaline had shot through the roof during the whole interview. The memory of his revenge on the two men still tasted sweet.

Chapter Fifty-Three

SUDAN, 1897

The Khalifa sat in his tent, surrounded by his closest advisors. Hashish filled the air as they smoked from the hookah in the middle of the large canvas enclosure.

"A spy from Cairo has passed along a message, Holy One," one of his advisors said. "The English are making plans to build a railroad south, into the Sudan. There is word that they are coming with a large army," he added. "He also sent several English newspapers, which, I am afraid, I cannot read."

"Take them to my translator," the Khalifa ordered. "I will have her read them to me later." He paused, letting out a slow stream of smoke.

"So the British have not learned their lesson," the Khalifa continued. "The infidel and his pious Christian soldiers are fools who have not learned from the lessons of the past. Thousands of years of war with Islam, yet who sits on the throne in Constantinople? We conquered them in the Crusades, and we have conquered them here in the Sudan. Let them come. We will give them another welcome," he said to his advisors. "We will teach them once and for all that Allah is almighty, and Islam is the light of the world."

Later that evening he went to Syrah's tent. He commanded that she read every column of the newspapers to him, even the articles describing the nightlife, theaters and book reviews. He listened silently as she read. How did you learn to read and speak English so well, he wondered?

The Khalifa was fascinated with the newspapers. He learned more about his enemy from the press than any spy could ever tell him, save the Austrian Slatin.

Slatin's escape cut him to the core. He had relied upon the Austrian to teach him all about the European world, and the English. He had given him a tent, a woman, and his life. And now in return, he had escaped. And no doubt, he was providing the infidel with everything he knew about the Khalifa and his forces.

Let them come, he mused. We will massacre them the way we did Gordon.

Syrah read on, trying not to show the terror she felt inside. How much longer could she live before the Khalifa discovered the truth, that she was Gordon's daughter? Someone would talk.

"Tell me again how you speak and read such good English," the Khalifa demanded.

Syrah felt her heart race.

"I told you Holy One, I don't remember. I was a slave," she said defiantly.

"Nonsense!" the Khalifa roared.

Syrah shrunk back away from him.

"I have never heard of a slave who was taught to speak English," he said accusingly.

Of course, he had never heard that Gordon had married a black woman, a Sudanese, who had given birth to his child. He made inquiry after inquiry of all his advisors. No one had heard anything. Why is she lying, he wondered? If she were not so valuable, he would have cut her head off himself. After he had raped her, of course.

Allah give me strength not to touch this woman, he prayed. She is poisonous. She has such beauty; she could enchant his entire army.

Chapter Fifty-Four

LONDON, 1897

"We have a problem," Lord Salisbury announced to the men seated around the table in the conference room at Number 10 Downing Street. "To be more precise, we have another Arab problem."

"What's happened in the Sudan now?" asked Lord Lansdowne. There was a hint of exasperation in his voice.

"Not the Sudan," Lord Salisbury corrected him. "Afghanistan."

Silence fell over the room. Afghanistan had been a painful thorn in the side of the British Empire, and especially its empire in India. The British Empire was at its zenith. The sun never set on the empire, which stretched from the dominions of Canada to the vast expanse of India and the Far East. Their military might had conquered all.

Except for Afghanistan.

No one in the room had forgotten the lessons of the past. And no one had forgotten the massacre at the Khyber Pass.

British foreign policy had always dictated that the empire would accept no challenges to its might. Afghanistan had poppy fields and many a British nobleman had made a fortune from them. But treachery was in the air. The Russians were scheming to take over the opium trade and replace the British. Therefore, when Dost Mohammed, the ruling emir, secretly accepted a Russian envoy in 1838, the empire had to strike back.

And it did.

Lord Auckland, the British Viceroy of India, led an invasion into

Afghanistan, captured Kabul, and placed the former ruler, Shah Shuja, back in power. Dost Mohammed was imprisoned. There were 4,000 Indian soldiers, a hundred British officers, and another 12,000 camp followers. The British occupation of Afghanistan was complete.

Or so they thought.

Someone forgot to inform the tribal leaders in the mountains that they had now become part of the British Empire.

These tribes loved to fight. They loved to fight each other. The Pathans, Swatis, Waziris, Mahsuds, Afridis, Bunerwalis, Chitralis and Gilgitis had honed their warrior skills on each other for ages. They viewed cunning and deception as art forms. The more devious one was in battle, the more respected the leader was. They were utterly ruthless.

When news came that the British were building forts and blockhouses in Kabul, they had a change of heart.

Enter Mullah Mohammad Akbar Khan.

He persuaded the barbarous tribal leaders that they could always go back to killing each other later, but it was in all of the tribe's best interest to get rid of these pale white men and Indian soldiers who had invaded their land.

And they did.

Mullah Mohammad and his men swept down from the mountains and surrounded Kabul. The Mullah sent word to the English commander of the Indian forces, General Elphinstone. Evacuate the city of Kabul or be destroyed. He even went so far as to guarantee safe passage. Dost Mohammed was returned to power.

The general had few options. He agreed, and led his 4,000 soldiers and 12,000 camp followers, many of them women and children, back towards India. They made it as far as the Khyber Pass.

It had been a trick.

Mullah Mohammad Akbar Khan had no desire to see the British army and its Indian soldiers return. The tribes swept down on the retreating column. They were sitting ducks, trapped between the stone walls of the pass. Only one man escaped to tell the story. They slaughtered the rest, woman and children included.

There would be no more British occupations of Afghanistan. Instead of trying to occupy and imperialize the tribes, they set out to punish them.

In 1878, the Indian government, a British surrogate, declared war on Afghanistan. The British soldiers went in with their Indian allies. Thousands of tribesmen were killed, and their villages burned to the ground. Led by General Roberts, the soldiers burnt eleven villages in Kandahar alone. The women and children were forced out into the open. They perished in the winter snow.

This time, however, the British did not stay. They withdrew back inside the borders of India. They had learned the dangers of trying to occupy Afghanistan.

"The mullahs are back," the prime minister told his ministers. "We just received word that they have attacked the fortress at Chakdara, and nearly captured it and the bridge across the Malakand Pass. The attack was turned back, and they have returned into the mountains."

Again, silence fell over the room. No one wanted to be the first to say it.

The Duke of Devonshire, Spencer Cavendish, had served in the British army and fought in Afghanistan before turning to politics. Now, as the lord president of the council, he sat at the large conference table with his peers. He felt a growing flame of anger inside. British foreign policy had always demanded an eye for an eye. Sometimes a life for an eye. The gauntlet had been hurled. If they turned their backs, the empire would only be challenged again.

"Well, I think another punitive expedition is in order," Cavendish announced, breaking the silence. "I realize we are already taxed with the Sudan expedition, but a punitive expedition has none of the cost of nation building. We hit and run. Again."

There were murmurs of approval. But what would the prime minister say?

Someone had stepped on the emperor's toes.

"I agree," Lord Salisbury said without hesitation. "We cannot let this challenge to the might of the British empire stand."

The prime minister was no fool. He had already given the matter serious thought before the meeting and had already arrived at the same conclusion as the Duke of Devonshire, but for additional, selfish reasons. If he showed weakness now, when the empire had once again been attacked by an old foe, his opponents would castigate and castrate him in the next election. Lord Salisbury had no intention of letting a Muslim mullah knock him off his seat of power.

"I propose an expeditionary force go into the Valley of Swat. The mission of this force is to be punitive only. We will teach them a lesson, and then we will leave behind a smoking hole," he said.

"Here, here," said various voices around the table.

"All for?" the prime minister asked. Every minister in the room raised his hand.

"Lord Lansdowne, at the direction of her majesty's government, as War Minister, you are to form an expeditionary force. It shall be called the Malakand Field Force. I want this force to be under the command of your very best general, and his orders will be to seek out and destroy the mullah and his men and then return home. There is not, and I repeat not, to be an attempt to occupy or hold any territory in Afghanistan."

"Yes, prime minister," Lord Lansdowne answered.

"Do you have someone in mind to lead the force?" Lord Salisbury asked.

"Yes. General Bindon Blood," Lansdowne answered without hesitation. This time he was ready. Lord Salisbury had pulled him aside before the ministers' meeting.

"Appropriately named, and a good choice indeed," the prime minister agreed. "Let's get to work," he said. The room broke out in excited conversation. British honor was to be upheld once again.

CHAPTER FIFTY-FIVE

ENGLAND, INDIA, AFGHANISTAN, 1897

Winston sat in the reading parlor at Blenheim Palace, sipping tea and reading the daily paper. He was on holiday, visiting his uncle, the duke. He nearly spit up his cup of tea when he read an article that Britain was sending an expeditionary force into the Malakand Pass.

"Bloody hell!" he exclaimed. Could it be? It was! The expedition was to be led by General Bindon Blood, a close friend of his father. He had met the general on more than one occasion, as recently as the year before his father died. The general had assured him that if he went into battle, Winston would and could be at his side.

"Bloody hell!" Winston yelled again.

The Duke of Marlborough came into the parlor and looked at his nephew. "I say old chap. You are rather excited," the duke noted.

"The bastard left without me. He's going to Afghanistan, to put down the bloody Arab rebellion, and he didn't invite me," Winston complained.

"Who is going to Afghanistan?" asked the duke. He hadn't read the paper yet.

"Bindon Blood," answered his nephew.

"Ah, Bindy. Swell chap. Back into the fray again? I say, Winston, I realize that you are a trained soldier, but those bloody savages in the hills of Afghanistan are dug in like ticks. No one has ever been able to conquer them. You wouldn't want to be there anyway," he offered.

"Like hell," Winston replied to his uncle. "I'm going. I've got to catch the first train out of here and get cracking!" he exclaimed. "Uncle, I may need your help."

The Duke of Marlborough looked at his young nephew. So much like your father, he thought of his late brother. So much energy. So much intelligence. So bloody goddamn immature and naïve.

"I stand at your service," the duke said. Besides, once Winston made up his mind to do something, he was going to do it, come hell or high water.

"I've got to get to London today," Winston said. "Uncle, may I borrow your fastest carriage?"

"Of course," replied the duke. "Where is your first stop?"

"I need to send a telegram," he said. "Then I've got to get back to my unit and get permission to join up with General Blood," he said.

"I thought you were going to spend your holiday here in England," the duke said. "Your mother will be none-too-pleased to hear about this."

"I will write her a letter," Winston promised his uncle.

When he arrived back at Aldershot, Winston was disappointed to see that General Blood had not yet replied to his telegram from London requesting immediate assignment to the Malakand Field Force.

Winston sat in his spacious quarters, sipping brandy, smoking a cigar, and venting at his housemate, Reggie Barnes.

"Damn Reggie, he left without me," he complained again.

"Winston, he didn't need to ask your permission," Reggie teased.

Reggie liked trying to keep young Churchill in check. Churchill was a cocky, arrogant little bastard who only thought about himself and what he could do to advance his career in politics.

"I didn't mean it like that, you prick," Winston said. "It's just that I was at the track one day with father and we were talking to Blood, and he promised me a slot on his staff if I ever asked."

"Wasn't that right after we graduated from Sandhurst?" Reggie asked.

"Yeah, so?"

"So maybe he forgot," Reggie replied.

"That's not okay," Winston fumed. "I sent the telegram on July 27th, and here it is the middle of August and I still haven't heard from him!"

"Maybe he's busy fighting a war," Reggie baited.

"Yes. Without me." Winston said with disgust. He drew deeply on the cigar and let out a slow cloud of smoke. "How are we doing on these Cubans?" he asked Reggie.

"We've got two cases left," Reggie replied, clipping off the end of his cigar. Churchill might be a pain in the ass but he was connected, and Reggie had finally grown fond of smoking a cigar. The trick is not to inhale, he learned. Churchill's liquor supply wasn't bad either, he thought, sipping his brandy.

"Winston, have you thought this through?" Reggie asked his friend.

"What do you mean?" Winston queried.

"I mean this whole Afghanistan thing. It's a different kind of war than Cuba," he said. "It might be more dangerous. We studied the massacre in the Khyber Pass at Sandhurst. You know how those little rag heads can fight," he warned.

Winston leaned back in his chair. "Any fool who has studied modern warfare knows that you do not attempt to occupy Kabul," he said. "And Bindon is no fool. I'm sure this is a seek and destroy mission. Kill as many of those pesky tribesmen as he can and then retreat to India. Besides, Afghanistan is a good buffer against Russia. To get to India, the Russians would have to go through Afghanistan. Let them try," he added.

"All the same, the expeditionary force will be sitting ducks for their marksmen in the mountains," Reggie said.

"Blood's not that stupid," Winston said. "He won't get bogged down in a firefight." Winston jumped to his feet, cigar stuck in his mouth as he began to shadowbox.

"Hit and run, hit and run," Winston laughed. He started to playfully jab Reggie's shoulder as he danced around him on his toes.

"They're better shots than the Cubans," Reggie continued.

Winston raised his eyebrows feigning surprise. "Better than the blackamoors?" he slurred.

Churchill didn't like Arabs or Negros.

"A bloody sand flea can shoot better than a blackamoor!" Winston exclaimed again, still dancing around Reggie's chair.

"Those sand fleas are dangerous," Reggie said. "Religious fanatics, every last one of them. Ready to die for Allah and go to heaven and receive seven virgins," he warned.

"Seventy-two!" Winston exclaimed. "Not seven!"

"Winston, you're drunk, and you're not listening to what I'm saying," Reggie pleaded.

"Of course I'm drunk," Winston agreed. "And I never listen to you, even when I'm sober," he laughed.

"That is true," Reggie agreed. Forget it. Hopeless situation. He sat back and sipped his brandy. The real question is what do I say if he asks me to go with him? Reggie could still hear the gunshots on the river in Cuba ringing in his head.

Reggie wasn't a coward. But he wasn't an idiot either. He possessed excellent survival instincts. Churchill was a publicity-seeking medal hound. It was as if Churchill thought he was immortal and could not be killed. People like that are very dangerous to be around, especially in a war. There will be other battles to fight, more wars to win. The Malakand Field Force was just going to be one more quick campaign in the history of the empire to punish savages who did not submit to their rule. Reggie decided he was going to sit this dance out.

The next two weeks passed quickly. Churchill kept himself amused playing polo and working on the manuscript of a book he was trying to write. Writing was an outlet for him, a way of expressing his superior intellect.

In fact, despite his somewhat arrogant prose and opinions, his dispatches from Cuba had been well-received. He caught a lot of ribbing from the men in his unit, but he didn't care. Besides, he liked the extra money. In reality, his father had not been wealthy and his mother's income was limited. The real money in the family was with the duke, and he wasn't the squandering type. The duke also knew that Churchill couldn't save a shilling. Churchill had hopes of selling his first novel.

Finally, he received a telegram from General Bindon Blood.

"All staff positions filled. I should advise you coming to me as a press correspondent, and when you are here I shall put you on the strength on the 1ˢᵗ opportunity.... If you were here I think I could, and certainly would if I could, do a little jobbery on your account. Signed, BB."

Churchill danced around their living room that evening in excitement. He waved the cable about.

"A member of the press, in a war," he said to Reggie. "This is Cuba all over again. I'm a bloody war correspondent!" Winston chortled with excitement.

"Yes, it is," Reggie agreed.

"Reggie, I need your help," Winston said sincerely.

Here it comes, Reggie thought.

"You are Colonel Ramsay's adjutant. I know there is no way he will let you go with me. But since you are on his staff, could you arrange a six-week leave for me?" he asked his friend.

Reggie let out a sigh of relief. "I suppose I could help out just a little," he said.

A week later, Churchill was on a 4,500 mile journey to join General Blood in the upper Swat Valley at his camp in Mingora. He travelled by steamship from England; through the Mediterranean Sea and the Suez Canal, finally arriving at Bombay on the Indian coast. Then he spent a week on the train, traveling through mountain passes, plains, and deserts. He wrote his mother a letter, acknowledging the dangers of his journey, but reminding her of his desire to take risks to gain popularity for public office.

The heat was stifling as he got closer to his destination. Finally, the train wound its way through the mountains and he reached his destination, a frightfully dirty and depressing little town called Nowshera.

The train engineer's eyes rolled as Winston unloaded his baggage. A lot of baggage. His "kit" was fully stocked with uniforms, clothing, cigars and brandy. He also had two horses and his tack. And finally, of course, he brought his manservant, Haj. After all, he was there on assignment and didn't have time to cook or clean.

Winston hired a carriage, and with his gear stowed and his horses in tow, set out on the nine-hour journey to the Malakand Pass and General Blood. As he traveled through the steep mountain passes and cascading terrain, he made verbal notes of his first articles for the Daily Telegraph in London, as well as the Allahabad Pioneer in New Delhi. He felt a great rush of exhilaration and excitement. Sweat dripped through his tunic, but he was too excited to care. This is a real adventure, he thought. This one should fetch me a very lovely medal indeed. A service medal and frontier medal at a minimum. A nice gong for the ride, he mused.

Finally, he reached the general's camp. He unloaded his gear and introduced himself to the general's adjutant, Lieutenant Victor Hughes.

"Winston Churchill," he said, shoving out his hand. "War correspondent on leave from the 4th Hussars," he said proudly.

The adjutant eyed him with dismay. How could one be with the other? You were either in the cavalry or worked for the newspaper, but he had no idea you could do both.

"Where is the general," Winston asked, looking around the camp.

"In the upper Swat valley," the adjutant replied. "He told me you were coming. We have a tent ready, and of course, you are now a member of the staff mess so you will be eating with the other officers. I see you have your man, so make yourself at home. I'm in the next tent over if you need anything," Hughes offered.

"See you at mess," Winston agreed. "Thanks." While his manservant was setting up his quarters, Winston took a stroll around the encampment.

It was set up by the book. He expected nothing less from General Blood. It was a giant square, with the men, animals, and artillery centered in the middle. All their tents, supplies, and ammunition were in the "safe zone." A defensive perimeter of trenches rimmed the outpost. It was a place to find shelter from "sniper" fire. On the other side of the trench were rows of concertina wire.

That evening Winston joined Lieutenant Hughes and the officers in the mess. The blistering heat was fading and would be soon replaced by the chilling cold. The extreme temperatures were new to him.

"Try some of this, mate," Hughes said, offering him a shot of scotch.

Winton recoiled as if bitten by a snake.

"Is it top shelf?" he asked. "I only drink the finest Scotch."

"Of course it is, mate. This is the drink of the British officer," Hughes laughed. "Down the hatch," he urged.

"Hmm," Winston growled. But the warm pull of the whiskey settled in nicely in his gut. He held out his glass to Hughes for more.

"I say, not bad, not half bad at all," Winston agreed.

He ate a good meal in the mess, and then sat back in a chair by his tent, smoking one of his Cuban's, sipping his scotch. He looked out at the brilliant stars above the camp. They were surrounded by an endless sea of mountain ranges capped with snow. He could see his breath in the air. Moonlight bounced off the crags and cliffs that surrounded him. This is indeed an adventure, he thought happily.

Haj came up to him. "Master, you need warm clothes. I have your bed ready," he said.

Winston took in a deep breath of the frigid mountain air. Blistering heat by day, freezing cold at night.

He snored loudly that night, drunk with both whiskey and his excitement. Haj slept in a bedroll on a mat at the foot of Winston's tent, exhausted.

Winston spent the next five days waiting for the general's return. General Blood had led a detachment north to punish the Pathan tribe, whom he believed was partially responsible for the attack on the British outposts. During those five days, Churchill took in as much information and scotch as he could absorb. And he could absorb a lot of both.

"We have approximately 7,000 soldiers here at the moment," Hughes briefed him. "Most of that is infantry, with about 700 cavalry troops. We also have 24 four field guns," he added proudly.

"An impressive show of force," Churchill noted. "How many are white?"

"I would say we have about a thousand British soldiers," Hughes answered. "Mostly with the Royal East and West Kent regiments and the 10th and 11th Bengal Lancers. The rest are Indian, mostly Punjabis."

Winston nodded. The Indian soldiers were fierce fighters and loyal to the empire. He felt his excitement growing.

"The enemy is comprised of several warlike tribes in the Mohmand Valley," Hughes said. "The valley is approximately a mile wide and ten miles long. The Watelai River runs down the middle. All of the tribes are Muslim, led by various mullahs and warlords. They believe they are fighting a holy war against us," he added. "They are merciless and take hostages only to torture them for information. Most of the time, they kill off the wounded," Hughes said.

"Remind me not to get captured," Winston said seriously.

"They are fierce fighters, and their tactics are cunning," Hughes continued. "They are well-armed with rifles, and they are excellent shots. We're having a devil of a time digging them out. They stay up in the mountains, using the high ground to their advantage, firing down on us."

"What tactics are we using in return?" Churchill asked. This was starting to sound like Cuba. Instead of hiding in the jungle the enemy was dug into the mountains.

"Slash and burn," Hughes replied. "Seek out their villages, burn them and their crops to the ground. Lure them into a firefight and kill off as many as we can. We are planning a strike into the valley as we speak, and will execute it if the general approves the plan."

Winston nodded his head sagely. "That's a mission I want to go on," he said.

Hughes looked at Churchill with disbelief but held his tongue in check. There had been a great deal of talk in the mess when Churchill wasn't present. After his exploits in Cuba, many officers labeled him as a "glory hound," and Hughes wasn't sure that they had missed the mark.

The next day, General Bindon Blood returned, riding into camp on his black stallion. He cut an impressive figure with his handlebar mustache and his dark brown eyes underneath his pith helmet. He went directly inside his tent and about an hour later, he summoned Churchill. Winston entered the tent and smiled at General Blood.

"Sir, a pleasure to see you again," Winston said.

Bindon Blood wrapped an arm around the skinny shoulders of his young friend and squeezed him.

"You too, young man. You too! I was sorry to hear about your father. He was a good friend of mine," Blood added warmly.

Churchill's face clouded. "It was a horrible loss," he lamented. He was still adjusting to his father's death.

"I know, and I'm sorry for your loss," the general sympathized. Then his voice picked up. "But now you are here, and I am putting you on my staff," the general proclaimed. "I am sending you out with Brigadier General Jeffreys and the 2d Brigade. He's leading a punitive raid on the villages in the Mohmand Valley. We're going to pay those little bastards back in spades for their attack on the brigade two nights ago. So gear up and be ready to move out," he said cheerfully.

Churchill's mood brightened considerably. "Outstanding, sir," he said smartly. They shook hands.

"And Churchill," the general added. "Be careful. This is some bloody intense fighting."

"Yes sir," Churchill said happily. At last! War! And a chance to prove my valor and earn a medal perhaps, he thought gaily. He ran back to his tent.

"Haji! Prepare me for war!" he ordered.

Mounted on his grey charger, Churchill rode proudly with his escort of Bengal Lancers to the 2d Brigade's position. He looked the part; the quintessential British cavalry officer replete with his swooping khaki topee, Sam Browne belt and spurred riding boots. The brigade was camped out on a plateau on the side of a mountain.

That night, he attended the officer's briefing in the command tent of the 2d Brigade. Lieutenant Colonel Thomas Goldney, the commander of the 35th Sikhs, gave the briefing.

"We are on a mission to teach these religious fanatics a lesson," Goldney began. "We will traverse the valley and destroy the villages of Badelai and Shahi-Tangi, here and here," he said, pointing to the map on the stand.

"Burn the villages, burn their crops, destroy their water supply and reservoirs, blow up any fortified buildings, and in general, wreak havoc and mayhem," he said. "You can expect sniper fire at all times, so be alert. We'll take three columns of men up the mountain. I will lead the center column."

"Do we have any intelligence on the number of tribesmen we might encounter?" Lieutenant Hughes asked.

"We don't know the exact numbers of Pathans in these two villages. I don't expect much resistance. They will most likely flee into the mountains and not return until we are gone," the colonel predicted.

"Damn it!" Churchill exclaimed.

"What?" the colonel asked.

"I'm spoiling for a fight," Churchill said eagerly. He didn't see the number of raised eyebrows in the tent.

"Be careful what you ask for," the colonel warned. What a naïve young man, he thought to himself. "The Pathans are fierce warriors. The mullahs have convinced them that they are fighting a holy war in the name of Islam. We are the infidel, the invaders. They want us dead. They use the word 'jihad' to describe their cause."

"Troublesome wretches," Churchill said.

"Dangerous fighters," countered the colonel.

"Yes sir," Churchill said smartly, proud to have contributed to the briefing.

Idiot, the colonel thought to himself.

Early the next morning, Churchill rode at the front of the column. Haj had laid out a clean and pressed khaki uniform. His pith helmet was polished, as were his Sam Browne belt and his leather boots. Winston dressed carefully. His lower legs, from ankle to knee were wrapped in leather gaiters. Strapped to his side was a model 1882 Webley-Wilkinson six-shot revolver. He also wore a thirty-inch long saber in its scabbard. He felt like a mighty warrior.

The journey into the valley was quiet, with no sign of the enemy. They would have to dismount and climb the last mile up to the villages. They split groups, and Churchill's group of Sikh soldiers reached the village in two and a half hours. It was a tough climb, and he felt the sweat dripping from his body.

When they finally reached the village, he was crestfallen. It was empty. He was with five British officers, including Lieutenant Hughes, Lieutenant Fincastle, and Captain Ian Smith. They had eighty-five soldiers with them. They set fire to the village, throwing torches in the mud huts. Three of the soldiers set a charge on the well at the center of the village and blew it to pieces.

"That's it then, mates," Captain Smith said with approval. "Time to leave."

As they turned to begin their descent, a shrill trill broke out above them, and suddenly heavy rifle fire opened upon them. They were sitting ducks in the village.

"I say, we're rather up in the air here," Smith said calmly. They dropped to the ground and began to return fire. Churchill could see they were outnumbered. So did the captain.

Churchill picked up a rifle next to him and started collecting cartridges that had fallen out of a wounded soldier's kit.

"Retreat, and quickly," Smith ordered.

Winston was determined to return fire. It saved his life. As eight men around him jumped to their feet flee, five of them were cut down instantly by a massive barrage of rifle fire. Winston continued to fire back, but when he saw the advancing tribesmen, he too got up and started back down the mountain.

Suddenly, Hughes cried out in pain and clutched his eye, blood spurting through his fingers.

Several of the Sikh soldiers picked Hughes off the ground and began to carry him out of the village. Churchill saw a dozen Pathan tribesmen leap out from behind the huts. The Sikhs panicked and dropped the lieutenant. Hughes let out a scream as the tribesmen got to him and hacked him to ribbons with their swords.

"Bastards!" Churchill cried out with rage.

One very large Pathan looked his way and advanced towards him, his sword dripping with Hughes's blood. Enraged, Churchill reached for his saber, but then had a better idea. Out came the revolver. He fired several shots into the advancing tribesman and dropped him like a rock. Winston turned and ran back down to where the others were waiting at a knoll below the village. They lay down covering fire for him, and he reached them safely.

"That was a tad bit hot," Churchill said, panting.

"Let's get the hell out of here," the captain agreed.

They ducked and ran down the mountain, shots firing all around them, plumes of dust spitting up around their feet. A bullet struck a young Sikh soldier, and his turban flew off with pieces of his skull. Another Sikh went down, and Churchill grabbed him by the collar, dragging him down the hill with him. The man was screaming in pain all the way. Must hurt, Churchill thought grimly, as he made his way down the mountain. But he got the man down the mountainside safely.

They finally reached the foot of the mountain and received covering fire from the embedded infantry there. The Pathans retreated into the mountain. Several hours later Lieutenant Colonel Goldney rode up with around three hundred men. They went back up the now deserted mountainside to gather up the wounded and the dead.

Later that evening, back at camp, they buried the dead in a solemn ceremony. Churchill looked down at the bodies wrapped in blood-soaked blankets. They had lost thirty men, including five officers. Eighteen more men were unaccounted for and presumed dead on the field of battle. No one expected them to remain alive. Churchill's normally boyish face was flushed and dirty. His uniform was splashed with blood. His hair was messed up, and he had pieces of flesh still on him from the bodies of other men. So this is war, he thought grimly, looking down at the dead.

The next day they broke camp and left the Mahmoud Valley. They burned every village, every field, and leveled every structure they came across. A great plume of smoke stood sentry over the valley as they made their way out and back to their camp at the Malakand Pass.

Later, before Winston came to mess, several of the officers recounted the battle at Shahi-Tangi. Churchill's actions the day before had not gone unnoticed. The fact that he had stood his ground when Hughes was hacked to death and was the last man out of the village gave the other officers new respect for the slight lieutenant with the famous name. The fact that he dragged a wounded Sikh soldier to safety also caught their attention.

When Winston entered the mess that evening, he was met with a newfound respect. He gained even more respect when he returned to England after writing an account of the Malakand Field Force for the *Daily Telegraph*. It was even a hit with the future king of England. Winston finally had blood on his hands. Randolph would have been proud.

CHAPTER FIFTY-SIX

IRELAND, 1897

Issac Parnell set down his copy of the Daily Telegraph.

"No fuckin' way," he fumed. The son of Randolph Churchill had become a celebrity. The Fenian s had been well-played by the well-healed.

Some things just weren't right. And this didn't sit right. The article in the Telegraph was about the adventures of Winston Churchill in the northwest frontier of Afghanistan. His dispatches seemed like he was out of breath – writing on the run.

It seemed entirely unfair to Issac. His family had been destroyed by the treachery of Randolph Churchill. His brother had been captured and murdered under the very same Sedition Bill that Randolph Churchill had promised his father would not pass. Churchill was a bloody hero and his brother Ben was dead. All because Churchill had a rich and famous father who unfortunately died several years earlier, or Issac would have assuredly killed him with his bare hands.

"Christ almighty" Issac cursed. He pulled on his top woolen coat and frayed wool cap and slammed the door behind him as he stepped into the bitter cold of an Irish winter night. He kept his head down, into the wind, as he made his way to Wrens Public House.

He felt the familiar warmth from the large stone hearth when he stepped inside. The smell of smoke and whiskey filled the air, along with the drunken chatter of red-faced workers. He searched the crowded room and saw the man he was looking for.

Michael. Joe Brady's son. The same Joe Brady who had been one of the masterminds behind the Phoenix Park murders sixteen years ago. Time had passed, and many more men had died in the cause. But Michael Brady and Issac Parnell were determined that they did not die in vain.

He sat down on an oak bench at the table near the hearth. Michael looked up from his pint of ale. No smile on his face. All business.

"Issac."

"Michael." They shook hands warmly.

"What mischief have you been up to lately?" Issac asked.

"Making new friends."

"Good friends?" Issac asked. He motioned to the pretty waitress. "I'll have a pint of whatever my friend is drinking," he ordered.

"Useful ones," Michael said. "Very useful ones. The War Office in London," he added.

Issac felt his body relax in the warmth of the room and drank deeply from his mug. He and Michael had been conspiring for years. They were both active members of the Fenian movement, determined to rid Ireland of the hated British army. They had made a pact to avenge their betrayal by Randolph Churchill. They had planned to kill Randolph himself, but the grim reaper beat them to it. But after his death, Issac thought of his brother's cold, lifeless body lying six feet under a pile of dirt, while Churchill's son was busy gallivanting around the world, writing about his exploits as if he were Jesus himself. His hatred for Winston Churchill burned stronger than the logs in the nearby hearth.

"There will be an expedition to Khartoum," Michael Brady said. "Lord Kitchener himself will be leading the expedition to avenge General Gordon's death."

"I've heard the talk. He is building a railroad from Cairo south to the Sudan," Issac replied. How ironic. They were in the same tavern where the Phoenix Park murders were conceived. He would be part of a new conspiracy to commit murder.

"Yes. They've already started," said Michael. "They are building a bloody train track from Cairo all the way to the Sudan," he marveled.

"This is a huge commitment by the government, and it will be very well-publicized."

"Yes it will," mused Issac. "I'm sure the press will be covering it like flies on shit," he added.

"One particular little shit, I'm sure," Michael said.

"Do we know where he is now?" Issac asked. He didn't need to say the name.

"India, I believe. He was posted there after Afghanistan." Michael looked around the crowded room. It was all the regular customers. "But he has apparently expressed an interest in the war office to join Kitchener's campaign," he added.

"Of course he would. And I dare say he will be successful," Issac agreed. "He's a fuckin' publicity hound just like his old man. He can't pass up a chance like this. I can see it now, his breathless dispatches from the Sudan, telling everyone how wonderful and brave he is."

"Our friends in the war office say that the general's staff is well-aware of Churchill's ambitions," Michael said. "It won't be easy for him to get on board."

"His mother would fuck Kitchener himself if she hasn't already," Issac hissed. "He'll go."

Michael nodded in agreement. "Yes. I agree. We have many of our people in the army. We'll make sure that they are posted to whatever regiment he joins."

"Do we make it look like a casualty of war, or do we make a statement?" Issac asked.

"We will have plans for both. As events unfold, they may dictate that themselves. But Winston Churchill must die, one way or another," Michael answered.

"Yes, that he must. And I hope it's a painful and prolonged death," Issac swore.

They clanked their mugs together in a toast and drank deeply.

CHAPTER FIFTY-SEVEN

LAKE CITY, 1897

Cora Baker ran happily down the path to the modest wooden home behind the town post office. Her younger brother Willie raced behind her. Cora was fast, and Willie was learning to his horror that his big sister could beat him in a footrace.

"Ha!" Cora laughed happily as she tagged the white picket fence surrounding her home. "Beat ya, beat ya beat ya," Cora taunted her younger brother.

"You did not," Willie protested. "You got a head start!"

Cora laughed again and reached down and rumpled Willie's hair.

"Okay, little brother," she said soothingly. "You won."

"I did I did I did," the seven-year-old cried out happily, bouncing and spinning around on his feet like a top at high speed. She took his hand and together they walked up the short dirt path to their house. Their mother, Lavinia, heard the ruckus and was already pouring a cold glass of water for each child. She feigned surprise when her children bounced happily into the kitchen.

"Mommy, mommy," Willie yelled happily. "I beat sister in a foot race."

His eleven-year-old sister looked at her little brother with nothing but love in her heart. His bright brown eyes were so proud. She loved him too much to set the record straight. She could always tell her mother later. She liked seeing her little brother happy.

"He won," she agreed happily. Her little brother stuck his tongue out at her.

"Well aren't you the fastest little boy in the world," Lavinia said. "Now drink your water and then go wash up," she instructed. She had already heated some water and it stood ready with a bar of soap in an iron tub at one end of the kitchen.

"Cora, your father brought home a chicken today," Lavinia said proudly. "I cut off its head and it's hanging upside down by its feet on the line. I need you to pluck it and clean it for me," she said.

Cora wrinkled her nose. She hated that chore. But at least she didn't have to chop its head off. One time a chicken got up off the stump without its head and ran around the yard. She shuddered as she remembered the sight.

"I'm making dumplings," Lavinia said. "So don't dilly dally. I want to have supper ready when your father gets home from work," she said proudly.

Lavinia was very proud of her man. Not every woman got to be married to a postmaster. Her husband was a federal employee. An officer of the United States government no less. Her husband was a very important man, in charge of the post office in Lake City, South Carolina. He got paid every week to prove it.

Later that evening, Postmaster Frazier Baker closed the door of the post office, fixed his collar, and began his short walk to his home in back of the post office. It was February, cold, and already dark. Three-day old snow lay in patches on the ground, hardened and slick. A gas light glowed faintly in the darkness. Frazier stepped carefully. He didn't want to slip on the ice.

He heard footsteps running up behind him. He tried to turn, but in his haste, one foot slid out from under him on an icy patch. He fell to the ground.

"Get up, nigger!" a voice yelled.

Frazier Baker, the first black postmaster in the history of Lake City, South Carolina struggled to his feet.

"What is the problem?" he asked. "It's me, the postmaster," he said, fear in his voice. He knew that there had been quite the uproar when he had been appointed. Most of the people in Lake City were white, and they didn't like a black man in charge of their mail.

"You're the problem, Frazier," a voice said in the darkness.

Frazier turned and ran as fast as he could for the door of his home. Lavinia had heard the commotion outside and opened the door. He rushed into the house and slammed the door behind him.

"Gather the children!" he yelled to his wife.

"Burn the place down!" a voice called out.

Frazier peaked around a curtain and looked out the window. There was a mob of white people outside the house, carrying torches and yelling. Some of the men wore hoods. He saw rifles, and quickly let the curtain close. They were surrounded.

Flames shot up from the shed behind their house.

"Oh my god!" he exclaimed.

"Frazier, Frazier, what should we do?" Lavinia called out.

"Put out the damn fire!" he roared. He grabbed a bucket and headed to the back door of the kitchen. The pump was outside.

Lavinia followed his lead, with baby Julia in her arms.

The loud burst of a rifle was followed by several more shots from different locations, and to her horror, Lavinia saw Frazier drop to the ground in a heap.

"Frazier!" she cried out. The air around her erupted in gunfire and the wooden frame of the house began to shudder under the impact. One slug tore through her right hand, striking baby Julia in the head. The blast ripped the baby from her arms and at the same time Lavinia felt the burning impact of lead in her leg. Both she and the baby fell to the ground.

"Sister, sister!" Willie cried out in horror as bullets passed, whizzing through the house.

"Willie, get down!" Cora screamed. She threw herself on top of her little brother, just in time to take a bullet to her back.

More gunfire erupted. The attackers were ignorant of the frightened screams of little children. The house erupted into a fireball. Cora could only lie on top of Willie trying to shield him from the flames. Suddenly she felt a hand grab her by the collar and her fourteen-year-old sister Rosa pulled her and Willie out the front door into the street.

The street was ablaze with light from the burning house. The mob was gone. Rosa looked around in horror. She could hear her mother's cries, and she ran around the corner of the house. She saw her father lying on the ground, a crumpled, bloody heap.

"Poppa!" she cried out. She saw the blood pumping out of her mother's leg. She was torn between which one to aid first. Something told her it was too late to save her father, so she ran to her mother's side.

"Why, why, why?" Lavinia cried out. Her eyes fixed on baby Julia, who lay dead in a bundle on the porch. Her little white blanket was now red with blood.

Chapter Fifty-Eight

Washington D.C., 1897

K ip pulled up the collar of his greatcoat and turned his back to the wind as he got out of the carriage in front of the White House. It was a cold grey afternoon and smoke billowed out from chimneys on the brick townhouses that lined Pennsylvania Avenue. There was snow on the ground.

He had been to the White House before, but not alone. He had received a note signed by General Hanson. He took the first hired hansom that drove by his office building.

He checked in with the guards at the back gate, presenting his credentials and the written order. He waited while one of the sentries went inside to verify his credentials and his invitation. The sergeant came back and saluted him briskly.

"This way, sir," he said. Kip followed him inside the staff entrance to the White House, grateful to be out of the freezing cold. He followed the guard through the grand hallway and into the main briefing room. He felt a moment of relief when he saw General Hanson's face. But he also felt his heart pounding at the stress of such an important summons.

"Take a seat, Major," General Hanson said, pointing to a leather chair at the long cherry conference table that took up the center of the room. Kip did as he was told and then looked around the room. A comfortable fire in the stone hearth warmed the room.

"Gentlemen, the President of the United States," the sergeant-at-arms called out. Everyone in the room came to attention.

President William McKinley walked through the doorway from the Oval Office into the briefing room.

"Take your seats, gentlemen," the president said as he settled his large frame into his leather chair.

"Proceed, James," he directed.

James Gary, the United States postmaster general, cleared his throat. A stout man, his most noticeable feature was his enormous white beard. With his bushy white eyebrows, he would have made the perfect Santa Claus. He had ten children and had spent his life building a fortune in the textile business. He had run for governor of Maryland ten years earlier but had lost. He was a very devout man, and he looked distraught.

"Sir, as you know, at the urging of many Republican leaders, we were able to secure the appointment of Frazier Baker as postmaster of the small town of Lake City, South Carolina. It has been a long-standing practice of our party to move colored people into positions of responsibility as part of the Reconstruction," he began.

"Unfortunately, the citizens of Lake City did not share the same enthusiasm as the Republican Party," interrupted Joseph McKenna, the Attorney General of the United States.

"Yes, so I understand," said the president. "Please, continue James."

"Mr. Baker was murdered by a mob. So was his infant child. His wife and their surviving three children were injured," Gary briefed.

"And who was the mob?" inquired the president.

"We don't know, sir," McKenna interjected.

"We believe it was a group of white citizens," Gary countered.

"Initial reports say it *may* have been, but it was dark and no one was identified," McKenna said tersely. "For all we know it could have been a group of disgruntled niggers who were jealous that Frazier got the job and they didn't."

"What has local law enforcement learned?" the president asked, ignoring the attorney general.

"No one is talking," Gary said.

"That could be because no one knows anything, couldn't it?" McKenna said. "If there are no witnesses, then no one would be talking, would they? Because if they were talking, and they weren't witnesses, they would be making up evidence, correct?" McKenna was a former prosecutor.

Kip sat at the table and tried not to let his face show any emotion. If he had heard the attorney general correctly, he was making an argument that since no one was talking, there were no witnesses. Of course, that was a completely illogical assumption. More likely, witnesses were not talking because they didn't want to get murdered too.

Several of the other cabinet members echoed their approval of McKenna's argument.

"Who was in charge of the initial investigation ?" the president inquired.

"The town marshal, of course," said Gary.

"Patrick Alexander is a capable lawman," McKenna said. "And he worked hand-in-hand with the Williamsburg County Sheriff, Mortimor Crow," he added.

"I see," said the president. "Is the investigation ongoing?"

"No sir," McKenna said. "Without any witnesses, there is nothing left to investigate."

Kip could tell the president was troubled. When he was Governor of Ohio, McKinley had spoken out against the practice of lynching in America. Although lynching had been a time-honored tradition for horse thieves and cattle rustlers, it was becoming an increasingly common outlet for white anger against black citizens. McKinley was no civil rights advocate, but he was well aware that white Democrats were eager to regain power in the south following the Reconstruction. The Democrats were using paramilitary groups to dissuade black Republicans from voting.

"I see," the president said. "Gentlemen, this meeting is adjourned."

The president stood up and the room immediately snapped to attention. As the various cabinet members and staff filed out of the room, the president motioned to General Hanson.

"General Hanson and Major McDuran, if you would be kind enough to please remain behind, I have some follow-up questions concerning Cuba," the president said. The sergeant-at-arms closed the door.

"Take your seats, gentlemen," the president instructed. "Major, I commend you for the work you did in Cuba. President Cleveland spoke highly of you. You have a keen eye, good ears, and you keep your mouth shut. Unlike Mister Churchill, who reported his glorious exploits to the press and anyone else who would listen," smiled the president. "Your insight in Cuba was of great value to the United States." the president said sincerely.

"Thank you, sir," Kip answered. So why am I here? Kip wondered to himself.

"So you are probably wondering why you are here," the president said.

"Is he a mind reader?" Kip thought.

"The murder of any federal official appointed by the president is a serious matter. I gave that man his job, and I do not appreciate him and his family being butchered because of my attempt to make this country better off. Nor can I ignore the fact that little, if anything, has been done to bring the killers to justice. Nor can I ignore the reality that certain federal officials don't either have the stomach or the desire to answer that question," the president said gravely.

"I appointed that man, and as a result of my actions, he is dead. I need an unbiased and unprejudiced opinion as to what took place down there so I can direct traffic here in Washington. The Justice Department needs a kick in the ass and I intend to do it. But I need some evidence," he directed.

General Hanson joined the discussion.

"Kip, this assignment will put your life in jeopardy. Racial hatred and bigotry run deep in this country, even in Washington. I have told the president that you can be trusted to get to the truth, no matter how painful it may be. And that's what we are asking for. The truth."

"Yes sir. I will do my best," Kip said. "But," then he bit his tongue.

"But what?" asked the president.

General Hanson's face looked as if he was going to throttle Kip right there at the conference table. It was one of his protégé's notable attributes to ask intelligent, insightful questions, but did he have to question the goddamn president of the United States? General Hanson always said that if Kip had an argument with God, he would state his case.

"Why not send a civilian, a member of the justice department?" Kip asked.

"Because the justice department does not share my displeasure," the president answered honestly. "Son, you ever heard of Senator Benjamin Tillman?"

"Pitchfork Tillman?" Kip quipped. "Yes sir."

"Well, in addition to being an outspoken critic in favor of white supremacy and lynching, he is also a member of the Democratic party. The other party," the president said forcefully. "You do know who I'm talking about, don't you Major?" he asked, his voice rising.

Here we go, General Hanson thought.

"Sir, if I'm not mistaken, Senator Tillman was the leader of the Red Shirts at the massacre of Hamburg."

"Enlighten me, Major," the president said.

"Sir, in 1876, a group of Negroes marched through the streets of Hamburg, South Carolina. They were being led by Captain Doc Adams and were drilling in uniform as members of the National Guard. It is alleged that they purposefully blocked the main street of the town as an act of defiance to the white people in the town."

The president smiled. "General Hanson did say that you were smarter than both of us. So what happened, Major?"

"The white citizens formed their own militia and ordered the National Guard to turn over their weapons. When they refused, a paramilitary conflict took place and a lot of people were killed, both black and white," Kip said.

"Correct, Major," said the president. "And who investigated the incident?" he quizzed.

"Sir, that incident was investigated by Attorney General Joseph McKenna," Kip answered truthfully.

"And was anyone ever charged with a crime ?" the president asked.

"No sir," Kip replied.

"And who claimed to be the leader of the white folk's militia?"

"The senator. 'Pitchfork,'" Kip deadpanned.

"That's right, Major," the president said sarcastically. The same 'Pitchfork' who is now a sitting United States senator, and, coincidentally, considers himself my successor. He became the governor of South Carolina by playing upon the fears of white southerners, and he sure as hell is going to try to get elected president of the United States by continuing to do so. He also happens to be Chairman of the Senate's Oversight Committee, which oversees the Attorney General's Office. "Senator Tillman was quoted as saying that Baker's death was *understandable* given the proud people of Lake City didn't want their mail delivered by a nigger," the president continued, and not too softly.

"I read about the senator's unfortunate remarks," Kip said.

"A lot of people did," said the president. "And if you think anyone from the attorney general's office is going to give me the straight skinny, you are full of shit. The bottom line here is there is a political war taking place in Washington, and my enemies in the Democratic Party have no intention of letting the blacks get to vote," President McKinley continued, incensed.

"And Tillman is going to make sure that never happens, even if it's over my dead body, which I'm sure he would like to see. So get your ass down there and let me know what in the name of God is going on!" the president thundered.

"And by the way," General Hanson added. "You *will* be under the guise of a civilian investigator from the justice department. You and I will have a further briefing at my office this afternoon to work out the details," General Hanson advised Kip.

"You are excused until then," Hanson said.

"Yes sir," Kip answered, snapping to his feet at attention.

"Safe journey, Major," the president said. "And if you need to kick a little ass to get the job done, you have my full support," he instructed. "This will not happen again on my watch," the president said angrily. "I want heads!"

"Yes sir," Kip replied. He walked out of the conference room with the weight of the world on his shoulders.

The irony of the situation was not lost on him. He was a murderer investigating a group of murderers. Who better to give chase? *If I had it all over again, I would love to kill those miserable bastards Larkin and Rodriguez. Give me the chance,* he swore to himself. *I'd take it. I'd even do it three times if I could.*

After Kip left the room, the president turned to General Hanson.

"John, explain to the major that in addition to answers, I want an example set," he said.

"How much of an example, sir?" General Hanson asked politely.

"Unforgettable," said the president.

CHAPTER FIFTY-NINE

LAKE CITY, 1897

Sheriff Mortimor Crow set the telegram down on his desk and sighed. He was a small man, slight of build, with gentle, feminine hands and features. Crow would have made a pretty woman but for having been born a man. But what he lacked in size, he made up for in ambition. Crow was a climber. If he thought he could get what he wanted by using your back to boost himself, he wouldn't think twice. It was how he rose to power as the sheriff of Williamsburg County. And he wasn't planning on stopping there. And that was why the death of Frazier Baker was causing him a great deal of concern.

The telegram stated he was to give his full cooperation to a federal investigator. Some dick named Gardner. The order was from the justice department. And he was arriving by train today.

"Deputy Peak!" the sheriff called out.

Peak immediately popped into his chief's office.

"What's up, boss man?" Peak asked.

"Get over to Chief Alexander's office and tell him we got a visitor coming and I need to talk to him, now," he ordered.

Crow could have walked over to the police station to speak with Alexander himself, but he knew that by summoning Alexander to his office he was continuing to establish his power over the police chief. Power was very important to Crow. He obsessed about it.

Chief Alexander was none too happy when Deputy Peak walked into his office and passed along the invitation to speak with the sheriff. But if he insisted that the sheriff come to him, as opposed to the other way around, he would appear petty and weak. Petty county politics.

"Tell him I'll be there in an hour," Alexander growled. He was a big man, heavy, with a round head and a prematurely balding scalp. But he had soft brown eyes and a kind heart that he masked with his gruffness.

"I'll make the bastard wait," Alexander decided.

An hour later he walked into the sheriff's office and hung his hat on the wooden peg rack just inside the front door. Deputy Peak was seated at his desk just outside Crow's office. Alexander knew that Peak was a lackey. A born ass-kisser. But like all ass-kissers, you didn't turn your back on them. That's when they are the most dangerous.

Alexander walked over to Crow's door and stuck his head inside. "You wanted to chat, Mort?"

Crow grinned broadly and waved the chief into his office, motioning to the chair set in front of his desk. He won!

Alexander wanted to roll his eyes, but he sat down in front of Crow's desk.

Crow's face grew serious as he handed Alexander the telegram. Alexander looked it over, and his face became concerned.

"We don't need this," he said solemnly.

"I agree," Crow replied. "But the question is, what, if anything, can we do about it?"

As Alexander sat there silent, thinking, Crow felt his impatience growing. He wanted an answer, and he wanted it now. Alexander was just too slow, Crow thought. Which was why Alexander was *only* the chief of police and not the sheriff.

"He's going to be asking a lot of questions," Alexander began carefully. "Not only about the investigation. He's going to want to know about the grand jury as well."

Crow nodded his head in agreement. "Precisely what I was thinking," he lied. "We need to talk to the district attorney. We all need to be on the same page," he said.

Alexander looked at him quizzically. "I thought we already were?" he said.

"Yeah, but we got to be precise," Crow said excitedly. "I want that snooping dick out of here in no time, because we've got nothing to hide, and the sooner those bastards in Washington hear that they'll leave us the fuck alone. We don't need their help, and we sure as hell don't need them acting like we can't do our jobs."

"Right," Alexander agreed. Sheriff Crow was right about that. Besides, all Alexander could think about was the dinner he knew his wife was fixing. Fried chicken, mashed potatoes, apple pie and ice cream. Alexander loved food almost as much as he loved his wife.

"So what do you propose?" Alexander asked.

Crow let out a sigh of exasperation. "Get over to the DA's office and let him know we need to meet, now. Best to hold it here at my office," Crow said.

"Right," Alexander agreed. He got to his feet and paused before walking. Both of his knees had been torn up playing football, and they ached. The extra hundred pounds he carried didn't ease the workload on his knees either. Alexander walked across the street to the Williamsburg County District Attorney's office. This was getting way out of hand.

Wanda Smith sat guard at her desk. No one went in to see her boss without her permission. She was the gatekeeper. The only people that went into her boss's office were people the district attorney wanted to speak to, and her boss hadn't said shit about wanting to talk to the chief of police, so he wasn't going to.

"I'm sorry, Chief Alexander," Wanda apologized. "But Mr. Ludwig is in a meeting," she lied.

"Wanda, I know this is the spur of the moment, but it's important," he insisted.

"I'm sorry, chief," she said. "I'll let him know you stopped by."

Alexander felt his blood pressure elevate.

"Wanda," he said calmly. "If you sit on this until later, you won't have a job," Alexander said honestly.

Wanda felt both offended and threatened at the same time. Alexander was a big man, but she was an enormous woman.

"Are you threatening me, Patrick Alexander?" she snarled. Patrick had been a bully in grade school. She didn't take it then and she wasn't going to take it now.

"Jesus, Wanda, no," Alexander said, backing down. "I mean this is serious. Mr. Ludwig will have both of our heads if he doesn't learn about this right now." He handed her the yellow telegram.

Wanda looked down at the telegram and saw that it was from Washington.

"I'll be right back," she said. She lumbered into her boss's office.

The Honorable David Ludwig, the District Attorney of Williamsburg County, sat behind his desk with his feet propped up, reading yesterday's edition of the Williamsburg County Record. Ludwig was an elected county official and elections were coming up the next year. He liked his job and had no intention of losing it. And this whole lynching thing had gotten entirely out of hand.

The editorial section of the Record was calling the postmaster's murder "the darkest blot on South Carolina's history." Which was easy for them to say. Because they knew damn good and well that "lynching" had been around for a long time, Ludwig thought. Hell, lynching was almost as American as apple pie.

The truth was, Ludwig had seen more than one lynching in his day, and most of the time it was well-deserved. He approved of vigilante justice. Who had the time to investigate every white cattle rustler or horse thief? If they had possession of the cow or the horse, that was evidence enough. Who had time for a trial? Why should it be any different for an uppity nigger? String the bastards up, Ludwig thought. After all, the land and everything on it belonged to the folks that owned it. And even though the folks up north thought that a nigger was a person, he didn't have to. So long as no one knew. And he made sure no one knew his prejudice.

He had already convened a grand jury in secret. No one had seen anything and he had a court reporter's sworn transcript to prove it. Ludwig was a political animal who worked closely with the United States Senator, 'Pitchfork' Tillman.

"Mr. Ludwig, Chief Alexander is outside your office, and he says he needs to speak with you," Wanda explained.

Ludwig held up his hand to cut her off. "Christ, Wanda, you know no one is to see me without an appointment first," he growled.

Wanda thought about slapping his arrogant face but decided she didn't want to lose her job. Instead, she handed him the yellow piece of paper. Ludwig snatched it out of her hand and read it with a scowl. She saw his jaw clench when he set it down.

"Tell Crow to get over to my office now," he ordered. "And have him bring his good-for-nothing kiss-ass deputy with him."

"Yes sir," she said. She went out to her office and called out for her assistant, Nancy.

"Nancy, run over to Sheriff Crow's office and tell him Mr. Ludwig wants to meet with him and Deputy Peak right now," Wanda ordered. She arched her eyebrows and sat back down in her chair in a huff. Men, she thought. Now they were going to do the dick dance of death to see who had the bigger prick. They are all pricks, she groused. But just the same, I'd better make a fresh pot of coffee.

"I'll wait," Alexander said.

That afternoon, while Ludwig held court in his office, Kip was seated comfortably in the first-class club car headed south to Charleston. He had paid for the upgrade out of his own money. Actually, it was Jacks's money, to be precise. It was hard to get used to the fact that he was rich.

He reviewed the file with the reports made during a previous investigation. His instincts told him the answer was right in front of him, in the reports. No one had asked the right questions.

Williamsburg County was sixty-three percent black, but Lake City was ninety-nine percent white. Most of the white people in Lake City were not happy that the power and prestige of the position of postmaster had been handed to a black man. The mail, along with the newspaper, was how Americans communicated with each other. The concerned citizens held a town meeting. The whites decided to boycott the post office and start up their own mail service with the neighboring county. When Washington heard about their discontent and the upcoming boycott, they sent postal inspector Bruce Butler to Lake City to investigate.

Butler's report stated that after conferring with District Attorney Ludwig and the sheriff, Ludwig later met with him privately. During that conversation Ludwig told him that the postmaster, Frazier Baker, was a member of the Colored Farmers' Alliance, and had intentionally cut mail delivery from three times a day to one time a day.

According to Ludwig, Baker used the excuse that cutting delivery from three times a day to one made it easier for him to get all the mail out in one day. But the townsfolk knew better, Ludwig had suggested. He told Butler that Frazier Baker wanted to throttle the white man's communication with the rest of the country. When Butler asked for proof, Ludwig supplied him with a police report from Deputy Peak. He had a statement from Henry Stokes. Stokes said that according to one of his house servants, Baker was planning revenge on all the white people in Lake City. He also was planning to rape some of the white women.

Butler returned to Washington with his report and Stokes's statement. His recommendation was to shut down the Lake City post office and move it out of town. Let the good people of Lake City have their own private mail service if they wanted to pay for it.

A month later, Baker was dead, and there were no witnesses.

Senator Tillman spoke glowingly of the hard work of the investigators following the murders and singled out both Ludwig and Crow, praising them for their intense and honest investigation and their sage and wise leadership through a difficult time.

Butler, now back in Washington, joined the crowd, and opined that although he couldn't prove it, he thought that the Colored Farmers' Alliance had killed Baker because he wasn't doing enough to make life terrible for the white man. Senator Tillman made sure Butler got a promotion.

The Democrats were pleased. But the president was not. "Unforgettable," was the word General Hanson used. An example had to be made.

Kip closed the file and ran his hand through his hair. He watched the countryside roll past his window. Kip had not spent any time with Negroes. There had been some mulattos in Cuba, but he hadn't given it any thought. There were no black people in Monterey and none at West Point. He had read about slavery and the deep prejudice against the black man in the South. But Kip had not seen it with his own eyes.

Kip was all too familiar with the plight of the Orientals, having witnessed the murder of Chow Lin at the hands of the white man. And his father had been murdered because he had tried to help the Orientals.

Kip saw little distinction between what happened in Monterey and Chivington's raid. Both had taught him all he needed to know about the slaughter and conquest of the red man and the yellow man. It repulsed him, along with the use of the Christian religion to justify the slaughter.

Slavery was no different in his mind. The black man had suffered the same fate as the red man and the yellow man in America. And for that fact, the brown man had been kicked out of California and Texas for good measure. The white man wasn't about to share power.

Which put Kip in an awkward position. He was a white man. But because of his childhood and life experiences, he didn't see color. He saw attitudes, bias, and most of all, tribalism. And it bothered him.

For everything that made America great, tribalism was its Achilles' heel. The love and safety of family was a tradition. The traditions of the family came from the tribe. But then, so did the culture of the tribe. And those teachings, whether they came from a white man, red man, brown man or yellow man were fraught with superstition, fear, bias, hatred and a desire to conquer.

In Kip's eyes, if you coupled tribalism with the abuse of religion and power, the human race was quite pathetic and uncivilized.

He had learned life's cruel lessons at a very early age, and he never forgot those lessons. He had raised himself up and survived his parent's death by stealing and struggling. Only to be saved by the kindness of a member of his tribe.

And so the circle goes, Kip thought, just like the endless line of trees whizzing by his window. He was headed deep into the heart of the white man's tribe. They would be none too happy with his arrival. Of that he was sure.

Chapter Sixty

LAKE CITY, 1897

Deputy Peak met Kip at the station. He was holding up a small sign with the name Randy Gardner on it. The deputy had weepy green eyes set above a large dirty brown mustache.

"You must be Mr. Gardner," Peak said, holding out his hand.

"I am," Kip said. "Randy Gardner, a pleasure to meet you."

"Same here," the deputy lied. "We always love a visit from folks in Washington."

"Do you get a lot?" Kip asked innocently.

"Not since General Sherman came down and wiped us out," Peak joked. He started laughing.

"Just a little Southern humor," Peak said. He couldn't stop laughing. "Love to tell that one to Yankees."

Apparently extremely nervous, Kip thought to himself.

"So how do you like being a federal investigator, Mr. Gardner?" Deputy Peak asked. His eyes were squinting, but the sun wasn't out. Peak was already jealous. He was sure he could be one too, if he wanted.

"Love it," Kip replied. He took his bag off the luggage rack. "You got a carriage or are we walking?" he asked.

"Right this way," Peak said, still amused at his joke. "Sheriff said to tell you that it's yours as long as you are down here," he added.

"I appreciate that," Kip said. "Going to need a horse as well," he added.

"Why?" Deputy Peak asked. His face grew suspicious.

"Going to be interviewing a lot of witnesses," Kip said.

"Weren't none," Peak said helpfully.

"Still going to need a horse, deputy," Kip said.

"I'll check with Sheriff Crow," Peak replied. "He only okayed a buggy."

Kip stepped up to the boot of the carriage and set his bag down.

"Deputy Peak," Kip started, but then he paused. He was already irritated. Next thing you know he was going to have to ask permission to go to the bathroom.

"Never mind. I can hire one at the livery stable. Thanks for meeting me with the horse and buggy," Kip said pleasantly, emotions under control.

"Sir, Sheriff Crow wanted me to stay with you and show you around the town," Deputy Peak protested.

I'm sure he did, Kip thought. No doubt they would love to know what he was up to.

"No need, deputy," Kip answered. "I've got a map," he motioned to his breast pocket.

"Well," Peak stammered. He was frustrated that the federal lawman was not cooperating with him. That was not very polite at all. Were all Yankees so rude?

"Do you know where you're going to be staying? I've reserved a room for you at the Wilderness Lodge. It's nice," Peak added.

"Thanks, deputy, but I already have a reservation," Kip said. "Thanks for meeting me. Please tell Sheriff Crow I look forward to meeting with him. I'll drop by later this afternoon after I get washed up," Kip said.

"Oh, golly, of course," Peak said. He was supposed to escort the lawman over to the sheriff's office as soon as he got to town.

"Sir, the sheriff was hoping to meet with you as soon as you arrived," the deputy advised Kip.

"Tell the sheriff I said thanks. I will stop by, but I need some time to wash up," Kip said firmly. "Have a pleasant day, deputy," he said.

Kip shook the reins, and the horse began to draw the carriage down the dirt street. Deputy Peak glared after him and then walked briskly towards his office.

Kip parked his carriage in front of the Charlotte Inn and went inside the old brownstone structure. He walked up to the registration desk and presented his identification to the elderly attendant.

"Do you have any mail for me?" Kip asked.

The attendant looked through a folder on his desk.

"No sir, Mr. Gardner," he replied. He looked at Kip sourly. "Yankee investigator, eh?"

"Yes," Kip said.

"What are you investigating?" the old man pressed.

Kip smiled. "When I figure it out, you'll be the first to know," he whispered.

The old man's bushy eyebrows went up.

"Room 3, second floor," he said to Kip.

"Thanks," Kip said. He took the key and walked over to the bellman's desk on the other side of the lobby. An older black man sat behind a desk, wearing a traditional blue bellman's uniform with white gloves.

"Got luggage in my carriage out front," Kip said. "Can you give me a hand?" he asked.

George Walker eyed the tall, good-looking young white man standing in front of him. He couldn't quite place the accent. George flashed an enormous grin and hopped to his feet.

"Yes, sir," he agreed. "I'll follow you, sir." They went outside to Kip's carriage.

Kip pointed out his carriage. "If you'd be kind enough to park that too, I'd appreciate it," Kip said. He handed George a nickel. George smiled happily.

"Will you be needing anything else, sir?" George asked.

Kip held out his hand. "Gardner, Randy Garner," he said. They shook hands.

"George Walker," the bellman said.

"Nice to meet you, George," Kip said. "What's the best livery in town?" he asked.

"Most white folks go to Newham and Son's," George said quickly.

Kip tried to figure out how old George was. Probably in his fifties, he decided, though he carried it well. George was a big man, and packed a lot of muscle underneath that bellman's uniform, Kip thought.

"Where do most black folk go?" Kip asked.

The question caught George off guard. So did the fact that Kip's eyes were locked on his. Most white men had a problem looking a Negro in the eye. George knew it was fear. But not this white man.

"Well, you know, Peter Jefferson has a stable down the road. But it's quite a ways from here," George said.

"Thanks," Kip replied. He turned and walked across the street.

George watched him, wondering what the man was up to. A few minutes later, as he finished parking Kip's carriage, he saw Kip riding away from the livery stable. Wonder where he's headed? George thought to himself.

Kip rode to the edge of town, to Peter Jefferson's modest stable. Jefferson was also an older black man, who was busy trying to calm a cantankerous mare who was throwing a snit.

"Easy baby," Jefferson called gently while maintaining control of the reins. The horse's eyes were upset. Kip saw a lot of white in her eyes.

"What upset her," Kip asked. He dismounted his horse and tied it to the hitching post.

"Not sure," Jefferson replied, never taking his eyes off the horse. "Easy Miss Milly," he gentled. After a few moments, the horse settled. Jefferson turned to face Kip.

"What can I do for you, sir?" he asked.

"My name is Randy Gardner," Kip answered. "I was hoping to speak with you for a few minutes," he said.

"What about?" Jefferson asked.

"The postmaster," Kip said evenly, watching Jefferson's face and eyes.

Jefferson winced. "Don't know what you are talking about, sir," he said.

"I'm with the federal government, Mr. Jefferson," Kip said. He handed him his identification card.

"A man could get killed talking to a Yankee investigator," Jefferson said. He handed the card back to Kip.

"Especially a Negro talking to a Yankee investigator."

"I'm going to be talking to a lot of Negroes," Kip said honestly. "They can't kill all of you."

"Yes they can," Jefferson said without a pause. "And their families too."

"Like they did Frazier Baker?" Kip asked.

Jefferson looked away.

"Don't know nothing about that," he said. "Please, mister. Just you talking to me now is enough to get me killed," he begged.

Kip saw fear in the man's face.

"Only because you know something," Kip pressed.

"No sir," Jefferson said. "I don't know anything, sir. Please, I'm begging you. Leave now. They'll kill you too if they catch you snooping around," Jefferson pleaded.

"Give me a name, and I'll leave now," Kip said.

"Mary Walker," Jefferson whispered.

"She related to the bellman, George Walker?" Kip asked.

"His wife, sir. Now leave me alone, please."

Kip nodded his head. "Okay. Thanks. Don't worry. You didn't know anything," Kip smiled.

Jefferson grumbled and walked back to the barn.

Kip rode back to the center of town and tied his horse up outside the Office of the District Attorney. The brick building had a brass plaque on the front. Kip pushed the door open and went into the lobby. A pretty woman with brown hair and big brown eyes sat behind a window.

"May I help you, sir?" she asked while she busied herself shuffling papers.

"My name is Randy Gardner," Kip said. He slid his identification through the slot at the bottom of the window. She looked over the identification.

"Very impressive, Mister Gardner," she said. "I'll be right back." She got up from her desk and walked down the small corridor. Minutes later she reappeared.

"Mr. Ludwig asks that you wait a few minutes," she said smiling.

"Of course he did," Kip smiled. He took a seat in the small lobby.

Ten minutes later a rather short, stocky man with dramatic silver hair but a youthful face stepped into the lobby. He smiled at Kip.

"Mr. Gardner," he said confidently.

"Mr. Ludwig," Kip smiled.

"A pleasure to meet you," Ludwig grinned, holding out his hand. His eyes said otherwise.

"Pleasure is mine," Kip said. "Thanks for taking time from your busy schedule to meet with me."

"No problem," Ludwig said, motioning Kip to follow him through the open door. "Let's go to my conference room," he led. "I've got some other people that want to meet you as well."

Kip followed him down the hallway lined with portraits of past district attorneys staring somberly down on all who passed. They walked into the conference room and Kip saw three men seated at the table. They all stood up when he walked into the room.

"Mr. Gardner, this is Sheriff Mortimor Crow," Ludwig introduced him. They shook hands. Kip noticed that the sheriff's grip was a little limp, almost feminine. Odd for a cop, Kip thought.

"Chief Alexander, our town's chief of police," Ludwig said, continuing the introductions. "And Deputy Peak," he said. They shook hands.

"We've already met," Kip said to Peak. "Thanks again for the carriage."

Ludwig took a seat at the head of the table. Kip noted that the others waited to sit down until Ludwig had taken his seat.

"The telegram from Washington asked us to help you out in your investigation," Ludwig began. "So here we are. What can we do to help?" he asked.

"A list of witnesses would be nice," Kip said.

Crow burst out into laughter and slapped his knee.

"Good one," Crow laughed. Peak had waited to see how his boss reacted and then he laughed too.

Ludwig, however, was not amused.

"Unfortunately, there were no witnesses," Ludwig said. He made a fist and softly pounded the table.

"I wish the hell we had some," he said earnestly. Crow nodded his head in agreement; Peak followed suit. Alexander just sat stone-faced.

"The postal inspector's report says differently," Kip bluffed.

Ludwig smiled. "Did it provide any names?" He had a calm demeanor. Too calm.

"Not that I can share at this point," Kip answered.

"Shouldn't we be working together?" Crow said smoothly. "I mean, what do you think the people will think if they knew that the federal government was keeping secrets from local law enforcement?"

"I don't give a shit," Kip answered evenly. "That's the way it works."

There was an awkward pause in the conference room. Kip knew that he would get no help from local law enforcement. But he wanted to find out just how deep the conspiracy went. And make no mistake. It was a conspiracy. A mob of white men had murdered a father and his child and burned down his house.

Obviously, there were witnesses. They were either too scared to talk or already dead. Kip knew he wasn't going to get any answers by playing nice. Kip let the silence linger. He would not be the one to speak first. He used the silence as a club.

"Sounds like the folks in Washington got the wrong impression somehow," Crow finally said. "You can see how that could happen, couldn't you Mr. Gardner? I mean, they weren't here, so they don't understand the situation," he explained.

"Which is?" Kip asked.

"It was dark out. Whoever did this blended into the night. It was probably some of his friends from the Colored Farmers' Alliance," Alexander offered.

"Hard to make out a nigger's face in the dark," Crow said. "Until he smiles." Crow broke into laughter at his own joke.

Ludwig silenced the laughter with a glare. "Ain't nothing funny about this, Mort."

"Got to have a little humor once in a while," Crow replied.

"Gentlemen, if you have nothing to offer, then I'd best be on my way," Kip said, standing up. They were idiots. They were also hiding something. Crow's joke infuriated Kip. He made a mental note.

"We are not going to invent evidence that does not exist," Ludwig said smoothly. "I took an oath of office that won't allow me to fabricate the truth."

"I too took that oath," Crow agreed.

"So did I," Peak weaseled in.

"Wouldn't expect anything less," Kip agreed. "Good day gentlemen," he said as he left the room.

"Goddamn nigger lover," Peak hissed after Kip left the conference room.

"Just a minor inconvenience," Ludwig said. "No one is going to talk."

"Nobody white, you mean," Crow glowered.

"Better talk to Henry, none-the-less," Ludwig suggested.

Henry Stokes sat back in the plush leather chair in the judge's chambers, admiring the sumptuous furnishings of the judge's office. Sure must be nice to have such a beautiful office and all that power, he thought to himself. Of course, Henry had some power too, but most folks in the county didn't talk too much about it. He had the kind of power that was only whispered about by town folk. A practice he encouraged. Fear was a great motivator and an even better weapon than violence itself.

Talk around town was that Henry was in charge of the Knights of the Klu Klux Clan, a tribe of white people dedicated to the principle that their race was the superior race. All others were not only inferior, but also a threat to the white race's existence. "If you ain't white, you ain't right,'" Stokes used to say.

Behind the desk sat the Honorable Judge Michael Taylor, a

god-fearing man. Judge Taylor was often known to preach on the pulpit in church and on the bench where he sat. In Judge Taylor's mind, God was justice, and he was God's instrument. This was why Judge Taylor listened to the voices in his head. It was God speaking out to him. He was explaining that to Henry Stokes as they sat in his chambers.

"And God made man in his image, the Bible says," Judge Taylor stated. "So the only logical conclusion is that the Negro is not god-like," he continued. "So if he is not like God, what is he then?" he continued with his soft southern drawl.

"A nigger," Stokes said.

"Well, you and I have something in common with Senator Tillman then," Judge Taylor agreed. "And the senator is very upset with what's going on in Lake City."

There was a knock on the door. It was the judge's clerk. She was a lovely brunette with an even more attractive body. Judge Taylor prayed to Jesus every day to give him strength because she was just so darn pretty.

"Sir, Mr. Ludwig is here to see you," she said.

"Send him in," the judge ordered.

Ludwig came into the room.

"Henry, good to see you," Ludwig said.

"So what brings you by, David?" the judge asked warmly.

"We got a little problem," Ludwig said.

"How little?"

"We've got a Yankee investigator sent down by the justice department snooping around asking questions." Ludwig handed the telegram to the judge. Judge Taylor adjusted his glasses and read the fine print.

"Hmm. Obviously, he's hoping someone will talk," Judge Taylor said. He turned to Stokes.

"Henry, is someone going to talk?" the judge asked.

Stokes shook his head.

"No. The only person who saw anything was Henderson Williams and we ran his black ass out of town. He knows that if he opens his mouth the same thing will happen to him," Stokes said resolutely. "No witnesses, no case," he added.

"So what do we do about this federal asshole they sent down?" Ludwig asked.

"Nothing," said the judge. "Unless someone talks."

"And if someone talks, we're going to have more feds down here than rode in with Sherman," Ludwig warned.

"Only if they find out," the judge said.

"I'll make sure they don't," Stokes said.

After nightfall, Kip waited for George Walker to make his way home. He watched the bellman walk down the street. Kip followed him on foot, strolling nonchalantly, pausing to look into the various storefront windows. Kip assumed he himself was also being followed. He knew he would have to clean his tail.

As the light from the gas lamps began to fade, Kip slipped into an alley and waited. He could see the tall figure as Walker continued down the street into the darkness.

Kip heard footsteps approaching the entrance of the alley. He saw the shadows flicker on Deputy Peak's face as his eyes darted around the alley. Kip stepped out of the darkness and brought a weighted lead sap down on the back of Peak's head. The deputy crumpled into a heap.

"Sleep it off," Kip said. "You're going to have one hell of a headache in the morning." Then he stepped back out into the street and continued after Walker.

George Walker stepped into the entrance of his shack on the edge of town. He could smell beans cooking over the fire, and his stomach growled. He also smelled fresh bread. His wife Mary came up to him and kissed him on the mouth.

"Hi baby," she cooed happily. She put her arms around him and gave him a big hug. She barely came up to his chest. She was wearing an apron and a scarf wrapped around her head.

George Walker wrapped his arms around his wife and hugged her back. He was happy to be home, where he could relax and be himself.

But when he heard the front door open and felt the wind come in from the darkness, he grabbed the iron poker that rested next to the hearth.

"You can put that down, George," Kip said, stepping into the room. He closed the door behind him.

"Like hell I will mister," George said. "What are you doing in my home?" he demanded. "You go near my family, and I'll bash in your skull," he warned. "I thought you said you were with the feds."

"I am," Kip said. "Sorry I didn't knock. Trying not to call attention to the fact that I'm here," Kip answered. "I had to make sure no one saw me coming to your place. If they did, you and your family would be at great risk."

"And how do you know that no one followed you?" George asked, with the iron poker still clenched in his fist.

"Because Deputy Peak is now taking a nap in an alley in town," Kip replied. "And I'm guessing he's going to be out all night."

George looked at him, astonished.

"I don't get it, mister. You can't hurt a deputy sheriff," he said, disbelieving. "Not unless you want to get hurt yourself. Not in this city, not in this county. Not in the South, period," he hissed.

"I can," Kip said calmly. He walked over to the hearth, trying to ignore the iron poker still clutched in the big man's fist. He held out his hands to warm them.

"George," Mary asked. "Do you know this man?" She tried to keep the fear out of her voice.

"I don't know yet. Go into the bedroom," George ordered.

"I'm told she is the one I should speak with," Kip advised, careful to keep any emotion out of his voice.

"Who told you that?" George asked. He was having a hard time keeping his anger in check.

"He wasn't white," Kip said. "So relax."

"No one should be talking about my wife!" George's voice grew louder.

"You'd better keep it down or they will be," Kip warned. "I'm not here to get you or your wife hurt. I'm here to find out who murdered Frazier and his little girl, Julia.

"You're a white man. Why would you care?" George asked.

"My boss isn't too happy with someone killing a federal employee," Kip said evenly. "Even a black one. Up north things are different than down here." Kip paused, eyeing the poker.

"Now, are you going to put down that poker and let me talk or shall I just leave your house whistling Dixie for everyone to hear?" Kip asked.

George lowered the poker, but still kept a firm grip.

"George, I know this is hard to believe, coming from a white man, but what happened here, what happened to Frazier and Julia, is not okay. I was sent to seek justice for their murders, and to make sure that whoever committed this horrible act stands trial."

"What is your name," Mary demanded. She stepped forward into the room.

"No Mary," George warned. "Don't trust him."

"I don't," she said. "But I'm not going to live in fear keeping my mouth shut about what I saw. They murdered that child in cold blood."

"On that we agree," Kip said. "My name is Randy Gardner. Can we talk?"

George looked at Kip. He let the fear drop, and he set the poker back on the hearth. "Have a seat," he said.

The next morning found Kip at the livery stable. He stepped into the office and smiled at the man behind the desk.

"Can I help you?" the man asked.

"Yes," Kip said. "I'm looking for the owner, Joseph Newham."

"You found him," Newham said.

Newham was balding and had a bushy brown beard. He was heavy set and wore wide suspenders to keep his trousers up.

"What can I do for you?"

"I'm from Washington," Kip said easily. "They sent me down to ask a few questions. Very routine matter," he assured.

"What about?" Newham asked. He looked back down at the sheaf of papers he held in his hand when Kip first walked in.

"Just following up on the killing of the postmaster," Kip said.

Newham stopped shuffling the papers. "And why are you coming to me?" he asked.

"There was some talk that some of the people involved were on horseback," Kip said. "I was wondering if you had rented out any horses about the time that happened?"

Newham shook his head.

"Nope. Sheriff Crow asked me the same question, and I gave him the same answer."

"Is that right?" Kip said. He felt his anger grow inside. Mary Walker had told him different.

"Yep," Newham answered. "Say, you got some kind of identification on you that proves you are who you say you are?" Newham asked uneasily. He set his paperwork down on the roll top desk.

"Sure do," Kip said. His Colt .45 came out of its holster and he aimed it at Newham's face.

"We're taking a ride in my wagon," Kip said. "It's parked out front. I'll follow you," he ordered. "You fuck this up, and I'll kill you and your family. I got two men watching your house right now," Kip lied.

Newham's eyes grew wide. He did as he was told. He climbed up into the carriage and Kip followed, gun down by his side. "Now drive," he said.

"Where to, mister?" Newham asked. His eyes darted along the street. No one paid them any notice.

"Wolf Creek," Kip ordered. "And don't try anything stupid."

They arrived at Wolf Creek thirty minutes later. It was a lonely place, surrounded by a dense canopy of trees.

"Pull up by those rocks," Kip ordered. He kept his pistol trained on the other man. Newham did as he was told.

"Now get out, and tie off this wagon," Kip instructed. As the man complied, Kip stepped down onto the ground.

"Climb up on those rocks," Kip ordered.

"I ain't doin nothing you say," Newham challenged.

"Fine, I'll drop you right here and me and the boys will have some fun with your wife," Kip growled. "Arlene, right? Pretty little filly with bright green eyes and big tits," Kip continued. "Then they'll butcher those two cute little daughters of yours."

Newham's face broke. "Ok, mister. Please don't hurt my family," he begged.

"You do as I say, and I won't hurt them," Kip promised.

"What about me?" Newham asked, climbing up onto the rocks. The rock formation was about six feet high, underneath a large pine tree.

"That depends on what you tell me," Kip said. He motioned upwards with his revolver. "Look up," he ordered.

Newham did so. He saw a hangman's noose hanging above his head.

"Pull that noose over your head," Kip ordered.

Newham froze. Any man would. Kip pointed the gun at his head.

"Put it around your neck, you sorry son of a bitch," Kip said coldly.

"You're not going to hang me, are you?" Newham pleaded.

"I haven't decided," Kip said. He pulled back the hammer on his revolver and aimed it at Newham's sweating forehead.

"Pull the noose down around your neck and tighten it," Kip menaced.

Newham's hand fumbled with the rope. His hands were shaking, but he got it over his head.

"Cinch it," Kip said coldly.

Newham tightened the noose around his own neck. His entire body was trembling. His pants grew dark as he urinated in his pants.

"There ain't no one around for miles, so you had better get this right the first time," Kip said. "Put your hands behind your back," he ordered. He tied the man's wrist behind his back.

"First wrong answer and I give you a kick" Kip promised. "You'll be dancing on the end of that rope, got it?"

Newham nodded his head.

"I understand you have a little experience with lynching," Kip stated. "Especially when it comes to black folk," he added. "Like the postmaster, for instance."

"He wasn't lynched, he was shot," Newham gasped.

"Same thing," Kip said. "Look it up in Webster's Dictionary. It means to murder without a trial, as in hanging," Kip continued coldly. "Kind of like what is happening right here, if you don't tell me the truth."

"And if I do?" Newham asked.

"You'll be granted immunity, and turn state's evidence," Kip said.

"They'll kill me."

Kip put the muzzle of his revolver in Newham's back.

"I'll kill you right now. Talk or swing." Kip prodded the man towards the edge of the rocks. "I don't like you anyway, and Henry Stokes is already singing like a canary," Kip bluffed.

"Goddamn it, man, stop pushing me," Newham cried.

"Sorry, you little prick," Kip said. "It's my job to push. Now, what happened that night?"

"If Stokes talked, you already know," Newham cried.

Kip pushed him harder. The toes of Newham's shoes poked over the edge of the rocks.

"Alright, I'll talk," Newham said with desperation in his voice.

"Then talk, because you're going to hell in five seconds if you don't," Kip growled.

"Stokes was the ring leader," Newham stammered. Kip prodded him towards the edge again.

"I know that," Kip lied. "But who was pulling his strings?" he prodded the off-balance man again with his revolver.

"Judge Taylor," Newham whimpered. "Judge Taylor, the DA, Ludwig, Crow. They were all in on it. They're all Red Shirts," he added. "They said they were following orders from Senator Tillman."

"And so did you," Kip said.

"Yes," Newham whispered. "Yes. Now I told you the truth mister, please don't kill my family or me," Newham begged.

Kip shoved him off the rocks.

Newham screamed as he fell to the ground, landing in a heap. His right arm snapped as he hit the earth. The rope tumbled down from the branch above the rocks, falling on top of him.

Kip climbed down the rocks and took the rope from around the man's neck.

"Guess I forgot to tie it off," Kip said. "This time."

"There won't be a next time," Newham cried. "I promise."

"Good boy. Alright. Get on your feet. We'll take you to see the doc. Then you go about your business until you get your subpoena," Kip told him. "You talk to anyone about what happened today, and all bets are off, and your family is dead," Kip warned.

"I won't," the man promised. He believed the man from Washington.

"Use your good hand to get up into that surrey," Kip ordered. "I'll drive."

It came as no surprise to Kip that the top law enforcement officials in Williamsburg County were instrumental in organizing and carrying out the murder of the postmaster. Even Judge Taylor's involvement came as no surprise. The question in his mind, and in the president's mind, was whether they could connect the dots to Senator Benjamin Tillman. Tillman himself had bragged about his involvement with the Red Shirts in his early years. He had even suggested that he led them in the Hamburg Massacre in 1876. He was a dangerous man indeed. But no less dangerous in Kip's mind than the men he had inspired.

When Kip went to the courthouse that afternoon, he already had a plan in mind. He waited across the street at the Early Saloon. He sat at the bar, keeping to himself, waiting for the courthouse to close down.

Judge Michael Taylor stepped out from the small tunnel underneath the courthouse steps. He adjusted his collar, slicked back his hair and pulled his hat firmly down over his head. His thoughts were divided between his secretary's tight ass and what his wife was cooking for dinner. Spring was in the air, and the lush Carolina countryside was beginning to show its true colors. The judge lived on a ranch five miles from town. He set his horse into a steady canter once he got out of town. The horse knew the way. He would be home in thirty minutes.

Taylor's thoughts were interrupted when he passed Wolf Creek and saw a man on horseback blocking his path fifty feet ahead.

Taylor guessed the man to be in his late twenties. There was something about the way the man sat in the saddle that made the judge uneasy. Taylor slowed his horse to a walk as he approached the man. Impertinent bastard, the judge thought to himself. Why the hell is he blocking the road? Cloaked in his sense of judicial power, it never occurred to him to be afraid. He was simply annoyed.

The man tipped his hat when the judge pulled up to the horse.

"You alright, young fella?" the judge asked.

"I'm afraid I'm a little lost," Kip said.

"Where are you headed?"

"Looking for Judge Michael Taylor's place," Kip smiled.

"You found him," Taylor stated. Something didn't seem right. He was glad he was wearing his revolver around his waist. Do I know this man, the judge wondered. Did I send him to prison?

"Randy Gardner," Kip introduced himself. "Justice Department."

"What's a Yankee doing in these parts?" the judge inquired politely.

"I keep asking myself the same question," Kip laughed. "But I'm here on official business. Just got a few questions."

"I'm a busy man, son," the judge said. He was. Supper was waiting. His annoyance was beginning to show. His arrogance will follow, Kip thought.

"So I hear," Kip said evenly.

Judge Taylor looked at Kip as if he had just slapped him.

"I don't like the tone of your voice, Mr. Gardner," the judge said. He set down the reigns. "Do you know who you are talking to?"

"Yes," Kip answered. His .45 caliber revolver appeared from his side, pointed directly at the judge's head.

Judge Taylor looked at him with indignation.

"You just pulled a gun on a superior court judge, son. You can't do that. It's a felony offense."

"So is lynching, judge," Kip answered. "Now step down off the carriage and into the woods and walk to Wolf's Creek," Kip ordered. "I want to talk in private."

Kip motioned to the judge with his pistol. "You can leave that revolver on the footboard." The judge slowly removed his revolver and set it on the floorboard. Then he carefully stepped down off the carriage.

"I don't know anything about a lynching, but I do know that you ain't no federal investigator," the judge said. He felt his adrenaline surge. "No one from the justice department is going to interrogate a state judge at gunpoint. So who are you and what do you want?" Judge Taylor asked. "Money?"

"Keep walking and shut up. We'll talk when we get to the creek," Kip commanded. He got down off his horse and wrapped the reigns around a tree with one hand, keeping his gun trained on the judge the whole time.

Judge Taylor was dumbfounded. He could not believe that a man with a gun was ordering him into the forest. He was a superior court judge, after all. Did this fool think he could get away with this?

"Son, this has gone far enough," Taylor said, standing his ground. "Put that gun down unless you're ready to use it," he said defiantly.

Kip stepped up to him and smiled. "I am," he said. Kip slammed the butt of his revolver against the side of the judge's head and he dropped unconscious to the ground.

The judge came to minutes later, surprised to find his hands bound tightly behind his back. He was lying on his side on top of some large boulders. Something was around his neck, but he couldn't see what it was.

"Get to your feet," Kip said.

The judge struggled to his knees; then he stood up. There was a rope with a noose knotted around his neck. The judge's eyes followed the rope up to a massive tree limb hanging over the rocks.

"That's right," Kip said.

He took in the slack from the rope and placed the noose around the judge's neck and cinched it tight. Judge Taylor cried out in pain as the rough hemp cut into his Adam's apple. His eyes grew wide with terror.

"Jesus help me," the judge whimpered. "Are you mad?"

"This whole town went mad when you murdered the postmaster," Kip said. "I'm just here to clean up the mess."

Judge Taylor swallowed hard. "I don't know what you are talking about," he coughed. He realized that his feet were just a foot from the edge of the rocks. He tried to step back, but the rope around his neck wouldn't allow him too.

"I wouldn't move, if I were you," Kip advised. "You might lose your balance."

"Damn you man, get me the fuck down from here," the judge ordered.

"Not until you answer some questions," Kip said coldly.

"I'm not saying shit," the judge snarled.

"I didn't expect you to," Kip answered coldly. He kicked the judge off the rocks.

Judge Taylor fell forward and the rope snapped his head back. He couldn't breathe. He kicked for the rocks with his feet. Gravel slid down the side of the rock cliff. The more he struggled, the more the noose tightened.

Kip climbed down from the rocks and walked over to Sheriff Crow and took the gag out of his mouth.

"You're next unless you talk," Kip said honestly.

Judge Taylor's feet began to drum in the empty air. Finally, they stopped, and his body went limp. His bowels opened and excrement flowed out of his pant legs and onto the ground.

"I'll tell you everything you want to know," Crow said, wide-eyed. He was tied up, watching the horror of the spectacle unfold in front of him. The Yankee had murdered the judge. Crow knew he was a dead man if he didn't talk.

"I'm sure you will," Kip said. He listened patiently while the sheriff unraveled the plot to murder the postmaster. He named Stokes as the ringleader and gave the names of a dozen other men who were involved. It matched what Newham had told him. It was clear to Kip that Stokes was the ring leader. It was also clear what had to be done next.

Newham was already scared shitless. When word spread that the judge had been murdered, Newham would keep his mouth shut until the time came. What else was he going to do? And when the time came, no one was going to care about his allegations that a federal investigator had roughed him up.

Crow was a different matter. He would talk. As soon as Kip left town, Crow would high tail it to town to meet and confer with Ludwig. Together they would plan their story, and plant the blame on someone else. Crow would also spill the fact that a man claiming to be a federal investigator had murdered Judge Taylor.

Kip was the messenger. He had delivered the message. Judge Taylor's lifeless body swung at the end of a rope. Kip wanted the people of Lake City to wonder and worry about who and why Judge Taylor had been murdered. Who could wield such unspeakable power with impunity? The white people would whisper among themselves. Kip wanted to leave them guessing. Justice had been served.

Kip put his revolver up against the side of Crow's skull. The sheriff had to go.

"The president sends his regards," Kip said softly. Then he blew Crow's brains out.

Crow crumpled to the ground.

They would all get the message.

Kip rode back to town, checked his time piece, and took the evening train to Washington. They would discover the bodies by morning. By then, he would be back in uniform.

Kip removed the blond wig he had been wearing and took off the fake mustache, wincing from the glue tugging at his skin. He took the clothes and shoes he had been wearing and put them in the bag with his disguise. He would burn the whole bag when he got home. He settled into the plush cushions in his private cabin and watched the stars and trees fly past in the moonlight.

What have I become? he wondered. Was I just following orders or does part of me enjoy this? Am I delivering the message the president wants, or am I sending my own?

He thought about the little two-year-old girl that had been butchered in her mother's arms and decided that he was sending his own.

CHAPTER SIXTY-ONE

CAIRO, 1897

Lady Churchill was in Cairo, staying at the Continental Hotel with her current lover, Major Carl John Ramsden. She had taken the weekly P. and O. steamship from London. Twelve days at sea had been an excellent tonic, as had the attention of Major Ramsden. He was returning to Cairo to his post on Kitchener's staff. Jenny had decided to travel with him to visit the Great Pyramids and to personally deliver a letter to Kitchener from the prince.

A single woman traveling with a British military officer from London to Cairo would have been an insult to both man and beast alike. So Lady Churchill traveled with her dear friend, Lady Maxwell, whose husband was already in Cairo.

Now they both sat behind a clean cotton table cloth adorned with fine silver and china in the main dining room. They were surrounded by windows, and they watched the donkey boys ride their burros down the street.

"They have everything here," Lady Maxwell gushed. "I can't believe they have trolleys and trams, electric lights, even electricity in the hotel."

Cairo had become a boom town. It was the boiler room of the British military machine advancing south along the Nile. There was a battle coming, but it was to be on British terms. The lines of communication were being drawn patiently as engineers and workers built a sword of steel deep into the Sudan, to be plunged into the heart like a bullfighter's sword. The power of the steamboat and the locomotive had advanced the ability to provide rations, munitions and every material needed for war deep into the heart of Africa.

Not that Lady Churchill was thinking in military terms that afternoon. But she was thinking tactics. Winston wanted to join the expedition that was going to crush the dervish. The problem was no one wanted him along for the ride. Jenny knew Kitchener. But he wasn't listening. It was causing her a great deal of worry.

"Oh look, Jenny, that donkey boy is riding his ass," giggled Lady Maxwell.

"Well, we have something in common then," Jenny laughed, without missing a beat. "Because I was riding an ass last night named Major Ramsden."

Lady Maxwell howled and snorted so hard a booger shot out of her nose onto the clean linen table cloth, which immediately sent both women into an absolute frenzy of laughter.

"Oh my god," Lady Churchill gasped. "Oh sweet Jesus!" she howled.

Her high cheekbones flushed. She quickly swiped the offending cornflake off the table cloth with her napkin and onto the floor, which made them both howl all the louder.

Heads began to turn in their direction, but the two women could not regain their composure. Lady Maxwell's shoulders were heaving as she tried to breath, but she couldn't.

"Oh god, make it stop," she gasped to Lady Churchill.

Tears washed down Lady Churchill's face. "I, I, I, I cannnnnnn't," she gasped.

The maître d' walked over to their table. "Is everything alright ladies?" he asked politely.

"Tahaaahaaahaha!" Jenny howled. She pounded the table with her right hand. "Bring us whiskey, please," she begged.

"Yes ma'am," the maître d' replied without missing a beat. He was used to drunken English folk.

"Oh my god, Jenny," Lady Maxwell chortled. "I shall never be the same."

"Don't look at me Maxie," Lady Churchill implored. Which of course made their eyes meet again and they burst into helpless laughter.

After three shots of whiskey apiece, they finally regained their composure, though now entirely smashed.

"Is your husband joining us for dinner?" Lady Churchill asked.

"Yes, in fact, Robert said he and Carl would both be joining us," Lady Maxwell replied, dabbing at the corner of her eye with her napkin.

Lady Churchill eyed her friend, noticing her swelling breast and curved hips. With her blue eyes and blonde hair, she was somewhat stunning. Not that Lady Churchill was any less so, with her raven hair and deep brown eyes. Her lips and her breast were equally full. Still, she felt that familiar pang of female jealousy spring from her heart. Lady Maxwell was a few years younger.

"Maxie!" boomed Robert Maxwell as he walked up to the table, resplendent in his khaki dress uniform and pith helmet.

"Lady Churchill" called out Carl as he strode up to the table next to Robert.

Both men were the stereotype of the quintessential British army officer. Sunburned, neatly trimmed mustache, intelligent eyes and high English cheekbones. They were in full field uniforms that made most women moist in their most private of areas.

"Cocktails," Carl ordered the maître d'.

"Of course sir," the maître d' replied. A native Egyptian, he tolerated the British with a sense of humor. They could be very amusing.

"Gin and tonic, all around," added Robert. He removed his pith helmet, and leaned over and gave his wife a passionate kiss.

"Please, Robert, stop," implored Lady Churchill. "She still has to wash her face. You have no idea what just came out of it."

At which, both women slumped down in their chairs, lost in laughter and alcohol.

Robert looked at Carl, and Carl looked at Robert.

"We missed something," Carl said slyly.

"Oh yes," Robert agreed. "Ladies, tell us all," he implored.

And of course, they did, and soon they were four Brits howling with mirth. Finally, the laughter subsided, and they sat in the evening air watching the carriages and dog carts weaving down the road.

"I have some interesting news," announced Carl. "It seems I am headed south to the railhead at Merawi."

A hush fell over the table. Merawi was near the front. It was the furthest most point of the railhead. It was also fraught with danger. Dervish forces had been attacking the extended outpost of the British advance, testing their defenses and gathering intelligence.

"Oh my Carl," Lady Churchill gasped. "That's wonderful news. As you know my son, Winston, is a cavalry officer and war correspondent. He would love to get on board the expedition," she said.

"My lady, that is up to Kitchener himself, and I am afraid that I don't have much pull with the Sirdar," Carl replied.

"'I've written three letters to that bastard, and he won't say yes," Jenny pouted. "I even danced with him at the prince's royal ball two years ago in London," she huffed. "See if I ever dance with him again."

They all laughed at her lighthearted humor.

"Robert, I want to see the pyramids tomorrow," Maxie begged. "Can you go with me?"

"No," her husband replied. "We are inspecting a new shipment of engines tomorrow. They are coming in by way of Alexandria. I'm afraid I will be on the road for a few days," he announced. Maxwell didn't notice the expression on Carl's face.

"Well I am off to the museum tomorrow," Lady Churchill announced. "I'm taking the tramway to Ghizheh." She lowered her voice to make it mysterious. "I am going to see the mummy of Ramses II, the Pharaoh of the Oppression," she whispered.

"They've got a lot of stiffs there," Carl added. There was lighthearted laughter around the table. The night was clear, and the stars were out in full force.

"It is a beautiful evening," Carl said. "I wish that we had more time to enjoy the city like you, Jenny. Unfortunately, things are getting busy."

"That they are," Robert agreed. "We are moving sixteen steam engines by rail to Merawi. Which is why I have to inspect each one personally before they are shipped out," he boasted. Robert was an engineer.

"And I will be personally supervising their transfer when they arrive at Merawi," Carl added. "Along with ten lathes, fourteen cutters, a dozen or so punching or sheering machines, 300 miles of steel rail, 200 trucks, along with 5,000 tins of biscuits and beef," he added. "Not to mention 1,000 gallons of oil."

"Shh," cautioned Robert. "Too much information for one evening," he cautioned.

"Ah, good point," Carl added. Both men were loaded.

"Will it be dangerous?" Lady Maxwell asked breathlessly.

Carl gave a confident laugh. "War is always dangerous my dear lady. But I'm sure all will be right," he added. He flashed her a brilliant white smile.

Jenny looked across the table at Maxie. Was she flirting with Carl?

"Without saying too much," Carl said, eyeing Robert Maxwell, "the journey is long and tedious."

In fact, the journey was both long and dangerous. It was a 340-mile journey by rail to reach the first steamers at Nagh Hamadi. Once in Nagh Hamadi, the equipment, supplies, and soldiers would travel another 205 miles to Assuan. From there, they transferred back to the rail for a short ride to Shellal, where they embarked on the steamers to Halfa, a mere 226 miles. From there, they picked up the military railway which took them deep into the heartland.

It was a hot, dusty journey, and danger loomed at every point. The Khalifa's men could attack from the rear in an attempt to sever the supply lines.

It was this dangerous journey that Winston Churchill was imploring his mother to make possible for him. The next day found Lady Churchill taking the tram to the museum. But she had a slight detour on her way. She was still deeply involved with the Crown Prince of England. The prince was her lover and her friend. And Lady Churchill herself was well connected with the military. She hired a small carriage to take her to Kitchener's headquarters.

The soldiers at the gate let her pass after they checked her credentials, verifying the signature on the letter she carried for personal delivery to the British general from the prince.

She followed the orderly down the long busy corridors of the military headquarters and into the smoke-filled waiting area of the general's office. She took a seat on a leather couch and smiled at several officers who tried not to stare.

A young major came out of the general's office. "Lady Churchill, the Sirdar will speak with you now. This way please," he gestured towards the open doorway.

Letter in hand, Jenny walked confidently into the office of Sir Horatio Herbert Kitchener.

"Ah Lady Churchill," Kitchener said smiling. "You are as beautiful as ever, my lady." He took her hand and let it gently touch his lips. "It's always a pleasure to see you."

"It is good to see you again as well, general," she said. "I have a letter for you from the prince." She took the letter from her purse and handed it to Kitchener.

"Ah yes," he sighed. "Have a seat."

He motioned her to an overstuffed leather chair in front of his desk. He briefly eyed the wax seal before slitting open the envelope with an ivory blade. He sat down behind his desk and read the letter.

"It seems that the prince would like your son to join our little expedition," the general said politely.

Inside, however, the general felt his blood pressure go up like mercury in a thermometer under the desert sun. Kitchener was well aware of Churchill's desperate wishes to join the campaign. And after having read Churchill's dispatches regarding his exploits in Afghanistan, including his criticism of his own military leadership, Kitchener had no intention of ever allowing Churchill to set foot in Egypt. The little bastard would stab him in the back by publicly questioning his tactics.

"My son is a brilliant writer," Lady Churchill gushed. "As well as an experienced, battle-tested cavalry officer. I'm sure he would be an asset to your campaign," she added.

"Of course, my lady," Kitchener replied, ever the gentleman. "But we have no open billets here," he said gently. "They have been filled for months, and there is already a very long line."

Jenny could see his mouth curl in a smile beneath his heavy waxed mustache.

"The prince would consider it a favor," she pleaded. It was beneath her dignity to beg, but she was determined to have her way.

Kitchener nodded. "I understand," he said. "I will have one of my men check again to see if anything can be done."

He got up from behind his desk and walked to his open door.

"O'Connor, come into my office please."

Lieutenant Scott O'Connor, of Belfast, stepped into the general's office and snapped to attention smartly.

"Sir," he waited.

"I would like to you check all available billets for an opening for a cavalry officer," Kitchener said as he sat back down behind his desk.

"Or correspondent," Lady Churchill blurted. She immediately turned red. How embarrassing, she thought. I'm giving orders.

Kitchener broke into a wide grin.

"Of course, Lady Churchill," he said graciously. He turned back to the young Irish officer. "Or war correspondent," he added politely. "It seems that young Winston Churchill would like to join our outfit."

O'Connor smiled.

"Sir, I would be honored. I will have an answer by tomorrow," O'Connor said. Secretly, the young lieutenant was already planning how to get word back to Ireland that Churchill was going to attempt to join Kitchener's expedition.

Kitchener stood up, and so did Jenny, following his lead.

"There Lady," he said. "It is done. We will have an answer by tomorrow. Where are you staying?" he inquired politely.

"The Continental," she replied.

"O'Connor will bring you word tomorrow at your hotel," Kitchener instructed. He took her hand. "Have a safe journey home," he added.

"Thank you, sir," she blushed. She walked out of his office, her shoulders high. Her flowing black mane cascaded down her back.

"A rather handsome woman," the general mused.

O'Connor allowed himself a moment of familiarity with his general. "Yes sir, she is striking."

"And O'Connor," the general added. "Don't bother checking about room for Churchill; we're full. I'm not going to let that publicity hound use my expedition to further his political fortunes. And please pass along my regards to Lady Churchill tomorrow."

"Yes sir," O'Connor said. Inside he cursed.

That afternoon, Jenny returned to the Continental Hotel after touring the museum. The museum was a massive stone building with countless rooms full of artifacts, relics, and mummies. But she was exhausted from the stress of her meeting with Kitchener and left the museum hours before she had planned.

She opened the door of her suite, and there before her in all his naked glory, stood Carl. And equally as naked, her legs wrapped around his waist, was a very naked Lady Maxwell.

"Oh dear," Carl said. "You came early."

"It seems you came early yourself," Lady Churchill quipped.

Lady Maxwell's mouth was already open, and she couldn't seem to close it.

"Bitch," Lady Churchill hissed. She turned and fled the room.

Chapter Sixty-Two

WASHINGTON, D.C., 1897

Kip sat down in a comfortably cushioned chair in the main briefing room of the army's Military Intelligence Division. In past staff meetings he sat in the chairs with their backs against the wall, where all staff officers sat. Now, he had a seat at the main conference table.

As a result of his exploits in Cuba and Lake City, Kip had been promoted. His official duty title was Inspector, Military Investigations. His unofficial duty title varied depending on the assignment. His surveillance of the situation in Cuba proved vital to Edwin Atkins and J.P. Morgan both. Major McDuran was now a very hot commodity in Washington D.C.

He looked out the large bay windows of the brick stone building on G Street. Horse-drawn carriages cruised up and down the busy avenue as the nation went about its business. And once again, Kip knew he was going to be asked to get involved.

The meeting had been unexpected. Kip was sitting behind his desk, getting ready to read the paper when his secretary, Miriam, came in and informed him his presence was required immediately in the main briefing room. It was unusual for a woman to be in the workplace. But he had learned that Miss Boydstone was an extraordinary woman.

"What is the meeting about?" Kip politely inquired.

"I don't know," Miriam answered.

Kip smiled. "Did you ask?"

"No."

"Who called the meeting?"

"He didn't say," she smiled innocently.

Kip noticed her eyes. She had big blue eyes under a head of chestnut hair just waiting to be unclipped and tumble over her shoulders.

"Who is *he*?" Kip asked. He noted her perfect white teeth when she smiled.

"The president's chief of staff," she answered.

Nice breast, Kip thought. He tried to imagine her naked; then his brain clicked in.

"The president's chief of staff? Holy shit, I'd better get moving. Where's my jacket?" he said in one breath.

Ms. Boydstone handed it to him, dusting off his new insignia.

"The theater after work?" she reminded him.

"Of course. Dinner first at the Thirsty Bull," he agreed. He left for the meeting.

President McKinley's chief of staff walked into the briefing room. The head of army intelligence, General Hanson, was at his side, resplendent in his beige khaki tunic and medals. They were engaged in an intense conversation when they walked in. Their voices dropped, but the intensity was still present.

Kip jumped to attention. He was about to call the room to order, but General Hanson motioned for him to sit.

"Kip," General Hanson said, "this is Boyd McKenzie, President McKinley's chief of staff."

"Sir," Kip said.

"It's a pleasure, Major," McKenzie said. He was balding, with a comb-over plastered to one side of his head, and an unkempt grey beard.

"The president was very pleased with your reconnaissance in Cuba and your investigation in Lake City," McKenzie added. "So much that he has another mission for you," he smiled.

General Hanson looked over at the sergeant guarding the entrance to the briefing room.

"Secure?" he asked.

"Yes sir," the sergeant replied without hesitation.

"Major, it has come to our attention that a very important person in the British Empire is facing a plot to have him killed," McKenzie said.

Oh god, Kip thought, not the British again. And who cares, he wanted to say.

"It might seem odd that we would have an interest," General Hanson explained. "This individual is extremely important to some very dear friends of the president."

"And British Intelligence and Scotland Yard are very accomplished," Kip noted. "So why aren't they handling this?"

"British Intelligence believes they are compromised on this matter," the general said. "They have a mole." General Hanson could sense his young protégés concern. He wouldn't lead him on. He knew better.

"Winston Churchill is the target," Hanson said softly.

"Oh Jesus," Kip blurted.

"I know," McKenzie said sympathetically.

"No," Kip said. "He's a prick. Whoever wants to take him out is doing the world a favor."

McKenzie sat back in his chair, stunned.

General Hanson tried very hard not to burst out laughing.

McKenzie looked at Kip's face. It was poker.

"Perhaps you're not the man for the job," McKenzie taunted, his voice insinuating a weakness.

Kip smiled politely at McKenzie's insult.

"You are correct, sir" Kip replied. "I'm not."

Kip stood up and looked at his boss.

"Will that be all, sir?"

Nipped that one in the bud, Kip thought. Churchill? He remembered the pouting lower lip and the air of insouciance that Churchill carried about him in Cuba. Kip despised anyone born with a silver spoon in his mouth. They usually walked about as if it were stuck up their ass.

"No Major. President McKinley will not accept your declination," General Hanson told him.

"Kip," he said gently, "I briefed the president. I told him you would not accept the assignment. But he *will not* accept your resignation."

The general paused, rubbing his hand on his chin.

"The president personally asked me to convey to you that he would very much appreciate your assistance in this matter. It's a political issue." He watched Kip's face. No reaction.

"And the president also said that if you still declined his request, he was prepared to make it an order," the general continued.

Kip frowned. He knew better than to insult the president. The fat bastard was meaner than a snake. Heaven help me, he thought, no chance for retreat.

"I am at the president's service, as always," Kip surrendered gracefully.

"Yes," smiled Hanson. "I thought you would be."

"So what is the mission?" Kip asked with resignation in his voice.

Hanson paused to allow McKenzie back into the conversation.

"We have it through very good sources that Churchill has been assigned to Kitchener's campaign in the Sudan," McKenzie began. "Irish terrorists have pledged to assassinate Churchill in retribution for his father, Randolph Churchill's, betrayal of Robert Parnell, years ago."

"Do we have any idea which Irishman is attempting to save humanity?" Kip asked dryly.

"I say, that's absolutely uncalled for," McKenzie blurted out.

"You wouldn't say that if you had the pleasure of meeting him. Have you had the pleasure?" Kip asked.

"No, unfortunately not," McKenzie replied tightly. "We suspect it will be an Irish man or woman, but they could hire anyone. A worst-case scenario is a member of the British army assigned to Kitchener."

"That wouldn't exactly narrow it down, would it?" Kip parried sarcastically. Something about the chief of staff rubbed him the wrong way. Like Churchill.

"You will proceed to Cairo immediately," General Hanson interjected. "You will report to Kitchener's headquarters upon your arrival. The Sirdar himself will be your point of contact. No one else can be trusted."

"I thought Kitchener was going to be the point of contact," McKenzie blurted out.

Kip tried not to let his eyes roll.

"Sirdar is the title General Kitchener carries as the commander of the Egyptian army," Hanson said drolly. Political appointees like McKenzie usually didn't know their head from a hole in the ground. That was another reason the meeting was being held at the MID. There were too many prying eyes and politicians around the White House.

"You will have access to dispatches from Kitchener's office," General Hanson said. "You will also have access to Scotland Yard, but they can make no guarantees. You will go wherever Churchill goes. Do not let him out of your sight," Hanson instructed. "You are a military advisor to the British, courtesy of the United States government," Hanson continued.

"Kitchener is not going to acknowledge that you exist publicly. Or for that fact, that he is even aware Churchill has been assigned to his forces. He was furious when he found out that Churchill had finagled his way in. He doesn't want Churchill along for the ride. He considers him a bore and a glory hunter."

"In which case, Kitchener is very astute. I like him already." Kip agreed. "And what is my specific assignment?" he asked.

"Identify the threat and terminate it. If you cannot identify the threat, protect Churchill, and make sure he comes home from the campaign alive, even at the cost of your own life," Hanson stated. "You will have to pick and choose your allies carefully, but you cannot and will not divulge the nature of your mission to anyone," Hanson added. "That is a direct order from the president."

"Churchill must have some friends in very high places," Kip mused.

"He does. And as you may know, his mother is an American. She gained information about the plot to murder her son while visiting Cairo. A good friend of hers, a Major Ramsden, owed her a favor it seems. He heard wind of the plot and told Lady Churchill, who in turn notified her very close friend, the Prince of Wales, the future king of England," the general said. "She may still be in Cairo when you arrive."

"And the future king is a very close friend of my boss, the president of the United States of America," McKenzie said with satisfaction.

"And if the intelligence is wrong, and there is no plot?" Kip asked.

"Then you will report to the president regarding the manner, forces and capabilities of the British army in carrying out this expedition, much as you did in Cuba. The president also wants a firsthand assessment of these religious fanatics who worship the Mahdi," the general instructed. "He's alarmed by these Islamic religious fanatics. He is also extremely interested in the British tactic of building a steel horse into Africa."

"From the president's point of view, this is a win-win," McKenzie said.

"That's easy for you to say," Kip deadpanned.

McKenzie ignored the insult.

"The information you gather will prove invaluable. A firsthand assessment of the military capabilities of the British as well as the Arabs by itself justifies your mission. The fact that it will also result in the future King of England owing the United States a favor is not lost on the president, or the goodwill this will foster in future diplomatic endeavors. If there is no plot, and you return home with this information alone, your mission will be considered a success. If there is a plot, and you successfully protect Mr. Churchill, then the latter will prove the icing on the cake," McKenzie concluded.

"The U.S. consul-general, Jack Harrison, will be briefed as to the intelligence aspect of your mission, but not the plot against Churchill. He will provide assistance to your mission, including making sure you have the proper financing, equipment, and arms," McKenzie added.

"You will use his telegraph office for your dispatches," Hanson cut in. "Just tell him what you need. You will obtain passage through Thomas Cook and Son. You will be departing New York tomorrow. Upon arrival in London, you will meet with your contact at Scotland Yard. You will receive information from your contact but you will not provide any information to them."

"One question," Kip interrupted. "If I die protecting Churchill, you lose my intelligence, and I my life. How is that a win-win?"

"You better not get killed then," McKenzie smirked.

Kip frowned. Asshole, he thought to himself.

"Kip, you will send weekly dispatches via telegram," General Hanson instructed. You will be provided the proper codes tonight. After this briefing, you will remain behind for a thorough briefing from the head of our Egyptian intelligence unit."

So much for dinner with Ms. Boydstone, Kip sighed to himself.

"One last question," added Kip. "Does Churchill know anything about the plot or my assignment?"

"No," the general stated.

That figures, Kip thought. Leave the worries to me.

CHAPTER SIXTY-THREE

CAIRO, 1898

Kip sat on the wooden bleachers overlooking the hard- packed clay parade ground. A British officer marched his troops in close formation. The faces of the Egyptian soldiers marching in their khaki dress kits were intense underneath their red fez with a white tassel. Their light blue uniforms, with yellow trim and a red sash were impressive. Memo to self, Kip thought, they are well-dressed and march well. But can they fight?

A lone British officer casually strolled towards the bleachers alongside the parade field. He too was watching the battalion as they marched proudly. The bright blue diamond patch on the side of their fez displayed prominently.

Kip eyed the officer approaching him. Khaki uniform, freshly pressed stohwasser gaiters, leggings perfect. Chin held high under the pith helmet. Field glasses hanging casually around his neck. Pistol prominently displayed on his Sam Brown belt on his right hip. Yep, it was Churchill alright. The intelligence officer had briefed Kip that Churchill carried a Mauser pistol on a silk lanyard. He was right, Kip noted. He also noted it was brand new and not army issue.

Kip had inquired of the orderly where he might find Churchill that morning. The orderly told him that Churchill enjoyed watching the troops being put through their paces. Morning drill, Wednesdays, and Thursdays, the orderly noted.

Predictably, Churchill was late. They had been drilling for a half hour. Score another point for army intelligence. Kip was briefed that Churchill was always late for everything.

"Ah, Major Kip McDuran," Churchill called out as he approached. "I was told you were looking for me," he said, bounding up the bleachers.

Same red cheeks, pouty lips, girlish shoulders and the enthusiasm of a puppy, thought Kip.

"Good to see you again," Winston stated, hand outstretched.

Kip smiled diplomatically, stood and they shook hands.

"You too," he replied, eyeing Churchill carefully.

"So what brings you to our party?" Churchill asked. They sat back down on the bleachers.

"Same mission as Cuba," Kip answered. "The United States wants to learn everything it can about this dervish insurrection and your tactics to defeat them."

"Odd fellow, this Khalifa," Churchill said. "He was the handpicked successor of the Mahdi, and he knows better than anyone where his power came from." Churchill paused, lighting up a cigarette. He offered one to Kip. "And it sure as hell wasn't from Allah."

"I don't smoke, but thanks," Kip declined politely.

Cigarette hanging from his lips, Churchill continued. "Interestingly enough, after the Mahdi died, Abdullah had a hell of a time dealing with the Mahdi's family. He had a few of them killed to make his point. Now his power is absolute," he said.

"But it would appear not for long," Kip noted.

"No. Not for long. The Khalifa will pay the price for murdering General Gordon," Churchill said calmly. "He was the Mahdi's second-in-command. And I for one look forward to seeing the noose knotted about the bastard's neck," he added succinctly.

Kip had other ideas about the motivation of the British expedition. If they were truly out to avenge Gordon's death, they would have started a long time ago. Instead, thirteen years had passed. Kip wondered if Churchill suspected the real reason behind the British expedition. His briefing at MID revealed it was all about France and their intent to dam the Nile.

"Not to change the subject," Kip said politely, "but what is the latest news of Captain Marchand?"

"The Frenchman is in the Ivory Coast, where he belongs, collecting his ivory and his women," Churchill laughed.

"That makes sense," Kip smirked. "He, along with many other French officers, shares a love of all things ebony." If Churchill knew the French were coming, he showed no sign. Instead, he took the predictable path from Kip's prodding.

"Ah, the Negress. She can be charming," Churchill laughed excitedly. "Their areola are as large as silver dollars and their legs can crack you like a walnut," he joked.

"I wouldn't know," Kip said.

"Neither would I," Churchill added. "It's what the troops were tossing about on the passage here," Churchill explained.

Kip did not mention the French again. If Churchill had some insight from his vast collection of "friends," he wasn't letting on.

"When are we shipping out?" Kip asked innocently. He already knew the answer.

"I'm not sure," Churchill said. "But not for several weeks. Where are you staying?" he inquired.

"The Continental," Kip replied.

"Lovely place," Churchill said. "My mother is staying there too. I'm meeting her for dinner. You must join us," he invited.

Dinner with Churchill, Kip mused. A crazy Brit and his crazy American mother. This should be interesting. I can hardly wait. He tried to imagine what Churchill's mother looked like. He pictured hag hairs growing out of her chin beneath a mole and a disapproving scowl for the commoner.

I might have been wrong about the hag hairs, Kip thought as he walked into the dining room. Lady Churchill was anything but a hag. Her skin was flawless, not a line showing any hint of her age. Her hair was thick, dark and long, framing her high cheekbones and full lips.

Although well-bundled, as was the dress code of the time, her hourglass figure hinted at very large breasts and long, supple legs.

Kip found himself awed by her beauty. She had dark brown eyes, like a leopardess, eying her prey with a casual disdain before dining. He could only guess her age.

She, however, gave not the slightest hint of interest in the young American officer, dressed in his dress uniform. Not so much as a gaze at all in his direction.

But in her mind, she had already undressed the handsome young army officer with the chiseled jaw, the muscular shoulders, and the very tight and shapely ass. His piercing blue eyes were to be avoided at all cost. Lady Churchill had no intention of being read like a book. She was still smarting from being played by Carl.

"Winston my darling," she cooed, hugging her young son to her in a display of affection completely absent from his childhood.

Churchill blushed. "Mother, may I introduce Major Kip McDuran, United States Army, and West Point graduate."

"Charmed ma'am," Kip said, bowing slightly at the waist.

"It's a pleasure, Major," she said. She turned back to her son.

"I promised that you would be joining the Sirdar, didn't I?" she beamed.

"Yes mother, I can't thank you enough," said Churchill sincerely. "Of course I feel terrible about the demise of the man I am replacing," he said.

It turned out that Kitchener had an opening in his ranks after all. The man Churchill was replacing died unexpectedly of malaria. One man's misfortune, another man's gain, Kip thought. What Kip didn't know was Lieutenant O'Connor had already notified the Fenians.

Music began in the background. The haunting strains of a violin carried across the grand room. Dancing reflections of light from the immense candelabra played on the windows, making the setting rich. It was quintessential colonialism, Kip thought. While the impoverished masses struggled for food and water, here he was wining and dining with a beautiful American socialite and her spoiled-rotten English son.

I wonder what they would think if they knew I spent time living in the forest like an animal, stealing food from hotels and clothing from their lines? They wouldn't give me the time of day.

Perceptions were always tricky for Kip. His childhood had shaped him into the man he had become. But he was unsure of whom and what he had become. In his dreams, he could still hear the guttural grunts when the big fish struck Rodriguez. He could hear the old sea captain's screams. And he couldn't care less. He had felt a somewhat sharp sense of satisfaction when he fired his pistol into Larkin's forehead. No remorse. They deserved to die. Then, of course, the murderous folk back in Williamsburg County. The judge, the sheriff, they all had it coming, he decided. Just ask the president.

His intellect told him he was very disassociated from himself. His intellect also told him that he was also very unpredictable, even to himself. As he eyed the comely figure of Lady Churchill, the muscles in his loins began to stretch. Perhaps not completely disassociated.

The first course came and went, as did the first glass of alcohol. Churchill's perpetually flushed cheeks were even more so now. He waved a glass of whiskey in one hand and a cigarette in the other.

"There is an old saying," he began. "Some men are made to conquer; others are made to be conquered. One simply has to figure out where one fits in," Churchill boasted.

"And whom might have said that?" Kip asked politely.

"My father. A very wise man," Churchill beamed. "A toast to Randolph Churchill. A man who should have been prime minister."

Kip noticed several British officers at a table nearby. The restaurant was filled with British officers and their dates. They seemed to wince at the toast.

Take note of that, Kip thought. They all know Churchill by sight.

"To my late husband," Lady Churchill said, raising her glass.

The officers at the other table heard Lady Churchill. They stood and raised their glasses.

The lady indeed has a presence, Kip thought. He stood and raised his glass to join the toast. This is going to be a fascinating evening indeed.

They all toasted in merriment, and then sat back at their respective tables to chatter about the day.

"Another toast," Churchill said, in a voice meant only for their table this time.

"To life, liberty, and the pursuit of happiness," he teased. "Isn't that what your declaration of independence states?"

"Happiness is an interesting term," Kip replied. "The highest good, in all matter of actions."

Churchill raised an eyebrow.

"An American soldier quoting Aristotle?" he said, surprised. "Mother, Major McDuran is an educated man."

Lady Churchill raised her glass. "To educated men who quote Aristotle," she toasted. This time she looked him right in the eyes. They locked.

"To educated men," he agreed. He sipped from his glass.

"So Kip," Winston, began, "may I call you Kip?"

"Of course."

"Do you know Aristotle well, or was that an educated guess?"

Kip smiled. "Actually I never met him."

"Oh, I say that was funny," Churchill laughed, slapping his knee.

"The better question would be whether I understand Aristotle at all," Kip replied. "But I do think his observations about happiness still have relevance in today's world. According to Aristotle, the uneducated majority appear to think that pleasure is happiness," Kip explained. "I think that still holds true today. Technology may have changed, but people haven't. Everyone wants instant gratification."

"And the educated man," Lady Churchill intervened. "What is his idea of pleasure?" Her eyes locked with Kip. Churchill giggled. He loved watching his mother bait men.

"The feeling of pleasure belongs to the soul," Kip replied.

"Is that quoting Kip McDuran or Aristotle?" she inquired.

"Still stuck on Aristotle, I'm afraid," Kip replied honestly. "The pleasure of each consists of what he is said to be a lover of," he continued.

"Aristotle was a remarkable man. I get lost in his metaphysics, but his writings on ethics are spot on."

"And what are you a lover of, Major ?" Lady Churchill asked seductively.

"I don't really know," Kip smiled. Good wine and beautiful women popped into his head.

The friendly banter continued throughout the meal.

They stepped out of the restaurant and into the massive lobby with marbled ceilings and floors.

"I'm headed to the bar," Winston said airily. He waved them off with his hand. "Good night mother, Major," he said, as he staggered off.

"Would you escort me to my room?" Lady Churchill asked.

"Yes, of course," Kip replied.

At the door of her room, she turned to face him.

"Goodnight, Major," she said.

"Good night, ma'am," he said.

She smiled, leaned forward and kissed him, holding her mouth to his. Her lips were full, warm, and pleasurable. Kip's hands went around her waist and opened the door to her room. They moved inside, still kissing, but with more urgency.

His hand went to her breast, and down inside her bra. She was full, bursting with passion.

The kiss continued, but he moved down to the small of her neck.

"Uhm, I like that," she purred. Her hand came up between his legs. "Mmm, I like that too," she whispered. They undressed each other, slowly, until they stood naked, embracing. His hand traveled to her vulva. It was dripping wet. They fell onto the couch.

"No, wait," she said.

Oh, Christ, Kip thought. Now what ?

She got off the couch and onto her knees.

"Come here," she urged. "I want to show you my idea of pleasure." He stood and entered her mouth. When she sensed he was about to lose control she pulled away.

She lay back on the couch, legs inviting, breast taunting.

"Take me," she whispered. And he did. Over and over. Her soft moans turned to urgent screams as she climaxed.

Later in the evening, Kip dressed quietly so as not to disturb her. It would not be "proper" to be seen leaving her room in the morning. He was going to write her a note for when she awoke.

"Kip," she said softly. She was awake.

He leaned over the bed and kissed her passionately.

"Leaving already?" she teased. "Thank you," she said. "I enjoyed every second. But I think we should be discreet about this."

"Yes," Kip answered. "I agree." General Hanson would not be pleased, Kip thought.

"I'll let myself out, you stay in bed."

She sighed happily. "I will, beautiful man. When will I see you again?"

"Let me check in with the staff today and find out what's on my plate," he replied. "We've got a lot to do before we ship out." He reached for the door handle.

"Kip," she said. "Please protect my son."

He opened the door.

"I promise Jenny," he said softly. Then he left. He was troubled as he walked down the long hallway. If she knew his mission, who else did?

CHAPTER SIXTY-FOUR

OMDURMAN, 1898

Syrah sat in the darkness of her tent. She had long since extinguished the single candle she was allowed. Her knees were drawn up to her chest. She rested her head on her knees with her arms wrapped around them.

It was only a matter of time before she was discovered. The fear was palpable, like a giant fist squeezing her heart. She could not eat, could not sleep. There was only one solution, one way out. She, like Slatin, would have to escape.

A slight breeze whispered through the flaps of her tent. It was cool in the desert that night. She would need clothing to stay warm, food and water, enough to last until she could reach a safe place. And she would need stealth.

Because he was such a vain man, the Khalifa made no attempts to hide Syrah from his subordinates and loyal chieftains. In fact, he often showed her off. He did so by ensuring that she sat behind him and to the right in his war meetings. Everyone knew who she was. She was beautiful, young, desirable, and she spoke many languages. She was a valuable commodity, to be owned and if necessary, traded for something equally as valuable.

Earlier that evening, he had brought her to the jirga in his massive tent. She listened carefully. It was about the white men, the British. They were leading an army of Egyptians south, deep into the heart of the Sudan. She listened in silence as they spoke about giant steel horses and riverboats spewing smoke.

One of the emirs said the British had now advanced as far south as Berber, two hundred miles to the north of Khartoum. She listened to the Khalifa as he debated with his warlords about their plans to defeat the threat.

Of all the Khalifa's advisors, Mahmüd frightened Syrah the most. He was smart and ambitious. He led the dervish armies of the west in Kordofan and Darfur, and had been summoned to Omdurman by the Khalifa along with 12,000 of his men.

The Khalifa sat proudly upon his wooden thrown. His chieftains sat facing him. Mahmüd sat in the middle, directly in front of the Khalifa. Syrah kept her head down, but she could feel Mahmüd's intense gaze.

The Khalifa was not watching Mahmüd. He was watching the chief of the Jaalin, Abdalla-Wad-Saad. The Jaalin territories lay directly in the path between the English and Omdurman.

"Brother," the Khalifa said to Wad-Saad. "The Egyptian army, led by the infidel, is advancing south. Your villages and people will not be safe from their treacherous acts. I am sending Mahmüd and his army to Metemma to protect your people."

Metemma was the largest of the Jaalin villages. It was also Wad-Saad's home. He had no desire to see the bloodthirsty Mahmüd occupy his village.

"You do us a great honor," Wad-Saad said, bowing his head to the Khalifa.

"Say no more," the Khalifa replied magnanimously.

"But my people cannot feed 10,000 mouths," Wad-Saad added with apprehension.

The Khalifa felt his blood begin to boil. How dare the lowly leader of the Jaalin protest against his order?

"My people are humble servants, loyal to the Khalifa and the Mahdi. Praise be to Allah and the prophet Muhammad," Wad-Saad begged. "But Metemma is poor, the harvest weak and the people are hungry.

Forgive me my lord, but could you not find a stronger city with a leader much wiser than I?" he implored.

"You worthless piece of camel shit!" the Khalifa roared. The tent fell silent, and all sat trembling, confronted by the Khalifa's outburst. His anger and his rants were well-known. It was also well-known that they were frequently followed by the loss of human life.

"How dare you protest against my orders, against my wisdom," the Khalifa harangued. "You should die the death of a pig. Your miserable little village is a scourge upon the soil. Mahmüd will occupy your territories in my name and you will succumb or die," he ranted.

Wad-Saad bowed to the Khalifa, prostrating himself on the rug in front of him. "I did not mean to question the wisdom of the Khalifa," he apologized.

"Leave my sight at once!" the Khalifa roared. "Return to Metemma and prepare your people for Mahmüd."

Wad-Saad bowed as he crawled from the tent.

Mahmüd witnessed the humiliation of Wad-Saad with joy. The Jaalin had long been a nemesis to his ambitions. Now they would become yet another tool in his hand to forge the defeat of the English who led the Egyptians like cattle.

Mahmüd despised the Egyptians who fought alongside the infidel. How they could join forces with the soldiers of Christ sickened him. At least the Sudanese who fought alongside the white man were not followers of Christianity. They still worshipped their pathetic pagan gods. The white man, the supreme threat to his people and his religion, were soon to fall within his grasp.

After Wad-Saad crawled out of the tent, the Khalifa turned to Mahmüd.

"Take your army to Metemma," he instructed. "And take as you please," he added with a smile on his face. "Do not stay in the village. I have a new plan for you and your army, but I do not wish to share it with anyone, yet."

Mahmüd nodded.

That night, Wad-Saad rode his camel back to his village. The journey would take several days. His mind was occupied by the threat to his people. Mahmüd was a brutal warlord, bent upon destroying the Christians in a holy war. But he was also a cruel man, who would plunder Metemma, steal all they had, and rape their women. He vowed when he arrived at his village he would convince his people to throw themselves at the mercy of the English. Then he would throw his newfound friends into the face of the Khalifa.

After the jirga, Syrah sat in her tent, her mind racing. Metemma was a hundred miles to the north. If Mahmüd and his army were to lay siege and occupy the lands of the Jaalin, there would be little safety for her. If she escaped immediately, perhaps she could reach Metemma before Mahmüd's army. From there, she would find a way to travel north, to the English. She could tell them much in return for her safety.

As she sat in the darkness, she could trace the outlines of the city in her mind. Where the stable was, where she could steal a horse. She would steal dried kisru, dates and water skins. Once on the land, she could forage for nuts from the dôm palms. She would set out on her journey at night, traveling under the stars. She could read the stars, like a map, and knew which direction she would go. With luck, she would arrive at Metemma shortly after Wad-Saad. From there, she could plan her escape to Atbara, where the British were rumored to be encamped. She had no idea what to expect when she found the British, but it certainly could be no worse than her plight, held captive by the Khalifa.

That night, Syrah slipped from her tent past the sleeping guard, dressed in a full-length black burqa, her head covered by a niqab. Any woman out at night would arouse suspicion, but at least her face was not visible. She made her way into the shadows to the corral. There were horses and camels within the enclosure. She forced open the flimsy wooden door in the mud walls of a small storeroom. She found a bag of kisru and several empty water skins. She took the skins and filled them from the trough of water for the animals.

Alone, unarmed, and very much afraid, she led a black mare out of the corral and into the darkness of the African night. Only after several miles did she dare climb on the horse and urge it into a gallop. She would have to put as much distance as possible between herself and Omdurman before the Khalifa discovered her escape. There was no turning back. She threw her headdress off and turned her face into the night.

The moon was full. The beautiful black woman with the stunning physique and long braids that flowed down past her shoulder blades galloped across the plains. She felt as surreal as the surroundings themselves. Her heart pounded with excitement as she put more distance between herself and her captors.

Her biggest fear was that if she were captured, they would keep her alive and rape her. She would allow no man to take her against her will again. She tried to block out the nightmares of her mother's death at the fall of Khartoum, and her own rape when held captive by Kauūk 'Alī.

Never again, she swore to herself. She would die first.

CHAPTER SIXTY-FIVE

CAIRO, 1898

Kip found a seat among the officers assembled in the auditorium. It was their pre-departure briefing. They were headed south, to the war. He had been with Kitchener's staff for two weeks by day. By night he had found himself in bed with Lady Churchill. She was insatiable. He couldn't help smiling as he recalled the passionate lovemaking the night before.

He spent many an hour in the bar at the Continental, drinking with the other staff officers before he made his way up to her room. It had allowed him to make a few friends. Of course, Churchill was always at the bar with him. The man could drink.

Kip felt his shoulder jostled as the baby-faced lieutenant found a seat next to him.

"Cheerio, Major," Churchill greeted him.

"Top of the morning to you, mate," Kip replied.

"Room attention!" barked the senior officer. They rose to their feet in unison. General Benson strode across the stage and took his seat. An orderly uncovered several maps, and Colonel Wingate, from Kitchener's intelligence staff, took the lectern next to them.

"Gentlemen, this briefing is secret, and no word of it is to be spoken outside of staff officer meetings from this point forward," Colonel Wingate began. Wingate had a large handlebar mustache and mischievous eyes. "Take your seats." They sat in unison.

Wingate looked to the back of the auditorium. "Sergeant-at-arms, is the room secure?"

"Yes sir."

"As you know, the last year has been spent building a considerable fighting force to the south. The railhead is now established at Berber, approximately one hundred and fifty miles from the Khalifa's army at Omdurman. You are the last of the reinforcements to join the column as it advances south," Wingate briefed. "Your squadrons will depart over the next two weeks. The first group will be leaving tomorrow morning."

An excited rush went through the hall.

"A great deal of progress has been made moving steamers and gunboats past the Fifth Cataract north of Berber into the deep water of the Nile. You will be joining the main army there. All total, your forces will number just over 25,000 men."

There was a strong murmur of approval among the officers.

"You will have plenty of artillery support. The newest gunboats, *Zafir*, *Naser* and *Fateh*, have all been patrolling south of Berber," Wingate paused.

"General Benson would like to address you now," Wingate said. He took his seat and a distinguished looking officer with graying temples and a hawkish nose took center stage.

"You will be under the command of the Sirdar," General Benson instructed his men. "The British Division will be led by Major-General Gatacre. The Egyptian Infantry Division will fall under the command of Major-General Hunter. The Egyptian Cavalry will be commanded by Lieutenant Colonel Broadwood, the Camel Corps by Major Tudway, and the Artillery under Lieutenant Colonel Long."

General Benson paused.

"You should know who you are fighting. No doubt you have read the papers, heard the gossip. The enemy is fighting a jihad," he continued. "They believe it is a holy war, in the name of their god, Allah. They have their code of honor. Deceit and guile, cunning and ruthlessness, death and torture all are considered important attributes for their warriors. Above all, they despise the white man, and all he stands for. You will get a situational briefing upon your arrival at Berber. Good luck gentlemen," he said somberly.

"Room, ten -hut!" Colonel Wingate called out. General Benson walked off the stage and left the room.

"Take your seats, gentlemen," Wingate instructed. "Now, we will continue with an intelligence briefing on the capabilities and tactics of the enemy, and their command structure."

"The Khalifa remains in his holy city, Omdurman. His second-in-command is Emir Mahmüd. Mahmüd brought an additional 12,000 men, including horses and rifles, from the western provinces in Kordofan and Darfur. They have a well-trained cavalry and know how to use small artillery. We believe the Khalifa has also formed alliances with several other chieftains in the area," he continued.

"These chieftains are normally at war with each other, but faced with a common enemy, they have come together. They are fierce fighters, and their religion gives them a warlike frenzy that also justifies in their minds committing atrocities on enemies and innocents alike. Do not expect to be taken prisoner. They execute anyone weak enough to be captured," Wingate warned. *"After* torture," he emphasized.

There was an uneasy shift in the audience's mood.

Wingate walked over to a large map prominently displayed on the stage.

"Our forces are massed at Atbara, approximately 150 miles north of Omdurman. In between are the villages of Metemma and Shendi. They belong to the Jaalin, who are also allied with the Khalifa. The Jaalin are led by Abdalla-Wad-Saad, another one of the region's warlords. The Jaalin are only 1,200 in number, but their village stands directly in the path of our advance. There are rumors they are no longer allied with the Khalifa and may welcome us. Unfortunately, I can neither confirm or deny that rumor."

Wingate paused for a moment before continuing. So bloody much information.

"With the surrounding tribes joining the fight, the Khalifa's total forces will number roughly 80,000 men. Our intelligence reports indicate his main army of 60,000 is at Omdurman, his new 'holy city.' The remaining 20,000 are spread between Omdurman and Atbara under the command of the emirs Mahmüd and Osman Digna. In addition to those20,000 men, their women, children, cattle and possessions travel with them in caravan fashion," Wingate noted.

"Speaking of traveling, you will travel from Cairo to Atbara via steamer and the railway. The daily temperature will be around 110 degrees or higher," he added. "Consume plenty of water, and ration the whiskey."

A burst of laughter broke out from the officers.

"You will now break out into your individual units. We have detailed orders for each commander. Please have your unit briefings with your men, and ensure they are briefed on the rules of engagement. You are dismissed."

The audience hall broke into animated conversations. Finally, they were going to war.

"Let's grab some chow at the officer's mess," Kip suggested to Churchill.

"Indeed, let's do," he agreed.

Churchill watched Kip as he went down the buffet. His plate was overflowing.

"You certainly have an appetite," Churchill teased, piling slices of roast beef onto his own plate.

"Once we leave Cairo, I don't expect to get another good meal for a bit," Kip said. They made their way to a half-empty table where three officers were seated.

"Gentlemen," Churchill interrupted. "May I introduce Major Kip McDuran, United States Army," he waved with a flourish.

"Lieutenant Scott O'Connor, at your service, Major," one of the officers said, coming to his feet. "To what do we owe the honor of an American in our ranks?" he asked.

"O'Connor?" Churchill asked. "I've heard the name."

"That's because it's Irish," O'Connor laughed. "There's still a few of us running around," he added.

All the officers broke into laughter. Churchill looked embarrassed.

Kip laughed with them. "I'm afraid that my family hails from Scotland," he broke in. "Not that McDuran is a clan of any note."

"Ah, a Highlander," O'Connor teased.

"Not really," Kip answered. "A little town called Lundin Links, on the North Sea coast," he replied. "It's too cold in the highlands."

"Too many castles," O'Connor added with a smile.

Churchill bit his lip and thought about his uncle's castle at Blenheim. Not the time for it, he decided.

"So Major," asked one of the other officers. "Why do we have the pleasure of an American Army officer in our midst?"

"My government has a very keen interest in the dervish forces," Kip stated. He had been expecting such questions, but as always, felt a small knot in his stomach.

"Is your government expecting to get involved in the Middle East?" inquired another officer. "I realize you American's consider yourselves world players now that you are at war with Spain, but I wasn't aware you were at war with the Khalifa."

"We're not," Kip answered honestly. "But whether the war is in the Philippines or Cuba, my orders are to learn all I can about nonconventional warfare," he explained. "I'm just a reporter, here to document what I see and send a report back to the army, where it will wind up in a small little book tucked away in a dusty bookshelf," he said.

"Kind of like Churchill's writings," cracked the officer sitting next to O'Connor, Captain McAllister.

"I say........" Churchill sputtered.

"Just teasing, couldn't help myself. Ian McAllister, at your service, Lieutenant," said the Irish captain with a laugh. "And unlike poor O'Connor and McDuran, my family has a castle. We hail from Dublin," he said easily.

"Where do you hail from, O'Connor?" Kip asked politely.

"Belfast," the young lieutenant answered.

Belfast, Kip thought. Northern Ireland. Christ, he cursed to himself. I'm surrounded by micks and we're getting ready to ship out. I haven't got a clue who wants Churchill dead. How the hell am I supposed to protect the cheeky little bastard if I don't know where or when it's coming from? Thank you General Hanson, he thought sarcastically.

"When are you blokes shipping out?" O'Connor inquired. "I'm in charge of putting out the rosters, but I'm afraid I don't know everyone's departure dates by heart," he said.

"Not sure," Churchill said, "we have our unit briefing this afternoon."

"Squadron B is leaving tomorrow morning," O'Connor stated.

"I'm in A Squadron," Churchill said. "They haven't told us yet."

"Sometime in the next two weeks, I imagine," O'Connor said. "What about you Major?" he inquired politely.

I'm attached to A Squadron as well," Kip answered. "Perhaps we'll find out this afternoon."

"Well, we've already finished our lunch, and from the look of your plates, you may be here awhile," O'Connor said. The three officers stood up.

"Churchill, sorry about the joke," McAllister said. "I've read some of your stuff; it's quite good. It's a pleasure to go to war with you," he said sincerely.

Churchill beamed. "Thank you, sir. The pleasure is all mine."

McAllister gave them a wave and the three officers left the mess.

"That was awkward," Kip said.

Churchill smiled. "I get that a lot. I'm used to it. It comes with the territory, you know."

"No," Kip said. "I don't." Kip wasn't being rude, just honest.

"You should have seen the hazing I got as a kid," Churchill explained. "Everyone knew who my father was; everyone knew my name. It was like having a target on your back. Hello, launch the arrows," he laughed.

You have no idea, Kip thought.

"Now, I appreciate it," Churchill continued. "I almost revel in it."

"Why?"

"Because it's who I am. I believe in my destiny. Every man has a destiny."

"What is your destiny?" Kip asked.

"I will be the prime minister of England someday, as my father should have been. I am here to make a name for myself. I intend to win medals, distinguish myself on the field of battle, and use that famous name to get elected to Parliament," Churchill replied. Kip could tell he was dead serious.

"What would you do with your office?" Kip probed. Such an arrogant prick, he thought.

"Ensure the growth and well-being of the British Empire," Churchill replied without missing a beat. "And what is your destiny, Major?"

"I don't believe in destiny; I don't believe in fate. I believe that men are responsible for their actions and the consequences that flow from them," Kip answered.

"You American's are so pragmatic and so practical," Churchill said. "Now that your nation is becoming a world power, you have so much to learn about the world. You can learn a lot from us. The sun never sets on the British Empire."

"The British Empire is less one huge colony," Kip reminded him. "And since you are half American, do you ever get confused about your loyalties?" Kip smiled politely.

Churchill threw his head back and laughed. "Not in the slightest, Major. I am a loyal servant to the crown."

"I've never been too fond of any monarchy," Kip confessed. "It seems to tempt fate when power is passed on by birth. Who's to ensure that the monarch truly has the people's best interest at heart? How do they know he wasn't born a royal idiot?"

Churchill laughed again. "That's why we have Parliament, he pointed out.

"Well at least Cromwell got that part right," Kip said.

"And I truly do want to be a member of Parliament, and I truly do have the people's best interest at heart," Churchill added sincerely.

Kip looked at the steady blue eyes. *A future politician in the making wants me to believe him. No way.*

"I believe you Churchill," Kip lied.

"Now let's get to the regimental briefing before they start without us."

"Right."

The 21st Lancers were under the command of Colonel Martin, who stood on the stage in one of the smaller auditoriums. He watched his men file in and take their seats. *So bloody young,* he thought. The white officers and their non-commissioned enlisted leaders were a proud and eager outfit. The enlisted troops, mostly Egyptian, would have a briefing from their white noncommissioned officers later.

"Gentlemen, take your seats please."

The room grew quiet.

"The 21st Lancers will be divided into three squadrons. B squadron is departing tomorrow morning. Squadron assignments are posted on the bulletin boards outside the auditorium. Squadron commanders will have a list of their men," Martin informed them.

"You will be traveling 1,400 miles through the desert to reach your destination. Your journey will last 11 days. You can expect the daily temperatures once you reach the Sudan to be well over 110 degrees Fahrenheit during the day. You will depart Cairo tomorrow by train to Khizam. Men will ride in the carriages; the horses will ride in covered rail cars."

"From Khizam you will take the steamships to Assuan. These steamships are leased from Thomas Cook & Sons, so be sure to return them in the same condition you found them," he added. Laughter filled the room.

"At Assuan, you will disembark, and take time to exercise the horses. Then you will ride to Shellal and board steamers which will carry you to Wadi Halfa. From there you will ride aboard the Sudan Military Railway for a 400-mile trip across the Nubian desert to Atbara, just south of Berber where the expeditionary army is based."

Where in the name of God am I going, Kip thought. *The heart of*

Africa? Might as well be hell. Over 110 degrees by day? The men will be dropping like flies and so will their horses.

As Colonel Martin Colonel continued, Kip pondered when and where the battle would take place. His intelligence briefing in Washington had told him that the Khalifa would not attack the British at Atbara. The Khalifa was well aware of the deadly effects of artillery and the Maxim gun. While at first blush it might seem madness for an army of 25,000 men to attack a force of over 80,000 angry men defending their homeland, technology was the great equalizer. In fact, Kip surmised that it would be an old-fashioned ass-whipping.

The British gunships were deadly. The brand new 1898 Class armored screw gunboats each packed two Nordenfeldt machine guns, a quick firing 12-pound cannon, a howitzer that could wreak havoc from long range and 4 Maxims. The Maxim was a formidable weapon. The water-cooled recoil-operated machine gun could spew forth a cyclone of death, capable of firing 500 7.69 caliber bullets a minute.

The British artillery, once set up and established on land, was also a formidable force equalizer. The 40-pound cannons and 5-inch howitzers would lay down a wall of shrapnel long before the dervish forces were in range to use their rifles. They would also have 20 Maxims on land.

As long as no one did anything stupid, it would be a rout, Kip decided. Keeping Churchill alive, on the other hand, would not be so easy.

B Squadron was leaving for the Sudan tomorrow, and he still didn't have any suspects in mind, other than the obvious connection with the Irish officers at the mess. Logic reminded him that there was no shortage of Irishmen in the army. Where would the attack on Churchill take place? How would the attack take place? When, and by whom? The Fenians could have paid off anyone, including the Arabs.

The most likely scenario was in battle, Kip decided. There would be any manner of opportunities to kill Churchill, and either make a statement or create an investigation. The more publicity, the better. That's what terrorists want. It would also provide cover for the assassins. The chaos of the battlefield rarely reveals its hidden secrets, Kip thought.

The best lessons learned are learned by the vanquished. And they don't talk much.

One of many lessons life had taught Kip was not to wait for things to come to him. It could be a long wait. He didn't like being watched by an enemy he couldn't see. It was time to see if he could flush them out of the brush.

After the briefing, he excused himself from Churchill and went to the stable to get his horse. The ride to the residence of U.S. Consul-General in Cairo took an hour. The immaculately attired Egyptian officer seated at the entrance looked over his papers and sent him through.

Kip didn't have an appointment, but he doubted he would need one. He had a special request for the War Department in Washington. He had to send a telegram immediately. He spoke briefly with Consul-General Harrison, without divulging his mission. He was led to the telegraph room, where he handed his message to the operator.

Urgent for War Department, General Hanson Eyes Only. Contact the Prince. Request Churchill and I be reassigned to 21st Lancers, Squadron B, immediately for departure tomorrow.

Kip went to bed late that evening after riding back to the base from the Ambassador's residence. If his plan was successful, he might force their hand. He also made sure he was packed and ready for war.

Chapter Sixty-Six

SUDAN, 1898

The Khalifa rushed into Syrah's tent, his face contorted with rage. "Where is the woman?!" he screamed. "Where is the woman?!"

The guard assigned to watch her could only look down at the ground. "I do not know, my lord," he said.

"You do not know?!" the Khalifa shrieked. "You do not know?" He pulled his sword from his scabbard and held the blade to the man's throat. "Find her now," he hissed. The man slunk from the tent, bowing.

The Khalifa stomped out of Syrah's tent and back to his own. Although it was early in the morning, the sun was already beating down. If Syrah had escaped, he had no translator to assist him. It couldn't have come at a worst time. He had planned to call a jirga, a council meeting of all the leaders of the Arab tribes of the Sudan. Now he would have to act as if nothing was wrong. He did not want anyone to get wind that both of his translators had successfully escaped his grasp. To do so would appear weak.

"Tell the city I will speak to them today at noon," he ordered one of his aides. "Call the emirs to counsel, today, after I speak to my people," he barked at another. The aide went flying from the tent.

Later that day, at noon, the Khalifa rode his horse through the obedient crowd that had gathered in front of the city's largest mosque in Omdurman, which was also the resting place of his predecessor, the Mahdi. Thousands of his dervish soldiers thronged around. Boldly colored banners waved about, and the shrill tongues of the women and the roars of the crowd added to the excitement of the moment.

He dismounted his horse and walked up to the top of the stairs, turning to face the crowd.

"Allahu akbar!" he roared.

"Allahu akbar!" the crowd roared back.

"The infidel is coming!" he screamed. "The Egyptian traitors are bringing the English scourge. Their Christian army advances, intent to destroy our blessed city of Omdurman," he warned.

The Khalifa rested his hands on the wooden pulpit that he used to address his people, and he leaned forward as if he was seeking to bring them closer to him.

"Allah the Almighty, and the Mahdi, have brought me a great vision," he preached. "I see the bodies of the white man stretched out in the sand, obliterated by the armies of Islam. Birds pick at their bones, bleached white by the sun. And the jackal runs after the fleeing Egyptian as he runs from our advancing horde. The Egyptian will flee to his home, never to return. And in the blessed name of Allah, neither will the Christians!" he screamed.

Excitement spread through the crowd.

"The Mahdi came to me in my sleep," the Khalifa continued. "He told me that the hand of Allah is on my sword," he pledged. He pulled his sword out and waved it above his head.

"In the name of Allah and the name of the prophet, Muhammad, and in the name of the Mahdi, we will rise and destroy the infidel and the Egyptian whores who would seek to bring the white man to our land!" he roared. "And I will lead you with my sword!" he shouted. He could feel his excitement rise with the crowd.

"And I will destroy them with my sword!" he screamed, his voice reaching a crescendo as he waved his sword about his head in a circle. "This is a holy war," he commanded. "It is jihad! I command you to rise in the name of Allah and our glorious Mahdi. Rise!" he ordered.

The dervish horde scrambled to their feet and roared back their approval. Thousands of swords gleamed in the sunlight as they capered about.

"I command you, and Allah commands you, to defend your homeland. Defend your women from the devils who would have their way with them. Defend your crops and your belongings. Defend Islam and all that is holy!" he harangued.

"Fight in the name of Allah!" he screamed. "Islam will prevail, and we will rule the land victorious in the name of the prophet. The law of Islam shall be the law of the land, and all who stand against us shall die a horrible death!" he promised.

"Allahu akbar!" Spittle flew from his mouth as he incited the crowd.

"Allahu akbar!" the crowd roared back, a sea of blue and white jibbas made of cotton, red and blue patches and gores of navy blue and khaki wool facecloth. Glistening swords and rifles shook madly in the air.

The Khalifa mounted his horse and rode out into the worshipping throng. His skin had goose bumps, as he was caught up in the moment. Breathing heavily, blood coursing through his veins, he rode away from the crowd, closely followed by his bodyguards. He left the screaming mob behind him, and rode to his tent, to meet the counsel of emirs.

It was time to declare war.

He strode into the jirga and took his seat on his throne.

About him were the emirs of the tribes of the Sudan. Ahmed Fedil of Gedaref had traveled hundreds of miles to the capital to attend the jirga, as had the Ibrahim Khalil from Gezira and Osman Digna from Adsarama. They had brought their armies to Omdurman, to serve the Khalifa, and to destroy the infidel who dared to trespass on their lands.

Osman Digna had fought the Egyptians before. At the Battle of El Teb, his army inflicted heavy casualties and sent the Egyptians fleeing home. The Egyptians returned, but this time led by General Graham and the British.

At the second Battled of El Teb, Osman Digna nearly defeated the British as well, and was the only foreign commander ever to succeed in breaking the British infantry square. Osman Digna was no stranger to war.

"We have been betrayed," the Khalifa stated. "The Jaalin, the cowards of the river, have sought safety and comfort in the arms of the British."

A murmur of surprise spread through the tent.

"Mahmüd is on his way to Mettema as I speak," the Khalifa said. "He has taken his army to punish the Jaalin. He will leave behind an empty hole in the ground, filled with the blood and limbs of the traitors for the cowardly Englishman to find as an example." And for anyone else who would dare think to betray me, the Khalifa thought silently.

"Begin preparation for war," the Khalifa ordered. "We outnumber our enemy four to one. We too have rifles and artillery. We too have horses, we too have soldiers. Begin preparing your armies, and be ever vigilant. We must double the number of scouts and spies that we have watching the infidel. I want to know their every move."

He paused while he took a sip of tea from an ornate copper chalice. He set it down on a brass tray.

"Is there anyone here who wishes to be heard?" he asked.

There was silence in the tent. They knew better.

"Go then, and prepare your armies," he ordered.

After the emirs had left his tent, he turned to the leader of his personal guard, Mohammed-ez-Zein. "Find the woman, and bring her back to me, alive," he ordered.

His trusted lieutenant bowed and left the tent.

"Alive!" he yelled after him.

Abdalla-Wad-Saad arrived at his village at dawn. He went to every hut, arousing the Jaalin from their slumber, imploring them to meet him in the village square. Within fifteen minutes, all of the tribal leaders had assembled. As the morning light broke over the village, Wad-Saad informed them of their plight.

"There will be no mercy," he told them. "The Khalifa will seek to destroy us, rape our women, murder our children," he warned.

"We must flee," one of the leaders said.

"They will cut us down in the open," Wad-Saad replied.

"They will cut us down here," argued another.

"We have no idea of how many men he will send against us," Wad-Saad said. He was trying to convey confidence. In the pit of his stomach, he feared the worst. The village sat in a small clearing next to the Nile. The Jaalin had constructed a small mud and stone wall around the entire village and had built up several small ramparts at each corner.

"We have rifles," he said. "We will send out scouts to warn of their advance. We will be waiting for them."

The Jaalin set out busily fortifying the walls and gathering every weapon in the village. A count of able-bodied men reached 2,500. But only 80 working rifles could be found, along with 1,500 rounds of ammunition. The rest would have to make do with knives, spears, swords, clubs, rocks and anything else they could get their hands on.

Abdalla-Wad-Saad sent a rider to the British carrying a message pledging his allegiance to Egypt and imploring them to come to their aid immediately.

CHAPTER SIXTY-SEVEN

CAIRO, 1898

The next morning Kip took a seat in the back of the auditorium, intentionally avoiding Churchill, who was in the front row. There was excited chatter in the hall. B Squadron was leaving later that day, and the rest of the men might find out their departure dates as well. He could see Churchill's pink cheeks flushed with excitement. Kip was excited too, but for a different reason.

Colonel Martin took the stage. "Take your seats, men," he ordered. The nervous chatter died down.

"B Squadron will meet with their officers immediately after the briefing to prepare for departure. A and C squadron commanders will stay after the briefing to meet with command staff for their departure dates," he continued.

"There are a few last-minute changes to today's departure roster," he added. "Your commanders will brief you after we finish up with the command staff. Plan on returning to the auditorium in one hour's time," he instructed.

The room broke into an even louder chorus of excited chatter and banter. Kip remained behind for the command staff briefing. He moved down to the front row and found an empty seat.

"Gentlemen," Colonel Martin said, addressing his commanders and senior noncommissioned officers. "A squadron will depart in three days time, on August 3. C squadron will depart three days after that, on August 6. A and C squadron will gather at the rail station today to see

B squadron depart. Once we are all at Atbara we will proceed as one unit again."

He paused as he took a sheet of papers off a table. "Some minor changes in the departure roster," he noted. "A squadron is losing Lieutenant Churchill to B Squadron, along with Major McDuran, the American observer. A squadron will pick up Lieutenant Smythe in return."

Kip looked around the room for a reaction from anyone. There was none.

"Also, B squadron is picking up Sergeant O'Leary and Corporal Mackenzie. A squadron will receive Sergeant Patterson and Corporal Michael in return."

"I say, seems to me there is some cherry-picking going on," joked the A squadron commander.

"Don't look at me," said the C squadron commander.

Kip wanted to raise his hand. Why were O'Leary and Mackenzie switching squadrons? His message to General Hanson had requested Churchill's reassignment only. The transfer of the two non-commissioned officers, O'Leary and Mackenzie, to B Squadron could be a coincidence. Or it could have been the knee-jerk reaction he was trying to discover. He waited until the briefing was over and approached Colonel Martin.

"Sir, a word with you?" he asked politely.

"Of course, Major," the senior officer said. They retreated to a small office. "The Sirdar was very clear that I am to accommodate you in any way possible," Martin said. He looked at the American army officer with curiosity.

"What do you want?"

"Just a question about the roster," Kip said.

"I doubt the United States government gives a shit about the roster," Colonel Martin smiled. "And if you are going to ask me why you and Churchill are reassigned to B Company, I can't tell you because I don't have an answer. And if you have a problem with leaving today, there's nothing I can do," he added. "We received a cable this morning from the War Office in London reassigning you and Churchill to B Squadron," he went on. "That's it. I hope you're packed."

Kip smiled back. "I've been ready since I got here." "Are there any special instructions for me in that cable?" Kip inquired.

"Not unless it's in code," Colonel Martin replied. He was serious. He took up a folder and rifled through its contents, pulling out a yellow piece of paper. "Take a look for yourself," he said, handing the cable to Kip.

Attention Col Martin, 21st Lancers. American advisor Major McDuran and Lieutenant Churchill transferred to B squadron effective before scheduled departure.

"Nope, doesn't say a word. Oh well, I'm sure someone in London has a reason for the transfer," Kip said casually. "What about the noncommissioned officers, O'Leary and Mackenzie?" Kip asked innocently.

"That was purely a local staff function," Colonel Martin said. "You'll have to ask someone on the Sirdar's staff about that. I believe Lt. O'Connor is in charge of the roster. Ask him."

"None of my business, that won't be necessary, sir. I was just curious," Kip said in return. He handed the dispatch back to the commander of the 21st Lancers. Bullshit. O'Connor was from Belfast. Someone in personnel had made the switch for a reason.

"Guess I'd better grab my gear," Kip said as he left the room, taking care to salute first.

He went back to his quarters. When he had first arrived in Cairo he met with the quartermaster and obtained uniforms for the 21st Lancers. It was the standard British army khaki field uniform for overseas service. He also had the standard issue helmet, a Wolseley-style cork helmet covered with khaki. It had a quilted cotton sunshade extending the brim of the helmet. He also had a quilted cloth "spine pad" that he would wear on his back to protect his brain and his spine from the crippling rays of the sun.

After the standard issue khaki uniform and helmet, the rest of his gear was courtesy of the War Department in Washington.

As noted by name, the 21st Lancers indeed carried spears. It was a fact that Kip found disturbing. In this day of modern warfare, a man with a pointed stick was little match for a man with a loaded rifle, even if it was an old-fashioned musket. Put the man with the sharp stick on a horse, and he was still an easy target for a patient marksman. The day of the cavalry was numbered, Kip thought. A man on a fast horse was best used for reconnaissance, not combat.

The Lancers were also armed with the 1896 model Lee-Enfield carbine firing a .303 caliber bullet, and a Webley revolver.

For once, Kip was in complete agreement with Churchill on a military matter. Churchill carried a brand new 1898 Mauser self-loading pistol. This German firearm had a box magazine which held ten 7.63 mm bullets and could be fired as fast as one could pull the trigger.

Kip thought that the American fascination with the revolver was foolish. Especially given the advances in technology with self-loading pistols. The Colt firearms company apparently agreed, and they had developed a prototype model based upon the design by John Moses Browning.

Kip smiled as he held the .45 caliber pistol in his hand. It was beautiful and deadly. It was designed to knock men down so that they did not get up. The rifled five-inch barrel could send out a lead slug that would tear a man's arm off. With seven rounds in the magazine and one in the breech, the pistol featured a double action, which allowed one round to be chambered at all times. The lead bullets were hollow point and lethal. It had been handcrafted for Military Intelligence officers. It was not available to the public.

For his rifle, Kip had thought long and hard about the type of combat he would encounter and how best to arm himself. The army was using the new Krag-Jorgensen bolt action repeating rifle built by Springfield. It was accurate but only had five rounds in its magazine.

However, the Winchester Repeating Arms Company had been refining its popular Model 1866 rifle for years, experimenting with different cartridges and calibers. The rifle Kip carried fired a modified .45 caliber cartridge and could hold up to ten rounds in its tubular magazine.

It also had a loading gate on the side that allowed for easy reloading. Thus, both his pistol and rifle had stopping power and capacity. An edge Kip was counting on.

It took most of the day to get the horses and supplies loaded onto the steamers for the nearly 1,400-mile journey to the railhead at Berber. Kip was impressed with the logistics employed by the British to move such a large fighting force over a long distance.

A military band was playing "Auld Lang Syne" as they finally got seated on the coach. Excited chatter and banter filled the cars as they pulled away from the station. Huge billows of smoke hurtled up from the engines as they roared to life.

Kip found a seat next to Churchill, and they watched out the window as the crowds disappeared and the train picked up steam.

"We are going to Assuan to board the steamships for Wadi Halfa. It's going to take a great deal of time to unload the railcars," Winston said. "We should take advantage of the delay and go to see the Egyptian ruins."

"I have always wanted to see the Pyramids," Kip answered honestly.

Churchill giggled. "Sorry mate," he laughed.

Kip felt himself growing annoyed. "What's so amusing?" he asked.

"No Pyramids in Assuan, mate," Churchill teased. "Didn't they teach you yanks that at West Point?"

Kip felt his blood pressure rise. "I must have been absent that day," he replied. The little prick was making fun of him.

"There is, however, a remarkable structure, the Temple of Philae," Churchill continued. Churchill reveled in his moment of glory. The American had a weakness, he thought. He doesn't like to be teased. And he needs to work on his history lessons.

"It is also known as the Temple of Isis, the goddess of motherhood, magic, and fertility. Rather an amazing woman," Churchill continued with a mischievous grin.

"Much like my mother."

"I know the story of Isis," Kip interrupted. "Ideal mother and wife, patroness of nature and magic," he added. "Mother of Horus, the god of war." He paused. "Hey, by your account, you must be Horus," he joked back.

"Indeed," Churchill replied. He patted the butt of his pistol. They both laughed.

They reached Assuan the next day. The two men hired a carriage and followed the road towards the temple, which sat on an island in the middle of the Nile. Kip tried to enjoy the ride but was distracted. Were they being followed? He was uncomfortable with the idea that someone was watching Churchill ; much like a lioness watching her prey, waiting for the right moment to strike.

But Kip was soon overwhelmed by the stark beauty of the temple. He had seen photo plates and lithographs in his studies at West Point. But nothing prepared him for the incredible sense of history he felt as he wandered the ruins. He admired the sculptured towers rising towards the sky. He marveled at the temple hieroglyphs carved into stone. They spent several hours wandering through the temple before reluctantly heading back to the railhead. Their small Arab guide deftly guided the carriage along the dusty road.

"Remarkable, truly remarkable," Kip said.

Churchill nodded in agreement. He took a flask of whiskey out of his hip pocket and took a swig. He offered it to Kip, who politely declined.

"A remarkable civilization," Churchill said.

"And like all great civilizations, *past and present*, destined to fall," Kip replied.

Churchill looked at him with bemusement. "Surely you are not suggesting the rise and fall of the British Empire?" he took another sip of whiskey. It was on.

"Jesus," Kip said, exasperated. "You're not going to start with that holy empire shit again are you?"

"England is not a holy empire," Churchill replied calmly. "And you started it. You are confusing the Holy Roman Empire which conquered the ancient Egyptians with the Empire of the Realm."

"If I'm not mistaken, the Holy Roman Empire built a few forts on your land as well," Kip stated.

"Yes, but that was before we became an empire," Churchill said.

"All great civilizations fall," Kip said.

"Not England," Churchill said. His lower jaw set, not unlike a bulldog. They rode in silence for a few minutes, each man reflecting upon the ruins of the fallen Egyptian pharaohs.

"Where did you grow up?" Churchill asked, switching topics.

"Monterey," Kip answered.

"My father liked Monterey," Churchill reflected. "He took a vacation there when he was ill. He stayed at the Del Monte Hotel."

"A small world," Kip noted. Too close to home.

"Indeed," Churchill replied.

"What brings you here, Major?" Churchill asked.

"Orders," Kip answered honestly. "What about you?" he countered. "You certainly aren't here for the money. And you certainly aren't here because someone forced you," he added. "Why are you here?"

"Why am I here?" Churchill mused. His boyish face broke into an infectious grin. "I told you already. To kill as many dervish scoundrels as I can, win a few medals, and get elected to Parliament," he laughed.

"Glory hound," Kip said.

"Ambitious," Churchill replied.

"So was Caesar," Kip countered.

"And political," Churchill added. "Don't forget. Very political."

"Yeah, I get that about you," Kip snorted. "Born with a silver spoon in your mouth," he stated. He wanted to add that Churchill was an arrogant ass as well but decided to be diplomatic.

"True," Churchill nodded. "And why shouldn't I take advantage of my good name? It's my bloodlines."

"Because you didn't do shit to earn it," Kip said honestly.

"Nobility is passed from generation to generation," Churchill lectured. "A commoner couldn't be expected to understand that. That's why we have a sovereign, a living, benevolent monarch, a symbol of our people and our race."

"You are a tribe," Kip said. "With a village idiot and a group of elders holding all the power."

"We are a tad bit more civilized than that, dear chap," Churchill laughed.

"Not really," Kip stated calmly. "You call this expedition civilized?" Your tribe is going to fight their tribe because your tribe believes in a different god than their tribe."

"They are a pestiferous breed," Churchill said.

"This is nothing more than a crusade. History repeats itself," Kip said. "Islam versus Christianity."

"This is not a Holy War," Churchill argued.

"It is for them," Kip pointed out. "So it is for you. You are fighting a holy war whether you like it or not."

"The white man has long had the responsibility of bringing order to chaos on this continent," Churchill maintained.

"You may not want to go out on a limb for the white man," Kip advised honestly. "Your tribe is going to burn their village and take their women," Kip pushed. "That's what tribes do. And the only thing that is different today from the past is the technology. And in your case, your tribe has quite the edge."

"You Americans have a remarkable way of simplifying things," Churchill said. Brutal, but honest. An effective approach, his mind logged.

"It's that simple," Kip maintained. "Each tribe has its religion, its own beliefs, and values. If you are not with them, then you are against them."

"Surely you are not placing Christianity on the same plane as Islam," Churchill bridled.

"All religions are nothing more than a means of obtaining and holding power," Kip argued.

"That's blasphemy," Churchill said. "Now you've gone too far." His cheeks flushed.

"That's the truth. Religion plays upon each man's weakness, which is each man's fear of death," Kip continued.

"Every single living being is born with a death sentence in place," Kip hammered. "You can't appeal it, and there is no clemency. Promise life after death and you obtain a following. Obtain a following, and you obtain power. To keep power, promise no life after death if you don't believe."

Their carriage rolled to a stop in front of the encampment. "You get a lot of believers that way. Fear is a wonderful motivator," Kip added.

Churchill listened intently. It went against everything he learned as a child.

Kip jumped down from the carriage, his boots kicking up a cloud of dust.

"Be they priest, imam, high priestess, cardinal, pope or medicine man, they all claim one thing.…. to be the one true religion with the one true God," Kip said.

Churchill dismounted the carriage.

"You express some alarming views, Major," he said stiffly.

"It's called freedom," Kip replied.

"You're going to rot in hell," Churchill warned seriously.

Kip could only laugh. "I'm not going to rot in hell," he smirked. "It's too damn hot. I'll be incinerated. There won't be anything left to rot."

"Bloody yank," Churchill snorted. The two men walked silently back to camp, where they joined the rest of the squadron to walk the horses around the first cataract of the Nile.

CHAPTER SIXTY-EIGHT

METEMMA, 1898

Syrah reached Metemma three days later than she planned. She rode her horse slowly through the village, wholly absorbed by the horror that surrounded her. Smoke was still billowing up from the torched huts. Burning thatched roofs fell into the pyre. She was no stranger to atrocity, but her blood ran cold as she absorbed the scene.

Scorched, mutilated bodies were strewn about, some piled on top of one another, others lying halfway inside huts. Flies gathered around the dead heaps with lustful excitement. Burning flesh stumps with smoldering sandals protruded from doorways. The stench of iron and charred corpses nearly overcame her, burning her eyes and the insides of her nostrils. She clenched her jaw, stifling her gags as she slowly made her way through the carnage, transfixed.

Syrah saw the body of a headless baby impaled on a wooden spike and gasped in horror. Old women laid lifelessly on the ground, mangled in the blood and dirt, partially disrobed, their limbs akimbo, legs forced apart. No doubt the young women were still alive, kidnapped, destined to a life of slavery and rape.

There was no one alive here. Mahmüd and his men exterminated every one of the Jaalin. Apparently, the law of Islam did not apply to warring tribes.

Syrah snapped out of her stupor when she rode out the other side of Metemma. Leaving the billowing smoke behind, she ruminated on how men could such be such animals, so sadistic, so ruthless. All of her life she had seen nothing but hatred, annihilation and destruction. It was a disease.

She decided to ride north, towards Atbara. She stopped to fill her water skin from the Nile. The sun was high and the rushing water looked inviting. She looked along the river banks for tracks from the crocodiles, but there were none. She looked around the tall grass by the river. She was alone.

She changed into more traditional Sudanese clothing, a tob she found in the village. It still had dried blood on it. Sudanese woman usually wrapped themselves in fifteen feet of material, with one end thrown over the left shoulder, and the rest wrapped down to their ankles. Syrah's tob was more like the Dinka, shorter, ending just above her knee. She took off her tob and set it on a rock. She left her sandals on the shore, and walked into the water, completely naked.

With the water up to her waist, she ducked her body entirely underneath, reveling in how refreshing it felt. She rubbed sand from the river bed over her body, scrubbing away dirt and sweat. She was desperate to get the smell of Metemma off of her body.

After she bathed, she washed her clothes in the river and put them on wet. They would be dry within an hour. She wrapped her head in a hijab to protect her head from the sun's scorching rays.

She thought about what would happen when she encountered the British. She feared they would not be accepting of her. She was half white, but her skin was mahogany, dark from the sun. Her hair was thick and black, but straight, which made it easier for her to braid. Thank god she had blue eyes. It would add evidence to her incredible story.

She knew that the British would be impressed that she could read, write and speak English. She could only hope they would listen and give her shelter. Perhaps she could find work.

She was hungry, so she ate a kisru biscuit. It would have to last the day. She had only one left, and at least two days travel ahead. She would follow the river north and pray that she would not encounter men. She secured her water bag and kisru and mounted her horse. It would be a long, hot, dusty ride. But there was nothing for her back in Metemma. There was no one left alive.

CHAPTER SIXTY-NINE

WADI HALFA, 1898

The squadron reached Wadi Halfa just before the second cataract and began the enormous task of transferring men, animals, supplies and weapons from the steamers to the train. The coal-black steel engines stood silently under the afternoon heat, unyielding and unconcerned. It was a different story for the sweating men and animals, almost feverish from physical labor and the sun's relentless burning rays. But finally, it was done, and the men boarded the Sudan Military Railway.

They fired the engines and the locomotive built up pressure. An hour later, they began their journey through the desert.

Kip gazed out over the vast expanse. The horizon was lost in a shimmering mirage of water underneath a cloudless blue sky. A sea of ocher stretched out endlessly ahead of them. Mother of God, he thought to himself. I'm a long way from home.

Sweat dripped down every inch of his body; his uniform was completely drenched. The windows were open, allowing hot air and dust to rush through the cab. I'm in hell, Kip thought. Churchill walked down the aisle, a flask in his hand.

"Care for a tipple?" he offered.

Jesus, Kip thought. Does this guy drink from dusk until dawn?

"Nope, I think I'll wait," Kip responded dryly.

Churchill mopped his brow with a sweat rag and stuffed it back into his pocket. "Well, before you know it, we'll reach Atbara," he said.

"The day after tomorrow," Kip replied.

"And then the real fun begins," Churchill smiled. "From there, we march to Wad Hamed."

"Insane," Kip said, wiping away sweat with his collar.

"You know what they say, only mad dogs and Englishmen go out in the noonday sun," Churchill agreed.

"That I believe."

"We are going for good reason," Churchill assured him.

"What's that?" Kip asked. "The good of the empire? For the royal idiots?"

"Avenging Gordon," Churchill smiled, ignoring the dig. "That's more than enough reason."

"This isn't about avenging Gordon," Kip disagreed. "It's about projecting power. Your government is making a demonstration of its ability to advance a line of communication deep into the heart of Africa. The military is an instrument of national power, period."

"Spoken like a true academic," Churchill mused. "You just don't see the romance, the adventure in all this?"

"Romance," Kip said, incredulous. "For Christ's sake, you've been in the sun too long. And don't get any ideas."

"Not that kind of romance, you dolt," Churchill laughed. "You need to work on the King's English," he chided.

"Keep it up," Kip growled.

"Romance," Churchill said softly. "A long medieval tale in verse or prose, originally written in one of the Romance dialects about the adventures of knights and other chivalric heroes," he recited, in the increasing agitation of his American friend.

"Great, so you memorized the dictionary," Kip muttered.

"I spent a great deal of time mastering the written word," Churchill said lightly. "However, I cannot say the same of mathematics."

"Well, we have something in common then, don't we," Kip agreed.

"Not my cup of tea," Churchill smiled. "But then, who's going to elect a mathematician to Parliament, after all?"

"You don't have to be a mathematician to figure out why we are here," Kip retorted. It was hot. He got out of his seat and walked over to the thermometer on the wall of their car.

"Only one hundred and five," he announced. "And it isn't even noon yet." He looked around their railway car. The excited chatter of the squadron in the morning had died down, and now many of the men were napping.

He came back to his seat.

"So Churchill, if I understand you correctly, you plan to go to war, win medals and fame, go home, get elected, and be a politician?"

"Yes, I believe in my destiny, and that is my destiny," he said matter-of-factly.

"You're certain you will survive this little war we find ourselves in?"

"I could be killed," Churchill said thoughtfully, "but I rather doubt it. I have many things to do in this life and death would be a severe inconvenience."

"Really?" said Kip, eyebrows raised. "A severe inconvenience?"

"My father left behind a great deal of unfinished business," Churchill continued.

"Boy howdy," Kip said sarcastically. If only you knew how much unfinished business, he thought.

"I feel it is my destiny to finish his business and my own," Churchill added.

"And that is?" Kip asked.

"I've told you before, to preserve the empire, the British way of life. We are the most civilized people in the world. We are a system of laws and integrity."

"The rich get richer? Hardly my idea of integrity."

"The laws in my country exist to ensure that the rich keep what they have earned and can pass it down to their children," Churchill answered.

"You can have all the money in the world and it still won't buy you a first-class ticket to heaven," Kip said. "What about the rest of the people, the common folk?"

"They need that sense of structure, of organization. People need to belong to something. Our way of life, our values, our history provides that."

"So long as no one upsets the balance of power," Kip pointed out. "Once power is obtained, tribal leaders will justify anything to ensure they maintain power, even to the detriment of the tribe."

"Why should they give it up?" Churchill asked. "If a man spends his whole life working to achieve power, why should he forfeit his work?"

"Why should his children inherit that power?" Kip challenged. "What makes them qualified to inherit any power in the first place?" he added, his volume increasing. "What makes you qualified to inherit power?"

"Me?"

"Yes, you," Kip snapped. "You have this need to finish your father's work, but what makes you think you are qualified? You're not your father."

Churchill sat in silence. He pulled out another cigarette and lit it, drawing deeply.

"I say, old man," he said, letting a slow stream of smoke out his lips. "That was a tad bit aggressive, don't you think?"

No shit, Kip thought to himself. I'm in this godforsaken land, dying of dehydration, simply so I can babysit some spoiled-rotten aristocrat who thinks he is God's gift to the world, and protect him from the very people whom he expects to hold reign over.

"Yes, it was aggressive," Kip admitted. "But the point remains. You are not your father."

Churchill reached inside his tunic and touched his father's watch, as if he needed to reassure himself that it was still there.

"I feel compelled, driven," he said. "I'm being completely honest. I can't explain it. It's the way I grew up."

He looked at Kip. The handsome American soldier sitting next to him seemed sincere. It was the custom of men to bond before a fight, Churchill reasoned. To share stories of home and girls. To argue and curse, and ultimately, to become brothers-in-arms.

"I never got to know my father," Churchill continued. "I wanted to.

I was desperate for his attention. The harder I tried, the more distant he seemed to become. I was never good enough. I was never good at anything. He pointed that out on more than one occasion up until his death."

They sat in silence for a moment.

"And you Major, your father, your destiny?"

"My father was murdered when I was a child, and my mother died shortly thereafter. I'm an orphan."

Churchill sat silently, trying to absorb the idea. "You grew up in an orphanage?"

"No," Kip said.

"Who too raised you?"

Kip felt himself becoming defensive. The little bastard was digging. But some part of him actually wanted Churchill to understand him.

"After my mother died, I pretty much kept to myself," he said.

"How old were you?"

"Ten."

"Who raised you?"

"Actually, for a few years, I did."

"You raised yourself?"

"Yes."

"Where did you live?"

"In the forest."

Churchill sat back in his seat. "Pardon my asking," he said after a pause. He was trying to get his mind around the idea.

"You're kidding?"

"No."

"Like a wild animal?"

"Fuck you."

"I didn't mean it like that," Churchill apologized. "I mean, though, as in sleep in the forest, eat in the forest, go to church in the forest, and go to school in the forest?"

"Yes, for a while. But there was no school for me then."

"How in god's name did you survive?"

"I don't know," Kip answered honestly.

"How the bloody hell did you get here?" Churchill asked.

"By train," Kip answered dryly.

Churchill let out a laugh.

"Seriously mate, your story is fascinating. How the hell does an orphan who grew up in the wilderness grow up to become an intelligence officer, a graduate of one of the most prestigious military academies in the world? I mean, who the hell opened your doors?"

"It was simply a matter of luck," Kip admitted. "Eventually I was adopted, by a very good man. He was wealthy, and he took me in."

"What was his name?"

"David Jacks," Kip answered.

"Bloody hell, I've heard of him. He owned the whole town of Monterey at one point, didn't he?" Churchill exclaimed.

"Yep," Kip answered.

"Holy shit," Churchill said. "I remember reading his obituary. He passed away a few years ago, didn't he?"

"Aye, that he did."

"And who inherited his fortune?" Churchill asked.

"I did."

"I see." Churchill sat back in his seat. He took another drink from his flask.

"So instead of being born with a silver spoon in your mouth, you tripped and fell, and the spoon lodged in your ass. As in, you lucked into it?"

"Pretty much."

"So if you have money, why the hell are you here?" Churchill asked. He was becoming increasingly interested in his new friend's story.

"I was already in the army when Jacks died," Kip answered honestly. "This is all I know."

"But it must be tempting, the high society life?"

"I wouldn't know," Kip replied. "I'm not sure I want to."

"Now I feel like a little devil, sitting on your shoulder," Churchill joked. "Should I tempt you with stories of the wealthy elite?"

"No. I've already had dinner with you and your mother. That was more than enough."

"It's as if the world revolves around you," Churchill pressed.

"I believe it," Kip answered sharply.

"*Everyone* wants to be your friend," Churchill prodded.

"Was it that way for you?" Kip asked.

"No, actually. You see, I was already in the circle. Everyone in my circle already had a birthright. We all knew that growing up. So in that sense, I was just run of the mill."

"With a massive insecurity complex?"

"Quite," Churchill admitted. "And actually, my family is a bit tight on cash. The duke has all of that. That's why I write."

"And now?"

"I have a lot of lost time to make up for," Churchill said.

"While still carrying that massive insecurity complex?"

"That's my fuel, my energy."

"Driven."

"Yes. Precisely."

"Hmm." Kip reached over and gestured towards the flask. Churchill handed it to him with a boyish grin.

"To the devil on your shoulder," Churchill toasted.

"To the devil on my shoulder," Kip toasted back. He took a long drink, then looked back in surprise at the flask.

"Not bad, actually," Kip said approvingly.

Churchill grinned.

"I'm growing on you, Major."

"So is this fungus in my crotch," Kip replied. He took another swig.

CHAPTER SEVENTY

ATBARA, 1898

Churchill's heart froze when he heard the area called to attention. They had only just arrived at the main base camp that morning. The bugle announced the arrival of the commander. Sir Herbert Kitchener, the Sirdar himself, rode into the camp, resplendent on a white charger. His cadre followed him to the stage constructed at one end of the field next to headquarters. All heard the bugle call as it sounded out formation. The men dutifully stopped their chores and made their way to the parade ground in front of the stage.

Kitchener was legend. He was the Commander of the Armies of Egypt. Like an ancient pharaoh, he ruled the land. It had been a long road. The oldest son of a British officer, he had entered the Royal Military Academy at Woolrich, training to join the Royal Engineers. He spent ten years as a staff officer. During an assignment to Cyprus and Palestine, he took the time to learn Arabic. When the British secured Egypt, he was a natural pick for posting there. He steadily rose up through the ranks. He was brilliant, and he knew it. His knowledge of Arabic and his energy made him a natural for the Intelligence Department. During his career, he had even written to General Gordon but never received a reply.

Kitchener was no stranger to the Islamic radicals. He had been wounded in combat in 1888 battling the dervish forces led by Osman Digna. He was then assigned to the War Office in Cairo, where he spent four years rebuilding the Egyptian Army. His efforts had not gone unnoticed, and in 1892, he was promoted again. He was the quintessential British commander. And his men revered him.

"Assemble the men," ordered the camp commander.

Kip followed from behind. There was more to learn. He moved to the back of the crowd and found Churchill standing at the very rear of the assembled troops.

"I say old chap," Kip teased. "I do believe the 21st Lancers, having just arrived, are supposed to be sitting up front."

"Well, old chap," Churchill countered. "If the Sirdar finds out I'm here, I'm bloody well certain he will send me home." He turned his head away from anyone directly in his path. He refused to make eye contact with anyone. He wished he could become invisible.

"Do you really think he gives a shit? He might have more important things on his mind than you," Kip said, annoyed by Churchill's self-importance. "Like the war?"

The Sirdar made his way to the stage. The sergeant-at-arms called them to attention.

"Gentlemen, the commander."

The men rose to their feet as one.

"Take your seats," the Sirdar ordered. The men sat down on a row of wooden bleachers.

"Welcome to the 21st Lancers!" Kitchener announced loudly.

"Hoorah!" they roared back.

"As you know, we are about to engage the enemy in battle," he said seriously. His bright blue eyes glistened above his fierce mustache. "Our scouts and intelligence officers have briefed me that the Khalifa's main army remains entrenched in Omdurman. His army there is estimated at 60,000 men." He paused to let the number sink in. "But he has another 20,000 in reserve nearby."

"Our combined force, British, Egyptian and Sudanese, is twenty-five thousand. We are outnumbered nearly 4 to 1. Therefore, at the outset, let me say we are happy to see you," Kitchener said, grinning at his men. His confidence was contagious, and the 21st Lancers roared back their approval.

"At daybreak tomorrow, you will join the main strike force camped at Wad Hamed. It will be a nine-day march, under grueling conditions, so take care of yourselves and each other. It will be hot," he warned. "Hydration is a must."

"Speaking of hot," he continued, "Wad Hamed is only sixty miles from the dervish capital at Omdurman. Upon your arrival at Wad Hamed, we will begin the final phase of the expedition. We will ride on Omdurman, and destroy the enemy!"

"Hoorah" roared five hundred men, confident and ready for battle.

Kip stood in the back of the crowd, searching for faces. He picked out Mackenzie seated in front with the rest of the 21st Lancers. He was easy to spot with his flaming red beard. Mackenzie's attention was not focused on the Sirdar. Instead, he was looking around the gathered formation.

Kip didn't see O'Leary next to the big Irishman. He scanned the crowd of men. He spotted O'Leary on the right side of the formation. O'Leary seemed intent, first looking at the 21st Lancers assembled in the front of the crowd, and then looking around the rest of the men that encircled them.

That's because he's looking for Churchill, Kip thought to himself. He should be sitting up front with the rest of the Lancers.

"Gentlemen, good luck, Godspeed, and God save the Queen," Kitchener concluded.

"God save the Queen !" the men roared back.

"Area attention," called out the sergeant-at-arms. The Sirdar left the stage, and with his cadre in tow, walked to the headquarters tent and went inside.

General Gatacre, the commander of the British Division, took the stage to continue the briefing. Kip listened with one ear while he briefed the men.

Neither Mackenzie nor O'Leary paid attention to the briefing. They were too busy looking around the crowd. Kip watched with interest when O'Leary finally spotted Churchill, standing next to Kip. He saw O'Leary's face reflect something akin to relief. O'Leary's eyes traveled from Churchill to Kip. Their eyes met, and O'Leary immediately looked away.

"Got you," Kip whispered to himself.

Kip woke early the next morning. It was still dark. He could smell the cooking fires as he sat on a folding canvas chair next to his tent, a mug of steaming coffee in his hand. The smoke hung in the air as the men broke camp and got ready for the final march to join the rest of the force. Kerosene lanterns flickered throughout the encampment as the men readied for war.

Kip finished his coffee and then made his way over to Churchill's tent. Churchill was drinking a cup of tea and smoking a cigarette. His gear was still unpacked.

"Good morning," Kip said.

"Yes, it is," Churchill replied. "Kitchener left yesterday, and I am still here," he beamed. "I almost feel a bit cheeky."

Kip looked around the encampment. "I've got to give you Brits credit," he said. "Quite the force."

"Wait until we reach Wad Hamed," Churchill mused. "Twenty-five thousand men armed to the teeth, ready to meet a host of 80,000 hostile dervish savages. This will be a battle that will be remembered long after it is over."

"Aye, I imagine so," Kip agreed. "I'm heading over to headquarters to catch General Gatacre before we start the march," Kip said. "I've got a few letters for him from my government."

"Ahh, you're a courier as well?"

"Jack of all trades, master of none," Kip answered.

In fact, he did have some letters for the general. But Kip also wanted to set up surveillance on Mackenzie and O'Leary during the first part of the march. Kip was sure his cover was still intact, and he wasn't entirely sure that the two men were a threat. He wanted a chance to mingle with them without Churchill present. If they were assassins, he wanted to get to know them better. It would be easier to stay alive that way.

Once assembled, the column stretched out for a mile. In addition to the 500 men and horses of the 21st Lancers, there were additional Egyptian troops and artillery. Thousands of pounds of ammunition, food, water, and supplies were loaded onto wagons and carts pulled by 1,400 mules, donkeys, and camels. They left at the break of dawn. A cloud of dust followed the formation as it left the camp.

For Kip, it was a pleasure to be back in the saddle, even for a long ride. It gave him time to think. He rode comfortably midway in the column, keeping O'Leary and Mackenzie roughly a hundred yards in front of him.

As the sun rose higher on the horizon, so too did the mercury. By noon it was 116 degrees, and the rays of the sun showered down on them like arrows, digging deep into their stamina and testing their willpower.

Even Kip grew concerned. He was accustomed to the heat and had continued his childhood obsession with running, even in the humid summer heat in Washington. But all men were not equal when it came to the temperature.

Shimmers of silver lay on the horizon. Kip had never seen a more dramatic mirage. A vast ocean of sand stretched before them, broken only by occasional dark boulders jutting up through the earth.

Steep ravines slashed the plain. They were called "khors," formed by water flowing over millions of years during the rainy season. It would be a hazardous march by day, but impassible at night due to khors that dug deep into the terrain.

Kip drank deeply from his canteen. If a firefight broke out, he didn't want to die of thirst. He rode forward until he reached the group of men next to O'Leary and Mackenzie. Kip made it a point to go by a water wagon to replenish. Then he settled his horse to match the pace of the column. Both man and beast were laboring, and he could hear the heavy breathing of both.

He pulled his horse up next to Mackenzie.

"Howdy," Kip said.

The big Irishman looked startled at first, then he smiled.

"Hello indeed," Mackenzie said with a grin. "What brings you to this godforsaken place?" He mopped his forehead with a rag and then stuck it back in his waistband.

"Orders, same as you," Kip said. He motioned around them. "This is a very well-organized expedition with the latest technology and weapons. I'm a spy sent here to steal every last secret I can and pass it on to my army," Kip laughed. "My government was thrilled when your government gave me permission to tag along. I guess we're getting to be close friends," Kip added.

"Hey, who's your new friend," O'Leary said, feigning jealousy as he rode up to join the two men. He was a small and wiry man with short, curly red hair.

"Kip McDuran," Kip answered, reaching out to shake the outstretched hand. "United States Army. I've been sent here to learn everything I can about this expedition."

"It's a pleasure, sir," O'Leary said, eyeing Kip's rank on his lapel.

Suddenly Kip heard a voice cry out, and he looked to his right in time to see a young private fall off his horse, hitting the sand like a sack of concrete.

"Private Bishop!" Mackenzie yelled out. He rode over to the fallen Lancer and dismounted. Several other soldiers joined him, and they immediately began rendering aid to the fallen soldier.

"He's not breathing," Mackenzie called out. "Somebody get the surgeon!"

"Get some water on him," O'Leary said. He poured water from his canteen over the fallen soldier's pale face.

Officers quickly noted the fallen soldier and diverted the column around him. The aids worked on him for several minutes without any success. Several of the men crossed themselves. The surgeon arrived, and after a quick examination pronounced him dead.

The men were sweating profusely, but they gathered up their fallen comrade and lashed him over the back of one of the burros for a proper burial when they made camp.

They rode on.

Kip's section moved silently, miserable from the heat and the sight of

Bishop dying. Kip rode with them for another hour before breaking off his surveillance and heading back down the column to locate Churchill. It was no time to talk.

He found B Squadron, but no Churchill in the ranks. Puzzled, he rode over to the squadron commander.

"Sir, have you seen Lieutenant Churchill?" he inquired.

"He stayed behind to chat with some old friends at the camp headquarters. He said he would catch up with us later this evening."

"Yes sir, thank you," Kip replied. He settled his horse into pace with the column. This evening?

Not good. O'Leary and Mackenzie in front of him, Churchill behind him. There was nothing else to do but ride on and survive, Kip decided. He adjusted his clothing and water intake to make himself as comfortable as possible.

Finally, they made camp. The tired men took care of the animals before they tended to themselves. They set up a bivouac at the edge of the river. The men not assigned to the first watch gratefully ate a dinner of tinned bully beef, biscuits, and warm beer.

As dusk settled in, Kip found the B Squadron commander. No one had seen Lieutenant Churchill. Kip volunteered to ride back to find him. The commander gratefully accepted his offer.

Kip headed out into the twilight along the trail they had left behind. His horse startled a herd of gazelle and sent them leaping into the dusk. Using the stars and his compass, he was confident he could always find his way along the river. Somewhere he would discover Churchill in between.

Churchill left camp at dusk, much later than he intended. He had been drawn into a long and complicated argument about politics. That topic, along with several drinks, had him pleasantly buzzed as he set out under the moonlight to join the column. He knew he shouldn't be traveling alone at night in the desert, but he was confident in his horse and his ability to find the column under the moonlight. Just follow the river, he decided.

In three hours, he was utterly lost, wandering about the African desert at night under a moonless, cloudy sky.

"Damn," he cursed. It would do him no good to travel further in the darkness. He brought his horse to a halt and sat, listening to the sounds of the night. He couldn't help but feel a little adventurous, despite the fact that he had no food or water. Or compass. He remained calm, confident he could find his way to the river and pick up the trail at daybreak.

He heard a sound. It was soft and faint and came from the side of a massive black boulder rising from the earth. Curious, he urged his horse forward toward the sound. What if a spy was following the column?

Winston silently dismounted his horse and made his way forward on foot. If he returned to the column with a captured spy in tow, he would undoubtedly earn a medal.

He made his way stealthily around the rock.

"Umph," he groaned, as a figure came out of the darkness, knocking him to the packed sand. He jumped to his feet only to be knocked down again, this time by a water bag that slammed into the side of his head. Churchill dropped like a hammered steer, and the lights went out.

He came to minutes later and noted with mild curiosity that the sky had now cleared. He tried to rub the back of his head but realized that his hands were tied. With his rope.

"I am sorry, but I have to make sure you are an English soldier before I untie you," a woman's voice said from behind him. "Do not turn around."

Churchill frowned. He had been captured by a female spy.

"What is your name?" she asked.

"Major McDuran," he lied.

"Why are you following me?" she asked.

"Why are you spying on the column?" Winston countered.

"Because I seek refuge," she said honestly. Syrah stepped out in front of him, into the moonlight. "I am half British," she said.

"Oh," Churchill said, brow furrowed. He saw a beautiful woman standing before him. Her skin was mahogany, but her eyes were a brilliant sapphire blue.

"So am I," Churchill said truthfully.

"We have something in common then," she replied. "That's a good start."

"Your English is good," he noted.

"My father taught me."

"Your father?" Churchill asked.

"He was a British officer," Syrah said quietly.

"Oh, do I know him?" Churchill asked. I've been captured by a siren, he mused. I must be dreaming.

"He's dead."

"And you will be too, ma'am," Kip said, stepping from the darkness, his pistol pointed directly at Syrah's head.

"If you move an inch."

"Major McDuran," Churchill gasped. "Thank god man, um," he paused. He looked embarrassed. "I just captured this female spy."

Kip eyed Churchill's roped hands and rolled his eyes.

"I can see that," Kip said dryly. "Ma'am, since you speak such good English, would you kindly identify yourself?" he asked.

"My name is Syrah," she said.

Kip took out his knife with his free hand and cut Churchill loose.

"Thanks mate," Churchill said.

"Don't mention it," Kip smiled, gun still on Syrah.

Kip was stunned by her beauty. The almond shape of her eyes, deep-set above the most incredibly high cheekbones he had ever seen. Her face was all ovals. Her skin was like burnished mahogany. She had full lips and the most brilliant sapphire eyes he had ever laid eyes on. Her large, full breast jutted proudly upward under her tob. Long legs, Kip noted. Incredibly long legs. Long black braids flowed over her shoulder and down to her waist.

"Major Kip McDuran, United States Army," he introduced himself. He put the knife back in his sheath and lowered the gun. He wasn't ready to holster it right away.

"What is your English last name?" Kip asked.

"Gordon," Syrah said proudly.

Churchill was helping himself to Kip's canteen when Syrah said her last name. Water sputtered out his mouth.

"As in?" Churchill challenged.

"You wouldn't believe me," she said.

"General Gordon did not have an illegitimate half-breed child," Churchill spewed venom, and not very politely.

"Yes he did," Kip said calmly.

Churchill looked at him in amazement. "How the bloody hell do you know that?" he asked.

"Intelligence briefing right before I left Washington," Kip answered honestly. "It was mentioned. If by chance I picked up any information as to her whereabouts, the Brits wanted to know. Even if it confirmed her death," he added.

"What the hell else do you know?" Churchill said, embarrassed and angry.

"Don't ask," Kip said. He looked at Syrah. "Tell me your mother's name," he ordered.

"Sindella," she said.

Kip holstered his gun. "I was not expecting to find you," he said.

"More like I found you," she countered.

"No, you found him," Kip said seriously. "And I found you both," he added with emphasis.

She grinned broadly. Her teeth were white and perfect. Kip noted dimples in her cheeks and then instantly brought himself back to reality. Slow down soldier, he thought. But truth be told, he was absolutely floored by her beauty.

"Fair enough, Major," she said.

"So if you are Gordon's daughter, where the hell have you been all this time?" Churchill asked with disbelief. "If that's true, your story is too incredible to be true," he said, tripping over his own words.

"Omdurman," she replied. "I was the Khalifa's translator," she added. "I sat in on all of his meetings," she offered. "I can give you his plans, everything. I know much," she pleaded. She was putting all her cards on the table. It was now or never.

"Prove it," Churchill hissed.

"I helped Slatin escape," she said calmly.

Churchill was stunned. Intelligence had briefed that Slatin had escaped. Kip eyed her cautiously.

"What do you want?" Kip asked.

"My freedom."

"Done," Kip replied.

"Wait a minute," Churchill interrupted. "You can't grant her asylum on behalf of her majesty's government," he bristled.

"I'm not, Churchill," Kip sighed. "I'm granting her asylum on behalf of the United States. You know, that other country that kicked your ass in 1776. Ever hear of them?"

"Oh," Churchill noted. He tried to act unimpressed.

"We want to know *everything* that is going on here," Kip reminded him. "I'm an observer, remember?"

"More like a spy," Churchill said.

"I'm in uniform, you dolt," Kip said. Hah, got you. My turn.

"Ma'am, I do accept your offer on behalf of my government," Kip said smoothly, his composure regained. "I would ask that you remain with the column when we rejoin it today, and I will offer your assistance to the Sirdar's intelligence staff, with myself acting as your escort. After we complete our business here, you will return with us to Cairo for debriefing and a determination by the American Consul-General as to what to do with you," he ordered. "And if you value your freedom and your life, *you will* be honest," he added.

"I have no choice," she said. "I have nothing else to offer."

"I will ensure your safety and your virtue," Kip said. And he meant it. She was the most beautiful woman he had ever seen.

"I don't know," Churchill said. He kicked at the dirt.

"You don't have a need to know," Kip said bluntly.

"Wait a minute," Churchill said. "I'm part of this too."

Kip looked at him in amazement. "You are?"

"Yes, I most certainly am," Churchill added. "I am not going to assist you in returning this valuable spy that I captured without credit for my share of the work," Churchill stated.

"She captured you," Kip pointed out.

"That doesn't matter. You need my help getting her to the front."

"No, I don't."

"Yes you do," Churchill insisted.

"You want a medal," Kip said matter-of-factly.

"Of course I do," Churchill replied.

"Okay, we captured her together," Kip said.

"No you didn't," Syrah said. She looked at Churchill. "But Lieutenant, if I were to add to my debriefing that you did *help* capture me, would you ensure my safety as well?"

"Of course," Churchill said. Now she was talking.

"I think we have an arrangement," Syrah said.

"I think so," Kip said, wondering who was in charge. "I have a compass," he said to Churchill. You might want to tag along with me," he suggested.

"Indeed," Churchill added proudly. This was turning out nicely after all.

They rejoined the column by noon. Syrah was relieved to see the reassuring presence of the soldiers but also felt fear. She found it difficult to trust any man, but she knew she could not survive in the desert alone for any length of time.

The heat was back, and even Kip was relieved to see the shimmering water of the Nile. Gone were the telegraph poles, he noted. Palm trees and gazelle lined the riverbanks, along with dense green foliage.

That night, as they made camp by the river, a new menace attacked. Hordes of biting, stinging insects joined the falling sun, swarming about in the sky.

Kip dug into his rucksack and took out a tube of ointment. He rubbed it on his hands and face and was happy to note that the bugs stopped biting. Supply was right about this repellant. He went down to the river. One of the gunboats lay moored just offshore. Several crewmembers tossed wooden cases down to men standing knee deep in the river.

"Champagne," they called out happily.

"You've got to be kidding me," Kip said.

"Of course not," Churchill called out cheerfully. He splashed into the river up to the gunboat. "I say, pass me one of those would you," he asked politely.

A case landed in his arms.

"I say, thanks, old man," Churchill called out. He pushed it to shore.

Cheerio, thought Kip. Jesus, these English bastards drank a lot.

He had handed off Syrah to Colonel Wingate with instructions as to her status when they first entered the camp. He decided to make his way back to the command tent to check on her. Churchill would have to be on his own for a few, he decided.

Kip found her sitting on a stool, eating a plate of food. A guard stood watch.

"I was hungry," Syrah said.

Kip nodded. So was he, for that fact.

"You're English is very good," Kip complemented her.

"Thank you."

"How does an American know of my existence?" she asked.

Kip sat down next to her on a large rock. "My country has a powerful connection with this country," Kip said.

"I don't understand," she said.

"We too have our slaves," Kip said. "Word traveled as more family members came to our country," he added. "People talk. I interviewed a man and a woman in America. They were freed slaves originally from the Sudan. They were Dinka."

"Are you a spy?" she asked.

"No," Kip replied. "I'm in uniform."

"What if you were not in uniform?" she asked.

"Then I would be a spy," he agreed.

"I would rather you be an army officer," she said, finishing her meal.

"Why?"

"Because I don't think I could trust you if you were a spy," she said with a smile.

"You are foolish to trust me, period," Kip said, standing up.

"Likewise," she quipped.

Kip looked into her eyes. He saw no fear. She smiled. That's a dangerous smile, he warned himself. He admired her long, jet black hair.

"Alright, we will debrief later," he said quickly. "Let me know if you need anything. We've got a long ride tomorrow. And you will be riding with me. The commander doesn't have men to spare and doesn't want to assign any of his fighting force to be your escort."

"Thank you," Syrah said.

"Don't thank me," Kip said. "Thank Churchill. He's sure he will get a medal for your capture. He insisted to his commander that he too was responsible for your safety. You are now a very valuable asset to their army. They believe you can give them a great deal of information about the Khalifa's intentions."

"I can," she assured him. "I can."

That night, she spent over three hours debriefing with Colonel Wingate and his intelligence officers. She told them everything she knew about the Khalifa and his men, the jirga, and who attended. They peppered her with more questions, which she answered truthfully.

Kip sat in the background during the debriefing. He listened carefully, watching her every move with interest.

The intelligence officers interrogated her at length.

When she was finished, Kip knew she had assured her future. But there was one more question that needed to be asked.

"When the Khalifa is captured or killed, will you identify him for us?" Kip asked.

"Of course," she answered.

Kip knew that some of the British officers were offended by the idea that Gordon had engaged in a sexual tryst with a black slave while in

Khartoum, but they were eager to avenge him, so they forgave him. It didn't hurt that she was beautiful. The Brits were so keen to be perceived as gentlemen. Kip left the tent, confident that she was an important asset, and would be treated as such.

He made his way over to Churchill's tent. He found the young lieutenant smoking a cigarette with one hand and drinking from a champagne bottle with the other.

"Buy you a drink, Major?"

"Yep."

Churchill handed Kip the bottle, and he drank deeply. It was cold, bubbly, and tasted delicious.

"I could get used to that," Kip said.

"I am," Churchill answered. "How did the debriefing go with our spy?" he asked.

"Very good," Kip said. "She can describe the military fortifications at Omdurman, his order of battle, and she will cooperate in identifying the Khalifa."

"And then what?" Churchill asked. "What are they going to do with her?"

"Political asylum in America or Britain. Once she identifies the Khalifa she will be dead if she remains here."

"Do we care?" Churchill asked.

"I do," Kip said.

"She is lovely," Churchill teased. He suspected that Kip liked her.

"Aye, that she is," Kip said.

"As black as coal," Churchill added.

"More like mahogany."

"A beautiful negress. Feisty too. But a blackamoor is a blackamoor," Churchill said.

"A what?"

"Blackamoor, you know, Negro. I believe you refer to them in America as niggers."

"I see a beautiful woman," Kip said. "The color of her skin is irrelevant to me."

Churchill laughed aloud.

"You Americans. So eager to atone for your sins. You want everyone to love you," Churchill said.

"I never owned slaves, so I have nothing to atone for."

"Your country would not have been built without slave labor," Churchill challenged. "Who else are you going to find to tend to your tobacco fields and cotton plantations?"

"They are free men now," Kip said. "They work for wages just like anyone else."

"Oh god, so simple," Churchill said, amused. "Well I'll tell you what, why don't you take the charming negress back to America and see how she fits in?"

"Not my job," Kip said. He yawned. "Long ride tomorrow, I'm going to grab some shuteye."

"Good night sweet prince," Churchill teased.

"Fuck off," Kip answered.

Chapter Seventy-One

THE JOURNEY TO WAD HAMAD 1898

The ride out was beginning to look a lot hotter than the ride in. Kip mopped his brow. His khaki field hat blocked the sun but not the heat. His uniform was drenched with sweat. There would be more casualties.

The 21st Lancers were providing escort to thousands of horses, cattle and pack animals moving south along the river.

Syrah threatened to escape if she had to ride in a wagon for eight days. She rode a brown Arabian horse next to Kip, who rode an Arabian charger as well.

"You ride well," Kip noted. It was an understatement. She declined a saddle and rode bareback with just a bit and a bridle. She steered the horse with her muscular legs. She wore a long flowing white cotton tob wrapped around her athletic frame. On her head was a royal blue hijab. Kip thought she looked stunning. But then, she would look good in anything, he decided.

"Thank you, so do you," she said glancing sideways. "You have a western saddle," she noted.

Kip smiled easily. "Some habits die hard," he admitted. "I've been lugging this thing around the world," he added. I wouldn't know what to do without a pommel."

"I would," she said. She smiled innocently.

Kip coughed and looked out over the desert that surrounded the river. Perhaps it was the heat, he thought. Or perhaps it's just me, he smiled to himself. Did African women know how to flirt, he wondered?

"That's why I ride without a saddle. I just want the horse beneath me," she said matter-of-factly. "I like being on top."

Kip blushed. He was relieved to hear approaching hoofs from behind. It was Churchill.

"Cheerio," Winston greeted them, his boyish face flushed from the heat. He was grinning ear to ear.

"Why the shit-eating grin?" Kip asked.

Churchill let his horse fall into rhythm with the other horses. "Because I have successfully avoided discovery by the Sirdar, and now he is riding ahead with the officers and staff in the steamers," Churchill boasted.

"Why are you hiding from the Sirdar?" Syrah asked.

Churchill looked annoyed. "I'm not hiding from anyone," he said sternly.

"Yes you are," Kip laughed out loud. He was surprised by the hurt look on Churchill's face. Ah, he didn't like being called out in front of a woman. It was a weakness Kip could exploit.

Syrah laughed as well. Churchill flipped the reigns and moved ahead to join up with some fellow officers.

"Sensitive fellow," Kip said.

"Is that a trait of the Englishman?" she asked.

"I don't know them well enough to say." They rode next to each other in silence for a few minutes.

"And I don't know anything about you either," Kip finally said. "What was your childhood like?"

"Before or after?"

Kip shook his head. "I don't know what you mean. Before or after what?" He could see the immense sadness in her eyes.

"My parents' death," she answered.

It hit a chord. Something inside of him resonated.

"It's not something we plan for," Kip said. The slow rhythm of the horses walking along the river bank and the warm air lulled him into a thoughtful mood.

"We?"

"I too lost my parents, as a child," Kip replied.

"What happened?" she asked.

She studied his firmly cut jaw line. She found him extremely handsome.

"My father was murdered. My mother passed away not long after," he said bluntly.

"Life is always cruel and seldom fair," Syrah responded, her face solemn. "My father was murdered too. My mother as well."

"We speak the same language," Kip answered. He knew they did. They rode on in silence, each acutely aware of the other's presence.

Three days out of Atbara they saw the first signs of the enemy. Shots rang out in front of the column as they passed a small rocky mountain. Puffs of smoke rose from the enemy positions on the cliffs and lead slugs slammed into the hardened-earth along the riverbank.

"Shit!" Kip yelled out as sharp gravel shrapnel sprayed into the air. There was no cover and no time.

"Deploy the Maxim!" Churchill yelled out. "Cover fire on the rocks, now!"

Two horse-drawn Maxims running escort on the column opened up on the cliffs, sending thousands of rounds smashing into the rocks and ricocheting among their positions. The dervish guns were quickly silenced.

But the deafening roar of gunfire had sent the horses galloping in a panic.

"The horses!" one of the men yelled out.

"Relax," Churchill replied. "It's too hot for them to go far. They'll be right back, I assure you. They too need the water." His words proved true. Minutes later the spooked horses ambled back to the herd.

"Tragedy averted," Churchill chirped as he rode up to Kip and Syrah.

Kip eyed him with newfound respect. "That was quick thinking on your part," Kip said approvingly.

"Thanks. A little trick I learned in Afghanistan," Churchill said modestly.

"You've changed since Cuba," Kip said seriously.

"No, I didn't change," Churchill said, equally as serious. "I went to Afghanistan."

"Tell me about it," Kip offered. He was astounded when Churchill broke into a grin.

"No need, my good fellow. I wrote a book about it." He dug into one of his saddlebags and pulled out a hard-covered book.

"Really," he said, offering it to Kip.

Kip took the book from his outstretched hand. "The Malakand Field Force," he read off the cover. "By Winston fucking Churchill. Jesus, you did write a book about it," Kip said, dumbfounded.

"I know, I've read it," Syrah said.

"You've what?" Kip asked incredulously.

"The Khalifa obtained a copy and ordered me to read it to him," she replied. "He found your critical assessment of the English mistakes useful," she said.

"Thank you," Churchill replied.

"This is getting weird," was all Kip could say.

CHAPTER SEVENTY-TWO

WAD HAMED, 1898

Eight days later, they reached Kitchener's army camped at Wad Hamed on the banks of the Nile. The encampment was right out of the textbook. It stretched nearly two miles along the river, guarded on its western perimeter by a wall of thorn bushes. Nature's barbed-wire was useful.

Kip rode his horse from one end of the perimeter to the other. Maxim machine guns bristled the zeriba, facing west. Ten gunboats guarded their eastern and southern flanks, armed with Maxims and twelve-pound guns. Five steamers loaded with supplies also rested in the water, surrounded by a pincushion of masts from the small boats accompanying the flotilla.

Kip was impressed. He saw little chance of defeat at the hands of the dervish. On the other hand, he was bothered by what to him was an example of the stubbornness of man.

With such massive firepower, such superior technology, the Brits were willing to let men ride into battle armed with spears on horses that could be cut down with a sword. It was as if this was a sporting event to them. Like horses and hounds chasing a fox. Did they have any idea of how bloody this was going to be?

Nearly one hundred-thousand men were going to smash together in a violent collision. Blood would soak deep into the sands of the desert. It was not the place to be on a horse armed with a spear. It was also the most likely place for an assassin to strike. Churchill's death would appear to be merely a casualty of war.

Kip rode back to the camp and found himself drawn to the tent where Syrah was discreetly tucked away, along with two armed guards. They did not want her to be a distraction for the men.

He tied off his horse, nodded to the guard and walked to the entrance flap.

"It's Major McDuran," he said. "May I come in?"

He heard a rustling inside the tent, and then her voice a moment later.

"Yes, of course, Major," she said.

He removed his hat, brushed aside the mosquito netting and stepped inside.

She was still wearing the long blue tob but had removed her hijab. Kip admired her finely cut features. She was breathtaking. He tried not to notice the swell of her breast and the curves of her hips beneath the fabric.

"How are you being treated?" he asked politely.

"Very well," she said. "I am afraid my English is not good enough though."

"Your English is fine," Kip replied. "It's better than my Arabic."

Syrah laughed. "I don't want to hear you speak Arabic. I am enjoying being in the company of Englishmen," she said. "And American men," she added.

"How long did the Khalifa hold you captive?" Kip asked, changing the subject.

"Too long," she answered.

"Does the Khalifa know what he is up against? You said he read Churchill's book."

"No. The Khalifa only knows his hatred for the white man, and his desire to follow Allah's will," she said. "They have beaten the British army before. They believe they will do so again. Allah will be their guide."

"Yes, of course," Kip answered.

"You sound cynical."

"When it comes to religion, I am," he replied honestly.

"You have no faith?"

"Not when it comes to man," Kip answered.

"What about when it comes to God? Do you believe in God?" Syrah asked. She looked into his eyes.

"I have my faith, but I don't practice organized religion," Kip answered. "Man has taken a beautiful idea and turned it into another instrument of power. All religion does is give false hope to the hopeless and power to those who would exploit it."

"I believe in God," Kip continued. "But I don't believe everything I read. I don't believe that Jonah lived inside a whale, and I sure as hell don't buy into the argument that if you don't believe in the Christian God, then you don't get to heaven. My god never told me that."

"Eighty-thousand dervishes are waiting to die for Allah in Omdurman," she reminded him. "They believe in their god."

"And you?" Kip asked. Time to turn the tables.

"And me what?"

"Do you believe in God?"

Syrah paused. She shook her head.

"No. Life is too cruel for there to be a god," she answered. "I see the way men behave, *the evil they do* in the name of their God."

Kip nodded in agreement. "I know. I've seen it too."

"You told me what you don't believe about God. Now tell me what you do believe," she urged.

Kip smiled. "The way I see it is, when I die, there is either life after death or there isn't. I'll either be pleasantly surprised, or I won't know the difference."

"Do all Americans think like you?"

"No. I grew up a little different than most folks."

"Ah," she said. "That I can understand," she said honestly.

Kip knew that he had been seen going into her tent, and did not want to stay too long. She was under his authority, but he didn't want to appear "improper."

"Well, anyway, I should be going," he said.

Syrah took a step forward. She reached out and touched him on the arm.

"Thank you," she said. "I was hungry and frightened. You saved me."

"I doubt that," Kip answered. "And besides, Churchill saved you, not me," he smiled.

She threw her head back in laughter. "And how is my hero ?"

"Probably a little tipsy right now, explaining to the men how he allowed you to handcuff him as a ruse to keep you occupied while I snuck up behind you."

"Go keep him company," she said.

"Yes ma'am," Kip replied. He bowed and stepped out of the tent.

He walked to his horse, baffled. It was undeniable that he was attracted to this woman. But he was in the middle of a war. He didn't have time for emotions. Or romance. And yet he was feeling something he could not explain.

Meanwhile, Syrah was in a similar state of puzzlement. She was surrounded by thousands of British and Egyptian soldiers. She had endured only violence in the hands of men. Nonetheless, there was something about Kip that reached a part of her that had never been reached before.

Kip went to the officers' area. Another British tradition offered itself to him. Tables with white linen, hot food and beer awaited the British officers. They sure know how to live, he thought. They were in the middle of Africa. It was the eve of battle, and it almost seemed as if they were throwing a party.

He eyed a pitcher of beer. When in Rome? he thought. Just one. He helped himself.

"What's that, drinking on the eve of battle?" Churchill said. He had walked up behind Kip.

Kip eyed the glass in Churchill's hand. Whiskey of course.

"Just want to fit in with the crowd," Kip said smiling. He sipped his mug. It was delicious. All the men were dripping with sweat that night.

It was hot, and the mosquitoes fought to take more blood out of the men than the dervish ever could.

"The men are excited," Churchill said. "They are ready for battle."

"Do they know why they are fighting?" Kip asked.

Churchill looked at him with bemusement. "For Queen and country. For England. To defend the borders of Egypt. For Gordon," he said succinctly. "We're still kind of pissed off about that, you know."

Kip smiled. "Anger may in time change to gladness; vexation may be succeeded by content. But a kingdom that has once been destroyed can never come again into being; nor can the dead ever be brought back to life."

"So sayeth Sun Tzu," Churchill agreed. "But frankly, England can do without the Khalifa, and the Sudan is better off without that religious fanatic running around butchering people. Speaking of savages, how is your Nubian princess?" Churchill chided.

Kip ignored the dig.

"Extremely valuable," Kip said truthfully. We already knew a lot about the Khalifa and his organization thanks to Slatin. But she was able to corroborate that intelligence and added a few things that we didn't know."

"Such as?" Churchill asked.

"That's classified," Kip smiled. "And you don't have a need to know."

"You are a bore," Churchill said.

"Yep," Kip answered.

"And more than just an observer, I might add," Churchill said.

"What makes you say that?" Kip asked.

"The fact that you were allowed to sit in on an intelligence briefing with a spy for three hours. British intelligence wouldn't allow a so-called 'observer' to sit in on that. Who are you, Kip?" he asked.

"I am an intelligence officer with the United States army," Kip answered honestly. "Our two governments decided I could be of some use here."

"We don't need any help fighting, and British intelligence has been collecting information for the last ten years. We already know the location and position of every emir in the Sudan. We have spies everywhere, Kip." Churchill took a deep drag off his cigarette.

"I know you think I'm an ignorant child, but I'm very smart," Churchill continued. "I've been watching you watch me since we first met on the parade ground. Why are you watching me?"

General Hanson's instructions still rung in Kip's ear.

"Because I find you fascinating," Kip said sarcastically.

"Bullshit," Churchill said. "Mother told me."

"She told you what?" Kip demanded.

"That some Irishmen would like to see me dead. It seems that a few of them might be here," he said proudly. "You are my bodyguard."

Kip's face showed no emotion. It came as no surprise. He had long wondered whether Jenny had warned her son. Like all mothers, she loved her son more than life itself. Too bad if it got Kip killed.

"No worries," Churchill laughed. "Your secret is safe with me."

"Look," Kip said. "We don't know if there is anyone here or not."

"I know that too," Churchill said. Their voices had dropped almost to a conspiratorial whisper, even though they were twenty yards from the nearest soldier. "And as far as I can tell, I'm the only one here that knows your *real* mission." Churchill rubbed his hands together gleefully. "Do you have any suspects?" he asked excitedly.

"Jesus, Churchill, this isn't a bloody game," Kip scolded.

"Oh yes, it is," Churchill grinned. "Life itself is a game, and this will be a grand adventure. History will be kind to me because I intend to write it."

"Well let's just make sure you are not history just yet," Kip said. And he meant it. He looked up into the stars. Heaven help me. The man was insane. He couldn't keep it in any longer.

"Churchill, you are either the biggest fool or the bravest man I've ever met. Why in the hell are you here? Why the hell aren't you back in England hiding somewhere? I mean Jesus man, you not only volunteered to come to this hellhole to fight a war, but you did so knowing full well that assassins were out to kill you?" Kip looked at him with amazement.

"I want to be here," Churchill said. "I've never felt more alive in my life."

Kip could only shake his head.

"If you had stayed home, I wouldn't be here, you stupid son of a bitch," Kip laughed. "Christ, I can't believe this."

"I don't need a babysitter," Churchill said.

"Tell that to the Nubian princess that captured your ass," Kip said.

They both started laughing. It was the eve of battle.

CHAPTER SEVENTY-THREE

THE ADVANCE, 1898

The next morning, the army advanced towards Omdurman. A great cloud of dust rose into the air as the cavalry horses and camel corps rode out ahead of the foot soldiers. The flotilla of boats moved in a giant mass down the river, gunboats bristling at the front of the fleet. The supply barges and gyassas followed behind. A vast sea of wooden mast and metal steam engines moved together as one.

The horse-drawn artillery followed the formation, sending up yet another vast cloud of dust. All total, 8,200 British soldiers and 17,600 Egyptian and Sudanese regulars advanced towards the enemy. Artillery and Maxims, 40-pound howitzers and quick firing 12-pound guns were ready to unleash a hail of metal into and above the enemy. These engines of death would quickly right the enemy's numerical advantage.

Across the rocky plains and desert sand they advanced. They could see the mountains of Jebel Royan in the distance, and they knew they were getting near. Kip and Winston, riding with the 21st Lancers, headed out across the desert to go around the rocky hills that lay in front.

The entire force would move to Royan, where a zeriba had been set up in advance. The flotilla reached it ahead of the ground forces. Hospital tents were set up on an island, and stores of supplies were stacked up. The men unloaded the barges, and the battle kits and supplies seemed unending. The surgeons readied themselves to receive the wounded. There would be blood on the field of battle.

The tribes of Christ rose to meet the tribes of Muhammad.

Chapter Seventy-Four

OMDURMAN, 1898

The jirga assembled, and the Khalifa faced his tribal leaders who had gathered together to stop the invasion of the white man and his Egyptian whores. He listened as each leader spoke of the coming war. The Khalifa had many spies who had been watching the British advance. He knew where they were and how many they were.

He had an army, 60,000 strong, with another 20,000 spread out in reserve. He had rifles and ammunition. He had cannons, swords, and pistols, long knives, and spears. He had fought the white man before and left him for dead on the field of battle.

The faces of the emirs bore determination.

"Tomorrow, we attack," the Khalifa announced. "The Mahdi came to me in a dream last night. He said we will be victorious," he said confidently.

"The enemy is outnumbered. Our army is strong and fierce and ready to die for Allah. The prophet Muhammad has blessed us. The Mahdi told me so. The time for jihad is here. The time for Islam to rule the Sudan is here. The time for those cursed mongrels who call themselves Arabs and have joined ranks with the white man has come. Leave none alive. Take no prisoners. The black men who have joined the white man and defied Allah will be slaughtered, to the last man. As must the Egyptian traitors!"

The emirs growled their approval.

"As for the white man, the Mahdi has pronounced that he must feel the pain of our weapons, and suffer for his insolence. An example must be made. The Mahdi has told me that we must teach the white man never to come to our lands again. The Mahdi said the white man is a plague that threatens us all. He must be exterminated."

An almost guttural rumble went through the tent.

"We know that to die for Allah is to reach heaven above earth. Islam teaches us that to die for Allah guarantees each man seventy-two virgins to carry on his lineage in heaven. We know there will be no white man there waiting for us. To die for Allah and Islam in a jihad is the holiest of deaths. Fear not. The Mahdi has told me we will be victorious!" he roared.

The emirs roared back. The vast sea of dervish warriors encamped nearby heard the roars and began roaring themselves. They screamed to Allah, invoking his name and his strength. Multi-colored banners waved in the air. Spears glinted in the morning sunlight. Swords shook, and shots fired into the air. The women in the encampment began to utter their shrill screams, using their tongues to make a high pitched whistle. Sixty thousand warriors stood ready to advance on 25,000 enemy soldiers with another 20,000 held back in reserve.

Osman Digna, the leader of the Hadendoa tribe, emerged from the tent to the roar of the crowd. His face was fierce, his jaw set underneath his resplendent headdress. His men would join Mahmüd and his men, creating the reserve force at Adaramra, awaiting orders from the Khalifa.

Osman Sheikh-ed-Din and Osman Azrak followed behind him, wearing their dark green headdresses proudly. They brought 25,000 Arabs soldiers to the fight. They would be a massive force at the center of the attack. Another deafening clamor from the assembled army broke out as they watched their leaders emerge from the tent.

Ali-Wad-Helu emerged next. He brought his warriors from the Degheim and Kenana tribes. These Mulazemin warriors would guard the left flank of the force under the light green flag, and lead the advance to engage the enemy's cavalry.

Emir Yakub, whose men fought under a black flag, came next. More roars came from the worshipping throng.

Emir Sherif followed. The crowd cried out in approval. His Dongola tribesmen would reinforce the right flank under their red banner.

And finally, the Khalifa appeared. He would ride in the center of the army, guarded by 2,000 personal bodyguards, and surrounded by the rest of his army.

The roars of the men and the shrill whistles of the women were deafening; it seemed as if the earth itself was vibrating.

Drums began to beat and the horns began to blare. The gathering horde assembled under their different colored banners. They started their advance on the plains of Kerreri.

CHAPTER SEVENTY-FIVE

NORTH OF KERRERI, 1898

It was early in the morning. Darkness still hung over the expedition as it began to rain.

"You've got to be kidding me," Kip said, holding out his hand to feel the drops. The wind picked up, and thunder and lightning broke out overhead.

"That's fitting," mused Churchill. "The storm of battle approaches as well. We will either meet the enemy today or ride all the way to Omdurman untouched."

"Don't count on that," Kip said. He was finishing up lashing his gear to his horse. They were surrounded by a sea of tents and soldiers getting ready for battle.

"We're close. They'll be waiting for us. Today is the day," Kip said. His face was tanned and his eyes ablaze. The endless hours of lecture at West Point about great battles of the past came to mind. Countless hours of reading and writing about the art of war now became a reality. He prepared his mind for combat and said a silent prayer to his god.

Churchill too was feeling the moment. He was up before the rest of the camp had stirred. He was already wearing his combat gear, his pistol confidently riding his hip. He lit a cigarette and offered one to Kip.

Kip took one from Churchill's outstretched hand.

"I thought you didn't smoke," Churchill said.

"I do now," Kip answered. He inhaled deeply and took in his surroundings. The encampment covered ten square miles, with the shadows of the rocky hills of the Shabluka Mountains behind them. Artillery guns stood ready, howitzers primed with explosive shrapnel that would rain down upon the head of the enemy long before they could reach the expeditionary forces. Maxims hedged the perimeter of the zeriba, ready to cut down any horde that managed to survive. The army took turns sleeping so that half the men were prepared to take up defensive positions at all times. The gunboats gathered nearby on the banks of the Nile, standing sentry as well; howitzers and cannons in position.

Kip exhaled a cloud of smoke. I am impressed, he thought. He hated to admit it, but the chief of staff was right. Kip's report on this war would indeed be of interest both to the civilian leadership and the military.

"If the assassins come, it will be today," he predicted.

"I agree," Churchill said. "I just wish we knew who the bloody hell they are," he added.

"I have my eyes on Mackenzie and O'Leary," Kip told Churchill. "I've been watching them watch you. But I'm not certain. Maybe they just think you're pretty."

Churchill just laughed. "So we will have to wait for them to make the first move?"

Kip nodded. "I'll have your back," he said.

Churchill reached out his right hand, and they shook warmly.

"And I'll have yours," Winston said grinning.

The bugle sounded, and the giant encampment came to life.

"Let's go kill some dervish," Churchill smiled.

"Aye," Kip growled. "I imagine quite a few."

The 21st Lancers rode out ten miles ahead of the expeditionary force. Kip could see a rocky peak approaching. When they reached the top, he looked out behind them. He could see the vast sea of the army stretched out below. Churchill and Kip scanned the distance with their field glasses. There was no sign of the enemy.

Colonel Martin sent a message by way of flags back to the Sirdar —no enemy was in sight.

They led their horses to the next observation point high up the steep hills.

"I say," Churchill said calmly. He was scanning the horizon with his field glasses from a rocky outcrop. "I can see Omdurman. And I can even see the dome over the Mahdi's grave."

Kip looked through his binoculars. He could make out a yellow dome amidst rows of mud houses. He also saw a single hill that rose between them and the city. There was a long, steep ridge partially blocking their view of the plains.

Every muscle in his body tensed. "Behind the ridge," he murmured. "The ridge between us and the city. That's where they'll be. The bastards are lying in wait."

Churchill nodded. "An ambush? How exciting."

Kip looked at Winston's face. He was grinning from ear to ear. Kip had learned by now that the Englishman next to him was absolutely insane. Churchill had no fear and no shame. He was who he said he was: an ambitious man who chose to follow his father's footsteps and was willing to stake his life on making his claim.

Kip saw a movement in the distance and squinted through his binoculars. It appeared to be a long black line, speckled with white. A mirage? He watched silently. It was moving, like a giant centipede.

"Churchill, look at the formation at your two-o'clock," he whispered.

Churchill peered through his binoculars. "They're riding fast," he said.

The mass of dervish forces was riding out to meet them on the field of battle. It was not an ambush. It was to be a collision of flesh and blood.

Kip could see that the gunboats had advanced down the river, and now they opened fire. Huge explosions broke forth as they sought to take out the Khalifa's artillery in the city. Smoke billowed from their engines and their howitzers as they pressed in. He could see the deadly precision of the artillery, and the city began to erupt in flames.

He heard the whine of an artillery shell passing overhead. Then the distant boom of the 40-pound howitzers. Swells of black smoke erupted from inside the city.

Waves upon waves of dark lines moved forward and spread out on their flanks. Standard operating procedure, Kip thought. Mass at the center, spread out the pincers, like the horns of a water buffalo, and try to flank them.

The Sirdar ordered his cavalry to pull back to the flanks of the main fighting force. The 21st Lancers retreated from the center mass of the enemy. They stopped momentarily to return a volley of fire at a dervish scouting party that pursued them. They were pleased to see that the range of their rifles exceeded that of the dervish.

The Sirdar placed his expedition in an arc, with their eastern flank protected by the Nile and the gunboats. They set up the artillery in the rear and sighted in the guns to lay down a barrage when the enemy came within 800 yards of their position.

But, much to the Sirdar's surprise, the advance stopped. They remained just out of range of the heavy artillery.

Watching the scene unfold from his vantage point, Kitchener quickly realized the enemy was not going to advance further. He called off the artillery barrage of the city. He wanted to lure them in closer. It was becoming a battle of wills.

The 21st Lancers and the rest of the Egyptian cavalry positioned at the center of the arc, on the riverbed. Trenches were dug around the perimeter of the zeriba, manned by Sudanese and Egyptian riflemen. They held their Lee-Medford rifles at the ready.

Regular patrols were sent out at intervals to reconnoiter the enemy's position.

Kip and Churchill rode their horses out to the tip of the arc, where Lyttelton's Brigade of fusiliers and grenadiers stood at the ready behind a row of mimosa hedges. Maxim guns had been drawn up on carriages and placed along the line.

"Looks like we're digging in," Kip said. "The Sirdar is daring the Khalifa to attack."

"Indeed. The lead patrols have retreated," Churchill said, peering through his field glasses.

The main dervish force also stopped its advance. They were five miles from the British encampment. Kip saw the sea of warriors fire their rifles in the air; then they broke ranks and set about establishing their perimeter.

"Looks like they aren't taking the bait," Churchill noted. "They are digging in as well."

Kip set down his field glasses and mopped his brow. He had a feeling that the Khalifa would choose to attack at dawn, before the heat of the day. They rode back to camp.

The 21st Lancers claimed an area to the rear of the zeriba, along the banks, to afford the horses some shade from the palm trees and water from the Nile. Four squadrons set about putting up tents and preparing an evening meal. But every man had his rifle nearby, locked and loaded.

B Squadron had bivouacked closest to the river. Their tents were close to one another, and space was at a premium. Privates Peddar and Smith were busy setting up the cooking fire. Privates Ives and Keys brought several buckets of water up for washing. Several folding canvas chairs were set up around the tents, and the Lancers hungrily devoured macaroni, tinned beef, sardines, and biscuits. Colonel Martin and his second-in-command, Major Wyndham, set up their tents a short distance from their men to give them privacy.

Sergeant O'Leary and Corporal Mackenzie were engaged with Sergeants Montecy and Carter, still debating the accuracy of the Mark II bullets. Several other members of the squadron joined them, and soon a rousing conversation was taking place. Kip could hear the excitement in the men's voices. Would the dervish attack under cover of nightfall? How well would the horses fight in a night battle?

Kip watched the two Irish soldiers carefully while Churchill acted utterly unconcerned. Churchill engaged young Lieutenant Robert Grenfell and his brother Harry in a debate about the number of dervish warriors they would kill the next day.

As night fell, the searchlights on the gunboats swept out over the plains. They could see the Khalifa's forces in the spotlights. They too had set up tents, including the Khalifa, whose black flag stood prominently in the center of the mass. The steamboat's searchlights fell upon the Khalifa's camp. Several of his riflemen fired at the lights, but with no effect. The gunboats were safely out of range on the river.

Sentries on both sides patrolled their respective positions, ready to sound the alarm in the event of a night attack. The Sirdar ordered his men to sleep in shifts to ensure they were at the ready. The Maxims were manned at all times, as was the artillery. The zeriba was lined with men, rifles in hand. Egyptian, Sudanese, or white, they were all one army now, on the eve of battle. They stood together, facing out across the plains towards the tribes of the Khalifa.

To a man, each contemplated his fate. Will I die in battle? Will I be afraid? Will I be brave? Will I kill or be killed? To a man, none openly discussed his thoughts or his fears. Instead, the cheerful banter continued.

While Churchill was occupied with the Grenfell brothers, Kip decided to visit Syrah.

"Syrah, it's Major McDuran," he announced from just outside her tent flap. "Do you have a moment?" he asked.

"Yes, come in," she said.

Kip looked around and saw that no one seemed the slightest bit interested in his presence. He went inside.

"So what brings you to my tent on the eve of war?" she asked. She was wearing a short tob.

Kip shook his head. "I wanted to make sure you have everything you need. I may not have time to talk tomorrow," he said.

"Thank you, Kip," she said, touched by his kindness. He was facing battle, and yet he was concerned about her. It was not something she was accustomed to.

"I have everything I need. You need to focus on yourself," she said seriously. "The Khalifa and his men are very dangerous," she warned. "They enjoy killing." She paused for a moment, unsure how to express her feelings the right way.

"I'll be fine," Kip replied honestly. "There are some things about me you don't know. And I don't want to frighten you. Let's just say killing is something I understand."

Christ, that sounds ridiculous, he thought as the words escaped his lips.

Her eyes looked puzzled.

"You are a warrior. Of course you would understand killing," she said. "I have known nothing else from men. My father was a warrior and he died in battle."

"Where I come from, there are people who live their entire lives without seeing violence," Kip told her. "Even now, there are many men in the military who have not seen combat."

"I have lived surrounded by violence my entire life," Syrah murmured, casting her eyes downward. "I cannot imagine such a thing."

Kip was touched by her honesty. She was not afraid to express her thoughts to him.

"There are many decent men in the world who abhor violence," Kip continued. "The man who adopted me was such a man. He was a good, decent man who wouldn't hurt a soul."

"You are fortunate," she said.

Kip nodded his head. "Yes. If he hadn't come along, I am afraid to think of the man I might have become." Kip paused. He was still holding back. Even he wasn't sure of whom he had become. She sees me as a warrior, he thought. I see myself more as an executioner.

"Who is the man you have become?" she asked, gazing deeply into his eyes.

He was transfixed. He was certain she could read his mind. He couldn't lie.

"To be honest, I don't know."

Syrah quietly studied the handsome soldier standing before her. She was moved by his vulnerability. Instead of boasting about his exploits, he was allowing her to see into his soul. He wasn't trying to impress her. He wasn't trying to dominate her. He wasn't trying to rape her. Instead, he was treating her as an equal. It was surreal.

"I see a kind and honest man who is also very strong," Syrah said to him. "You have both an air of kindness and an air of danger about you. I have never experienced both from a man."

"You deserve someone to be kind to you," Kip said quietly. "You are a very beautiful woman." He smiled. "And I suspect you are more beautiful on the inside than you are on the outside."

Syrah could only look away. No one had ever expressed an interest in what she was beneath her skin.

"I'm sorry," Kip apologized. "I wasn't trying to be offensive."

She looked back at his face and saw only kindness, and perhaps something else. But love wasn't something she had ever experienced, except from her parents. And that had been some time ago.

Syrah reached out and touched his face.

"Be careful tomorrow. I want to see you again," she said.

Kip gently lifted his hand and caressed her cheekbone.

"I will," he said finally. "And I want to see you again too," he admitted. They smiled at each other.

"I'd better go find Churchill and make sure he's ready for battle tomorrow," Kip said.

"He may act like a clown," she said. "But I watched him when we came under fire. He was very calm and very sure of himself."

"I noticed," Kip said. He wanted to tell her his real mission, but of course, he could not.

"Go. And please, come back to me alive," she said.

Kip nodded and left her tent. This time he didn't care who was watching. He went to find Churchill.

He found him where he had left him. Winston finally gave up on his argument with the Grenfell brothers and sat down next to Kip, drink in hand, cigarette dangling from his lips.

"Those two brothers are impossible," Winston sighed.

"Those two brothers are inseparable," Kip laughed. "You were outnumbered the minute you engaged," he said.

"So are we," Winston noted, arching an eyebrow thoughtfully.

"It will be a massacre," Kip ignored him.

"A steep price to pay for one's religion," Churchill mused.

"Yep," Kip agreed. "It is a shame. There is a passage in the Koran, from the Islam book of Abraham. It says 'Allah, unto whom belongeth whatsoever is in the heavens and whatsoever is in the earth. And woe unto the disbelievers from an awful doom,'" Kip recited. "Not much difference from Christianity is it? If you don't believe in Jesus, you are going to hell. If you don't believe in Allah, you are truly fucked. It's a great way to scare folks into being believers, isn't it?"

"You sir, are a heretic," Churchill joked.

"I plead guilty, my lord," Kip replied.

"On the eve of battle, many men seek solace in their faith," Churchill said.

"It is their faith that will result in their massacre tomorrow," Kip said.

"We will lose men too," Churchill warned.

"Aye," Kip answered. "But not like them. Not like them."

Churchill took a drag on his cigarette. Someone was playing their violin by a campfire, and the men grew silent. Gentle smoke hung in the air alongside the soft song from the violin that floated out over the plains.

A hundred-thousand men faced each other in the darkness.

But only one god watched from above.

Chapter Seventy-Six

THE BATTLE, 1898

The blast of the bugle sounded at 4:30 in the morning. Kip had already been up for an hour, gear packed, horse loaded, ready for combat. Unlike the Lancers, Kip liked his load light. He had one water flask, his rifle in its scabbard, and four bandoliers of ammunition. He also carried a small field dressing kit for battle wounds. The Lancers loaded up their horses with water bottles, saddle bags filled with picketing gear and tins of bully beef and biscuits. Kip would eat a good breakfast, but that was it. He wasn't planning on eating the rest of the day.

He looked around the immense zeriba set up the day before by the soldiers. The fortification was a semi-circle. The Nile ran the length of the eastern side of the encampment. The ever-watchful gunboats waited in the moving river silently.

The southernmost area of the camp, facing the enemy, was lined with deep trenches filled with black-skinned Sudanese riflemen and brown-skinned Egyptians. Behind them stood a wall of mimosa and thorn bushes.

Behind the mimosa and the thorn barricades stood the cream of the crop. The Lincolns, Seaforths, Camerons, Warwicks, Grenadiers, Northumberland and Lancashire Fusiliers stood ready, their Lee Medford rifles just waiting to lay down a withering hail of lead over the heads of the entrenched riflemen.

A full artillery battery sat on a small hill above their position with a complete view of the plains to the south.

The western side of the zeriba was a line of more trenches, running north to south. It too was lined with dense, thorny mimosa hedges. Rifle brigades stood ready, the men resting their barrels on the berm of their trenches. Maxim machine guns, field artillery and mortars were interspaced every hundred yards.

Kip and Churchill sat astride their horses in their full battle gear along with the rest of the 21st Lancers. The horses snorted and shifted restlessly. They fed off the adrenaline of the soldiers riding them.

As the first light of dawn broke, Major Fowler, B Squadron Commander, looked to his men.

"We are riding out south to Surgham Hill, to take a look at the enemy's positions. Stay together. No one goes out alone," he ordered.

The Lancers made their way through the opening in the mimosa. Kip noted that O'Leary and Mackenzie were riding next to each other as the squadrons moved out. Kip rode next to Churchill. He had two enemies to fight that day, the dervish and the assassins. The familiar cold, ruthless mentality he had experienced in his past settled in. Today was a day to kill or be killed. He had no intention of being killed.

Kip's thoughts turned briefly to Syrah. She waited in a small tent near the command center. She too had a fight in this battle. To identify the Khalifa and his various emirs as they were either captured or killed. Kitchener wanted no mistake as to the identity of his fallen foe.

Kip's feelings towards Syrah were conflicted. His military mind told him she was a valuable intelligence asset. His heart told him something else.

These and many other thoughts filled his mind as they set out under the growing daylight. The clatter of the horse's hooves on the hard-packed desert clay kept time with their advance.

They reached Surgham Hill quickly. They rode around the base of the hill, to the western side, where the clay gave way to sand. While the others dismounted and set up a perimeter, their Lee-Enfield rifles pointed towards the southern desert plains, Kip and Churchill climbed high up the hill with their field glasses-looking out through the morning haze above the desert.

"Holy shit," Kip said as the approaching dervish forces became focused in his lens. "That's a lot of pissed off rag heads."

"Indeed," whispered Churchill.

The two men rested their field glasses on a chest high boulder that blocked most of their bodies.

"Whatever are they thinking?" Churchill wondered out loud as they looked across the desert floor.

To the west, they saw a light green flag and a mass of dervish warriors moving northwest, away from the British encampment.

To the south, a larger mass of dervish advanced under a dark green banner.

To the east, another dervish horde surged forward under a white flag, headed directly towards the British stronghold.

"The light green force is going flank us," Kip noted. "If they can reach the ridge they will have the high ground to hide behind and set up look outs."

"And I suspect the warriors on the eastern flank under the white flag are going to be sacrificial lambs, drawing our attention," Churchill added.

"Which means the dark green forces standing between us and Omdurman are going to mass against us," Churchill continued. He continued to peer into the lenses, as did Kip.

"They are trying to draw us out," Kip observed.

"I think we had better get back and report what we see," Churchill said.

"Yes," Kip replied. The two men scrambled down the hill to their waiting squadron.

"Sir," Churchill saluted the scowling face of Major Fowler. "Request permission for the good major and I to ride back and brief the Sirdar on our observations." He smiled. "Time is of the essence."

"Brief me first, Churchill," the major ordered.

Kip felt his anger growing. "We don't have time, Major. The enemy is just over the ridge."

The two officers glared at each other.

"Ride," Fowler ordered.

The two men wheeled their horses and took off at a gallop towards the southern end of the zeriba.

"Get two more men up that hill on lookout," Fowler ordered. "I want to know what the hell is going on."

Both O'Leary and Mackenzie were watching Kip and Churchill ride off. Fowler glared at them.

"You two, get your asses up that hill," the major barked. "I want a godamn situation report!"

"Yes sir," O'Leary answered. He gave a shrug of his shoulders to Mackenzie and the two men clambered up the hill.

Kip and Churchill covered the distance back to the zeriba quickly. They rode through the entrance between the mimosa and acacia trees. It had been reinforced with barbed wire. They found the Sirdar atop the hill overlooking the battlefield.

They pulled up their horses and saluted smartly.

"Sir, Lieutenant Churchill reporting along with Major McDuran," Churchill stated.

"Proceed," said the general, his eyes still out on the approaching mass.

"A flanking movement is headed northwest, probably to hide behind the southern Kerreri ridge under a bright green flag," Kip reported.

"That would be Ali-Wad Helu," Colonel Wingate stated calmly as he stood at the Sirdar's side.

"Just inside of them, to the west, a large mass of riflemen and spearmen under a dark green flag," Kip added.

"Most likely Osman Shiekh-ed-Din and Osman Azrak," Wingate said, looking at his map.

"Holding back in the center is another equally large mass of soldiers.

At least 3,000 are on horseback and clustered around several artillery pieces under a black flag," Churchill added.

"The Khalifa himself," Wingate noted. "Most likely with Yakub at his side. It would appear our intelligence asset was right about what she heard in the jirga."

"And a very determined group of warriors on the eastern most flank under a white banner, coming up the river's edge, headed right smack towards Lyttelton's Brigade," Kip finished.

"Well done," the general growled.

"Major McDuran, your assessment?" he asked.

Churchill looked hurt. Kip felt himself laughing inside. He was such a jealous little bastard.

"The forces under the white flag are a diversion. Sacrificial lambs. The flanking movement on the southwest will take up position on Kerreri Ridge and wait. No doubt they are hoping that after we slaughter the white force, we will abandon the zeriba and come out after them. While we pursue the remnants, the light green force will swoop down behind us while the dark green force attacks up the front, and we are caught between two pincers."

"Devilish plan," the Sirdar mused. "Churchill, what's your take?"

Churchill felt himself bursting with pride. "I concur," he stated succinctly.

Kitchener couldn't help but feeling a little surprised at Churchill's short reply. Good god, was the glory hound from Cuba and Afghanistan finally growing up?

"And the city itself?" the Sirdar asked.

"He will have a reserve force there as well, sir," Wingate interrupted. Churchill looked annoyed.

"Including I suspect, the majority of his artillery. They will attempt to open up on us as we advance, but we can easily suppress their fire with our own artillery and the gunboats," Wingate said.

The Sirdar nodded his head.

"Good work men, back to your post. That is all," he ordered.

Churchill and Kip saluted smartly and cantered their horses back toward the rest of the 21ˢᵗ Lancers.

"Perhaps the little bastard has grown up," Kitchener said to Wingate.

"Not possible, sir."

The general couldn't help but laugh. But then his face grew serious.

"And where the hell are Mahmüd and Osman Digna?" Kitchener asked his intelligence officer.

It had already occurred to him that the Khalifa was setting a trap. He knew their tactics from numerous battles in the past. So long as his men held steady and followed orders, he was ready to decimate his foe. It was why he stopped the artillery barrage. He wanted his enemy closer.

"I believe they are holding in reserve, somewhere north of Atbara. We've heard rumors, but we don't know exactly where they are," Wingate answered.

"That's comforting," Kitchener responded with irritation.

Kip and Churchill watered their horses on the river before rejoining the Lancers atop the crest of a small hill. It gave them a view of the battlefield. They watched the forces under the white flag take the lead, charging up the eastern flank of the zeriba along the river wearing white and blue cloth jibbas and turbans.

Suddenly two explosions in quick succession raised a huge cloud of red clay dust in front of the southern edge of the British zeriba.

"Those cheeky bastards are firing their artillery at us!" Churchill exclaimed. The main wall of the advancing white horde was now within less than 3,000 yards range, advancing behind their artillery.

The boom of the British howitzers broke the air, and at least a dozen projectiles whistled over Kip and Churchill's location, exploding above the advancing white horde.

Shrapnel rained down upon the charging dervish. Huge clusters of men were knocked to the ground, their flesh shredded by the sizzling steel fragments. The British gunners fired round after round; shrapnel exploded above the dervish horde and cannon shells exploded in their midst, sending out a spray of fury.

Nonetheless, the white horde advanced, into range of the riflemen. The riflemen opened up with volley after volley. Their firing was controlled and steady. Slug after slug found flesh, bone and sinew.

Within minutes, half of the advancing white horde lay dead upon the ground, but still more came. Then the Maxims opened up. A hail of bullets spewed forth into the air, cutting down swathes of white clothed dervish, swords and spears ripped out of their hands as they fell bloody to the ground.

Kip felt himself sickened by the carnage as the hard ocher sand ran red with blood. The bloodbath played out before them.

The artillery and the gunboats opened fire on Omdurman with their heavy guns. Massive explosions burst up from the city as they sought out the dervish artillery.

The Maxims on the gunboats also opened up on the white horde, and it looked as they were struck by a giant blast of wind, tossing them like ragdolls to the ground. Flesh and blood flew into the air, spattering on their white cotton tunics as they fell in mass.

The remaining white forces climbed over mountains of mangled bodies, trying to advance. But as their numbers dwindled, the advance slowed and then came to a complete halt. They could not move further. A barricade of corpses lay in their path.

"That didn't go as they planned," Kip deadpanned.

"Gruesome," Churchill agreed.

Suddenly they heard the bugle sound the advance of the horse cavalry and the camel corps. Colonel Broadwood led his men out of the zeriba, west towards the bright green flag of the flanking force. He was not going to let them get behind the zeriba. Nine squadrons moved out on horses and camels to intercept the flanking light green forces.

Osman Shiekh-ed-Din saw the British horses and camels emerge from the zeriba. The British were taking the bait. They were going after Ali-Wad-Helu's flanking movement.

Osman Sheikh-ed-Din turned to Osman Azrak at his side. "Their western flank is exposed," he said.

"The Khalifa said to wait for his signal before attacking the western flank of the zeriba," Azrak warned him.

"No, the time is now," Sheikh-ed-Din disagreed. He quickly barked out orders to his subordinates, and his force swung northeast, towards the western side of the British encampment. He would cut off the cavalry retreat and ride unimpeded into the British zeriba.

Osman Azrak shook his head. He would keep his men in position as planned.

Colonel Broadwood quickly saw he was outnumbered and recognized the shifting danger. If he continued to pursue the flankers, the main dark green force would take him from the other side.

Kitchener, atop the hill, field glasses in hand, also recognized the danger and signaled to his heliographers to send new orders to Broadwood.

They flashed out the message, "WITHDRAW IMMEDIATELY TO THE ZERIBA".

"Sir," an aide called out to the colonel. "Orders from the Sirdar, withdraw immediately!"

"Damn right!" Broadwood cursed. He turned his force northeast, with 15,000 screaming dervish chasing them from behind.

"Let's take them for a ride," the colonel growled.

There was just one problem. The camels couldn't keep up with the horses. The horse cavalry left the camel corps in the dust. Broadwood saw that his men were in danger of being caught. He wasn't going to be able to outrun them after all.

"Shit!" Broadwood yelled out again.

There was a dip between the two ridges, forming a small plain. The dervish caught the tail end of the retreating camel corps, and a bloody altercation ensued.

Realizing they were caught, fifty soldiers dismounted, took cover behind the rocks and opened fire. The forward mass of the surging dervish stumbled as bodies fell in front of them, but they surged forth after the retreating camel corps. Some broke off to deal with the riflemen, who were soon engaged in hand-to-hand combat and then quickly overcome. Only 400 yards separated the dervish and the remainder of the camel corps. But the action of the men who took cover bought some extra time for the fleeing camel corps.

Broadwood grimaced. He signaled the nine horse cavalry regiments to prepare to charge the advancing horde. It was his only chance of saving the camel corps.

"On my command!" Broadwood shouted. The white tunics of the dervish army marked with their multi-colored patches quickly whitewashed the black rocks of the southern Kerreri Ridge as they closed in like water flowing over a dam. Thousands of dervish warriors sprang from nowhere, threatening to cut them off.

Lieutenant Beatty watched the unfolding drama from the deck on the gunboat *Tamil*. So did the rest of the naval officers on the other four gunboats. They had only dreamed of such a chance as this.

"Give me hell!" Beatty screamed to his gunners.

The quick firing 12-pound howitzers erupted on the dervish horde chasing Broadwood and his men, followed by the Nordenfeldt machine guns and the Maxims letting loose as the dervish force came within range. They fired just above the approaching camel corps, who grimly kept their heads down as they rode for safety. Like a rake among leaves, the dervish were swept aside.

As the Maxims heated up, they had to refill the cooling water bladders to continue the rate of fire. Soon, they were pouring buckets of water over the barrels to keep them from melting.

The advancing horde of dervish collapsed upon a wall of the dead and the dying coming to an abrupt halt. The camel corps swiftly moved inside the safety of the zeriba, followed by the horse cavalry.

"Bloody navy saves the day," Broadwood muttered gratefully.

Kip and Winston had joined the 21st Lancers gathered at the southern tip of the zeriba. They had a close-up view of the carnage taking place.

"Jesus!" Churchill exclaimed.

Kip watched the advancing white-clad men tumbling and falling as bright red, gaping cavities opened up in body after body. Heads burst open like watermelons from the fire and shrapnel, spilling onto the dirt in a pulp. And still they came, tripping and stumbling over their dead brothers and comrades. The gap closed.

Meanwhile, the dervish warriors advancing under the white flag were reinforced by Osman Azrack, who also was caught up in the bloodlust. The British had not come out, so he would go in and take them instead. He ignored the Khalifa's battle plan and instead led fourteen thousand warriors towards the southern end of the zeriba. They were headed directly towards the waiting rifle brigades, Maxims and artillery.

Several of the British officers next to Kitchener had to look away for a moment in horror. "Oh god," one of them said.

The Sirdar looked at the advancing army. He too felt sickened at the unfolding massacre, but stood resolute in carrying it out.

"Obliterate them," Kitchener ordered. The signals flashed. When the advancing horde approached 1000 yards, shell after shell rained death down upon them. Bodies were flung into the air as the explosions ripped among them.

The Sudanese rifles and the British brigades behind them opened up. Their aim was deadly. Their rifle barrels grew hot from the rapid fire and the barrels of the Maxims turned a burning red.

Sheik Osman Azrak was enraged as his men were cut down. He rode his horse forward into a gallop, getting to within 150 yards of the zeriba. Hundreds of rounds surged forth in unison. His body convulsed from the vibrating impact, ripping him from his horse as he tumbled backward, the horse collapsing beneath him. He was dead before he hit the ground.

"Cease fire," the Sirdar ordered, and suddenly the deafening roar of the British guns grew silent.

Ears ringing, smoke and gunpowder searing their lungs, the soldiers stared in awe at the scene before them. Thousands upon thousands of lifeless corpses littered the field, submerged in vast pools of blood.

In their own ranks, they had suffered casualties as well, but only minimal. Several officers had been killed by random bullets that had whizzed into the zeriba. All total 150 men on the British side were wounded. Some received treatment where they lay; others would be assisted to the two field hospitals.

Slowly, small pockets of dervish soldiers moved about under the momentary lull. The white army lay decimated. But the battle was not yet over. The British gunners took aim as small clusters of dervish rose up from the ground.

"Hit them again," the Sirdar ordered. The cannons roared back to life and the marksmen put their eye to the sights. The enemy attempted to hide in the swells of the rolling plains, but the artillery dug them out.

"I do not want them to retreat to the city," the Sirdar announced to his staff. If they could retreat in large numbers to the city, they would have to dig them out, house by house.

CHAPTER SEVENTY-SEVEN

THE CHARGE OF THE 21ST LANCERS, 1898

General Gatacre rode his horse to the 21st Lancers position and found their commander, Colonel Martin. Kip and Winston were by his side.

"We are going to take the city. But first the Sirdar wants to know what is behind Kerreri ridge. Take a good look and report back," he ordered.

"Yes sir," Colonel Martin saluted. He turned to his squadron commanders. "Mount up!"

Finally, at last, the 21st Lancers were going to take the field of battle. Kip could feel their excitement.

The Grenfell brothers slapped each other on the back. Robert's usually serious face was plastered with a grin.

"Churchill," Colonel Martin ordered. "You and Major McDuran take Sergeant O'Leary and Corporal Mackenzie out on the western flank. Lieutenant Robert Grenfell, you and your brother take Corporal Swarrick and Private Ives on the eastern flank. Get up on those ridges and set up a look out while the main force comes up the middle. And watch out for the khors. They may be infested."

"Let's ride," Kip said, turning to Churchill.

"Indeed," Churchill agreed.

They set their horses to a trot as they turned to the southwest. Kip set sight on the edge of the ridge that stood sentry over the vast desert. They rode four abreast, with Kip on the left edge, Churchill on his right. The two Irishmen, Mackenzie and O'Leary, held their lances at the ready. They crossed the half mile to the ridge quickly. The horses picked their way carefully through the rocks as they climbed the crest of the ridge.

The ridge stretched out ahead of them, but once past the rocks, the view opened up to the flat desert. Between the ridge and Omdurman was an open plain, dotted with retreating dervish. Heat waves rose up from the hot sand, partially obscuring their view.

The rest of the regiment waited at the base of the ridge while Colonel Martin and his staff came up to Kip's location. The British colonel peered through his field glasses out onto the plain. The retreat of the wounded and disenchanted flowed in one continuous line all the way to the city.

Rifle fire broke out and chips of rock flew up into the air around them.

"Snipers," Colonel Martin said calmly.

Down the ridge, the main body of Lancers drew their rifles and returned fire.

The snipers retreated back into the rocks.

"Signal the Sirdar that other than a few snipers the ridge is clear and that thousands of the enemy are retreating to the city," he ordered. The heliographer flashed out the signal.

"Now we wait," the colonel said. But within a moment, the Sirdar flashed back his reply.

"Advance and clear the left flank. Use every effort to prevent the enemy from reentering Omdurman."

"That's it, men," Colonel Martin said. His faced was flushed with excitement.

"Fight's on. Same two patrols set out, same orders, report back quickly."

Kip and his men broke away and down the hill.

As they rode down the ridge, they encountered wounded and dying dervish soldiers lying on the hot sand. One of the wounded raised a rifle and was quickly shot by the big red headed Mackenzie. Two more dervish rose from behind the rocks and fired at the men.

Kip drew out his .45 and it barked into action. Two shots, two dead men tumbled backwards into the rocks. Churchill made a mental note that both kills were head shots.

"Getting a little hot here," Sergeant O'Leary observed.

"Let's get up on this dune and take a quick look," Churchill ordered. They galloped up the hill. Both officers quickly surveyed the field and they then rode back to Colonel Martin. Grenfell's patrol was also back.

"All clear," Churchill reported.

"About two hundred dervish gathered in a khor at the bottom of the ridge," Lieutenant Robert Grenfell reported. Three quarters of a mile to the southwest."

"We'll take them," Colonel Martin ordered.

The Khalifa sat in his tent at the southern base of the Jebel Surgham ridge. His plan to draw the British out in the open had failed. To his dismay, Ali-Wad-Helu had disobeyed his orders and attacked the western flanks of the zeriba. That force was cut to ribbons, and now left stragglers all over the plains. The Khalifa and his men were now the only thing between the British and his holy city, Omdurman. He left his tent and unhitched his horse.

The Khalifa was determined that his path to retreat to his city would remain open, and had posted 200 Hadendoa tribesmen in a khor below the Kerreri Ridge. It was these 200 warriors that Lieutenant Grenfell had observed and reported to Colonel Martin.

But what Lieutenant Grenfell did not observe, or report, was that the Khalifa had seen the 21st Lancers advance, and had been informed by his scouts that the British cavalry was advancing to cut off his retreat.

As the Khalifa now sat astride his horse, underneath the black flag of his personal army, he saw an opening.

"Ibrahim," he ordered. "Come to me."

Emir Ibrahim Khalil rode his horse to the Khalifa's side, his dark face scowling under the desert sun.

"Take 2,000 of our men from the black flag and reinforce the Hadendoa at the khor beneath the ridge. The British horsemen are coming to cut the road to Omdurman. Kill them all and take no prisoners," the Khalifa ordered.

"Yes my lord," the emir answered immediately. He screamed to his lieutenants, and four regiments, each five hundred men strong, broke away from the black flag and scrambled towards the khor.

The Khalifa motioned to his fastest messenger waiting nearby on horseback.

"Ride to Adaramra. Tell Mahmüd and Osman Digna we will hold Omdurman, and they are to attack the infidel from behind. Go now!" he yelled. He watched in satisfaction as the messenger rode off in a cloud of dust.

The battle was not over.

The 21st Lancers formed a line as they left the ridge and advanced onto the field of battle. The horses galloped forward, and the men leaned ahead in their saddles, lances at the ready.

Small groups of dervish warriors fell backwards from their advance. They scrambled to safety in the rocks. Smug satisfaction crossed the Lancers' faces under their pith helmets. Each thought to himself, "they'd better run!"

The only man not feeling smug was Kip. This was his worst nightmare.

Three hundred men on horses, armed with spears, were now advancing in the open across the plains of Kerreri. They saw a small pocket of dervish warriors in the distance, a small black smudge of men gathered on the road to Omdurman.

Kip rode on Churchill's right side. Behind them rode the rest of B squadron, including Mackenzie and O'Leary. All of the men held their lances at the ready, save Churchill and Kip, who both chose to have their pistols at the ready.

As they closed in on the men guarding the road to Omdurman, Kip saw the dark jagged line of a khor in front of them. The dried-up waterway could be ten to twenty yards wide, or bigger, and just as deep. But from this distance, it was impossible to tell.

The dark smudge became clear. Several hundred dervish riflemen, now clearly visible, dropped to their knees, rifles at the ready. Kip could see their brightly colored banners behind them. The dark blue cloth patches on their white cotton tunics shimmered under the sun.

Kip saw smoke erupting from the rifles before the first crack of a rifle shot reached his ears. The whole dervish line of rifles erupted, and bullets whizzed through the line of advancing men.

"Charge!" screamed out Colonel Martin, waving his saber into the air.

Three hundred horsemen spurred their horses to a gallop, thundering across the hard clay.

Kip kept his horse on Churchill's right flank. He could see Churchill's face from the side. He looks like a man possessed, Kip thought. Churchill's eyes were mad with rage, his face flushed red with excitement as he roared at the top of his lungs.

"This is fucking grand!" Churchill shouted over his shoulder, briefly glancing at Kip.

The line of dervish riflemen were now only two hundred yards away. Bullets kicked up rocks and dirt around the charging horses. The dervish held their line and continued to fire into the approaching horsemen. The 21st Lancers bowed their heads forward and urged their horses on.

Suddenly, the black line that Kip had seen in the distance opened up. It was a large khor, wide and deep. And out of its maw sprang two thousand enraged dervish warriors, many on horseback as well. They flooded up from the depths of the khor to face the charging Lancers.

Three hundred charging steeds slammed into the midst of the swelling horde. The collision of horses and bodies sent a shockwave across the plain like a clap of thunder. Back in the zeriba heads turned in amazement at the unfamiliar sound that swept over them.

Men were torn from their horses and dismembered by the shrieking dervish. Bright flashes of steel and large sprays of blood filled the air.

Gasping for breath, horses and men alike clashed, screamed and flailed in a maniacal frenzy.

Colonel Martin's second-in-command, Major Wyndham, rode directly into the center mass of the emerging horde. A wild-eyed dervish thrust his rifle into the chest of his horse and pulled the trigger. The horse went down and the major was thrown over its head into the screaming mass. Sword in one hand, pistol in the other, he began to slash his way out.

Lieutenant Robert Grenfell steered his horse directly into a ring of dervish warriors with their rifles raised. A volley of fire from the rifles toppled him off his horse; his pith helmet tumbled off his head as he hit the ground. Unsteady on his feet and seriously wounded, he was able to struggle to his knees, his blond hair streaked with blood that ran down his face.

His brother Harry screamed and tried to steer his horse to his brother's aid. But before he could reach his fallen kin, a dervish warrior raised his sword high and slashed Robert's head completely clean from his body. Robert Grenfell toppled to his side, his legs and feet twitching engulfed in a pool of blood.

Harry, now completely insane by what he had just witnessed, plowed over the warrior with his horse. The beast's massive chest mashed into the dervish, flinging him aside. Harry leaped off the horse and landed directly on the chest of the warrior who had just killed his brother. He swiftly yanked a knife from his scabbard and plunged it directly into the man's heart. Again and again, he gouged the already dead, mangled body with all his might, ignoring the blood that spewed up in his face.

Another dervish warrior sprang into action and ran Harry clean through with his sword. Harry spun around in rage, drew his pistol and shot the man point-blank in the face. He ignored the blood pouring from his wound and charged directly into another group of dervish; his pistol snapping and his sword slashing.

Lieutenant Molyneux found himself swept off his horse in the bottom of the khor. He was immediately attacked by a group of dervish warriors. As he raised his pistol, his hand was slashed off by a swordsman.

The pistol fell to the ground and discharged. A sword smashed into the side of his helmet; the blade cut through clean to his scalp.

From out of the dust, Private Byrne rode into action, despite the fact he had already been shot in the shoulder. His horse knocked the dervish away from Molyneux, who scrambled out of the khor using his one good hand. A dervish warrior thrust his spear into Byrne's side. Byrne shrieked with fury and blasted the man in the face.

B squadron now found itself swept into the depths of this hell, drowning in a swarm of thousands of bloodthirsty dervish warriors. Kip fired round after round as the enemy tried to rip him off his horse.

More warriors leapt at Churchill, limbs aimlessly flailing in desperate attempts to pull Churchill from his saddle. Churchill's 7.63 mm Mauser cracked in rapid fire as he blew the bodies off him left and right.

Out of the corner of his eye, Kip saw the red-bearded Irishman Mackenzie toss aside the body of a dervish warrior that he had run through with his lance. The big Irishman caught a glimpse of Churchill surrounded, and smiled. He calmly drew his 1986 Lee Enfield rifle and aimed directly at the Wolseley cork helmet that sat on the head of Winston Churchill.

An instant before Mackenzie's finger squeezed the trigger, a soft-leaded hollow point slug tore into his forehead, leaving a gaping crimson hole; a spray of grey matter and blood blew out the backside of his helmet as the .45 caliber round from Kip's rifle expanded, tearing his brains from his skull.

Sergeant O'Leary, riding next to him, had also been yanked from his horse by the dervish warriors. He slashed back at them with a sword in one hand, and a revolver in the other. He saw Mackenzie fly backwards off his horse and he glanced in Churchill's direction.

"No!" O'Leary screamed. He cut off the hand of the nearest dervish warrior and aimed his pistol at Churchill's head.

After Mackenzie had drawn his rifle, Kip had focused on the big Irishman and was forced to ignore the fray around him. He grimaced in satisfaction when he saw the back of Mackenzie's head explode. He searched out O'Leary in the midst of the swirling, screaming horde. Kip's eyes found O'Leary in the chaos, aiming his pistol at Churchill. Kip's Winchester rifle roared again, sending a soft lead slug into O'Leary's right eye. His flesh flew into the face of a dervish warrior who was poised to cut off O'Leary's head with his sword. The spray of blood blinded the dervish warrior momentarily, and he missed his mark.

Kip fired once more. The warrior's body flipped backwards as if he had been kicked in the chest by a mule.

Churchill heard the distinctive roar of Kip's Winchester and glanced about. He saw the American shoot Mackenzie off his horse, and saw O'Leary raise his pistol at him. Churchill's eyes widened as he started to raise his own pistol in response, but a hand grabbed him and he kicked out with his stirrup, driving the steel into the eye of the attacking warrior. The man screamed and let go of Churchill's hand at the same moment O'Leary's head exploded.

Churchill looked back at Kip. He was now surrounded by ten dervish warriors who had taken advantage of his distraction with the assassins. In order to save Churchill, Kip had left himself exposed.

Kip felt himself torn off his horse and he fell into the mob of crazed men. He jumped to his feet and drew his .45 caliber pistol.

Churchill saw Kip's plight, slammed a new box magazine into his pistol and spurred his horse directly into the throng of men surrounding Kip. The rapid fire of his pistol was matched by the roar of Kip's Colt .45. Both men emptied their clips into the mass of the assailants. Eighteen lead slugs found their mark in the flesh and bone of the swarm.

Churchill bowled over two more warriors with his horse just as they flanked Kip. Kip took advantage of the brief opening, grabbed his rifle off the ground and leapt back onto his horse.

"Ride!" Kip screamed at Churchill. Both men kicked their horses into action and galloped through the mass of bodies still clutching at them. Kip thrust his foot at the head of one charging dervish and felt the impact of his boot crush the man's face. Another fell underneath his charging steed and shrieked in anguish as the horse's iron hoof tore off his nose.

Both men reached the top of the khor and rode onward to the open plain. They looked back down, bearing witness to a scene from hell.

Only half of the 21st Lancers had made it through the ambush and rode out the other side of the khor. Colonel Martin was one of them, unscathed. He ordered his men to form into another line, and readied them to charge back into the abyss of tangled bodies below. He saw the gaping, dirt-caked wounds in his men and their horses. Blood was everywhere. Spears and swords stuck out of man and horse alike. Entrails and organs dangled from abdomens, mangled limbs bled profusely, eyes hung out of their sockets. And yet the men prepared to charge back into battle.

In the swarming sea of flesh below, the scene was worse still.

Enraged dervish hacked off the heads off British cavalry soldiers who had been unlucky enough to be pulled from their horses. British soldiers fired back with their Lee-Enfield carbines and Webley revolvers at point-blank range. They too were howling with boundless, maniacal rage.

Looking at the carnage below, Colonel Martin swiftly changed course. The dervish and British soldiers in the depths of the khor continued to annihilate each other.

"Dismount and open fire!" he screamed. One hundred and fifty of England's finest marksmen took aim at the mass below and opened fire-many wiping the blood from their eyes just to aim. Many felt the searing pain of their own wounds, some with blades still in them. But their .303 caliber bullets found their mark in the sea of teeming flesh below.

The remaining 21st Lancers surrounded in the khor below could only gasp in astonishment as their attackers fell at their feet.

The barrel of Kip's rifle was ablaze as he fired continuously, matched by the other Lancers relentless gunfire. Slowly, the sea of men separated as the remaining dervish began to run for the cover of the nearby ridge, and the safety of Abdullah's black flag. The Khalifa spurred his horse back towards the safety of the ridgeline, spewing obscenities in a frenzied rage as he crossed the hard-packed plain.

"Cease fire!" Colonel Martin yelled out.

For a brief moment, smoke and silence hung in the air. Then the mass of bodies in the bottom of the khor began to move.

Kip and Winston stared down on the horror below, utterly aghast. Disfigured bodies, impaled by sharp steel, writhed in pain, releasing helpless groans of anguish. Dozens of horses kicked and flailed in agony. One British soldier slowly crawled on his knees out of the khor, a spear protruding from both ends of his torso. The 21st Lancers slowly got to their feet.

Lieutenant Harry Grenfell, still insane with rage, ignored his wounds and pulled his pistol from his scabbard. He walked down into the khor and began shooting any dervish warrior who moved. Several more officers pulled their pistols from their holsters, and they too waded into the khor among the wounded and the dead. Shots rang out as they coldly executed any dervish warrior who was still alive. The Sirdar's orders had been very clear. No prisoners, unless they were emirs.

Though, truth be told, it was bloodlust that arose from deep within the survivors that drove their actions, not their orders. Colonel Martin gave his men time to finish business.

After the gun shots ceased, Colonel Martin looked at his regiment, bloodied and weakening under the afternoon sun.

"Gather the dead and wounded," Martin ordered. The 21st Lancers gathered up their fallen comrades and made their way back to the British field hospital inside the safety of the zeriba.

Chapter Seventy-Eight

THE PLAINS OF KERRERI, 1898

While mayhem was unfolding in the khor, the battle on the plains raged on.

The Sirdar looked down on the battlefield from his observation post high above the plains. He had no idea if the green force still lurked behind the ridge, but the road to Omdurman was now his for the taking. He realized that the dervish, now regrouped, still outnumbered his own force. Over 35,000 enemy soldiers remained on the field of battle. And they were filled with an insatiable thirst for revenge. But, he had the modern weapons.

"Signal the men to prepare to advance on Omdurman," he ordered. "And have Colonel Wingate from Intelligence Branch bring the woman. I want solid confirmation that the Khalifa is dead," Kitchener instructed.

"Yes sir," his adjutant replied smartly with a salute. He left the overlook and went to the back of the zeriba, where Intelligence Branch had set up shop.

Smoke hung in the air from the cannons as Kip and Churchill made their way through the wounded men in the zeriba. They dismounted and let their horses drink from the river. Foam and blood spattered their flanks.

Orders were given to form two squadrons with uninjured horses and only slightly wounded men. Pistol shots rang out as several grievously wounded horses were put out of their misery.

Kip sat down on a rock and took off his helmet and poured the contents of the canteen over his head, washing blood, sweat and pieces of human tissue off his face.

Winston lit a cigarette and marveled at how steady his hands were when he lit the match. He took a deep drag off the cigarette.

"I'll have one of those," Kip said. He reached out.

Churchill handed him a smoke.

Kip lit his cigarette. Churchill noted Kip's hands were rock steady as well.

The bugles sounded, signaling the men to prepare to advance.

The two men looked at each other. The thought of more bloodshed to come was nearly overwhelming.

"I don't think Mackenzie or O'Leary will be joining us," Churchill said.

Kip let out a stream of smoke. "Nope, I reckon not."

"Thank you," Churchill said. He held out his hand, and the two men shook.

"Don't mention it," Kip said smiling. "And don't trust that we smoked out all of them," he warned.

"I dare say I will be looking over my shoulder for the rest of my life," Churchill agreed.

"You look over your shoulder, but I've got your back," Kip said warmly. "Churchill, when I first met you, I thought you were the biggest ass I'd ever met in my life," Kip said.

"And now?" Churchill interrupted with a twinkle in his eye.

Kip looked down. For a moment, he was silent.

He raised his head once more and looked Churchill in the eye.

"Even bigger," Kip said, his voice unfaltering.

Both men laughed.

"But I'll ride with you any day," Kip added.

"Likewise Major. Likewise." He got to his feet and crushed his cigarette under his boot. "It looks like we still have some work to do."

Kip looked around. The camp was packing up, preparing for the next phase of the battle, the attack on Omdurman, the Khalifa's holy city. Wagons were loaded, tents were folded away, rations stored. Men had reloaded and rearmed, horses were hitched to the artillery, and Maxims were mounted on their platforms.

"Saddle up," barked out Colonel Martin as the Lancers reformed.

"Signal the advance," the Sirdar ordered from the hill overlooking the zeriba.

The expression never changed on the Sirdar's face. He watched the bloodshed of battle with no sign of emotion on his sun-baked face. It had never been in doubt. The wildly attacking dervish forces were no match for the sophisticated weapons and tactics of a modern army.

Kitchener lowered his field glasses. "Well, I think we gave them quite the dusting," he remarked calmly to his subaltern. He turned to his second-in-command, General Gatacre.

"Take the city, find the Khalifa, and bring him to me alive," he ordered.

"Sir," Colonel Wingate interrupted. "We captured a messenger for the Khalifa. He was sent with instructions for Mahmüd and Osman Digna to attack us from the rear."

Kitchener smiled at Wingate.

"Nice work," he nodded. And he meant it. It had occurred to him that the Khalifa's reserve force would be called into action. But it was nice to have proof.

"General Gatacre, we'll take the city first. Then take five thousand men and whatever guns you need to Adaramra and wipe out the Khalifa's reserves," Kitchener ordered.

"Yes sir," the general replied. The advance on the city continued.

The 21st Lancers rode ahead as scouts, just ahead of the massive army now completely mobilized and approaching the outskirts of the Khalifa's city. They passed row after row of mud-walled houses with thatched huts and squalid alleyways that crisscrossed the neighborhoods outside the great stone wall of the city.

The British artillery from the batteries and the gunboats had decimated the population of the city. Disfigured bodies of women and children lay motionless in the streets. Limbs were missing, heads were missing. Scarlet hues of blood and body tissue seeped into the mud, creating a morass of death. The stench was overwhelming.

The Lancers hurriedly wrapped handkerchiefs around their faces. Several leaned sideways off their horses to vomit. From every street corner terrified soldiers and citizens alike rushed to the street and lay prostrate upon the ground in complete surrender.

Churchill and Kip exchanged glances. Neither could hide the pain in their eyes as they bore witness to the enormity of the calamity that had taken place. The horses moved slowly; alley after alley it was the same. Burned and charred corpses were everywhere, as were the pleading survivors groveling in the hard-packed sand.

The Khalifa's forces were either fleeing south or throwing themselves at the mercy of the enemy. The British army met little resistance as they rode through the gates and into the bowels of the decimated city.

Here, the damage was even more severe, as the heaviest concentration of artillery had landed round after round of heavy explosive in an attempt to silence the Khalifa's batteries. They had succeeded, but the civilian population paid the price.

Charred bodies protruded from the ashes of smoldering fires, belching the smoke of cooked human remains. It was a smell that no man would ever forget. One scorched body toppled sideways, leaving afoot stuck to the ground and a gaping pink maw of uncooked flesh where the bone had snapped at the ankle.

Inside the city, in the town's center, where the Khalifa had rallied his men, were the gallows where the Khalifa had hung anyone who dared challenge the law of Islam. Many were still there, bodies hanging stiff, rotting and motionless beneath the rope around their necks.

The British forces soon completely swallowed the city as they continued their advance. Only when they reached the Mahdi's tomb did they pause. It was the holiest of holiest places in the city, where the body of the "chosen one" lay in rest. Leader to millions, hope to the masses, his tomb lay in white marble.

"Destroy it," Kitchener ordered. "Dig up his foul remains and burn them."

And they did. Gordon's death was avenged.

Later that evening, the holy city taken, the men of the British expeditionary force finally took rest as the night began to fall. Sentries were posted, guard towers on the great wall were manned with soldiers, Maxims and torch lights illuminated the pitch. Exhausted men fell into a fitful sleep of nightmares.

"Well I guess we are all going to hell for this one," Churchill mused, a cigarette dangling from his lips and a stiff shot of whiskey in his mug. He and Kip had pitched their tents next to a corral reserved for the surviving horses of the 21st Lancers.

"Let me get this straight," Kip retorted. "Thousands of dead dervish martyrs are going to Allah to receive seventy two virgins, and we are going to hell? That hardly seems fair."

Churchill snorted. "Nothing fair about war, is there?"

"Nothing fair about life," Kip answered.

"I'm not sure my military training or my prior combat experience prepared me for this day," Churchill admitted, brushing his hand through his hair.

"Nor mine," Kip agreed.

"It was butchery," Churchill said.

"We nearly got butchered in the khor," Kip said, a solemn expression on his face.

He leaned forward to take another cigarette from the outstretched hand of his friend.

"It was disconcerting. Mackenzie and O'Leary were out for vengeance. For the actions of my father," Winston said thoughtfully. He paused, the rising moon catching his glowering jaw, jutted forward.

"And you still want to follow in his footsteps?" Kip asked.

"No. I intend to be the man my father never was," Winston replied.

Silence hung in the air as each man pondered his life.

"Did you know your father?" Churchill asked.

"Not well, he was murdered when I was ten," Kip answered.

"Did they ever catch who murdered him?"

"No." Kip paused. "But I did."

Churchill's eyebrows shot up.

"Judge, jury and executioner?"

Kip ground out his cigarette in the sand. "You might say that."

"How did it feel?" Churchill asked.

"Great," Kip said coldly.

"Oh my," Churchill said. "Remind me never to piss you off. And how do you feel tonight?"

"Cold. Your turn," Kip suggested.

"Satisfied," Winston replied immediately. "Gordon has been avenged. The enemy annihilated. The British empire rules supreme."

"What a waste," Kip said. "There are thousands upon thousands of rotting corpses; men, women and children lying out under the moon, their bodies being pulled apart by animals. There are thousands more wounded, crippled and helpless. A hundred years from now, who will care? What will it matter?"

"We had to set an example," Churchill replied honestly. "Religious fanatics were bent upon destroying all we consider civilized. The Sudan is better off without these people."

"Are they any worse than the Catholic Church which laid waste to innocent and happy people of the southern hemisphere?" Kip asked. "Who brought death, destruction and disease in the name of God, *and* took all their gold?"

"You think too much, Major," Churchill said.

"It is a problem," Kip admitted. "Let's get some sleep," he suggested. "I can hardly wait to see what tomorrow brings."

"Quite right," Churchill agreed. The two men placed their cots outside the tents that night. They stretched out under the stars, each alone with his thoughts.

Kip waited until he heard Churchill snoring. Then he made his way to Syrah's tent. The guard had fallen into a deep slumber on his stool.

"Syrah," Kip said softly.

She opened the tent flap and gestured for him to come inside. She turned up the wick on her kerosene lantern and gasped in horror. Kip's face and hands were stained with dried blood. Pieces of flesh and bits of bone remained onhis uniform, which was torn in several places.

"Are you wounded?" she asked with concern.

Kip shook his head. "No."

She touched his shoulder. "I was afraid you had been killed," she said. Her eyes searched his. "It must have been horrible," she added.

"Aye, it was that indeed," he said honestly. "And the Khalifa escaped."

"I know," she answered, looking down. "I went with Colonel Wingate to the edge of the city, in case they found him. I saw many dead bodies, but not his," she said.

Kip could hear disappointment in her voice.

"But at least you are safe," she whispered. "That was the longest day of my life, waiting to know that you were alive."

Kip looked into her eyes.

"I was worried for you too," he said. He reached out and caressed her face.

"I have feelings for you," she said. "I have feelings and emotions that I have never experienced before. I'm not sure what to do or say."

Kip was stunned by her admission. But deep within, he knew he too felt the same way.

"I too have feelings for you," he admitted.

They embraced, holding each other as if their lives depended on it. Kip could feel her heart beat against his chest. She looked up and he kissed her. Gently first, and then more passionately. Her lips eagerly sought out his mouth in return.

"I can't stay," Kip said. He wanted to, but he knew the sentries would talk. It was a matter of time before the sleeping guard would awaken.

She nodded. "Go."

Her heart was pounding inside her chest. She wanted to tell him that she loved him, but the words could not come out.

He left as silently as he had arrived.

Chapter Seventy-Nine

SUDAN, 1898

Kip took a seat on one of the canvas-backed chairs of the many lined up neatly in rows inside the main briefing tent. The Sirdar had assembled his key staff members for debriefing. General Gatacre stood at the podium, watching as the senior officers found their seats. Churchill was not in attendance, as he was not one of the Sirdar's favorites or senior staff. Which made Kip wonder why he had received a special request from Colonel Wingate?

"Gentlemen, the Sirdar," General Gatacre announced solemnly.

The senior staff rose to attention.

"As you were," Kitchener said briskly. Instead of taking their seats, the tent broke into applause. Kip almost thought he saw Kitchener blush at the attention. The commander looked at his men with gratitude.

"Thank you, I trust you are applauding yourselves," he mused. Laughter rippled through the tent. "And of course, your men," he added after a pause. Take your seats please. I know you want me to be brief, so sit the bloody hell down," he said with a smile.

A roar of laughter broke through the large domed tent. It felt good to laugh, it felt good to be victorious, but most of all, it felt good to be alive.

"I will let your commanders provide you with the details of your great victory at your respective breakouts. But let me just say how proud I am to have led such a distinguished group of men into the jaws of hell," the Sirdar said, his eyes blazing.

His sincerity sent a chill up the spines of his men. It felt good to make your commander proud. The men looked at each other and handshakes and slaps on the back went around the audience.

"We lost a great many dear friends and comrades on the field of battle, and a great many more are wounded. Let us have a moment of silence to pray for their salvation," Kitchener said, bowing his head.

"Heavenly father, bless the souls of those great warriors who sacrificed their lives to protect all that they hold holy and dear; God and country. Let them find eternal peace in your care. And give their families and loved ones the peace to continue life's journey without them," he paused. "Amen."

"Amen," the men repeated solemnly.

"I promised you I would be brief, and I will," the Sirdar continued. "We have some unfinished business to attend to." His face grew serious.

"We captured one of the Khalifa's messengers fleeing the battle. He disclosed the Khalifa still has 20,000 men held in reserve under the leadership of Osman Digna and Emir Mahmüd. They have moved north of Atbara to Adaramra. No doubt they intend to attack us from the rear. Major-General Gatacre will take his men and finish them off." Kitchener paused to let it sink in.

Kip could only image the torture the messenger endured. "Disclosed" was such a polite word.

"The Sudan is once again a protectorate of the Khedive of Egypt," Kitchener continued. "Egypt shall be responsible for maintaining order and conducting the daily affairs of government for the people. However, a small British contingent shall remain in Khartoum as military advisors after General Gatacre finishes off the remaining dervish. Volunteers would be nice, but not essential," he said.

"There are two other more serious matters we must attend to," he added.

"First, the Khalifa has managed to escape our grasp. He is not at Adaramra with his reserves. We believe he fled south on the White Nile with his personal guard. We are sending an expedition to capture or kill him. Capture is preferred, but not at the risk of British lives. I want to cut off the head of the snake," Kitchener continued.

"Dead or alive, we'll need positive identification. We must ensure the Islamic extremists are finished once and for all. We have an intelligence asset that will provide that for us."

"Second, and perhaps more importantly, the French have placed troops in Fashoda," he announced, to the surprise of his men.

A murmur went through the tent. The French? In the Sudan? The senior leaders quickly began to assess the possibilities. Armed hostilities with the French could be the beginning of another war. There had been many rumors, but never had it been officially announced.

"The French mission is insidious. Use the civilian labor available and build a dam, thereby cutting Egypt off from the Nile at its source," Kitchener added.

Finally, Kip thought to himself. That is why I am here in the first place. The president wants confirmation that the French expedition fails. It was not in the best interest of the United States if the Nile and the Suez Canal were to be held hostage. American shipping and the navy relied on the Suez Canal. Cut off the Nile and you cut off the life of Egypt and everyone who lives there, including the people that own and operate the canal. The United States would have to sail its ships around the cape of Africa to reach the Orient.

Kip had to admit it was a brilliant plan. The French would hold the world hostage. Ruthless and brilliant.

Thousands of bodies lay rotting on the plains of the Kerreri, their bones to be picked clean by the vultures, the sand and the sun.

This was not about avenging Gordon. This was about power, and the need to keep and protect it. It was that simple. Not that Kip had any love lost for the radical Islamic dervish led by their pompous holy man. The Sudan would be better off with the Khalifa captured or dead.

But war between France and England was a centennial event. It was like two tribes fighting over the same game trail through the forest. There was room enough for both, but neither wanted to share. Nor would either let the other pass. The cycle of violence would continue, and the grasp for power would tighten around the very people the governments were supposed to represent.

"I will lead the expedition to Fashoda," the Sirdar continued. "General Gatacre will give those of you who are going to Adaramra a complete briefing on your mission after I am finished," he paused. "But I want to add one more thing to those who are going with me to Fashoda. As you know, we captured a member of the Khalifa's staff. She is, or was, his translator. She has agreed to identify the Khalifa in return for her freedom."

"Therefore, her safety is essential to the mission to capture or kill the Khalifa," he instructed. "Brief your men to that effect. She is a mission essential resource to be guarded at all times."

Who will guard her after the mission, Kip wondered to himself? Who will guard her then?

He got his answer an hour later, after General Gatacre's briefing. Colonel Wingate walked up to Kip and stuck out his hand.

"Major, we've enjoyed your camaraderie and your bravery," Wingate said. "Lieutenant Churchill spoke very highly of you," he continued with a sly smile on his face.

"Thank you, sir, I think," Kip said, shaking his outstretched hand.

"So much so, in fact, that I have a personal request from the Sirdar," Wingate continued.

"Lieutenant Churchill informed us that you personally guaranteed to provide for the safety and well-being of the Khalifa's translator. In fact, you held out that you had the authority of your government to do so. The Sirdar would like that very much, and accepts your offer. He trusts that you join him on the expedition to Fashoda, and that you will ensure the safety and well-being of this high-value intelligence asset. Of course, members from intelligence division will also be on the expedition, and you can count on their support. You will be leaving tomorrow."

A million thoughts filled Kip's head at once. His mission was now over. He had kept to his end of the bargain. Churchill was alive and Mackenzie and O'Leary lay dead. Mission accomplished. He did not have authority to continue onto Fashoda to capture the Khalifa.

But if he didn't go with the expedition to Fashoda, Syrah would be forced to press ahead without him. He couldn't leave her.

"I will have to dispatch a cable to my commander on that issue," Kip said carefully. "I trust that will not insult the Sirdar?"

"I can assure you that has already been arranged for at the highest levels," Wingate replied. "I have been asked to pass that on to you from General Hanson. I am told that you would not object to continuing on to Fashoda."

"Of course not," Kip answered. "But I do need to send my commander a telegram regarding some further details," Kip said. Wingate nodded.

In fact, he needed to get a message to General Hanson to authorize funds and documentation for Syrah to travel to America with him.

"By the way, where is Fashoda?" Kip inquired politely.

"Hell," Wingate replied with a devilish grin on his face.

"That's comforting, sir," Kip smiled. "Thank you."

"Not at all, my pleasure," Wingate smiled wickedly.

Kip stepped out of the tent into the blazing sunlight. He made his way to where the 21st Lancers were encamped on the river. He found Churchill lounging in a canvass hammock fixed between two palm trees, a drink in one hand and a cigarette in the other, as usual.

"And what does the senior staff have to say?" Churchill said cheerfully.

"You are going home," Kip said. He took a cigarette from the pack that lay on Churchill's tunic.

"Help yourself," Churchill laughed. Something was troubling his American friend.

"And you?" Winston asked.

Kip sat down on a canvas chair next to the hammock. "I'm going to Fashoda," Kip said.

"What the bloody hell is in Fashoda?" Churchill asked.

"The French," Kip answered.

"Really?" Churchill said. His eyes widened in amazement. "What does that have to do with you?" he asked innocently.

"You dimed me out, you prick," Kip said.

"Whatever does that mean?" Churchill asked, feigning astonishment.

"You told them I guaranteed Syrah's safety and well-being," Kip laughed.

"You personally granted her asylum on behalf of your government," Churchill answered honestly."I was there, remember?"

"I know, but I didn't volunteer to take a goddamn trip into the jungle. Jesus. What have I gotten myself into now?" Kip said ruefully. "And where the hell is Fashoda anyway?"

"A good ways south," Churchill said helpfully.

"How far south?"

"Hundreds of miles," Churchill answered cheerfully. He sipped at his whiskey and took another drag off of his cigarette.

"I'm sure you'll go by gunboat," Winston offered.

"Yeh, well, I guess I set myself up for that one, Kip said.

"You are an officer and a gentleman," Churchill teased.

"And a bloody fool, too," Kip added.

"Quite." Churchill said. "But you did save my life, so that must count for something."

"I'm beginning to feel like a puppet on a string, and I'm wondering who is pulling my strings," Kip growled.

"The British government has no desire for the public to know that General Gordon fathered a child with a black slave while serving as the governor general of the Sudan. That would put a stain on his legacy," Churchill said.

"She needs a keeper, and that's you," Winston continued, his voice sincere. "Which means you get to spend some more time with the beautiful and charming negress," Churchill teased. "A little conflicted are we? Perhaps you are having a hard time staying professional with your feelings."

"Listen you prick, I am very capable of handling my emotions," Kip replied. He grabbed another cigarette from the pack lying on the hammock.

The problem was, Churchill was right. Kip could not forget her sapphire eyes framed by her flawless skin and high cheek bones. Nor could he forget her full, playful lips that turned upwards in the corners when she smiled.

"Perhaps," Churchill mused. "But she does exude a certain exotic appeal."

"Aye, that she does," Kip admitted.

"She is also a marked woman once she identifies the Khalifa. The British will simply release her and whatever is left of his army will ensure she is killed. Quite slowly I might add," Churchill said.

"I know, but I have not yet arranged for her safe passage to America," Kip said. And that meant a personal eyes only telegram to General Hanson in Washington.

"It's not that I don't trust my government, but unless I have his personal guarantee I'm not sure I can get her into the country. I know they've reached some kind of agreement to ensure her cooperation, but I don't know that they are interested in ensuring her safety," Kip said, his voice filled with concern.

"Well, if there is anyone who can keep her safe, it's you," Churchill said. "And by the way. The obvious. No one can know what happened in the khor."

"It will be in my report to my superiors," Kip said.

"Of that I am sure," Churchill agreed. "But no one else," he warned.

"No one else has a need to know," Kip assured him. "Except perhaps your mother."

"I'll take care of that."

"I'm not sure I trust you with that, but since I'm headed off to the deepest and darkest and you are headed back to England, I don't think I have a choice."

"Quite right," Churchill assured him. "I will pass along your regards to my mother," he smiled.

"Please do," Kip said.

CHAPTER EIGHTY

THE NILE, 1898

The next morning Kip loaded his gear aboard the gunboat *Sultan*. It was the Sirdar's command ship. All total the expedition would consist of five steamers, two battalions of Sudanese rifles, two companies of Cameron Highlanders, an artillery battery and four Maxims.

Kip stowed his gear in his cramped quarters. There was space for nothing more than a bed and a footlocker. He opened the hatch on the brass porthole and let the warm Nile air flow into the cabin. Christ, he thought, it's no bigger than a closet.

He heard a loud crash on the deck above. Kip rushed out of his cabin and looked up the gangway.

"Oh sorry, I dropped my chest," Churchill laughed. "Fortunately the whiskey is well-padded."

Kip could only smile. "What the hell are you doing here?"

Churchill danced lightly down the steps.

"I couldn't let you have all the fun now, could I?" His boyish face beamed. "Besides, mother would never forgive me if I let something happen to you."

"Right," Kip could only manage. "Where's your cabin?"

"Next to yours, of course. I don't go anywhere without you at my side," Churchill fawned. "I just don't feel safe," he continued to chide.

"More like you want another medal," Kip said sarcastically.

Winston smiled. "The thought did cross my mind. But I just want to be with my hero," he continued to tease.

"Fuck off," came the expected retort. Churchill just laughed.

"I'm going ashore to talk to Wingate and check on Syrah," Kip said.

"I've got a few loose ends to tie up as well," Churchill said. "I'll go ashore with you."

Kip made his way off the boat and down the gangway to shore and the telegraph tent. He handed his message to the operator, with clear instructions that it was to be marked "eyes only" for General Hanson. The telegram explained his request for asylum and funds for Syrah's trip to America, including living expenses once she arrived.

He left the tent and made his way over to the 21stLancers. He found Churchill engaged in a serious debate with several of the other officers.

"Mind if I interrupt?" Kip asked. "Lieutenant Churchill, do you have a moment?"

"Of course, Major. Gentlemen, excuse me for a minute," Churchill said politely. They walked back towards the wooden dock. Sailors and soldiers alike scurried about preparing to make way. Smoke was already billowing from the massive steam engines.

"Give me a smoke," Kip demanded.

Churchill gave him his pack. "I'm going to switch to cigars," Winston announced. "Much more fitting for a future member of Parliament," he cracked.

Kip couldn't contain himself any longer. It had been bothering him all morning.

"What the hell are you doing volunteering for this mission to Fashoda? Who's going to explain to your mother if you do not return alive? I'm not. I did my job. You're alive. Do I have to protect your sorry ass again?" Kip asked, raising an eyebrow.

"Right now I'm focused on keeping my ass alive," Churchill said honestly. "I'll worry about the rest if and when I get back to England."

"You're fuckin nuts."

"Perhaps," Winston answered nonchalantly. "Perhaps."

Kip could only shake his head.

"Actually old chap, I just crave the adventure," Winston said resignedly. "I love danger; I love excitement. It makes me feel, alive."

Kip combed his fingers through his hair in exasperation. The man was insane.

"I'll check in with you later," Kip said. "I've got some business to attend to." He didn't like the fact that Churchill was going with him. How many times could he ensure his safety? Eventually the odds would catch up.

But first he needed to talk to Syrah. Something else was eating away inside of him.

CHAPTER EIGHTY-ONE

SUDAN, 1898

Syrah heard footsteps outside her tent. She pulled her hijab close around her face. She was careful to cover her entire body with a black cloth chadur ever since she had joined the British expedition. She would have preferred a tob. It would have been cooler. But she was surrounded by men. Her guards were respectful, but she could see various emotions in their eyes. And the lust. The white men were the most courteous. She was a high-value asset, and they did not wish to incur the Sirdar's wrath. But they would not look her in the eye.

The Sudanese soldiers showed her the same respect as they would any woman in their tribe, which meant that she was a highly-valued cow or goat.

The Egyptians bothered her the most. She could see a combination of loathing and lust in their eyes. After all, she was a black woman, and she had value. It titillated them.

But when the dark-haired American came into the tent, she felt something entirely different. They embraced immediately without saying a word. They kissed passionately. Kip could have kissed her forever, but he had to tell her his plan. They pulled apart reluctantly.

"I've sent a telegram to my commander requesting funding and documentation for you to travel to America after this mission is finished," he said abruptly.

"Why would your country care what happens to an escaped black slave?" she asked. "Do they not have black slaves in your country?"

"Not legally. Not anymore."

"Is that yes or no?" she asked.

"It means like everything else man does, it's complicated," Kip answered honestly. "But black people are still treated like slaves in many parts of my country." The horrors of Lake City came back to his mind.

"After I identify the Khalifa, I am dead here," she said calmly. But her sapphire blue eyes showed no fear.

"Yes." He paused. It had been troubling him greatly.

"Where else would I go? To America, to be treated like a slave, or to England, to be treated like a whore?"

Kip grimaced. "Not England. They do not want you there."

"I was born in Africa, and I shall die in Africa," she said proudly.

"But I am attempting to make arrangements for you to live in America," he urged.

"To be your slave?" she asked.

Kip shook his head.

"No. But there is no other place for you to go. I've got to get you out of this place. You are not safe here. You have too many enemies," Kip said.

The idea of traveling to America frightened her. Where would she stay? Would she be respected or treated as a slave? But she could not stay in Africa, and she knew it. She looked at Kip, deep into his eyes. He seemed troubled.

"I can see your sadness. You killed many men?"

"Yes."

"I too have killed several men," she said proudly. "And they deserved to die."

"These men were following the empty promises of an empty man," Kip said. "That is what men do."

"They followed their god," she said.

"They thought they were, yes," Kip agreed. "But in truth, they were not."

"Does it make a difference?" she asked.

"No," he answered honestly. "I have killed other men, and it had nothing to do with God or religion." He paused. "The men I killed today, I killed because it was my duty. It was either them or me."

"As it should be," she said, staring at him intently. "That is the way of our land. Kill or be killed. It is the way of the lion, the leopard, and the cheetah. The water buffalo and even the hippo live by that code, as does the crocodile and the jackal."

For a moment, Kip was silent.

"We are men, not animals," Kip stated.

"I have not seen a difference," Syrah replied honestly. "Until I met you."

CHAPTER EIGHTY-TWO

THE JOURNEY SOUTH, 1898

From the moment he set foot upon the Sultan, Kip felt a sense of worry. This mission was even more treacherous than the war, and it concerned him greatly, even though they were armed to the teeth. The Sirdar was bringing 1,300 men, and of course, they brought artillery, including the armament of the gunboats.

The gunboats *Sultan*, *Sheik*, and *Fatah* led the way, towing barges loaded with supplies, animals and ammunition. Behind them traveled the stern-wheel steamer, *Dal*. Several more steamboats carried the rest of the soldiers and towed even more barges. Two more gunboats brought up the rear.

Unlike the other boats, the *Dal* was more like the riverboats that plied the American rivers. It had a large parlor, converted into a war room complete with charts and maps on the walls. It had a well-equipped galley and multiple staterooms for the senior staff.

Kitchener had pulled Kip aside when they first boarded the *Dal*. They sat in the war room alone. *(Wasn't Kip staying on the Sultan?)*

"Whiskey?" Kitchener offered.

Kip knew better than to refuse. "Of course sir, don't mind if I do," he smiled.

The Sirdar took a seat behind his desk and motioned Kip to sit down. He cut off the end of a Cuban cigar and carefully stoked it to life.

"Major, I received a dispatch from the War Department this morning. They have exchanged dispatches with your War Department in Washington. It appears that you already submitted a full report on the battle for Omdurman."

"Yes sir, I did get that out."

"Her Majesty's government wishes to convey its gratitude to you for looking after Churchill. His mother and prince in particular wish to convey their thanks."

"I wasn't aware my report was being shared with civilians," Kip said, somewhat annoyed.

"Perhaps it would comfort you to know that Churchill's dispatch was shared with your government as well. He too expressed his gratitude." He puffed on his cigar.

"Major, our governments share a great deal in common. Behind closed doors, our alliance grows stronger every day. Your president thinks very highly of your abilities. The queen is very fond of Churchill, as is the prime minister and the prince. They all owe you and your president a personal favor. I'm sure when the time comes the debt will be repaid, with interest." Kitchener paused to take a sip of whiskey and a puff of his cigar.

"We also appreciate your capture of the Khalifa's translator, and her ability to ensure the identity of the Khalifa. As expected, we have information that the Khalifa has men dressed and posing as him in several different locations to mislead us. Quite frankly, we don't have the time to waste chasing down false leads. We want our man, and we want him now. So your attention to the translator and ensuring her safety during the mission is deeply appreciated."

"Thank you, sir," Kip replied.

"The information she has provided to Colonel Wingate and Intelligence Branch has already saved lives and provided an immense pool of information in which to manage the reconstruction of Omdurman. She also gave us the names and locations of several more of the Khalifa's remaining strongholds. Operations are already underway to destroy them," the Sirdar continued. "She also has verified other sources as to where we can expect to find the Khalifa."

"Yes sir."

"After the capture and death of the Khalifa, your assignment will be complete, and you will return to America, along with the translator. She will not survive here in the Sudan, and she would not be welcome in England. Your General Hanson is making arrangements for her well-being in America. Of course, I know that is no concern of yours," the Sirdar said.

Kip saw a twinkle in his eye. Or was it sarcasm? he bastard had read his "eyes only" telegram to General Hanson.

"As to capture and death of the Khalifa, the answer is no, Kip said. "But as to the well-being of the translator, the answer is yes." Kip said honestly.

The Sirdar nodded. "Well then Major, I leave it to you and your judgment about how to proceed once the mission is complete," Kitchener said. "I repay loyalty in kind. Let me know how I can assist you. In the meantime, please keep her safe. I need her."

"Yes sir. Will that be all?"

"Yes."

Kip snapped to attention, smartly saluted the general, and left the war room.

The next two days passed quietly as the armada traveled slowly up the Nile. As the sun grew low on the horizon, they moored on the riverbanks and sent Sudanese soldiers ashore to gather firewood for the boilers and fresh meat and fruit. They brought back large quantities of mimosa and sunt, which burned like coal. Gazelle and antelope too were on the menu.

Kip spent the first two days watching the river with fascination. The muddy banks were lined with enormous crocodiles that slithered quickly into the river when they sensed the approaching gunboats. Hippos lay still, with only their eyes and the tips of the ears protruding above the water, observing. They were dangerous and unpredictable. Troops of baboon sat and watched in stoic silence as the boats cruised by. Spider monkeys flung themselves with abandon among the tree branches that lined the river. Kip had never seen such an abundance of strange new creatures in his life.

Several times each day, he invited Syrah to come up on the deck with him, and she happily explained to him the nature and habits of all the creatures that he saw. She always wore her black chadur and hijab, careful to cover her face. Her piercing blues grew excited and joyful as she pointed out all the wildlife. She animated her stories with quick punctuations with her hands. Kip enjoyed their talks about nature and about the various tribes of the Sudan. He was amazed at the depth of her knowledge.

In return, Kip told her the story of his life. It was a story he had told to no one. But something about her made him feel safe to share his emotions without being judged. He also was aware of the physical chemistry and electricity between them. It was something he had never felt before.

The days grew hotter as they traveled south towards the equator. The desert had given way to the grass plains of the savanna. After five days on the boat, Syrah began to feel trapped. Watching the passing grasslands, she longed to set foot on the earth again.

As the ships began searching the shoreline for a suitable place to lay anchor, Syrah approached Kip, who was scanning the river banks with his field glasses. Although the dervish horde had been soundly defeated at Omdurman, he knew that thousands had escaped south with the Khalifa. They would be angry, hurt and wounded. That would make them all the more dangerous, and he knew that it was a matter of time before they attempted an ambush.

"Major," Syrah interrupted. "May I speak to you?"

Kip lowered the glasses and faced Syrah. The mere sight of her made his knees weak. It was going to be a long passage, he thought to himself.

"Yes, of course."

"I need to feel the earth beneath my feet," she explained. "I am not used to being so long on a boat. May I go ashore with the landing party tonight?" she pleaded. Her large sapphire eyes looked sad.

"I'll check with the general's staff," Kip said. "I know it's been a quiet passage so far, but we are expecting trouble sooner or later," he explained. "I'll drop by your cabin later and let you know what they said."

"I would be indebted if they do," she answered. She bowed her head, and then turned and went back down the passageway to her stateroom.

"Oh boy," Kip muttered. She was a high-value asset. The request would not be-well received. He made his way to the bridge of the ship. Kitchener and Colonel Wingate were looking over a series of charts.

"Sir, may I interrupt?" Kip asked.

Kitchener looked up. "What is it Major?"

"The translator would like to go ashore with the landing party to get the feeling back in her legs," he said.

"What's wrong with her legs?" Wingate queried.

"She's not used to being confined to quarters. I'm afraid she may be cramping up. A walk on dry land would probably ease the discomfort," Kip answered.

"Fine, go with her, and make sure she returns safely," Kitchener said. His eyes pierced Kip's. He didn't have to say a word. Kip knew he was guaranteeing her safety.

"Yes sir." Kip left the bridge of the *Sultan* and went down to Syrah's quarters. A sentry stood watch outside her door. The sentry jumped to attention when Kip approached.

"As you were, Smythe," Kip said, saluting back.

He knocked on her door. "It's Major McDuran."

"Come in, Major," she said.

He opened the door and stepped into her cabin, closing the door behind him. When he turned to face her, he had a difficult time holding his composure. Gone was the chadur. Instead, she wore a colorful piece of material that wrapped around her body. It ended just below her knees. She smiled when she saw the look on his face.

"It is common in the Southern Sudan for the women to wear less because of the heat," she explained. "And this cabin is very hot. In many of the villages, the Dinka women only wear goatskin skirts and no shoes. They wear no top, just a string of beads," she said.

"You probably should keep the top," Kip said, trying not to gawk.

Her legs were long and muscular. Her breasts, full and protruding, pushed at the cloth.

"It's much more, how would you white men say, practical?"

Kip was no stranger to beautiful women, but she paralyzed him.

"Uhm," he stammered.

"Yes, Major?" she smiled, looking into his eyes. She put her arms around his neck and kissed him passionately on the mouth. She tasted of cinnamon and cloves.

Kip reached out one hand and caressed her smooth mahogany cheekbone. They embraced, and he marveled at the feel of her body pressed into him. He slowly removed the cloth from her body as she unbuttoned his tunic. She pressed her breast against him. He lifted her and carried her to the bed. Their lovemaking was hushed, urgent and passionate. They finally both collapsed on the bunk to catch their breath.

"I'm falling for you," Kip whispered, gazing into her eyes. "There's something I want you to know," he paused. "You asked me if you would be my slave in America. That's not what I'm looking for."

"What are you looking for?" she asked.

"Will you marry me?" he proposed. His heart was pounding. What if she said no?

"But what would your American friends say?" she asked playfully.

"The hell with them," Kip growled.

"Then the answer is yes," Syrah said. They embraced and their bodies intertwined again. They grew even more passionate, urgently seeking out each other's body. They kissed deeply as Kip entered her. Syrah felt her body explode as she experienced her first orgasm.

After they were both spent, they lay looking into each other's eyes. There was no turning back.

"I have a surprise for you," Kip murmured.

"You've already surprised me more than you will ever know," she assured him.

"We're going ashore," he said, smiling into her eyes. "Get ready, and dress appropriately," he added. They embraced again and then separated reluctantly. Kip opened the door and stepped out.

Corporal Smythe leaped to attention as Kip quickly exited the cabin and strode down the narrow passageway.

His life had forever changed.

The working parties went ashore as the blistering sun began to set on the horizon. The lulu, mimosa and sunt trees growing along the edge of the Nile burned hot and clean in the boilers of the steamships. The men would work through the night with large candles and the electric beam. Better to conduct heavy labor at night to escape the heat.

Kip stood on the deck of the *Sultan*. The skies were clear. It would be a good time to go ashore. He went down to Syrah's cabin and knocked.

She opened the cabin door, dressed in a full black chadur, her face covered. Kip smiled. She knew her presence among the crew already created a distraction for the men. He appreciated her changing into something less revealing.

"Follow me," he said. "I will take you for a walk."

He led her down the passageway and up the stairs to the open deck. They crossed the gangway, and Syrah nearly fainted with joy at the feel of solid ground under her feet. The boat had moored in a clearing on a river bank. A dense tree line was set back twenty yards from the shore. The hum of the insects along the river was music to her ears, as was the chatter of the colobus monkeys roaming in the trees.

"Thank you, Kip," she sighed. She uncovered her head and took a deep breath. The air was hot and steamy, but it tasted delicious. It chased the confined odor of oil, steel, coal and boilers from her lungs. She looked at the dense tree line.

"The men will have little trouble cutting wood here," she said. She pointed towards large pods hanging from the trees.

"Did you know that the lulu nut is strong medicine?" she asked.

"No."

"The nuts are also delicious to eat when one is hungry," she added with a smile.

Kip could only stare off into the distance.

"I'll remember that," he said. His attention was on the other side of the river. He saw the familiar bright patchwork of a dervish shirt in the dense foliage. The sun was dropping quickly on the horizon, but he could make out several men on the other side of the river, peeking up over a large group of rocks.

"We're being watched," Kip said calmly. "I take it the Khalifa still has friends this far south of Omdurman?"

"More than friends," Syrah assured him. "He owns this land. It used to belong to the people of the Shilluk tribe, but the Mahdi and then the Khalifa enslaved them. Those who resisted were murdered. He has spies everywhere."

"They are watching us from the other side of the river, and I'm sure they are watching you," he added. "We'd better get you back on board."

"Please, just a few more minutes. I'm not ready to go back inside that iron crocodile just yet," she begged.

Kip looked up and down the river. Sentries from the *Dal* were all around them. This was her last time ashore until the Khalifa was captured and killed.

"Okay, five more minutes," he said. He kept his eyes on the other side of the river.

Syrah rolled her eyes.

"I'm going for a walk," she announced.

"No, you are not."

"Fine," she said. She started to squat.

"Jesus!" Kip yelled, his eyes wide.

"Shall I take that as a yes?" she asked politely.

Kip gave in. "Yes, go behind that stand of trees."

He watched her arch her back as she walked away.

So too did the dervish patrol on the other side of the mimosa. When she left Kip's view, they moved in quickly. They had orders to capture the woman, alive. The leader came up behind her swiftly, put his hand around her mouth, and held a knife to her throat.

"You will be silent," he ordered her quietly in Arabic.

Syrah could only nod. He put a hood over her head and tied her wrists behind her back. They crept away as silently as they had arrived. But as they moved through the trees, they startled a flock of cranes, sending them into flight as they furiously beat their wings.

Kip heard the birds, and at first thought Syrah may have startled them. But they came from the second stand of mimosa, not the first. He pulled his pistol and ran towards the second tree line. He saw Syrah's figure being led away by five dervish warriors.

Suddenly Kip heard the burst of rifle fire and the soil in front of him exploded. He dove to the ground for cover and felt the hot lead whistle past his skin. He saw flashes from the rocks and knew he was cut off. They had him pinned down.

Enraged, he rose up from behind the rocks, but a bullet grazed his shoulder. He was forced to take cover or die. It broke his heart, but he knew he could not rescue her if he was dead. Only after the darkness came could he slip away.

CHAPTER EIGHTY-THREE

THE SULTAN, 1898

Kip walked briskly up the metal steps to the bridge of the steamer, his face contorted with rage. The Sirdar glanced his way.

"I imagine this isn't good news," the Sirdar said calmly.

"The translator has been taken hostage by a dervish raiding party," Kip reported. He was angry at himself for letting this happen.

"They've been watching us every time we stop for wood, just waiting for a weakness, and they found it," Kip continued, disgusted. Why did he allow her to go to shore?

Churchill came up the stairs onto the bridge along with Colonel Wingate.

"Our scouts are reporting that the dervish raiding party is already headed towards Kordofan, where the Khalifa is entrenched. According to reports, the Khalifa has received reinforcements from various tribes, and now has reconstituted his fighting force there to over 8,000 men," Wingate reported.

"Kordofan is 125 miles inland," Churchill said. "That's a long stretch without a natural water supply."

The problem was obvious. As long as they were near the river or the railroad, they could bring their technology to bear. But without it, they would need more men. More men meant they needed more water, and there wasn't any. Churchill knew it, and so did the Sirdar.

"Gentlemen, we are 2,500 miles from civilization," the Kitchener said. "Our primary mission now is to intercept the French at Fashoda and see what mischief they are up to. Only after we have accomplished the primary mission can we go after the Khalifa. I need every swinging dick I have to persuade the French to turn around. England doesn't want a war with France, but we will not allow them to shut off the water to Egypt." He turned to Kip.

"I cannot split my forces in half. A rescue operation is out of the question. After we deal with the French, we will deal with the Khalifa," he said resolutely.

"And the translator will have been raped, tortured and executed," Kip said, trying to keep the frustration out of his voice. He understood operational necessity. He would have made the same decision.

"You are most certainly correct, Major," Kitchener said. "I wish I had more men, but I don't. I know it sounds heartless, but the mission must come first. I'm sorry." He had seen the sparks fly between the translator and the American.

"She is the only one who can identify the Khalifa with accuracy," Churchill interrupted. "She is an important component to the secondary mission, which will eventually become our primary mission. Such a resource should not be wasted," Churchill added.

Kitchener glared at Churchill.

"Churchill, if I want your counsel I will ask for it. I read your book about your adventures in Afghanistan, and if you had stopped there, I should have thought it was excellent. Instead, you criticized the entire war department and General Bindon Blood's sagacity. Blood gave you the chance to exploit your political ambitions. You, in turn, stabbed him in the back," the Sirdar scolded.

"I have no intention of allowing you to do the same with me," he advised his subordinate.

"Well hell, I guess I'm just going to have to go fetch her myself," Kip announced. "I'll need my horse."

"I'm afraid I can't allow you to do that, either," the Sirdar replied. "You too are a valuable intelligence source, replete with knowledge about our war fighting strategy and tactics. If captured, you could compromise our entire operation."

"You just had *your* most important intelligence asset captured on this journey to Fashoda," Kip shot back. "She too knows your tactics and your intentions. Which means they already have that information, so your concerns for my well-being, though appreciated, are not in play."

"Everyone leave the bridge except for Major McDuran," Kitchener ordered. His face glowed red with fury. He would not tolerate insolence from a subordinate officer, but neither would he reprimand him in front of other officers.

The deck cleared immediately, except for Churchill, who hesitated, until he saw the look in Kitchener's eyes. He changed his mind and went down the stairs to the lower deck.

"I will not tolerate insubordination in a combat zone," Kitchener began. He intended to lace the American up one side and down the other with a good old-fashioned ass-chewing.

"I am not your subordinate," Kip said honestly.

Kitchener's eyebrows raised in astonishment.

"I work for one man, and only one man. *That* man is the President of the United States. And if you want to check that for accuracy, speak with your prime minister and your prince," Kip advised the stunned general. "None of them will be pleased to hear of your interference with *my* primary mission."

"Which is?" Kitchener demanded.

"Classified," Kip bluffed, clenching his jaw.

The two officers glared at each other.

"Send a telegram to your command if you don't believe me," Kip doubled down.

"The American is correct," Churchill interrupted. He couldn't help himself. He had been listening on the stairway. Kitchener looked at him as if he was going to kill him right there on the spot.

"Sir, I can confirm that Major McDuran is an agent for President McKinley," Churchill said calmly. "He came at the request of our government."

"I too can confirm that fact," Colonel Wingate spoke up. He too had been waiting nearby.

Churchill turned towards his general.

"Sir, I would not be able to criticize your actions in writing because there are no facts that warrant such words. Your campaign has been brilliant and history will reflect that fact, *as will* I," he added sincerely.

Kitchener paced the bridge. He turned on Kip.

"I don't want any more 'fuck alots'," the general seethed. He demanded perfection from himself *and* his men.

Kip and Churchill looked at each other in surprise. Churchill suppressed a grin.

"What's your plan, Major?" the Sirdar asked bluntly.

"Sir, I am going to survey and recon the Khalifa's position and locate the translator. If possible, I will secure the asset to assist you with the secondary mission," Kip informed the Sirdar. "I will also have a full and up to the minute report for you when you return from Fashoda. I'm sure that both of my actions would assist your secondary mission."

Kitchener had already made up his mind.

"Very well, Major. I will not get in your way under one condition," he warned.

"Which is?" Kip asked.

"Take Churchill with you," Kitchener ordered. Churchill's eyebrows shot up.

Kip looked the general in the eye.

"We both know the odds of my success or survival is not good," he said cautiously. "Your government will not appreciate Lieutenant Churchill's loss."

"How would you know?" Kitchener demanded. "Besides, I didn't authorize this cheeky bastard to be here in the first place. In fact, quite the opposite." He glared at Churchill as he spoke.

"He wouldn't even be here if I had my way. Ask his mother. His fate rests not upon my shoulders nor upon my conscience. If I want to throw him off my ship, your president can't bloody well say shit," Kitchener spat through gritted teeth.

"I did use the proper American there, didn't I? Shit? As in shit, shit, fucking shit!" he roared. He glared at Kip, just waiting for anyone to say a word. He would have them all shot.

There was silence on the bridge.

Finally, the general acquiesced. "Very well, Major. See the quartermaster. Take whatever supplies and arms you need to accomplish the mission.

"Sir," Churchill stammered.

"What Churchill? You don't want to go?" the Sirdar growled.

"No sir, quite the opposite, in fact." Churchill was embarrassed. "Sir, I want the record to reflect that I am volunteering to go. In fact, not just volunteering, sir. Pleading would be more accurate."

"You're fuckin nuts," Kip advised Churchill.

"We agree there," Kitchener agreed.

"You just want a bloody medal and publicity," Kip snapped at Winston. He could not let Churchill go with him. The president would not forgive him if something happened to Churchill at Kip's own doing. Contrary to mission parameters, he decided.

"We agree again," Kitchener said.

"Show me either a general or a politician without ambition, and I will show you a fool," Churchill interceded. "Kip, don't talk about me as if I am one. I have no intention of getting myself killed. One can't bloody well become prime minister if one is dead," he blurted out with fidelity.

Kip and Kitchener looked at each other in astonishment. Kitchener burst out laughing.

"What?" Churchill said indignantly.

CHAPTER EIGHTY-FOUR

ABA ISLAND, 1898

The two men stood on the river bank opposite Aba Island and watched the ships move south down the White Nile towards Fashoda. They were alone in the middle of nowhere. A sudden commotion in the water behind them made Kip turn. A giant crocodile slithered out of the water and onto the muddy river bank.

"Jesus, look at the size of that lizard," Kip said in amazement. It was over seventeen feet long with a head like a steam shovel. "I wouldn't want that pissed off at me," he added, eying the crocodile warily.

"Don't worry, mate, he won't follow us where we're headed," Churchill responded.

"We're headed into hell, and you are a fool for going with me," Kip pointed out. "The first water is over forty miles from here at the wells of El Gedid."

"You know what they say," Churchill said, pausing for effect. "Only mad dogs and Englishmen go out in the noonday sun."

"Are you suggesting I'm a mad dog?"

"Yes. And now you own it," Churchill said proudly. "Major 'Mad Dog' McDuran."

I am mad, Kip thought to himself. If only I hadn't let her go ashore.

They mounted their horses. The camels followed behind faithfully. They had three of the massive beast of burden; one for food, one for water, and one for gear.

It was indeed forty miles to the next watering hole. And as they got further away from the river, the landscape changed dramatically. Soon they were surrounded by barren plains of hard-packed desert clay, thorn bushes and rocks. It was over a hundred degrees Fahrenheit and the sun beat down without so much as a cloud in sight. Bleached bones of creatures that perished trying to reach the river lay scattered along the ground. Some were human.

The horses hung their heads under the heat. Kip and Churchill got off their mounts and walked alongside them for several miles to give them some relief.

"This is going to be a long journey," Kip muttered, mopping his forehead with a rag.

Churchill grinned. "You know what else they say? When you're going through hell, keep moving."

"I'll agree with you on that one," Kip answered. They kept the pace steady until night fell. Finally, they had to rest for a few hours. They slept like dead men.

When Kip awoke, it was still dark. He was going to sit up when Churchill hissed at him.

"Don't move," he warned. "Shhhh….."

Kip lay there wondering what the hell was going on. Suddenly a large black snake slithered out from under his armpit, across his chest and off onto the hard clay soil until it found a burrow and disappeared.

"African cobra," Churchill said nonchalantly. "They like to feel your body heat at night."

"Speaking of the heat, we're going to have to travel at night," Churchill advised. "Otherwise, we're not going to make it."

"They got a hell of a head start," Kip noted.

He was thinking of Syrah. Was she already dead? But he was convinced now that if they traveled by day, they would soon be dead. He ran his hand across his face. His lips were already parched. His face was dry as sandpaper.

Churchill could read his friend's thoughts.

"They will torture her until she tells them everything she knows,"

Churchill said. "And then they will kill her if she's not already dead."
He paused. "I'm not trying to be cruel. Just honest."

"I know," Kip answered.

He tried to keep any emotion out of his voice. He never liked dealing
with emotions. They got in the way and never made any sense anyway.
It was better to feel nothing. But this time, he couldn't escape into that
dark, cold place he was so familiar with.

Chapter Eighty-Five

THE KHALIFA'S CAMP, 1898

Syrah heard a voice in the fog.

"Allah has returned you to me for a reason." It was the Khalifa.

She recognized the voice and it jolted her to her senses. She lay bound and gagged on the floor of the Khalifa's tent. Her vision began to clear and her eyes focused. She saw his face. She was no longer in a dream. She was helpless again, and that enraged her.

"You will tell me everything I want to know about the British. Everything!" the Khalifa roared at her. He stood over her, fist clenched. He punched her in the face and kicked her brutally in the chest. She felt fire inside her body as her ribs broke.

"And after you have told me everything, I will take you until I am tired, and then I will give you to my men!" he screamed. "And when they are done, I will feed your ravaged body to the hyenas!" He kicked her in the ribs again.

"Tell me the truth, how did you learn English?" his voice was savage.

He ripped the rag from her mouth.

"Why are your eyes blue?"

For a moment she lay there silently, pain radiating throughout her body. Then she raised her head to look up at the Khalifa, her chin held high and her eyes flashing.

"I got them from my father," she said proudly. "His name was Gordon. And he has been avenged."

The Khalifa screamed with joy. "As will I!"

Chapter Eighty-Six

SHIRKELA, 1898

As they moved further inland, the color of ground changed from sand to ocher. Scrub gave way to an occasional mimosa tree. But the land was still barren of food, water, or life. It was seven days of hell, and the two men felt the strain.

Seven days later they reached the edge of the Khalifa's camp at Shirkela, 125 miles from the White Nile. They were in poor shape. They had hoped to replenish their water supplies and water their pack animals at the Wells of El Gedid. But the small amount of water that remained was topped with a green slime and smelled putrid.

Kip and Winston stood in exhaustion on a hill, looking down on the Khalifa's encampment through their field glasses. There was light from a half moon and the stars. The camp was lit by fires and torches. Thousands of grass huts were lined up in rows. They had water. Kip could see the outline of several wells set among the camp. And there was food. He could see goats and sheep in a thorny corral.

"I found it," Churchill said softly, peering through his field glasses. "A black flag is raised on the top of the Khalifa's tent."

Kip shifted his glasses to the direction Churchill was looking.

"I think you're right. And I bet that is where Syrah is being held," Kip agreed.

Churchill's jaw set. He looked determined. "Perhaps we should get a closer look," he said. Both men realized the perils they faced. Winston started to move down the hill.

"No, wait. I have a better plan," Kip whispered. "Let's capture a sentry and interrogate him as to her exact location and status."

"What are you going to do with the sentry after you're done torturing him?" Churchill asked.

"You know damn well," Kip shot back.

"Draw straws?" Winston asked. He was completely serious.

Kip was hungry, thirsty, miserable and hot. Neither man had slept for two days. And to top it all off, Syrah was most likely dead. The familiar coldness he had experienced all of his life suddenly returned.

"No." Kip pulled a sap weighted with steel bearings out of his knapsack. "The pleasure is all mine."

"Carry on, Mad Dog," Churchill said.

"I'll be right back."

Kip made his way down the hill. Fifteen minutes later he returned, carrying an unconscious body over his shoulder. The sentry was trussed like a turkey and had a rag stuffed inside his mouth held in place by another strip of cloth tied around his head. Kip hadn't bothered to blindfold him. There wouldn't be any need.

"Not bad," Churchill said with genuine admiration. He waited until Kip took the limp sentry and set him on the ground. Then he took the top off his canteen and poured water on the unconscious man's face. The sentry didn't react at first, but finally he came to. His eyes grew wide with fear.

"That's right," Kip said in Arabic. "You should be afraid."

"You speak Arabic?" Churchill exclaimed. Now he was really impressed.

The sentry looked at Kip with shock on his face.

"That's right, motherfucker," Kip said in English. He switched to Arabic. "I'm a white man who speaks your language. Tell me where the woman with blue eyes is. The Khalifa's translator."

The sentry tried to look away, but Kip grabbed his throat and put his knife to it. The blade just barely pierced the flesh of his neck. The man tried to scream in pain, but Kip held his throat with one hand, completely cutting off his air supply. His legs thrashed about until Kip eased off the pressure.

"Where is the Khalifa's translator?" he demanded again.

The sentry ignored him. Kip tightened his grip on the man's throat again until the man's eyes bulged out of his sockets and the veins popped out on his face. His feet began to drum. Kip eased off on the chokehold.

"I'll cut your throat," he warned in Arabic. "I'm going to let you speak, but if you call out for help, I'll make sure I take my time sawing off your head."

Kip pulled the gag out of the man's mouth, ready to silence him if he screamed out. The sentry began to cough. Blood came out of his mouth. I didn't stick him that deep, Kip thought. The little bastard bleeds easy. Kip struck him on the side of his face so hard that spit, blood and teeth flew out.

"Speak," Kip warned.

"She is dead," the sentry finally gasped.

Kip's eyes widened as he processed the words. For a moment he stared at the sentry, stunned. Then uncontrollable rage surged upward through his body. His heart pounded rapidly within his chest. At the same time, he was completely caught off guard by his vulnerability to pain. It tore at his soul. He knelt, one knee upon the man's chest, crushing him with his weight. His kneecap searched for the man's sternum. He pressed hard.

"Where is her body?" Kip demanded through gritted teeth, leaning toward the sentry's bloodied face. "I want proof."

The man held up his hands in surrender. Kip let him talk.

"The Khalifa tortured her in his tent. Then she was given to his men. Now she lies on the trash heap on the edge of the village for the hyenas to feed on."

Kip paused, and then snapped the man's neck with both hands. He rocked back on his heels and let go. The sentry's head thumped on the ground. Kip squatted next to the lifeless body on his haunches, holding his forehead in his palms, praying this was a dream. His face was pale. It reflected sheer agony.

He looks like a wounded animal, Churchill thought to himself. And, he is more dangerous now than ever.

Kip turned his head slowly towards Churchill. "I won't believe it until I see it," Kip said with dogged determination.

"I know she's still alive." He knew it was impossible, but he was determined not to give up.

They searched the perimeter of the village for hours under the darkness until the first light barely illuminated the trash refuge. The acrid stench was overpowering. Dead carcasses of humans and animals lay about, torn open by the hyenas and the jackals. Faces and bodies were unrecognizable. But there were no hyenas present when they first came upon the refuge, which Kip thought was strange.

"I'll never be able to identify her body," Kip finally said with resignation. His anguish was painfully discernable.

"We must return to the river to meet Kitchener," Churchill said softly. "He should be there in a week. Once we join up with them, you will have your revenge on the Khalifa." His voice was sincere. He felt no desire to patronize or placate his friend.

Kip just nodded his head, his eyes staring blankly forward. "Aye, I will. I will."

She was gone. He had to accept her death as he had accepted the death of everyone else he had ever loved. He felt cold again.

They slipped away from the perimeter of the camp and backed out into the scrublands. They found their horses and camels where they had tied them off, a mile away from the Khalifa's camp.

"We're going to have to keep traveling at night," Churchill said softly. His throat was dry from lack of water, but his brain was still functioning despite lack of sleep.

For once, Kip didn't disagree with him. He knew he was not in peak condition. It was morning now.

"We need to find a safe place to sleep, now," Kip agreed.

The problem was, there was no cover in sight.

They mounted their horses and began the slow march back to the banks of the White Nile. Even the camels were feeling the heat.

They reached a massive stand of thorn bushes seven feet high and a hundred yards long. It was thick, dense, and foreboding. But it was shade when the sun dropped on the western side. Both men pulled their machetes out of their scabbards and went to work. They cleared a tunnel deep into the scrub. It was exhausting work, and the sweat dripped off their faces. But finally, they were in deep enough where they were confident they would have adequate shade. They lay down on the hard desert floor and fell asleep.

Vibrations in the ground startled Kip. Churchill was still asleep next to him. He put his hand over his mouth and shook him. Churchill's eyes flew open. He was about to tell Kip to let him sleep, but the look on Kip's face told him that wasn't an option. He silently nodded his head. Kip lifted his finger to his ear and then pointed towards the opening.

It was twilight. Kip could hear their horses rustling about. They were spooked by something. Suddenly they heard a scuffling at the entrance to their cave, and they saw the face of a dervish warrior crawling towards them, knife in hand. The enemy had discovered them, trapped inside a giant thorn cage.

Kip fired a single shot from his .45 at close quarters, and the dervish warrior's head exploded. They heard yells and screaming outside the brush. Musket fire crackled in the air as the Arabs fired into the massive scrub.

"We are truly fucked," Kip said seriously.

Churchill's eyes darted around their enclosure. Everywhere was a solid wall of thick bramble and thorns. He picked up his machete and began to hack in the opposite direction of the entrance. He knew what he was looking for, and just prayed to God they would find it.

Kip heard voices shouting in Arabic.

"They're going to torch us," Kip warned. The thought of being burned alive in a massive bonfire did not appeal to him. He grabbed his machete and began hacking too. They could hear the dervish warriors laughing excitedly as they lit the brush on fire.

Chapter Eighty-Seven

FASHODA, 1898

The town of Fashoda sat on the edge of the western side of the White Nile. The desert and the savannah gave way to the edge of the jungle. The village perched on an island now, because of the winter floods. Only in the dry season did the water and allow passage by foot to and from the town.

Kitchener wasn't fazed. He had been expecting it. In fact, he had been expecting a lot of things. And as usual, his predictions were spot on.

He eyed the disheveled figure of the French officer sitting across the fire from him. He looked like shit. So did his men. In contrast, Kitchener's uniform was clean and ironed, and his men were well-fed and well-armed. The five gunboats sitting offshore added to the stark contrast between the two armed opponents.

"How was the journey?" the Sirdar asked.

Major Jean-Baptiste Marchand could only shake his head.

"Long, too long," he said in English with a heavy French accent. The truth was that he and his men were very sick. Malaria and dysentery are a hideous combination. They had travelled through the heart of Africa to reach their destination, and they were spent. They just wanted to go home.

"Fourteen months," Marchand added. "I lost many men."

Kitchener looked around the French camp. They weren't going to make it. He eyed a stack of rifles and a small howitzer.

"I have five gunboats, each armed with Maxims and artillery. I also have 1,500 soldiers with rifles."

"I have seven French officers left, and a hundred good men," the Frenchman replied. Kitchener could hear the disease in his voice. Marchand was fighting one hell of a fever.

"You realize of course, that my presence is an indication your mission has failed," the Sirdar explained with reason. There was no need to humiliate his enemy. Fashoda was no place for the white man, and the French had just learned that.

The major nodded his head.

"It was a gamble. We were well received by the Dinka and the Shilooks," he said. "They saved us. Please do not hurt them."

The French officer began to cough. It was several minutes before he could speak again. Kitchener waited patiently. It was over. The French had no choice.

"As long as you do as I say, I won't hurt anyone," Kitchener said with authority. "Your mission here is finished. There is no need to fight. I will offer you and your men safe passage with us to return to Europe. There is no further need for war or for slaughter."

Marchand nodded his head in submission.

"It was a foolish mission to begin with. And thank you for the offer of a ride home. But my men and I can travel east through Abyssinia to reach Djibouti."

"You and your men are in bad shape," the Sirdar warned.

"We made it this far," Marchand said stubbornly.

Kitchener nodded his head. It was over. Now all that was left was to capture and kill the Khalifa. And pick up Churchill on the way home, if he was still alive. Serves the bloody fool right. That ought to teach him to challenge authority, he thought smugly.

Chapter Eighty-Eight

SHIRKELA, 1898

It didn't take long for the smoke to reach them. Their shelter was about to become caged inferno. Kip could feel the heat all around him. He hacked desperately at the scrub. Their only hope was to find a game trail through the thicket. Both men were coughing heavily, choking on smoke.

"We're running out of time!" Kip shouted.

"I found it," Churchill said at the same moment.

It was a narrow game tunnel formed by years of use by creatures who were unlucky enough to call it home. It was just large enough for a man to slither through, like a snake. Churchill went first, with Kip behind him, pushing him forward. The dervish screamed happily, still clustered around the entrance, waiting for the white men to emerge.

The two officers struggled to find a way out. The smoke smothered them, making it impossible to breath. Behind them the fire raged, but they were finally putting some distance between themselves and the flames. Still, they had to get out of the thicket before the fire found them.

"Go, go, go," Kip urged.

"I bloody well am!" Churchill cried. The roar of the flames and the crackle of the inferno forced him to yell.

"Keep it down," Kip warned. "We're going to have to deal with them if we're still alive."

They slithered another hundred years before finally finding an opening on the opposite side. A massive conflagration lay between the two parties. The dervish warriors were still whooping on the other side.

They were confident their quarry had perished. They would find their bodies in the ashes once the fire burned through all of its fuel.

"Our horses, camel, and gear are on the other side, with them," Kip said, still gasping for air. He pulled his .45 out of its holster.

"Where are you going ?" Churchill asked, his voice hoarse from the smoke.

"To get them back."

"We don't know how many men they have," Churchill said incredulously.

"Hopefully a lot," Kip answered. "I'm in the mood. Let's dance," he said as he started jogging around the burning thicket, towards the other side, where the dervish capered about the fire.

"Bloody yank!" Churchill raged. He pulled his semi-automatic revolver out of his holster and ran after his friend. They circled the perimeter of the fire. They could see the dervish where they had left them. They were completely unaware that the two men were flanking them.

"I count ten," Kip whispered as they made their way behind the dervish.

"Eleven," Churchill countered. And they are all armed with swords and muskets."

"Fuck em," Kip came to his feet and calmly began walking towards the dervish.

Churchill could only grin. "Indeed. A last great gesture of defiance," he said, raising his pistol as he walked alongside.

Ali Muhammad stood with his men at the entrance to the burning thicket. They had found the body of the dead sentry with his head snapped on the outskirts of the camp. Ali wanted revenge. He listened intently for their screams as they burned alive.

Kip and Churchill had advanced fifty yards towards the men without being noticed, but they were still separated by twenty feet. Suddenly, one of the dervish soldiers turned and saw the two men with pistols advancing on them. He screamed out a warning and his men turned to face the danger.

Both sides opened fire at the same time. Kip dropped to one knee and quickly emptied his clip. He saw with grim satisfaction that he had dropped five of them.

"Out!" he screamed. He reached for his bandolier to reload.

Churchill stood up, arm and pistol extended in perfect marksmanship form. He emptied his clip, taking down three more dervish warriors.

Kip slammed a fresh clip into his pistol at the same time a musket ball tore through his chest. He let out a loud "umph" and toppled backward.

"Bloody hell," Churchill growled. He quickly reached for another clip with his free left hand but a musket ball slammed into his left shoulder. The clip fell to the ground. Churchill hit the ground next to it.

"Keep fighting," Kip urged.

Kip was prone on the ground but had his pistol reloaded. His gun roared as he shot the dervish, one by one. Churchill too was prostrate, firing with his one good hand. Both men emptied their clips. Finally, no men were standing on either side. The shots stopped.

Kip dropped his head onto his arm. He looked over at Churchill and saw the stain of blood spreading fast on his tunic. They were both losing a lot of blood. Churchill wasn't moving, and his face was in the sand.

It took all of Kip's strength to get to his knees. He felt dizzy.

"Churchill, get up," he said.

Winston Churchill lay on the desert floor, collecting his senses.

"Slave driver," he mumbled painfully.

Churchill slowly brought himself up to a standing position. He looked at Kip and his expression turned to horror. Kip was shot in the chest, and there was the sound of air sucking from the wound every time he breathed. Churchill struggled to his feet and put his hand on Kip's shoulder.

"Lay down," Churchill said.

Kip did as he was told. Churchill quickly pulled a sweaty bandana from his pocket and stuffed it into the wound. He didn't think his friend would last much longer. He was surprised that Kip was still conscious.

A dervish warrior stirred and Churchill walked over to him and coldly executed him in the head. He looked about and saw the camels. The horses were long gone. That actually might be best, he thought to himself. We don't have any water for horses anyway. They had another 100 miles to go before they reached the water at the edge of the White Nile.

Churchill walked slowly over to the camels and searched the saddlebags for the first aid kit. He too was losing a lot of blood. They were both in harm's way.

Churchill stuffed a rag soaked in alcohol into the chest wound and covered it with surgical tape. Kip screamed out from the pain. It was only a matter of time before infection set in. They would have to get the slug out soon. It was all he could do to get Kip onto one of the two remaining camels.

He got on top of his own camel and urged it to stand up. Kip's camel stood up too, and they slowly began to head east.

Five days later the camels dropped. Kip and Winston had carefully rationed their water to only a cup a day. But they too ran out as they drank the last drops from Kip's canteen.

"Any idea where we are?" Churchill asked as they sat on a small rock formation.

Kip tried to laugh but instead starting coughing up blood. He wiped his mouth.

"I'm pretty sure we're in hell," he answered. He looked curiously at the blood on his hand. "Bright red," he said valiantly. "Lung shot. Churchill, I'm not going to make it. Go on without me," Kip pleaded. "I'm deadly serious."

Churchill looked at his friend.

"Indeed. But I'm not going to leave you, and you are not going to die on me," he said matter-of-factly. We will walk the rest of the way."

Kip coughed again.

"Quite right," he quipped with his best British accent. It took him a full minute to get to his feet. He stood there swaying under the blistering sun, his lips cracked open, his tunic caked in blood.

Churchill slowly got to his feet. He felt himself grow faint. Then he crumpled over, losing consciousness from the loss of blood.

"Ah hell," Kip could only manage to say before he collapsed as well.

CHAPTER EIGHTY-NINE

THE WHITE NILE, 1898

The banks of the Nile were quiet in the still of the early morning. The creatures of the night were finding sanctuary from the blistering sun that would soon rise above them. Some dug into the muddy river banks. Others nestled in amongst the cool, thick reeds that lined the river. All were looking for sanctuary from the heat, including two men, whose near lifeless bodies lay in the mud.

The Nile crocodiles, fully aware that many animals would be coming to drink from the river at dawn lay silent in the river, just under the surface. Their nostrils protruded just above the water, searching the air for the hint of prey. One very large bull male, who was over fifteen feet in length, gently broke the surface of the river with his snout. Then his eyes emerged, followed by his broad, armored head. He waited patiently.

The two men fell at the river's edge. Kip was able to crawl to the water on his belly in the mud. He drank thirstily at first, but then began coughing and retching as his body took in water for the first time in five days.

Churchill too could only crawl. The left side of his body was no longer working as he slithered to the river bank to drink. But the cool water of the Nile soothed both men and eased their pain enough so they could crawl up the bank into the shade of a tree.

Kip could barely see. He squinted. He could just make out Churchill lying next to him.

"Hey, when do you think they'll get here?" Kip asked hopefully. He watched the river flow past them.

He heard a noise in the water to his right. He looked over and saw a fifteen-foot Nile crocodile emerging from the river, creeping their way. Its massive head swung side to side as it stalked its prey.

"Uhm, Churchill," Kip whispered in horror.

"I see it," Winston replied. It was all he could do to reach for his pistol. It wasn't there. The holster was empty. They were both out of ammo and had ditched their gear to lighten their loads.

"Well at least we made it this far," Kip said, trying to make a joke. He could see the eyes of other crocodiles watching the feast soon to be spread out in front of them.

Churchill could barely sit up. He found a rock and hurled it at the approaching reptile. It thumped off the armored skull. Unfazed, the massive beast with a mouth full of two- inch razors approached the helpless men.

"Churchill, you're the bravest man I've ever met," Kip could only cough out in admiration. He was too weak to move.

"Likewise," Churchill answered, his eyes fixed upon the approaching animal.

The giant crocodile was seconds away. It grew excited and scurried the last ten feet quickly. It raised open its mouth. In a moment, it would have one of them in its jaws, its teeth tearing first through flesh, and then with crushing force, deep through muscle and into the bone. Its massive tail would begin to thrash, and the energy would spin the thousand-pound creature into a whirling frenzy, tearing its prey in half, spilling blood and entrails into the river, whipped into frothy red foam by the churning reptile. The shock would paralyze the men's nervous system. But their eyes would register the horror of being eaten alive.

And then, miraculously, incredibly, Kip saw the steel hull of a gunboat coming around the bend. A Maxim machine gun opened fire, and bullets ripped up the length of the crocodile's body. Chunks of blood and flesh hurtled into the air.

"Not the ending you were expecting, was it, mate?" Kitchener said calmly, standing on the bridge of the *Sultan*.

"Nice shooting Sergeant Burba," Kitchener complimented the young gunner. The steamship pulled up to the river's edge. The two men lay in the mud along with the dead reptile. It was hard to say who was bleeding more.

"Thank you, sir," Sergeant Keith Burba answered. He kept his finger on the Maxim's trigger.

"Bring them aboard," the Sirdar ordered his first officer, who was standing nearby.

"Have the surgeons and the medical team ready just in case they're still alive."

EPILOGUE

Chapter Ninety

LONDON, 1898

"Kill me now!" Churchill cursed. He threw down the morning paper in disgust and poured himself a stiff drink. Lady Churchill walked into the room, alarmed.

"Bad news?" she asked with concern.

Winston walked to the window and stared out over his mother's garden. He had stayed at her London flat while he convalesced from his wounds, but now he was feeling quite healed. And bored.

"The bloody Boers have besieged Ladysmith," Winston informed his mother. "They are sending Kitchener to deal with the rebellion."

Jenny smiled. She already knew where this was going.

"Why the hell didn't he invite me?" he fretted.

"I'm sure he is very busy," his mother teased.

"I've got to get down there immediately," Churchill announced. "I'll speak with the editors at the Daily Mail and the Morning Post. I can get down there as a correspondent, and you can get cracking on finding me a military assignment with Kitchener's forces."

Lady Churchill wanted to say something but decided to acquiesce. She walked over to her son and put her arms around him.

"Shall I ask Lord Kitchener?" she said softly.

Churchill winced.

"Probably best not to tip him off in advance," he decided.

CHAPTER NINETY-ONE

WASHINGTON, D.C., 1898

President McKinley sat at the polished mahogany table in the briefing room of the White House. The oval table was fifty feet long, lined with empty chairs. In fact, the conference room was empty, save for the two men.

"I'm glad your back," the president said. "And I'm glad you've healed.

"I am glad to be back," Lieutenant Colonel Kip McDuran answered. "Congratulations on your re-election, Mr. President."

There was a knock on the door, and the vice president walked into the conference table.

"Teddy, I want you to meet Colonel McDuran," the president said politely.

"It's a real pleasure sir," Kip said, rising to his feet.

"The pleasure is all mine, sir," Theodore Roosevelt said warmly. "I've read all about your exploits." He sat in the chair across from the president.

"I have another mission for you," the president advised.

Chapter Ninety-Two

SHIRKELA, 1898

The sentry stood at the edge of the waste dump just outside the village. He was bored. He was hoping to watch the hyenas feeding on the wasted bodies that lay putrid on the ground. It was odd. They had been away for a month now. It was breeding season, but they would be returning soon.

Slowly, imperceptibly, there was movement amongst the dead. A woman's arm moved ever so slightly. Her eyes opened slowly. They were sapphire blue.

THE END

About the Author

Brock Walker spent a great deal of his childhood in Africa. His father was a diplomat posted to Libya, the Ivory Coast and Ethiopia. Brock studied creative writing at the George Washington University and graduated with a journalism degree from the University of Maryland. After college, Brock was commissioned as a navigator in the USAF. While in the military, Brock earned his law degree from the McGeorge School of Law. He left active duty to become a homicide prosecutor in California while also serving as a Staff Judge Advocate in the USAF Reserve. Brock is a decorated combat veteran who volunteered for a tour of duty in Iraqi Freedom, Enduring Freedom, and the Horn of Africa. Brock is married to Teresa Walker. They have four children between them. He is also a volunteer firefighter and scuba instructor.

CPSIA information can be obtained
at www.ICGtesting.com
Printed in the USA
FSHW011440080419
57052FS

9 781480 859210